SUMMIT AVENUE

Summit Avenue

~ A NOVEL ~

MARY SHARRATT

For Terri,
New Mexico Diva!
Mary Sharratt

COFFEE HOUSE PRESS   MINNEAPOLIS   2000

Coffee House Press is an independent nonprofit literary publisher supported in part by a grant provided by the Minnesota State Arts Board, through an appropriation by the Minnesota State Legislature, and in part by a grant from the National Endowment for the Arts. Significant support has also been provided by the McKnight Foundation; the Star Tribune Foundation; the Lila Wallace-Reader's Digest Fund; the Bush Foundation; the Target Foundation; General Mills Foundation; St. Paul Companies; Honeywell Foundation; Patrick and Aimee Bulter Family Foundation; the law firm of Schwegman, Lundberg, Woessner & Kluth, P.A.; and many individual donors. To you and our many readers across the country, we send our thanks for your continuing support.

Coffee House Press books are available to the trade through our primary distributor, Consortium Book Sales & Distribution, 1045 Westgate Drive, Saint Paul, MN 55114. For personal orders, catalogs, or other information, write to: Coffee House Press, 27 North Fourth Street, Suite 400, Minneapolis, MN 55401.

COVER DESIGN + ART Kelly N. Kofron
AUTHOR PHOTOGRAPH Torsten Rehbinder

Library of Congress Cataloging-in-Publication Data
Sharratt, Mary, 1964 –
    Summit Avenue: a novel / by Mary Sharratt.
        p. cm.
    ISBN 1-56689-097-7 (alk. paper)
    1. Young women—Minnesota—Saint Paul—Fiction. 2 World War, 1914 – 1918—Minnesota—Saint Paul—Fiction. 3. Saint Paul (Minn.) —Fiction. 4. German Americans—Fiction. 5 Lesbians—Fiction. I. Title.

PS3569.H3449 S8 2000
813'.6—dc21   00-022767

10   9   8   7   6   5   4   3

for Joske with all my love,
and in loving memory of my grandmother,
Cecilia Krippner Simons, 1905 – 1995

I refer to myths and fairy tales as essential psychic facts rather than as false stories or stories for children.

—Nor Hall,
The Moon and the Virgin: Reflections on the Archetypal Feminine

❦ ACKNOWLEDGMENTS

Enduring gratitude to everyone at Coffee House, especially to my publisher for his mentorship and patience. Gratitude and love to three dear
friends who believed in me and whose contributions to my work run
deep: Eileen Keane, Janet "Cat Lady" King, and Carolyn Morrow.
Special thanks to Mary Beth Maslowski, Mandy von Sivers, Cameron
Black, Ann Marie Hartmann, Jean François Berger, Katherine Clark, and
everyone in the Munich Writers Workshop, past and present. I would
also like to express my gratitude to Julie Popkin, Diana Voigt, Janet M.
McEwan, Maureen Reddy, Susan Tiberghien, Ruth Roston, Thomas E.
Kennedy, Scott Bartell, Eileen Boris, Jeanine Halva-Neubauer, Liz Jones,
Harmon Smith, R.P. Burnham, Cynthia Fogard, Jan Zita Grover, and
Flor and Jeanneke.

Prologue

THROUGH A DARK FOREST

How can you weave a life from fairy tales? This is what I do each night after the chores are done, the gardening and the canning. After the supper dishes are washed, dried, and put away. I put my little girl in her nightgown and hold her in my lap in the rockingchair by the window. Waxy yellow light from the kerosene lantern casts shadows on the walls as I move my hands to narrate my stories. Outside, the wind passes through the spruce trees like an invisible hand, branches scraping and clawing the tin roof overhead. The calendar over the sideboard shows a young woman clothed in an American flag, waving a Liberty Bond. Underneath, the month and year are printed in proud bold red: July, 1918. I have no idea when it will be over, this war that rages like a bloody phantom, like the ghostly shadows that dance on the walls as I tell my daughter the tale of the girl who walked all the way through the dark forest to the sorceress' house.

I am twenty-two but dress like a crone, all in black. My neighbors call me the Black Widow. I live alone with my little girl in a cabin in the woods like a witch in a fairy tale. Last month, when I first came to this place looking for cheap accommodation, I was nearly turned away. The farmer who rents out these cabins had raised an almighty fuss when he heard my German accent. I told him I was a pacifist, but these days pacifists are suspect, too. I told him, "I hate the Kaiser. I am an American now. I love this country." This made him soften slightly around the edges without really relenting. The next thing I told him was a story so fanciful, it could have come from one of my tales. Twisting the plain silver band on my left hand, I told him of losing my American husband in the war. "He died in the trenches of Montdidier." It was this that finally moved the old farmer. He let me and my daughter move into the most secluded of his three cabins, even let me plant a garden.

I don't think he regrets his decision. I am a good tenant, quiet and sober. I receive no callers and pay my rent promptly. I only go to town to buy supplies at the general store. On Sunday I go to the church up the road, but I leave right after mass without speaking to anyone. I will live alone in the forest with my daughter until my savings run out. Then I'll have to find employment of some sort. Cleaning other people's houses, taking in other people's laundry. But for now I wrap myself in my fairy tales and nurse the wound that no one can see. I let them call me the Black Widow, but it's not a man I'm grieving.

"And the girl walked through the forest for seven days and seven nights," I whisper to my daughter. "On the eighth day she came to Baba Yaga's house." I tell Russian tales, for they are the most beautiful. "Her house was like a castle. It was golden. It danced on hen's feet. Round and round, never stopping. So hard to find the door. How do you find the door of a house that's always moving?"

My little girl is drowsy now, her bright cornsilk head nodding off against my black blouse. Rocking her to sleep, I close my eyes. At moments like this, when the gibbous moon is rising and the kerosene lamp sputtering low, I can step out of this world, erase the past four years, erase the war. It's like looking in a mirror in a dream. Tracing my way back up the long road that led me to this cabin, this loss. Gathering the scattered threads and weaving them together, as if on a magic loom. Weaving them into a tale, my tale. This is how I mend what was broken, how I summon back the radiant thing I have lost.

Book One

MAIDEN: THE FIRE

1 ⁞ I was born in a forest even darker and more tangled than this one—in the Schwarzwald with its valleys deep as scars. My valley was so steep and narrow, we called it the Höllental, valley of hell. Enclosed by precipitous hills, it got very little sunlight. Bruised clouds shrouded the sun the morning in November, 1911, when I closed the coffin lid on my mother's face. I had just turned sixteen.

Lashing rain had turned the village graveyard into a quagmire. I stared down the hole they were lowering my mother into. A gash in the earth full of black water. I wondered if the coffin would leak, if the mud would stain the white paper rose I had placed between her fingers. Huddled under his umbrella, the priest spat out the final bless-ing as fast as he could. *He can't wait to get inside again,* I thought. *Can't wait to sit his fat behind in the plush chair next to the stove and fill his gut with apple cake.* I did not hear a word of his mumbling. I was studying our family headstone. My mother's name, newly chiseled, was at the bottom. Just above was my father's name. He had passed away last year. Above him, my brother, who had inherited his weak lungs. At the very top was a string of five sisters, vague recollections. Babies who had died before they were old enough to leave the cradle. *A cruel joke,* I thought, that I was the only one who had survived. What would I do now? I wasn't old enough to get married, wouldn't inherit a scrap of land. We had sold the farm to pay our debts.

Now my mother's coffin was at the bottom of the hole. Cloudy water closed in around it. The hole seemed to beckon me. The ground beneath my feet was soggy, uneven. It would be so easy just to slip and fall into that dark wet place. Cling to the unvarnished coffin, a ship on

an underground sea taking me to join the rest of them. I wanted to cry,
thought this would be so much easier if I could just throw back my
head and bawl thunderously like a bad actress in a village play. But I
could not. My eyes stayed dry. My tears would not come until much,
much later.

Uncle Peter, standing beside me and holding the umbrella over our
heads, was crying in the choked silent way that men do. My mother's
favorite brother, the village schoolmaster, the only bachelor over thirty
left in our valley, though none of the unmarried women favored him.
He was a bit of a laughingstock, a grown man who wept while his
young niece remained stoic, this man who lived only for his books,
who slept in the schoolhouse for lack of a proper home.

The priest slapped his missal shut and made the last sign of the
cross, and the guests dashed away to my aunt's house, where the
funeral dinner awaited them. I let them go without me. The thought
of food made my stomach clench like a fist. The thought of all those
people gawking at me to see how I was coping. I wanted to hide in
the forest like an animal.

"Kathrin, come away from that grave." My uncle was speaking to
me. "You'll catch your death in this rain." He led me into the empty
church, the only place we could be indoors and still alone. I didn't
bother wiping my feet at the threshold. My uncle sat on the back pew
and stared into his handkerchief with red swollen eyes, while I paced
up and down the aisle, my arms folded in front of me, wondering how
much of a mess I could make with my trail of dirty footprints. I found
my eyes resting on the statue of the Virgin, her sweet tender face bent
to the child in her arms. Swinging around sharply, I marched to the
back of the church and sat beside my uncle, who took my hand. How
could his hand be so warm? Mine was cold as a marble slab. All the fire
had gone out inside me. I thought I would never be warm again,
thought the blood inside my veins would freeze. My uncle looked at
me, his damp hair falling in his face. I brushed it back for him, and he
put his arm around me. "There's nothing left for you here, Kathrin. You
know that, don't you?"

I set my mouth in a firm grim line.

"I want to send you away from here."

At first I thought he was joking. "Give me your bicycle," I said, speaking for the first time since breakfast. "I'll ride to Switzerland and send you a card." The Swiss border was thirty odd miles away.

"No, Kathrin. You'll go farther than that. I'm sending you to America."

I turned away from him, looking at the cheap oil prints of the stations of the cross. America was a myth to me. Like the North Pole. As distant as the place my mother had gone to. Five years ago my cousin Lotte had gone over. She had sent a few picture postcards of tall buildings like the spires of cathedrals, then silence. America was a place that swallowed you up, and you were never heard from again.

"There's just enough money for your passage. You can live with Lotte. She'll look after you and help you find work. Anyone with half a brain can find work over there. *Here,*" he said with a sharp outtake of breath, "here you'd just be a servant girl until you're old enough to marry. That's not what your mother would have wanted."

I turned to him again, wrapping my arms around his neck, pressing my face against his wet wool coat. Already his voice sounded like it was coming from the other end of the world.

"You were always the best in school, Kathrin. You put the other children to shame. I didn't spend all those years educating you just to have you marry some farmer who'll treat you no better than a brood mare." He spoke plainly. That had been my mother's fate. Pregnant every other year until my father died. By that time her body had been too broken to make much use of her widowhood.

"You're a bright girl. Too bright for this place. We're different from the rest, you and I. We don't fit the mold. For a man it's hard enough, but for a woman . . . " He broke off. I thought again of my mother.

"You know you have to forget this place. Wipe it from your memory. Learn English as fast as you can. That's the most important thing. As soon as you step off that ship, you'll be an American."

2 ∽ April, 1912

A vast sweep of brick warehouses and factories flew past me. Smoke-stacks reared into the air. It was so flat here. The sky had never seemed so close. My first view of Minneapolis was from the window of a moving train. We crossed a bridge over the Mississippi, brown and wide, with flat-bottomed barges carrying timber. As the boy opposite me opened the window to get a better look, a blast of cool spring air hit me in the face, and then I breathed in the city's smell: the smell of coal smoke mingled with a musty, yeasty odor I could not ident-ify.

∽ When I stepped off the train, I saw a woman in her early twenties who was holding a piece of cardboard with my name scrawled across it in red crayon. I made my way toward her, this strange American who was the cousin I had not seen in five years. She wore a shiny pink dress with ruffles around the neck. Her waist was so tiny, cinched by her corset, I could have fit my hands around it, but her bosom rose above it, heavy and powerful. With a figure like hers, she belonged in the country. Baking bread and raking hay with her strong arms. How out of place she looked here, standing in a railway station with paint on her face. At home if you painted yourself, they called you a loose woman. She was smoking. Back in our village, only men smoked. I stopped a few feet in front of her, put down my suitcase, held out my hand for her to shake. Wondering what I could possibly say to her and whether I should say it in English or German. But my cousin made things simple.

"Du bisch d'Kathrin," she declared in a watered-down version of our old dialect. "I'm Lotte. That's your only bag? Come along, we have to catch the streetcar. I hope you have a nickel for the fare."

"Nickel?" I had never heard the word before.

"Five cents," she explained, already exasperated. "We'll room together at the boardinghouse. It's cheaper that way. And you'll work with me at the mill."

When Lotte said mill, I pictured the old water mill in our village. But the next morning she took me to cavernous brick grain mills painted white as flour, so immense I could have fit my parents' old farmstead inside them. The mills were clustered around St. Anthony Falls, straddling both sides of the Mississippi. Towering around me, they blocked the sun, just like the hills that surrounded the Höllental. They spewed smoke and pumped out that same yeasty odor I had noticed yesterday on the train. *Of course,* I thought. *This must be the smell of flour.*

"Don't stand there with your mouth wide open." Lotte tugged my sleeve. "People will think you're some stupid little farm girl who never set foot in a city before." E' dumm's Baremädele. She led me through an iron door into one of those brick fortresses. "This is the Pillsbury Mill, the biggest in the world," she said. "Write home and tell them that."

Following my cousin through a maze of electrically lit corridors, I thought of the story of the elves who lived inside the Zauberberg, the magic mountain. Red-faced, blue-shirted men pushed trolleys of grain. Watching them, I felt like a child at a fair. Even their curses sounded wondrous and strange, because they were in American English. I sneezed on the flour dust, which seemed to permeate every inch of the corridor. Like pollen, like snow in summer. The whole place hummed like a wasps' nest. The smell of flour and machine oil filled my lungs. "Come on, we'll be late." Lotte grabbed my arm and marched me into a room with an impossibly high ceiling. Walls of bare brick, grimy skylights at the very top. I thought how hot it would be in summer, how cold in winter. The wooden floor was littered with fabric scraps, dust balls, and odd bits of thread that got caught on the hem of my skirt. This was like a giant schoolroom, except where there should have been desks, there were sewing machines, women and girls hunched over them. Some of them looked so young—twelve or thirteen—but they already had the hooded, dark-circled eyes of old women. They were speaking all languages, not just American. They were pumping the foot pedals of their sewing machines like someone trying to ride a bicycle up an impossibly steep hill.

"You'll sit next to me," Lotte said, steering me over to two battered machines in the far corner, within sniffing distance of the lavatory. "We sew flour bags." She pointed to the crate of white cotton cloth on the floor between the two machines. "Take good care of everything. If you break a needle, they dock your wages. If you break the machine, they make you pay for it. You get five cents for each finished bag, so if you want to bring in five dollars a week, you better get cracking. If you're good, you can bring in six a week, but while you're new, you'll be lucky to get four or four-fifty. Your half of the rent at the boardinghouse is two-fifty," she added. "Just so you know."

I sat on the wobbly wooden chair. The seat, at least, was comfortable, worn smooth and deep by the seamstresses before me.

"Here's where you put the bobbins, and this is how you thread the needle."

Too transfixed to listen, I stared at the sign on the far wall, the red letters big enough to be seen from every corner of the room. I tried to decipher the foreign words.

No Smoking
No Gum Chewing
No Eating or Drinking
No Loitering
No Swearing
Five Minutes Late Means Fifty Cents Docked from Your Pay
Be in Your Place at All Times

"Kathrin, pay attention! You'll have to thread your own needle after this."

"Yes, yes." I ran a faltering hand over the machine and traced the gold letters stamped on the black cast iron, spelling out its brand name: *Phoenix*. What a name for a sewing machine! A firebird rising from the ashes.

"Kathrin, *what* are you looking at? Have you never seen a sewing machine before?"

"Mother never had one. I'm sure I could sew better by hand."

"Foreman's coming. Get to work." Lotte put two lengths of white cotton, already stamped with the Pillsbury logo, under her needle. Her foot flew to the pedal, then the needle burst into motion, the bobbins oscillating wildly. A blur of white and silver. The rattle and hum of two hundred Phoenix brand sewing machines in the same room. Two hundred women and girls sewing away like mad. I gave my cousin one last desperate look, but her face was a mask of concentration. The dots of rouge on her cheeks stood out like streetcar lamps. I found myself staring at her pink taffeta blouse with its plunging neckline, displaying her breasts like melons at a market stall. I looked away and took a deep breath, inhaling Lotte's perfume along with the stink of the lavatories.

I folded the edges of two pieces of fabric and pinned them together with the rusty pins sticking out of the cushion near my cousin's machine. Sewing straight seams to make flour bags. The task sounded simple enough. At home I had sewn complicated things by hand. Smocked blouses, gathered skirts, embroidered chemises. Smoothing the fabric out, aligning it to the path of the needle, I put my foot on the pedal. At first so lightly that nothing happened. Then I put a bit more weight on it, started pumping it back and forth. The needle moved up and down like a hen pecking seeds. I moved the fabric along. My hands were trembling. I was practically biting my bottom lip off. *Straight seams, any fool should be able to do this.* I started pumping faster, trying to get into the rhythm of it. I broke into a sweat, the back of my dress sticking to my shoulder blades like wet leaves. The blur of silver as the needle speeded up, the fabric bunching underneath it, the thread bunching together, the needle jamming. I took my foot off the pedal and examined my handiwork. A string of swear words emerged from my lips, a vocabulary I had never even known I possessed.

Lotte lifted her foot from her pedal, dug a seam ripper out of her pocket. "Rip the thread out and try again." Her words were cut short by a man's voice, a flood of abuse so elaborate, it made my cursing sound like Sunday school talk. He was screaming at me in a language half-foreign, half-familiar. I turned in my seat to see a squat man with a drooping, snuff-stained mustache. This must be the foreman. His embroidered name patch said Sepp Buchmayer. With a name like that, he could only be Bavarian, which accounted for his barbaric dialect. He was yelling at the top of his lungs, but his speech went through me like air. My eyes froze on the ropy strings of saliva between his yellow teeth, the net of broken blood vessels in his bulbous nose. He was bending over me, grabbing my arm to illustrate his point, attempting to lift me out of my chair.

Lotte sprang between us, sticking her cleavage in the man's face. I sank back into my seat and started jabbing at the bunched thread with the seam ripper. *This isn't America. This is a bad dream.* By the time I had torn the thread out and spread the material under the needle, Lotte was in her chair again, smoothing her hair back into place. I reached out to her, but she slapped my hand away. "I saved your skin. He's extra hard on new girls who haven't proved themselves."

How can you let that awful man come near you, I wanted to scream, but something in Lotte's briskness told me to leave the subject alone. "Why didn't he speak English to me?" I asked instead. "I could have been American for all he knew."

Lotte sighed so heavily, she blew her pin curls off her forehead. "No one would ever mistake *you* for an American. An *American* girl would *know* how to work a sewing machine. Besides, I told him I'd be bringing you in today to replace the last girl he fired. It doesn't take much to get yourself fired here. If you didn't have me to look after you, you'd be out on the street."

≈ When we left the mill ten hours later, following the stream of men and women out the metal doors into the darkness, I could hear the rush of the falls, could see the yellow streetlights on the other side of the Mississippi, distant with comfort and promise. Black water streamed under the Stone Arch Bridge, where a train snaked away into the night. Something leapt inside me when I heard it whistle. A westbound train. I thought of cities perched on the edge of the Pacific Ocean, fabulous as fairy tales. I imagined the sun setting on an endless expanse of waves. *This is America.*

If I were a man, I'd run away and live like a gypsy. If I were a man, I'd never let the likes of Sepp Buchmayer lay a hand on me. I'd throw him against the wall and give him a good pounding for what he did to Lotte. But my cousin seemed to have forgotten the incident. She was adjusting her straw hat with the red satin cherries. A hand-rolled cigarette was sticking out of her painted lips at a jaunty angle. "Come along to the tavern," she said. "It's the best part of the day."

Every night after work, Lotte went to Schmidt's Tavern in Northeast Minneapolis, just a few blocks away from our boardinghouse. A cramped bar packed with mill workers, mostly German, mostly men. A dim place with weak gaslights and clouds of blue smoke rising to the pressed tin ceiling. The sawdust on the floor was slick with spilled beer the night I followed Lotte through the swinging glass doors. Half the men turned to look at her, greeting her by name. There was one free stool in the rear corner. I headed straight for it, sat myself down, and crossed my arms in front of my rib cage to make myself look as small and inconspicuous as possible. I didn't like the look of those men. Eight o'clock in the evening and they were already drunk, pawing at my cousin, who didn't even bother to push their hands away. One of them lurched in my direction. "Wer is' denn de Gloane?" he asked Lotte. *Who's the little girl?* Lotte calmly placed herself between us and pressed a glass of beer into my hand. "Let her be," she said. "She's just a kid." Si 'sch nur e' Kind. "A good girl." E' brav's Mädele. "Not your type, at all."

I took a few sips of beer, but it was flat and lukewarm, acid in my empty stomach. Listening to the smattering of dialects around me, I wondered how I would ever learn English. "I don't like to drink," I said, passing the beer to my cousin.

"Suit yourself." She raised it to her mouth, took a long swallow, then resumed her banter with the men. From my perch on the stool,

I watched her flirting, teasing. When they flirted back, she seemed to open up and bloom. The flickering gaslight softened the rouge on her cheeks. At nine-thirty, when she finally whisked me off the stool, her eyes were luminous.

"We better go," she said, "if we still want to get some supper out of the landlady."

☘ We ate our supper in the boardinghouse kitchen. The meal that night and every night thereafter consisted of a plate of stew. Gray strips of some unidentifiable meat mixed in with slimy bits of cabbage, turnip, and plenty of gristle. Half an hour after downing my portion, I ran to the lavatory, where it came out again, out of my burning mouth and down the sewer pipe.

"It's because of the gristle," Lotte told me when I joined her again in our closet-sized room. "That happened to me, too, in the old days, but then I got used to it. You just need to toughen up a little."

I turned away from her and began to undress for bed.

"You know, for a kid, you're not bad looking." Out of the corner of my eye, I saw her stabbing out her last cigarette of the day into the overflowing saucer on the bedside table. "If you smiled a little more, you'd even be pretty."

I threw my nightgown over my head, wriggled my arms into the sleeves. I didn't feel the least bit comely. More like a stray dog with matted fur.

"You should be friendlier to the boys at the tavern." My cousin spoke decisively. "A few of them liked the look of you."

"I'm not looking for a boyfriend," I said and proceeded to give my face a vigorous scrub with white soap and cold water at the washstand.

"That's the only way you'll ever get out of the mill." Lotte pulled back the quilts on the iron-framed bed we shared, motioning me to crawl in beside her. "The only way out is by marrying. As soon as I find someone decent, I'll leave this place. Just keep that in mind, Kathrin. I won't be around to look after you forever. Sooner or later you'll have to get yourself a man. It's never too early to start looking."

She shut off the lamp. "Good-night," I said in English, just for the sake of speaking English. The only English I had spoken that day. I clung to my edge of the bed to keep myself from rolling into the sagging hollow in the middle. Shutting my eyes, I commanded myself to sleep, but every part of my body hurt. My neck and back ached from hunching over the sewing machine for ten hours. My stomach and throat were raw from the vomiting. I couldn't imagine ever eating again. I would turn into a ghost, a wraith. *Don't feel sorry for yourself!* I tried to use reason. Self-pity wasn't going to get me anywhere. I tried to lecture myself like a stern schoolmistress. *Lotte is right. You will grow a thicker skin. You will get used to this place. This is just the beginning.*

Kathrin, Kathrin. In my head I repeated my name over and over. First with the German pronunciation. *Kah-treen.* Then the American way. *Kath-run.* It made me sound like a different person. A person who could talk back to Sepp Buchmayer in perfect American English, making him ashamed. When I finally fell asleep, I dreamt of a hollow mountain made of flour. *Hollow mountains are full of treasure.* Two hundred girls and women lived inside that mountain. Running down mineshafts with picks and shovels, searching for diamonds, searching for gold.

☙ When I found out that the YWCA offered cheap English classes, I signed up immediately. This was what my uncle would have wanted. The teacher was a soft-spoken man in his early thirties who reminded me of him—a second-generation Swede named Peterson. I took that to be a good omen. I was determined to make him proud, make my uncle proud, too. The class was held four nights a week in a cramped room off Nicollet Avenue. There were too many students for the classroom's forty desks, so if you came late, you had to stand in the back for the whole three-hour lesson. My classmates were mill girls, factory girls, and seamstresses. One girl sat all day in a sub-basement making cigarettes.

We came straight from work, drained and exhausted, and also hungry, because attending class meant skipping supper. I thought that learning could feed me like nothing else, and for a while, it did. I studied my grammar on the streetcar back to the boardinghouse, studied all Sunday after church. Even in the mill, I memorized vocabulary, conjugated verbs in my head as I labored away on my flour bags. I don't know what inhuman energy was propelling me.

"Why?" Lotte kept asking me. "Where do you think it's going to get you? Do you think anyone at the mill cares if you speak good English or not?" I ignored her. From April, 1912, when I started my English lessons, to March, 1914, when Mr. Peterson told me I didn't need to come anymore, I was first in my class. I got a gold stamped certificate with my name penned in beautiful calligraphy. Only when my classes were over and my nights empty again did I begin to wonder if Lotte had been right.

Those spring nights in 1914, when the light stretched later and later into the evening, I began to take long solitary walks, going as far as the university. Those nights I asked myself questions, tried to answer them in my head. *What is the difference between hunger and longing?* On the surface the answer sounds simple enough. Hunger is a sensation of the body. Longing concerns the soul. But for me in that last spring before the war, before I became a woman and fell from grace, they were one and the same. I could not separate my hunger from my longing. I craved food, books, kindness, everything with a hunger that made me light-headed. Hunger and longing like a siren were leading me away from the straight and narrow, down the path of solitude and exclusion. My hunger drove me to ridiculous acts. By May, 1914, my hunger had grown unbearable.

3 ☙ I still have a photograph of myself taken in the spring of 1914. I keep it tucked away in my journal. A group portrait of some of the seamstresses at the mill. I am the skinny girl in back with the faraway eyes. Those days I spent most of my time somewhere else. Building, then inhabiting castles in the air. Walking to the university every evening after work, then taking the streetcar home was my only cure for hunger and longing. By the time I got there, the campus was deserted. I wandered the vast lawns and pretended my uncle was beside me, imagining the expression on his face as he took in those buildings with their pillars and marble floors. Once I mustered up the courage to go into the foyer of Walter Library, where I spent half an hour staring at the ceiling. It was like the ceiling of an old church, finely carved, painted blue, ivory, and gold, the colors of heaven. It was like the ancient Greek temples my uncle told me about. What was it he used to say? *"Beauty is not a luxury but a necessity. It feeds the soul. You can die from too little beauty."*

When the rumbling in my stomach made me dizzy, I sat on one of the stone benches outside the library and opened the paper bag that contained my makeshift supper of stale bread rolls and cheap waxy chocolate. Anything was better than the landlady's stew, which still made me sick. I took a bite of chocolate and let it dissolve in my mouth, eating as slowly as possible to fool my stomach that I was getting more. I wanted this bit of food and peace to last as long as possible. Those spring evenings I came back to the boardinghouse later and later. Sometimes I dreamt of never going back. Lotte kept teasing me about it. "Have you finally found yourself a boyfriend?"

Before taking the streetcar back to my boardinghouse, I often stopped at Jelinek's Antiquarian Bookstore, located on one of the side streets fringing the campus. In the front window they had the most beautiful goblets I had ever seen, made of brightly colored glass from Bohemia. That evening in early May when I came down the sidewalk, the last of the dying sunset was filling those goblets, making them glimmer like rubies, sapphires, emeralds, amethysts. I stopped and stared, holding my breath, until the brilliant colors danced and wove around me. Only when the colors were embedded in my vision did I turn and venture in through the noisy wooden door. The shop was like a cave. The area near the window was washed in the ruddy bars of the setting sun, but the farther you went into the labyrinth of bookcases, the more shadowy it got. In the very back they had electric lights burning the whole day long.

I was fortunate in choosing Jelinek's store as my sanctuary; any other shopkeeper would have shown me to the door. In my limp gingham dress and cracked shoes, I was unmistakably a mill girl. No matter how often I washed, I seemed to give off the odor of flour and sweat. But old Mr. Jelinek greeted me every night by name. "Evening, Kathrin." From the thickness of his vowels, I knew he was also foreign born. Night after night he greeted me, even though I never spent a penny in his store. He knew I had no money, but he let me look at his books just the same. I handled them respectfully, tenderly, as if they were infants. I couldn't afford to take any of the books home with me. It was enough to hold them, to leaf through their gilt-rimmed pages. I loved the dense tomes of Shakespeare with the lovely but impenetrable Renaissance English, those doomed heroines with their fanciful names. Desdemona, Cressida, Ophelia. Sometimes I glanced through the more modern novels and plays. Wilde, Shaw, and Zola. I knew these books were considered unseemly, even scandalous, but I never seemed to get far enough into them to understand why. Some nights I contented myself with more pedestrian works. That particular evening I was paging through *Sloan's Handy Hints and Up-To-Date Cook Book*. It was the section on etiquette that interested me most. I tried to memorize the rules of how people behaved in polite society.

"A gentleman should never take two ladies on his arm," I read, *"unless it is for their protection."*

From the other side of the store, I heard the door jangling open, light footsteps crossing the bare floorboards. Footsteps too light to belong to a man. A funny thing, Mr. Jelinek never seemed to get many women in his shop. *This must be an important customer,* I thought, because he was greeting her in his most cordial voice. The stranger was asking for a book she had ordered, a book in Russian, stating her request as if it were the most ordinary thing in the world. She sounded too old to be a college student. Her speech had depth and breadth to it. She spoke as confidently as a man. Never in my life had I encountered a woman like this. Uncle Peter once told me there were learned women in this country, not just female university students but female professors. Until now I had never believed him.

"Your book's right here, ma'am. Shall I wrap it up for you?"

"Yes, please. I'll just take a brief look around the shop if I may. I haven't been here in ages."

Swift footsteps coming in my direction. I forced my eyes to focus on the page in front of me. *"Your napkin is intended for your lips and beard only, not to wipe your face with."* The words hardly registered in my brain. I became aware of someone standing a few feet away. Slowly I lifted my eyes from the page until I saw the lady taking a book from one of the middle shelves and skimming through it, too immersed in her task to realize she was being observed. She was wearing a tailored suit of pale blue linen, the same color as the evening sky. I had never seen a woman's suit in that tender, fragile shade of blue. She had an elegant figure—slender, not scrawny, not broken by factory work or child-bearing. Her black hair was soft and waving, with a touch of silver in it, bound to the nape of her neck with a mother-of-pearl clasp. Her face was calm, serene even, like a statue of some symbolic figure: Peace or Justice. The book she was leafing through had colored illustrations of dragons, firebirds, and knights, but just then she shut the book, glancing up and meeting my stare head on. Her eyes were gray and starlike, quietly amused. Under her gaze my throat went tight, as if I were choking on a mouthful of dust. I hid my face in my book, my eyes moving up and down the page, the etiquette rules floating around like disembodied voices. *"When finished with your soup, do not turn the bowl upside down."* Behind these voices I registered the sound of the lady making her way back to the front of the shop, chatting again with Mr. Jelinek. I pricked my ears, straining to follow the conversation, but it was drowned out by the back door swinging open and a clatter of wing tip shoes.

Mr. Jelinek's nephew John came waltzing up to me with a broom in his hand. "The beautiful maiden of the mill!" he sang out, loud enough to startle the people on the street outside. I imagined the lady hearing that. *Beautiful maiden of the mill.* It was so ludicrous, I wanted to cover my face and burst out the door. John Jelinek was always inventing names for me. I put up with his teasing, because he reminded me so much of my dead brother. "How are you tonight, Kathrin?" he asked, a few decibels lower this time.

"Do you know that lady?" I whispered, nodding in the direction of the voices on the other side of the bookcase.

John whistled through his teeth. "The Professor's widow."

We viewed her through a gap in the shelf. Mr. Jelinek was wrapping up the Russian book for her. She paid him the full price of two dollars without even attempting to haggle.

"She's our best customer," said John. "If she ever moves away, we'll go bankrupt."

"She is not a professor herself?" I tried to keep the disappointment out of my voice. "A widow? Are you sure? She does not look like a widow." She seemed as unlike a widow as any woman I had ever seen. There was no air of loss about her.

"Her husband died six years back. You can tell she's lonely, all right." John narrowed his eyes and sauntered off.

"Thank you very much." It was the lady's voice, smooth and clear as a church bell. The door squeaked open, then shut after her. I put *Sloan's Handy Hints* back in its place on the shelf. *I'll go now.* But before leaving the store, I sidled over to the exact spot where the lady had been standing and hunted the spines of the books until I found the one she had been holding in her gloved hands. It was, of all things, a book of fairy tales. That explained the beautiful pictures. I leafed through them, one by one. A brooding knight was riding off into a purple forest of tangled trees. A mermaid was weeping, her salt tears falling into the salty waves. Then there was a picture of a woman in a meadow, her long dark hair sweeping down to touch the flower-starred grass. The woman was so stately, she reminded me of the lady. Her eyes were the same shade of gray. The lady was holding a wand, and from the tip of that wand, a river of silver was flowing, a river of silver turning into gold.

"You're so skinny, Kathrin." John came up to me again. "I bet I could lift you off the ground with one arm."

I snapped the book shut, then put it carefully back where I had found it. *He's just joking,* I told myself. *He means no harm.*

He was holding something behind his back. "Close your eyes and hold out your hands."

"I must catch my streetcar."

"C'mon, Kathrin. Have some fun for once."

Feeling like a child, I shut my eyes and held out my hands. I felt him putting something into my outstretched palms. Bread. I recognized the texture and weight. Opening my eyes, I saw a sandwich made of jagged slices of pan loaf with thick yellow cheese in the middle. My mouth filled with saliva. Before I knew what I was doing, I was bolting it down. There was sweet butter on the inside of the bread. Butter and not margarine. John hung by my side, eyeing me with an air of satisfaction. "Who feeds you when you're hungry, Kathrin?"

"Thank you," I said when I had swallowed down the last mouthful. Something about the way he was looking at me made me blink and glance away. "I must go. Your uncle will want to lock up."

"I'll walk you to your streetcar stop. You know you shouldn't be going around the city on your own after dark. Especially with those fraternity boys running around." He made a face. "Mama's boys with soft white hands who never had to do a day's work. They're the worst. Hey, Jan!" he yelled to his uncle. "I'm walking Kathrin to the streetcar."

Old Mr. Jelinek looked up from the ledger book. "You do that, John. Good-night, Kathrin." He smiled at me in such a way, I wished I were his kin, too. I imagined being John's sister, working in this forest of books. A grateful apprentice. I said good-night to Mr. Jelinek and followed his nephew out the door, treasuring their kindness, which was like an invisible shawl I could take home with me, a shawl shielding me from the cold stares I got on the street, the rude shouts at the mill.

"How are the flour bags?" John asked as we crossed to the street-car stop.

"They are the same," I said.

"Don't you ever get tired of the mill?" He took a pack of cigarettes out of his pocket and offered me one. I shook my head and watched him strike a match against a lamppost and light up. He smoked thin elegant cigarettes, the kind the college boys smoked. How could he afford them? They didn't make that much money at the bookstore. Maybe he filched them from the tobacconist on the corner. I wouldn't put it past him. He was so confident, he could get away with anything. Even in his faded shirt with the celluloid collar, he managed to look smart, managed to make the college boys walking up and down the street look like overdressed buffoons. He was five years older than I was but so full of life, he made me feel old. That's why I liked to think of him as a brother, teasing me and buoying me up. Not letting me sink too deep inside myself.

"That lady who came in tonight," he was saying. "You should see if you can work for her. Ladies like that have secretaries and assistants."

Sometimes John's sense of humor took me a while to grasp, but I made myself laugh anyway. "Oh, yes. She will hire a mill girl."

"I'm serious." He sounded annoyed. "With all your schooling, you could do better than the mill. Or do you want to sew flour bags your whole life like some peasant?"

I turned my back to him. Teasing was all very well, but he had gone too far. The streetcar was coming around the corner. "Here it is," I said. "Good-bye, John." Across the street, Mr. Jelinek turned off the lights in the bookstore. Something dimmed inside me, as well. Why did John have to spoil everything, spoil my vision of that lady with his crazy talk, and fill my head with longings that could never be granted?

"Wait." He grabbed my arm before I could walk away. I flinched a little. I wasn't used to being touched anymore. Lotte and I never touched. "I'm dead serious," he said, his hand on my arm, just above the elbow. "I'll talk to her and see if I can arrange something, but you'll have to get yourself a decent dress. That thing you're wearing now looks like an old tablecloth."

The streetcar screeched to a halt in front of us, silencing him and sparing me from having to think up an answer. I yanked my arm free and jumped in the back, clutching the rail. John was still standing there, looking at me. The expression on his face was somewhere between impatience and solicitude. He meant well, but he didn't know that he'd struck me where it hurt the most. That my education had been for nothing, that I'd spend the rest of my life at the mill.

An hour later, as I lay in bed beside my snoring cousin, I tried to picture my mother's face. I had no photograph, only memory. All I could see was the closed coffin in the muddy pit. When I tried to open it, I saw dirt, earth, a blank. It was hopeless. But I could conjure up the woman with the black hair. I could see her clearly as an image on a billboard. She was standing in a sun-drenched meadow with a wand in her hand, a branch of hazel, the wood used by diviners to find hidden springs, buried wells. I stared at the lady until she felt my stare, until she turned to me with those gray eyes like the Mississippi in November, but then I blinked, and she was gone. I remained alone in the meadow, except now I was holding the wand. It hummed in my hand like electricity, like a prayer.

I never expected to see that lady again. I even stayed away from the bookstore the next week, because I didn't want to break the spell, didn't want to hear any more of John's meddling, however well intentioned. I wanted that evening preserved forever in my memory. The dying sun gilding the Bohemian glass and the scholarly lady's voice echoing through the shop. The illustrations in the book of fairy tales, the colors as rich as if they had just been painted. And then John's outburst: *beautiful maiden of the mill.* In retrospect, I relished the sound of it. My life was bearable if I could think of myself as the maiden of the mill. I pictured myself mistress of an old-fashioned water mill, the big wooden wheel revolving with the tug of the stream. In my fantasy, I did not work in the mill but just sat beside it looking picturesque, wearing a red dress, the kind worn centuries ago, the kind I had only seen in books. My apron was full of soft white bread, which I tore into pieces and threw to the swans, who curved their graceful necks to devour it before the millpond current swept it away. My daydreams grew so ornate, I sewed one jagged seam after the next.

After work I went walking. I headed over the bridge and across the river, past the mills and factories on the West Bank, past the North Star Blanket Factory with its big upside-down star. I went downtown, toward Hennepin Avenue with the elegant buildings, the motor cars and delivery wagons, the businessmen bustling past shoeshine boys, the ladies with their powdered faces veiled against the sooty air. The smell of flour carried all the way downtown on hot and humid days. There was no escaping it. I tried to take comfort in the knowledge that even the rich had to breathe the same flour-smelling air as I did.

I walked as far as the downtown public library, but by the time I reached it, it was closed. They locked their doors at seven every night to keep out the derelicts. So I made my way back to the river, back across the bridge. Looking out over Nicollet Island, the big houses with their tidy lawns, the trees leafing out after the long winter, I watched the sun sink behind the smokestacks on the West Bank, the darkness falling over the river, the white walls of the Pillsbury Mills going russet in the sunset. If I hadn't had to work there, I would have thought they were beautiful.

That night my room had never seemed dingier. I couldn't lock or even close the door properly. The mildewed ceiling, the dirty pink wallpaper, the threadbare carpet, even the air was heavy and sour, smelling of the landlady's stew and Lotte's cigarettes. I sat on the edge of the bed, the mattress springs squeaking under my weight. As I leaned forward to unlace my shoes, I noticed an envelope lying on the bedside table, my name and address penned in a sloping, unfamiliar hand. The envelope was so crisp and perfect, I gave my hands a good wash before opening it.

Dear Cathrin,

When are you coming to the bookstore again? Did you forget what I was telling you?? I have good news. The Professor's widow will be expecting you at her house on Sunday morning, eight o'clock sharp, for an interview. I told her Sunday was the only day you have off from the mill. She has some things in German she needs translated. Here is her name and address:

Mrs. Violet Waverly
155 Summit Avenue
St. Paul

Get yourself something *decent* to wear.

Yours,
John Jelinek

My eyes froze on the lady's address. Summit Avenue in Saint Paul. Wasn't that where the rich people lived? I couldn't believe any of this. John had outdone himself. I should have been ecstatic with gratitude, but I couldn't help feeling that it must be some fluke, that I would only end up humiliating myself. Elegant ladies do not hire mill girls to do translations.

I slept fitfully that night. The next day I jammed the thread in my machine and had to spend nearly half an hour fiddling with it before it would run again. This did not escape Sepp Buchmayer, who came to stand behind me and breathe down the back of my dress. "Heiliger Birnbaum!" he screamed. "Stupid cow. If you don't shape up soon, I'll give your job to someone else." I straightened my spine and went on with my work. My eyes were glued on my sewing, but what I really saw was the woman with the wand.

4 ✒ Her house was like a castle built of golden limestone, with turrets and lancet windows half hidden in ivy. I stopped at the wrought iron gate and stared. Every residence on Summit Avenue was a mansion, each one grander than the next. This house was not the biggest or the most ostentatious, but I was afraid to step forward. Going through that gate would be like walking into a mirage. If I quietly turned around and caught the streetcar home, it would always remain perfect, like a remembered dream, an apparition that would sustain me every day for the rest of my life. But I forced myself into motion, walking up the flagstone path to the oak door carved with intertwining roses. I rang the bell. It was as if someone else had moved my hand.

I expected a servant to answer the door, but when it opened, I found myself face-to-face with the lady I had seen at the bookstore. She was wearing a white summer dress that made her skin glow like the inside of a shell. "Good morning, Miss Albrecht. I'm very glad you could come." The lady extended her hand for me to shake. Her grip was strong but cool and dry. "Please come in." As I stepped into the entry hall, the air seemed to vibrate with electricity. I tried not to gape at the fourteen-foot ceiling, the gleaming oak balustrade, the gardenias in their bowl. The scent of baking bread was coming from somewhere in the house. Baking bread mingling with the smell of gardenias.

"If you'll come up to my study," said the lady, "we can have a look at the manuscripts." I followed her up the curving staircase, through a labyrinth of paneled hallways. The memory will stay with me forever. I weave it into every story I tell my little girl. The splendid house with the oak door carved in a pattern of thornless roses in perpetual full bloom.

She led me into a room that looked like a slightly smaller version of Jelinek's bookstore, except it had an elaborately molded ceiling and a parquet floor covered in Persian rugs the color of pomegranates. One end of the room was taken up by an immense mahogany desk piled with papers, drawings, and books. On the other end, tucked into an alcove by the bay window, were two chintz armchairs and a low lace-covered table.

"Please have a seat," said Mrs. Waverly, and I lowered myself into one of the armchairs, sinking so far down I thought I would never be able to stand up again. She sat opposite me, her hands folded in her white muslin lap. "So tell me about yourself, Miss Albrecht. Have you been in this country long?"

"I have lived here just over two years, ma'am." I tried to hide my worn shoes beneath the hem of the green taffeta dress I had borrowed from Lotte for the interview. I clamped my forearms to my sides, so the dark patches of sweat wouldn't show.

"You must have been very young when you came over."

"I was sixteen."

"Did you come over with your parents?"

"No, ma'am." I lowered my eyes. "My parents have passed away." In my English class I had learned to say *pass away*, never *die* or *dead*. Americans think it's rude to say *dead*.

The lady reddened. "I'm very sorry to hear that. Are you here all alone, then?"

"I live with my cousin."

"Your English is good."

"I studied it for two years at night school, ma'am." I showed my certificate with the golden star.

"Very impressive," she said before handing it back to me. "Well, I suppose I'd better tell you a bit about myself. I'm working on a collection of fairy tales from different countries. I inherited this project from my husband, who was a professor of ethnography. He recorded these stories firsthand from peasants all over Europe. You see, he was quite gifted with languages. It took him years to collect these tales, but then he died unexpectedly before the anthology could be finished. He translated most of the tales before his death, except for the Russian ones, which I can handle myself, as I've studied that language, and the German tales, which I still need to have translated."

She left her chair and went to her desk, shifting through the piles of papers until she found a thick, watermarked notebook. Leafing through, she opened to a page in the middle. "Take a look at this, Miss Albrecht." She placed the notebook in my hands. "Can you make any sense of it?"

I squinted down at the handwriting running across the wrinkled page. The inked letters were cramped, spiderlike, barely legible. She expected me to decipher this? If it were a translator she wanted, surely she could find someone much more qualified at the university. I felt my face heating up like a brick in a hearth.

"Miss Albrecht?" I had expected her to be cross, but her voice was gentle, almost maternal. "Miss Albrecht, there's no need to be nervous. Just read the story and try to tell me in your own words what it's about."

My eyes settled back on the notebook. The garbled marks gradually formed themselves into letters and words, my mother tongue, and the hard knots in my stomach began to unclench. It was a familiar story, one I had heard many times at home, the kind of thing my mother used to tell me when I was still small enough to fit in her lap. "This is the story of a man who loves a Waldfee." Then I faltered. "I do not know the English word for Waldfee."

"Fay. Fairy. It's the same in English."

"A wood fairy," I said, looking up from the notebook.

"Very good. Now tell me the story."

"A man is cutting wood in the forest," I began. "He sees a wood fairy washing herself in the stream. She is beautiful, like no other woman. He goes to her and asks her to marry him, but she says, 'No, I am not like other girls. I am a wood fairy. Find a girl in the village.' But he loves her, and they marry. She makes him promise not to ask her any questions about her life in the forest before she met him. She makes him promise not to tell the neighbors that she is a wood fairy. She is a witch but a good witch. She brings her man luck and riches. Sometimes she is homesick for her old life in the forest, but she loves him. They have children, and they are happy. Because she brings her man such luck, he is soon the richest in the village. One day he has a big feast. He drinks too much. In front of all the neighbors, he asks her the forbidden questions. He says the forbidden things. 'My wife is like no other woman. She is a wood fairy. She can turn acorns into bread. She can turn river water into wine.' Then she must leave her man. She *must*. He has asked the forbidden questions and said the forbidden things. All his life he is sad, but she never comes back." I raised my eyes from the notebook until they were level with Mrs. Waverly's. I felt my face heating up again.

"Excellent, Miss Albrecht. I think you will be a great help to me. Can you type?"

"No, ma'am." Would Mrs. Waverly still want me? Being paid to sit and read the whole day in a beautiful house. It was too good to be true. "I can learn."

"I'm sure you can. You're every bit as clever as the Jelineks said. Ah, there's another thing I forgot to mention. If you like, I also have a guest room here where you could stay, just to save you the traveling and streetcar fare."

Invited to *live* in this house? I couldn't believe any of this. I imagined announcing my good fortune to Lotte. She would scrunch up her face in scorn. "Where's the hitch? There must be some hitch." My thoughts were interrupted by the maid coming through the door, bearing a tray of warm raisin bread, coffee, and cream. My stomach caved in on itself from hunger and longing as sharp as physical pain.

Mrs. Waverly thanked the maid, who set down the tray and silently swept out of the room. "Would you like some coffee, Miss Albrecht?"

I nodded fervently. When was the last time I had real coffee? My landlady only served Postum. Mrs. Waverly poured coffee from the silver pot into a blue china cup so translucent I thought it would shatter the instant I touched it. "Milk?" she asked. "Sugar?" I nodded to both. *Never again will I be gifted with such luxury and plenty.* I drank down the coffee so eagerly that it scalded my tongue, and I devoured the bread, dripping in fresh butter and strawberry jam. I thought I would never get enough to fill the cavity inside me.

When I had finished half the food on the tray, I noticed a portrait over the mantelpiece of Mrs. Waverly as a young woman. Her hair was arranged loosely around her shoulders, and the lace of her bodice framed an elaborate diamond necklace. She was holding a white rose. She looked so young in that painting, so green and untried, much as I felt at the moment—shy and overwhelmed, not quite believing or even trusting any of the remarkable events befalling her. The diamond necklace rested uneasily on her throat as if it were an undesired burden, a gift that was more like a curse.

"I see you've noticed the resemblance," said Mrs. Waverly, glancing up at the painting. "I must have been your age when it was done. My husband had it commissioned before we were married. Well, Miss Albrecht, have you had enough to eat?"

"Yes, ma'am." I was still savoring the residual flavor of the sweet milky coffee on my tongue.

"I know you're a very well-mannered young lady, but please don't keep calling me *ma'am*. It makes one sound so old. Now I suppose we'd better discuss the wages. How much do they pay you at the mill?"

"Between four dollars and five dollars-fifty a week. Depending on how many flour bags I sew."

She frowned, then folded her hands together. "Supposing I were to offer you ten dollars a week. Would you be willing to start with the translations today? And would the mill let you leave with such short notice?"

I clutched the armrests of my chair. "How long would these translations last?" My throat was so dry, I had to swallow. "How long do you want me for?"

She seemed to be expecting this question. "I have enough work to keep you employed until the end of August or September. After that we can see, but I'll be teaching you to type. You can go on to get a more steady job, say, in an office. I'll see to it that you get a good reference. Does this sound fair to you?"

I would never have to go back to the mill again. Ever. "Yes. Yes, that sounds very fair."

"What you can do is take this notebook and start translating for me. There's only one desk in this room, so I'm afraid I'll have to send you down to the dining room, which is never used unless I have company. Here's a German-English dictionary and some paper and pencils. I'd better go down with you. It's easy to get lost in this house."

Mrs. Waverly showed me to the dining room. "I'd like you to translate these first three stories. I'll come down in a few hours to look at your work. Don't be nervous, Miss Albrecht. Just do your best. Well, I'm going back upstairs now. I wish you luck." She quietly shut the door behind herself, leaving me alone in the vast room.

It was rather gloomy, I decided, despite its fine furniture: the long oval table, the exquisitely carved chairs and sideboard of darkly gleaming mahogany. I could tell the room was little used, though it was meticulously maintained, not a speck of dust anywhere. A lonely, neglected room. The claret curtains were faded now. The black marble fireplace had not been lit for quite some time. The walls were covered in dark still lives and photographs of stiff people wearing the stiff clothes of the last century. Over the mantelpiece was Mrs. Waverly's wedding portrait. She stood like a statue behind a chair on which an older man was seated. He was old enough to be her father and then some, no longer handsome but distinguished with his great, graying beard, that of a patriarch. I studied his face. He did not look harsh or commanding, but patient and protecting. His young bride looked shy and a bit uncertain, but not frightened. I decided they had been fairly happy together.

Next to the photograph was a bronze plaque dedicated to Professor Arthur James Waverly in honor of forty years of teaching and research. I could hardly wait to write to my uncle. *You were right when you told me that this was the land of miracles. I have found work in a professor's house.* Me, a mill girl, a farmer's daughter. I sat down with the books at the polished table, opened the ragged notebook, found a blank piece of paper and a sharpened pencil. *Ten dollars a week!* I would have to thank John and his uncle with all my heart.

Once I accustomed myself to the late Arthur James Waverly's handwriting, the stories delighted me. Witches and wayward children, talking animals, foresters with strange powers. But why would adults, especially scholarly adults, trouble themselves with these children's tales? I pored over the stories, translating them as best I could.

Around noon the maid came in bearing a pitcher of lemonade and a platter of sandwiches. Mrs. Waverly was right behind her.

"How has your work been coming along?"

I showed her the translations. "It is not so hard. They are simple stories."

Mrs. Waverly skimmed through the penciled pages. "The simplest stories are the most deceptive."

We ate our lunch companionably, and when we were finished, Mrs. Waverly asked me when I would be able to start. "How much notice do you need to give the mill?"

"If you like," I said, "I will start tomorrow."

When I returned to the boardinghouse and started packing my things, Lotte was even more scathing than I had anticipated. "Are you *mad*? You don't even *know* that woman. It just seems too *easy*. Nothing in life is ever that easy, Kathrin. Just you wait and see."

My new room at Mrs. Waverly's was round, built into a tower that looked out on a walled garden full of silver birch trees. Virginia creeper washed over the long windowpanes in a waterfall of shining spring leaves. My bed was narrow but sumptuous, made up with real linen sheets. When I lay down the first night and pressed my face to the pillow, the blood rushed in my ears like beating wings. It was a strange time. Dreamlike. Suspended from reality. I sent my uncle a five-page letter describing my new happiness, yet I scarcely believed a word of it myself. *This is all a sleight of hand.*

5 ⁓ My mistress was an enigma to me. I had never met a woman like her, could never decide which facet of her impressed me the most. Her elegance, her generosity, her wealth, or her formidable intelligence. Despite her warmth, I was in awe of her. She seemed aloof, not to me personally, but to the world in general, as if she did not inhabit the same earth as the rest of us. She was the personification of Dame Kind, the giver of gifts, and yet there was more to her. She was a woman of secrets. "She has something up her sleeve," Lotte had told me, conjuring up an image of Mrs. Waverly concealing her secrets like jewels in the folds of her white muslin dress. She was the woman with the wand. A sorceress of some sort. Not an evil sorceress. Her secrets were not of the malevolent kind. But she was one of those people who could hide whole worlds behind sophisticated manners and an ordered life. I wondered if I would stay in her house long enough to find out what any of her secrets were.

When she gave me my first week's salary, I had a yearning to buy a white muslin dress exactly like hers, but that would have been presumptuous. I settled on a pale blue muslin, cut quite differently. The skirt was shorter and not as full. The sleeves were short as well, edged with satin. Still, it was the perfect summer dress, the most beautiful thing I had ever owned. I felt like an impostor in the delicate fabric which lay against my skin, clean and soft from bathing in Mrs. Waverly's immaculate claw-footed tub. I didn't smell even faintly of work or sweat. I also bought a new hat, white straw with a pale blue ribbon to match the dress, and soft brown calfskin shoes, handsome but comfortable as bedroom slippers. One week at Mrs. Waverly's had turned me into a lady. After buying the dress, hat, and shoes, I'd even had enough left over to buy a bottle of orange blossom cologne for Lotte, whom I had promised to meet for church in our old neighborhood, and a box of toffees for the Jelineks, whom I planned to visit after church.

≈ "Well, look at you!" my cousin grumbled on Sunday morning when we met in front of St. Francis, right as the bell was ringing. I was nearly late. It's not a simple thing traveling from Summit Avenue to Northeast Minneapolis to be on time for nine o'clock mass. I'd gotten up at five in the morning and changed streetcars four times. But after the lengths I'd gone through to show Lotte my loyalty, she just shook her head, looking me up and down, clucking like a hen. "Nobody believed it when I said you went to work for some lady on Summit Avenue. They think you ran off with a man. Honestly, Kathrin, you look like a kept woman." But her scolding ceased when I gave her the cologne. She opened the foil package and dabbed some behind her ears as the organ sounded the first hymn. Then she tossed the cologne in her purse, and we flew through the doors and squeezed in on the end of the last pew.

I opened my missal, sang the hymns, and mouthed along in Latin as I had every Sunday before, but I couldn't concentrate. It was true what Lotte had said. The girls and women I had known from the mill were turning in their seats, craning their necks to stare at me, looking me over like I was one of those stuck-up charity ladies who came to the mill before Christmas to hand out stale sugar cookies and old clothes. It was as if I had deliberately betrayed them, bought this lovely dress just to make them feel doubly ashamed of their worn-out shirtwaists. One week away from the mill, one ten-dollar pay check, and I was already an outsider. *Kept woman!* I felt bee stung.

The bald old priest with the quavering voice began his sermon. Strange that I can remember it so clearly after all this time. He was speaking slow, simplified English for his congregation of immigrant mill workers: Poles, Germans, Italians, and the few Croatians. He was warning us young women—for the assembly was mostly female—not to pollute our souls with the temptations of the modern world. He preached against dime novels, moving pictures, and vaudeville shows. He derided the new fashions, the sheer stockings and rouge, the skirts that reached halfway up the calf, the strange new contortion dances and the ragtime music that accompanied them. He preached against alcohol, cigarettes, and sweet-talking men. "Purity is the crown of womanhood," he said, enunciating every syllable. "What do you call a woman who cannot keep herself pure?"

Lotte, who had indulged in nearly every one of those sins, nodded off to sleep, her chin digging into the yellow lace of her bodice. I began to feel a belated welling up of tenderness for her. My only kin in this country, and I had left her behind in the mills to go on to better things. "Did you find a new roommate yet?" I whispered, nudging her awake. I had already paid my half of the rent for May, but if Lotte couldn't find anyone to take my place, I should also pitch in for the next month. It seemed the least I could do.

"Alma Wilfahrt's moving in the first of June," she yawned. "Meanwhile," she added archly, "I'm enjoying having the bed to myself. You always whimpered in your sleep like a sick puppy. Anyway, I won't be staying in that boardinghouse much longer. Sepp's finally getting serious."

"Sepp! Lotte, *no!* Lotte, you wouldn't. Not with *him.*"

"Oh, listen to yourself!" Lotte raised her voice. "It's only because he's sweet on me that he didn't fire you a long time ago."

Heads were turning in our direction. The old lady in front of us turned around and made a loud shushing noise. It was a relief for both of us when the last hymn ended and we could step out into the fresh air. Flat-bottomed, curly-topped prairie clouds were sailing like steamships across the deep blue sky. It was warm enough not to need a cardigan but still seemed far from the stifling heat of summer, the days when the mill was like an oven, the sun pouring through the dirty skylights. I wanted to take my cousin's arm and say something that would smooth over the rift between us, but no words came to me.

"Are you coming along to Schmidt's?" she asked, though she knew very well I would say no. Sepp would be waiting for her there. Church was for women, children, and a few henpecked husbands. Working men spent their Sunday mornings at the tavern.

"You go on without me, Lotte. Have a nice time."

"Until next Sunday, then," she said, but she sounded dubious. We both knew that I would not be making the three-hour journey to the old neighborhood much longer.

"You better not get too used to the soft life," she told me. "It might be over quicker than you know. That lady won't keep you on forever." Before I could think of what to say, she had turned on her heel, already walking away from me. Her parting jab ricocheted in my ears on the streetcar to Jelinek's.

⤷ The bookstore was lifeless as a mausoleum. No glimpse of the Bohemian glass in the front window, just the dusty Venetian blinds pulled all the way down. I began to feel like a fool, standing in front of the locked-up shop with the box of toffees in my hand. Young unaccompanied women do not call on men. The proper way to convey my gratitude to them for helping me get my new job would have been to send a card, but now I was here, so I might as well make the best of it. I went to the narrow green door beside the main entrance. Tacked onto the wood was a faded piece of cardboard with *Private Residence* written on it, in what I now recognized as John Jelinek's handwriting. I looked up at the apartment over the shop. The curtains were open, so they must be awake. I rang the bell, which made such a racket that I cringed. Ringing their doorbell on Sunday morning. They probably thought it was a religious fanatic, or someone collecting money for the Minnesota Temperance Mission.

The ring was answered by silence. I was about to slink away when I heard footsteps descending the staircase. The door opened. Old Mr. Jelinek stood on the threshold in his gray felt slippers. "Kathrin," he said, drawing his hand across his forehead. "That's *you?*" A smile spread across his face. "My dear, this is a surprise. I see Mrs. Waverly's been treating you very well."

"I have you to thank. For everything." I was burning up with embarrassment, but a pleasant embarrassment, my misgivings melting away. I gave him the toffees. "These are for you."

"Thank you, dear. Please come in. John's just out to the bakery, but he should be back any minute." I followed him up the narrow staircase. The walls were covered in tattered paper, a pattern of golden Chinese roses that looked as if it were older than I was. "I hope you will excuse the untidiness," he said, opening the door at the top of the stairs. "When two men live on their own, Kathrin, it's not a pretty sight." He led me into the kitchen, also their main room, from the looks of it. There was a beat-up sofa in the corner and an ancient-looking walnut sideboard cluttered with old photographs in tarnished silver frames. In the center of the room was a round table covered in red oilcloth. Beside it were two mismatched chairs. He drew one out for me. "Would you like some tea?"

"Yes. Thank you." Then I gasped as something rubbed against my leg. A big orange cat with yellow eyes.

Mr. Jelinek laughed. "He's not even ours. He's the neighbor's, but he comes through the window to visit us. That's the thing about tomcats, Kathrin. You never own those creatures. They're not loyal to anything. They just come and go, but I think that one likes you."

I held out my hand, and the cat rubbed his head against it, purring.

"Mind that he doesn't shed on your skirt. That would be a pity." Mr. Jelinek filled the kettle and put it on to boil. Soon we were leaning over our teacups, as I told him about my new routine at Mrs. Waverly's and the fairy tales I was translating.

"She's a very good woman," he said. "I knew her husband in the old days, too. A pity you never met him, Kathrin. A distinguished and intelligent man, but not too full of himself the way some professors are."

Mr. Jelinek, I thought, was so like my uncle, or what my uncle would be like if he were my grandfather. I felt much more at ease sitting in his kitchen and listening to his thickly accented English than I had speaking my mother tongue with Lotte. He always treated me with an air of fondness and protection, as if he felt responsible for me. I liked to pretend we were related somehow.

"Have you ever seen her house?" I asked him. "It is so grand, like a palace, but also sad. She is rich and beautiful but all alone. No children."

Before Mr. Jelinek could reply, we heard the door opening, rapid footsteps coming up the stairs. "He's always in such a hurry," said Mr. Jelinek. "He runs up those stairs two at a time. Never does anything slow, that boy."

The kitchen door burst open, and John came in rattling a paper bag of bakery rolls. "It took ages this morning. I had to wait for them to get a new batch out of the oven." When he saw me sitting with his uncle, he looked me over like he'd never seen me before. "Kathrin. My, my." He dumped the rolls into a crumb-littered basket and held them under my nose. "They're still hot. The raisin buns are the best." Thanking him, I took one, then passed the basket to Mr. Jelinek. There were only two chairs, so John pulled an empty coal crate away from the wall, upended it, and sat down between us, blocking my view of his uncle.

"Kathrin brought us these," said Mr. Jelinek, nudging the box of toffees across the table. "She's been getting along very well at Mrs. Waverly's."

"I can see that myself."

I had never felt shy around John before, but now that I had every reason to feel grateful to him, I was tongue-tied. I could hardly look at him. Instead, I ate my roll. Mr. Jelinek got up to make some fresh tea.

"So you're happy there," said John. He tore off part of a steaming roll and stuffed it in his mouth, bolting it down with a hunger exactly like my own.

"Yes."

"You look like you just robbed a bank," he said, still chewing. "You look like you never set foot in a mill your whole life."

I laughed, dropping my guard. He was teasing me, and everything was the same as before. I took another roll and tried to eat slowly, discriminatingly, like a lady, but I was so hungry that I ended up wolfing it down in much the same manner as John. Mr. Jelinek put the fresh pot of tea on the table and brought a cup for his nephew. As John poured his tea and stirred the sugar in, I reached under the table to pet the cat, but my hand brushed up against flannel. It took me a few seconds to realize it was John's leg. I jerked my hand away as if I had touched a hot iron. If I could, I would have crawled underneath the linoleum.

John looked at me incredulously and burst out laughing. He scooped up the cat from under his feet and held him in his lap. "Here, Kathrin. Now you can pet him." Sensing Mr. Jelinek's eyes on us, I felt so preposterous, the only thing I could do was stretch out my hand and pet the cat. I ran my fingertips between his ears until he squeezed his eyes shut, purring as loudly as an unoiled sewing machine. I felt the bony ridges on his skull through the soft fur. It had been so long since I had held or caressed anything, human or beast.

When I finally drew my hand away, John tossed the cat on the floor and brushed the orange hairs off his lap. His uncle, who had been watching me the whole time, touched John's shoulder. "Kathrin," the old man said, "is the very image of our Nadja."

John covered his eyes with one hand. "Oh, don't you start on that."

"Who is Nadja?" I asked.

"My mother." John's voice was taut. The tendons in his neck were sticking out like ropes.

Mr. Jelinek left his chair and went to the sideboard, coming back with an old photograph, blurry and indistinct, more like a smudged sketch. The young woman in the picture had a heart-shaped face, thick and glossy hair, either light brown or dark blond. It was hard to tell. There was something written in Czech across the bottom of the photograph. The only words I recognized were the names: the one it was addressed to, Jan, and the one who had signed it, Nadja.

"She is pretty." I handed the photograph back to Mr. Jelinek.

"She was beautiful," he said. "She was too good for this world." He got up and put the photograph back on the sideboard. "I like to think," he said, his back to me and John, "that we don't really lose the people we love. They just come back to us in different guises."

"There's some rolls left." John handed me the breadbasket. I shook my head.

"I should be going." I got up and carried my empty teacup to the sink.

"Don't be a stranger, dear." Mr. Jelinek took my hand and held it in both his own. His hands felt dry, like parchment. "Maybe Mrs. Waverly will send you to the bookstore to pick up her orders, just to save herself the errand."

I nodded and smiled into his eyes. They were hazel, like my own. It was really hard to dispel the illusion that we were related.

John stood in the doorway, his hands in his pockets. "I'll walk you to the streetcar."

As I followed him down the stairs, I found myself wondering how old he had been when his mother died. I had never thought of him as an orphan before. Like me, like Lotte. "Your uncle is very kind," I told him as we crossed the street. Distracted by the thoughts milling around in my head, I nearly stepped into a splat of steaming horse manure. John grabbed my elbow, steering me around it.

"He's good-hearted," said John, "but once you get him started on those old stories, he'll go on the whole day. What do you do with your spare time now that you live on Summit Avenue?"

"It is too early to say. Everything is so new."

"Do you miss your sister?"

"My cousin." I hesitated. "A little. I—"

"Alone with the lady in that big house. Sounds lonely. This Saturday next," he said, "I'll come and visit you. Around seven. I've never been to Summit Avenue. You can show me around." He said this in a lightly facetious tone that made me laugh. When the streetcar came, I climbed in the back and waved over the rail at John and at his uncle, watching from the window.

⮷ By the time I got off the streetcar on Summit, it was late afternoon. Everyone was outside enjoying the fine May weather. Families were having tea parties and playing croquet on their endless mansion lawns. The women and children were dressed in white, the men in tan, pipes in their mouths, laughing. As the women sipped tea from porcelain cups, their servants stood in the background, silent as stones, waiting for their next summons. This I could see from the street. That was the oddest thing about American yards. They were open to the public eye, no wall or hedge to obscure the view of people walking past. It was as if they wanted an audience. Look at us drinking our tea. Look at our lace tablecloth. Look at us playing lawn tennis in our spotless linen trousers and white canvas shoes. Display was more important than privacy.

Only Mrs. Waverly's house was surrounded by a ten-foot stone wall, which itself was half hidden in grapevine. The big wrought iron gates in front were kept closed unless she was expecting visitors. Surely her neighbors regarded her as eccentric. A cloistered widow who lived alone with a single maid and over two thousand books. And now with an immigrant mill girl.

John had said I must be lonely at Mrs. Waverly's, but solitude was a thing that had never bothered me. After my years in the sewing room packed in with the other seamstresses and my years in the boarding-house, where I hadn't even had a bed to myself, it felt like a luxury. I still couldn't get over the vastness of this house, its elegance. Even as I unlocked the front door with the key Mrs. Waverly had given me, I felt a prickle of guilt, as if I were breaking in.

The house, when I entered, was more profoundly silent than any place I had ever been. The Oriental runners on the stairs seemed to swallow my footsteps. Going down the hallway on the second floor, I passed her study. The door was ajar, but when I glanced inside, the room was empty. Where was she? Visiting family? Friends? Did she have friends? I wound my way through the corridors, past all the closed doors I had never seen opened. I had no idea what lay behind them. Shut up rooms full of old furniture covered in sheets, carpets gone mildewed? The only rooms I had been in were the front entryway, Mrs. Waverly's study, the dining room where I worked, the lovely round tower room I slept in, the second-floor bathroom, and the kitchen, where we shared our evening meals.

As I opened the door to my tower bedroom, I found myself won-dering why Mrs. Waverly and her husband had never had children. The house would have taken on a completely different aspect if it had been full of children. Professor Waverly had been old when they mar-ried. Maybe that had something to do with it. Alone in my room, I blushed. The Waverlys' marriage was none of my business, yet in all my life, both here and in my old village, I had never known a married couple without children. I wondered if Mrs. Waverly had what my mother and aunts used to refer to as a female affliction?

I thought of the portrait of Mrs. Waverly in the study, the portrait done when she was my age. Then, as now, she was beautiful. She could have

married any man she pleased. Why an old man? Even with the affection
I felt for Mr. Jelinek, I could never imagine marrying him. Had she married the Professor for his money? No, I refused to entertain the notion
that Mrs. Waverly was capable of anything so vulgar, of stooping so low.

Lying on the bed, I studied the pattern of stars on the ceiling. Stars
flung around in constellations I couldn't name. There in the far left corner was the crescent moon. *No,* I told myself. Mrs. Waverly was a scholarly woman, and scholars are different from ordinary people. The life of
the mind was the most important thing for her, even more important
than a house full of children. Mr. Jelinek said that Professor Waverly had
been a brilliant man. She married him for his genius. She wasn't just
his wife but his assistant, his protégée, his right arm, following him on
his field trips around the world. She must have loved him deeply. Even
if she didn't wear black, she was loyal beyond the grave. A woman of
her beauty and fortune could find a new husband by snapping her
fingers, yet she hadn't remarried. She kept to herself, working on her
husband's last project like a chosen disciple, not handing it over to the
university. *Isn't that love?* I asked myself. *What is love, if not that?*

I wandered over to the curving windows veiled in Virginia creeper.
Every morning when I woke up, the room was full of leaf shadows, like
waking up in a forest. Elbows on the window sill, I pressed my face to
the glass. Through the curtain of vines, I could see the walled garden in
back. The high stone wall was what made me think of this house, more
than any other residence on Summit, as a castle, a citadel, a stronghold.
The walled garden was the most beautiful I had ever seen, full of
flowers and blooming trees, and yet it was hidden. No one on the outside knew it existed. On the far end of the garden, I saw someone
kneeling over a flower bed. Did Mrs. Waverly have a gardener who
worked on Sunday? I strained my eyes. No, it was Mrs. Waverly herself.
This was what she did with her Sundays. She didn't play lawn tennis,
didn't go to church. She knelt in the soil of her secret garden.

I should go out and say hello. I hadn't seen or talked to her all day,
having gotten up so early to make it to church on time. *Besides,* I
thought, winding my way back through the hall and down the stairs,
Mrs. Waverly hasn't seen my new dress yet.

6 ❧ Stepping out the back door, I made my way across the porch and over the lawn, which hadn't been mown yet that year. The thick grass was studded with small daisies, flowering red clover, and dandelions— more like a meadow than a city yard. It reminded me of the pastures I had known as a girl. My mother used to say that in May the world is like a beautiful dream. I moved forward slowly, savoring each step and the rustling noise the wind made as it moved through my new muslin skirt, molding and remolding it against my legs.

Mrs. Waverly crouched in the black earth like a peasant. She wore what were probably her oldest clothes, heavy brown cotton that would not easily show stains. Her sleeves were rolled up above her elbows, exposing her arms, ivory pale in the sunlight but less delicate, more muscled than I would have imagined. She was planting seedlings, digging holes with her trowel, putting the naked little plants in, and patting the soil around their roots. Though I was standing only a few feet away, she seemed not to notice me. She was singing something under her breath, something sad. *Something private,* I thought, overcome by a sudden sense of shame. What was I thinking of, sneaking up on my employer on a Sunday afternoon, intruding on her solitude? Perhaps she didn't want company. Perhaps I wasn't allowed in the garden without her permission. I was about to creep back to the house when she turned and saw me. Her face froze. She didn't scream but dropped her trowel, which fell noiselessly into the earth. Her face and even her arms were blazing red. She was as flustered as I was.

"You gave me a fright," she said. "I didn't expect you back until evening."

"I'm sorry. I did not mean to disturb you."

"I was dreaming again," she said before I could retreat. "You caught me in the middle of a daydream." She brushed the soil off her hands. "And yourself?" she asked, her equanimity returning. "How was church? Did you have a nice chat with your cousin?"

I murmured something polite and vague. It was easier than explaining I'd spent more time with the Jelineks than with Lotte.

"Your dress is lovely, Kathrin." She had never called me by my first name before. "Turn around. Let me see the back."

Feeling a bit silly, I spun around in a circle. The wind lifted my skirt, making it flare out around my calves.

"That's my favorite color," she said. "Blue like moonlight. Is it new?"

"Yes. I bought it yesterday."

"It suits you." Mrs. Waverly picked up her trowel again. "I'm nearly finished here. After I get cleaned up, we can have an early dinner. You're too thin, Kathrin. You need to eat more. Put some color in your face." She smiled at me before digging another hole, patting in another seedling. As I walked back to the house, my ears were ringing. The way she had spoken to me, more like a mother than an employer. Calling me by my first name. She had even pronounced it the German way, the first American I had ever met who knew how.

⟿ Since it was so mild, Mrs. Waverly decided we could eat at the wicker table on the back porch. Franny had cooked rosemary chicken, new potatoes, asparagus from the garden. Green asparagus, the kind I had never seen before.

Mrs. Waverly opened a bottle of white wine. When she poured it into the glasses, it glowed golden in the evening light, sparkling with a luminosity of its own. This was how I always imagined a magic potion would look. I felt like a mill girl again, a barefoot, unwashed mill girl who had wandered into a palace by mistake. I'd never drunk good wine before, ever. Sometimes my mother had made elderflower cordial, and I'd had the odd teaspoon of rum in my tea to warm up in winter and the weekly mouthful of sour communion wine, but never anything like this. "Cheers," she said, clinking glasses with me. I took my first sip. It tasted as golden as it looked. It burned inside my mouth.

She took my plate and piled it with asparagus, potatoes, chicken, and salad greens. The food tasted of spring, a distillation of the flowering apple and pear trees, the last daffodils and the first irises, and the many other flowers I couldn't even name. Back at the mill, whole springs had passed without my noticing much more than an absence of snow and a gradual accumulation of warmth, but now the season was unfolding around me everywhere I looked, and the chicken was the most tender I had ever tasted. I took this in with a wonderment so keen it bordered on pain, for I was afraid to trust any of it. Where was the hitch? What would move a lady like Mrs. Waverly to be so kind to someone like me? Why was she serving me this grand meal? She could have let me take my dinner in the kitchen with the maid. Not that I wasn't humbled by her goodness, but I knew she was concealing something from me, just as I was struggling to conceal my hunger and uncertainty from her.

I forced myself to eat the chicken with the silver knife and fork, tried to wield them as deftly as she did, though I really wanted to pick up the whole chicken breast in my hands and gnaw the flesh off the bones like the farmer's daughter I was. With one false move, one display of peasant coarseness, I would make the whole illusion shatter like a broken mirror. For this had to be an illusion, a spell, a dream. Despite her talk of helping me get an office job when the translations were finished, my secret fear was that sooner or later I would wake up and find myself back in the boardinghouse beside my cousin. That I would wake up hungrier and more desolate than I had ever been.

"Tell me about yourself, Kathrin," she said. "I don't even know what part of Germany you're from."

I set my silverware down, took another burning sip of wine. "My village was in the Black Forest, which is in the province of Baden." I used my best English and tried to banish my accent. "My valley is called the Höllental. In English the name would be Hell Valley." Then I cursed myself for being so uncouth. *Hell* is a bad word in English. "The nearest city is Freiburg," I added quickly. "There is a university there."

"Ah, yes." Mrs. Waverly nodded. "I was in Freiburg once. A long time ago. My husband had friends there, also professors of ethnology.

Höllental, you say?" She copied my pronunciation. "I'm surprised Arthur didn't take me there. It would be just the sort of place that would intrigue him. He was fascinated by the Black Forest, all the customs and so forth. Like those wooden masks they wear for carnival. I thought they looked a bit like African masks. Do you have them in your valley, too?"

"Yes," I said as diplomatically as I could. I had never liked those masks. Our carnival in the Black Forest was not some lighthearted affair with paper hats and confetti but something raw and very old. We didn't even call it Karneval or Fasching like they do elsewhere in Germany, because it was no carnival in that sense. We called it Fastnet, for those were the nights before Lent began, and our masks were not meant to be funny or quaint, but to terrify. "It is mostly the men who wear the masks," I told her. "They march at night with torches through the valley." When I was a child, those processions had given me nightmares. I thought the men with their masks lit up in the torchlight were evil spirits, the bogeymen my mother was always warning me about. "On the Tuesday before Lent begins, they march into the village square and make a big fire. Then they burn a witch."

Mrs. Waverly set down her glass, splashing some wine on her hand.

"Not a real witch," I explained. The way I talked, she must have thought I sprang from a race of philistines. "A big doll made of straw." I paused before going on. "But long ago they burned real witches. Well, not witches," I amended, lest she think I was superstitious, "but people . . . women they thought were witches. Not far from my valley is another valley called the Hexental, the valley of witches."

"I've read about the witch burnings," she said, cutting her asparagus into smaller and smaller pieces. She seemed to spend more time slicing her food than eating it and had barely touched anything on her plate. "I think that if I had lived back then, they would have probably burned me." From the tone of her voice, it didn't sound as if she were joking.

Picking up my knife and fork, I sliced one of the new potatoes into quarters, raised the fork to my mouth. *Yes, she is a sorceress,* I thought as I chewed and swallowed. *She admits it herself.* Maybe that was why I had never met a woman like her before. In my part of the world, they had been burned long ago.

"Tell me some more about the Höllental," she said.

"Once . . . one hundred years ago, Goethe came to our village. He spent the night in our inn." I didn't want her to think we were completely uncivilized. "And before that, the Austrian princess Marie Antoinette traveled through the Höllental on her way to Paris to marry the French king. She came through our valley with a train of fifty coaches."

"Marie Antoinette?" Mrs. Waverly was amused.

"Yes. In those days there were no proper roads in our valley, so the people had to build one just for her."

She laughed. "Oh, yes, I'm sure they did. Traveling through the Höllental on her way to be married. That's what I call tempting fate." She broke off, shaking her head. "It's such a pity Arthur never met you, Kathrin. He would have had all sorts of questions to ask you. Well, tell me something else, but not about carnival or anyone famous. Tell me something that you loved about your valley."

Something that I loved? What kind of question was that? I had to think a long while before I could answer her. "On the first day of summer, the longest day of the year, we rolled wheels down a hill into the mill stream. Burning wheels. They were on fire. They rolled and burned all the way down the hill, and then they fell into the water."

"We call them Catherine wheels," said Mrs. Waverly. "After the wheel St. Catherine was martyred on. Actually the custom predates St. Catherine. It's a pagan survival. Sun worship," she said, between sips of the shining wine. For a moment, she was silent. I used the lull in our conversation to finish my chicken, but even after cleaning my plate, I was still hungry enough to eat everything left in the serving dishes and the food on her plate that she had sliced with such care. But then, as if reading my mind, she started to eat. She finally seemed to have found her appetite.

"Tell me about your family," she said a few minutes later. "Do you have any brothers and sisters back home?"

That's when I dropped my knife and fork. What an ugly clatter they made as they fell against the polished oak porch. I leapt out of my chair, nearly knocking it over, and knelt to pick them up, wiping them on the damask napkin, making an ugly brown mark on the cloth. Kneeling on her porch with a stained napkin in my hand.

"Sit down, Kathrin. It's all right," she said. "I'll get you some clean silverware." She disappeared through the screen door into the kitchen. As I returned to my chair, I felt a dangerous prickling behind my eyes. How could I be such a clumsy fool? She came out again, handed me a new knife and fork, a clean napkin, then sat down calmly, as if nothing had happened.

"I have two brothers and a sister," Mrs. Waverly said. "Older than me. I'm the youngest. Next Saturday you'll meet them. They're coming by with their children. It will be a full house. I have nineteen nieces and nephews, if you can believe that. Kathrin, your plate's empty." She took it from me and filled it again, a generous helping of everything. Then she looked at me the same way she had when she'd asked me to tell her about something from home that I loved. "It must be bewildering for you, living over here. Everything so different from what you're used to. Do you get homesick?"

"No. Never." I ate my food so I wouldn't have to say anything else. She hadn't meant to wound me, but it had been a pointless question, like asking me if I missed my dead parents, when I couldn't even remember my mother's face. *I know I shall never see the other side of the Atlantic again. That old life is dead to me. That old life is buried.* I took a sip of the wine, an awkward sip, some of it spilling over my lip and down my chin. I wiped it away with the clean napkin, grateful that at least the pale wine wouldn't leave a stain, but the wine clouded my vision, making everything shadowy and dim. I bit my lip hard to steady myself.

"I remember Freiburg as a very pleasant place," she said, her voice drawing me out of the valley of my thoughts, back into the wicker chair in the sunlit garden. "Much prettier, I think, than Heidelberg, where all the Americans go. I had a hard time with the language, though. I learned French in school and Russian at home—my great-grandmother was born in St. Petersburg—but German was difficult for me. Arthur, of course, spoke excellent German. Languages were his specialty. Sometimes I think he should have been a linguist. He could pick up languages the way my nieces pick up the new slang."

She didn't speak of him the way most wives speak of their husbands, living or deceased. Not with the usual mixture of affection and
good-natured griping, but with a distant sort of reverence, the way my
uncle spoke of Schiller and Heinrich Heine. *It's because he was a genius,*
I told myself, *and no ordinary man.*

"He was a great professor, your husband," I said shyly. "Mr. Jelinek
said he was brilliant."

"Yes," she said, glancing across the garden. "He was very intelligent,
and he didn't mock me for being so bookish." She was silent for a
moment. "After he died, it took me a year before I could pick up a
scholarly book again without being reminded of him, of what I had
lost." Her eyes were somewhere else, seeing things I couldn't see, seeing things I couldn't even comprehend. For the first time, I had an
inkling of what John had meant that night in the bookstore when he'd
said, "You can tell she's lonely, all right." I began to sense her loneliness. The sadness she kept hidden.

"You know," she said, still gazing at the flowers and trees, "too
many men just want a wife for a piece of decoration. He was different." She turned to me with a half smile. "You're at the age when you
have to keep that in mind, Kathrin. I'll give you the same advice I give
my nieces." She was using a sisterly tone. "Before you settle on a man,
make sure he loves you for more than your pretty face."

Before either of us could think of what to say next, Franny came
out with a wheel of soft white cheese on a silver tray and a basket of
freshly washed peaches, droplets of water still clinging to their skin.
The peaches looked too perfect to eat. Mrs. Waverly picked up a silver knife and began to cut the cheese into wedges like a pie.

"When I went abroad for the first time, I was a grown woman,
twenty-one years old, with a husband to do the translating for me, but
even so, I was petrified. The way I looked and talked and dressed,
everyone knew I was a foreigner. I felt like a gawky young girl at her
first dance. I keep thinking how brave you were, Kathrin, coming here
when you were sixteen, all by yourself, learning the language from
scratch, speaking it so well after only two years. I envy your courage."
She spoke so sincerely, I was at a loss. I could not believe a woman like

her would see anything enviable in a person like me. *I wasn't brave, I was desperate,* I wanted to tell her, but, of course, I didn't. That would have been rude.

"Your uncle," she said, "must be very proud of you. Here, try a peach. They're from the hothouse, but still nice enough, I think." She reached across the table to hand me one. The fruit was heavy and moist in my palm.

"Thank you," I said and bit into it, my teeth sinking through the fuzz on the firm skin, into the sweet juicy flesh. I thought of the old stories of the gods eating nectar. This was nectar, this fruit, this kindness. I smiled at the woman sitting across from me and inwardly invoked Mr. Jelinek. I could smell her faint perfume, or maybe it was the scent of the garden.

"My great-grandmother came over from St. Petersburg when she was fifteen." Mrs. Waverly held out the silver tray so I could take a piece of cheese. Velvety on my tongue, tasting like raw almonds and wild mushrooms, the kind my mother and I used to pick in the forest every fall. "She came here alone, just like you. She arrived in New York and found work at a furrier's, fourteen hours a day. She was a wife and mother at sixteen, a grandmother by the time she was my age, and through her years of having babies, she kept working at the furrier's, because she had to, just to feed them. She saw to it that her daughters went to school and married well, and they saw to it that their children did even better." Mrs. Waverly stopped short, biting into a wedge of cheese.

"My father had a Russian name. Andresky. But he changed it to Andrews. That was my maiden name. Violet Andrews. When I was a girl, my father wanted us to speak only English, but my great-granny was living with us then, and she ignored the rule. She was over ninety and so ornery, nobody dared to cross her. She sat me on her lap and told me story after story in Russian. That's how I learned the language and how I came to love fairy tales, even before I met my husband."

Her eyes were so far away, you would have thought she could see across the ocean, as distant as they had been when I surprised her in the garden. Not wanting to intrude on her thoughts, I looked across the lawn, drenched in sunlight, dappled in shadow. My eyes came to rest on a delicate tree covered in pendulous gold flowers, shimmering in the sun, so radiant that it seemed to crackle, dancing and shifting like a fairy. "What is the English name for that tree?" I finally asked her. "In German we call it Goldregen. The flowers are like gold rain."

"The English name is laburnum," Mrs. Waverly said. "Untranslated from the Latin. Quite unpoetic, I'm afraid." We lapsed into silence, staring at the tree.

"Gold rain," she said a few minutes later. "That reminds me of the story of Frau Holle. The girl jumping into the well after her fallen spindle and winding up in Frau Holle's cottage. Do you know that one, Kathrin? It's one of the Grimms' tales. She keeps house for her and shakes out her featherbed every day, and at the end of the story, she's showered in gold."

I closed my eyes. That was my favorite story, the one I had begged my mother to tell me again and again. Something caught in my throat. I turned to Mrs. Waverly, feeling suddenly as nervous as when I'd first stepped through her front door last Sunday. Then she smiled at me, a disarming smile, like someone who had known me for ages. I took a long sip of wine, letting the garden and the laburnum tree blazing in the sun sink in. It was the most beautiful place I had ever been, the most beautiful place I would ever be.

≈ By day I sat in the sonorous dining room, translating for hours, getting ink stains on my fingers and cuffs. I practiced my typing, learning to pick out the letters by touch, practicing at least an hour a day. At the end of each session, my wrists ached and my fingers were like lead, but I kept telling myself that typing was the most important skill I would take with me from this job.

Our real life took place in the evenings, during the long meals we shared on the back porch. Sometimes we sat talking and sipping wine until the sun set and the moths came out. Those evenings we recited the fairy tales we had translated that day. I told her the German tales, and Mrs. Waverly told me the Russian tales. Those May nights are fixed in my memory like an engraving. Watching the sky darken to indigo, waiting for the first stars to appear, and listening to her stories. There wasn't enough light to make out her face, but her voice was an entity of its own, something she could shift into any shape she wanted. She could make herself sound like an old woman or a girl, like a harsh crow or a plaintive young man. The tales emerged from the darkness, tales I had never heard before. She told me the story of Marussia, who had the misfortune to marry a vampire. She told me of the Firebird, who carried the water of life, which could make the dead rise again. But the story I remember most vividly is the tale of the girl who walked into the thick of the forest to the sorceress' house. The story that was to become my story, shaping the rest of my life like a prophecy. The tale I shall carry inside me forever, like an old photograph hidden inside a locket. A secret icon.

This is the story as she told it to me. Even now, four years later, I can still hear her voice, every word and every inflection.

"Once there was a girl who lost her mother."

I shivered as she said this, pressing my hands together in my lap and leaning forward to inhale the lilacs in their crystal vase, white lilacs, ghostly in the sputtering candlelight.

"The girl's name was Wassalissa."

A name like music. I could see her. A skinny girl with long plaits. A girl who was always hungry.

"As she stood at her mother's deathbed, the good woman gave her a magical doll made of wood, a doll that would look after her always. 'Remember to keep her secret,' said the mother. 'No one must know you have her. Listen to what she tells you, and remember, above all, to feed her.' As soon as she had passed the doll into her daughter's hands, she laid her head back on the pillow and breathed her last breath.

"Wassalissa mourned her mother. So did her father, but not for so very long. Before the year of mourning had ended, he brought home a new bride, a handsome but spiteful widow with a mean-hearted daughter. As suddenly as he married, he went away on a long journey, leaving Wassalissa alone with her new stepmother, who made her do all the work while her own daughter sat idle. She was jealous of Wassalissa's beauty and wanted to break her with toil, make her hands rough and her face coarse, but the girl had her mother's blessing. She labored without complaint and only grew more beautiful. The more Wassalissa's beauty waxed, the more jealous her stepmother became. She plotted and plotted. How could she rid herself of this girl? Finally she moved the family to a cabin at the edge of a dense wild forest."

I was back in the Höllental. It was November, and the thin strip of sky we could see from the bottom of the valley was black, moonless, but full of stars.

"That forest was the home of the sorceress Baba Yaga, who ate human flesh and flew around in a cauldron shaped like a mortar, using a pestle for an oar, sweeping away her tracks with a broom made of dead man's hair. The stepmother sent Wassalissa into Baba Yaga's forest to gather firewood, yet the girl always came back unharmed, because the doll and her mother's blessing protected her. Finally the step-mother took the most desperate measure of all. She let the hearth fire go out. She let the fire go out in December, just before the winter solstice, the darkest night of the year. She let the fire go out, so in that house, there was neither light nor heat. Without fire they would per-ish. The stepmother accused Wassalissa of letting the fire go out. She thrust the girl out the door in the middle of the night into the freez-ing cold. 'Go to Baba Yaga and ask her for fire! Don't come back until you have a burning torch.'

"So Wassalissa set off at midnight through the forest of twisted trees. There was no moon. Thick clouds hid the stars, so dark it was. But the doll guided her on her way. Gradually the darkness began to pass. Suddenly she saw a man riding on a white horse, and it was dawn. Then a red man rode past on a red horse, and the sun rose. Wassalissa walked and walked through the forest until the doll said, 'There!' She stood in a clearing. In the middle of the clearing was a house set on hen's feet, dancing round and round in a circle."

It was too dark for Mrs. Waverly to see that I was crying. I would have died of shame had she seen my tears, but it was my mother's house that danced in that clearing. It was so real.

"The house was surrounded by a burning hedge of bare branches, and atop each naked branch was a flaming skull."

I *saw* this, as sharp and clear as if it were taking place in front of me. Except the skulls were our wooden Fastnet masks.

"Wassalissa wanted to run into the forest and hide, but then a black rider swept up on a black horse. He called out a charm to the hen-footed house, which immediately stopped its dancing and lowered its door to the ground. The door was made of dead men's bones. The door latch was a human collarbone. The lock was a grinning skull. The black rider jumped off his black horse, opened the door, and disappeared. Then it was night, the darkest night of the year. Her doll whispered, 'Go!' So Wassalissa stepped inside the strange hovel, and there was Baba Yaga herself."

The pictures inside my head began to diverge more and more from the story she was telling me. She was describing what a hideous hag Baba Yaga was, her wart-crusted nose touching her greasy chin, but the sorceress I saw was not grotesque. An older woman, yes. Twice as old as I was, with some gray in her hair, but not ugly. She looked like Mrs. Waverly, like the picture of the woman with the wand I had seen in the book of fairy tales at Jelinek's, her dark hair streaming loose.

"'Well, my daughter,' said the Yaga, 'who are you and what do you seek?'

"'Lady, I am Wassalissa. I have come because we have no fire in our house.'

"'You let the fire go out? That was a very foolish thing to do. For foolish acts, you must pay. You'll get your fire, but not for nothing. First you must do the tasks I set for you. To start with, you can get my dinner out of the oven.'

"Wassalissa ran to the oven and took out dish after dish, a feast for at least a dozen people, but the hag ate everything herself, leaving only a crust of bread for the girl. 'Tomorrow when I go out, you must sweep the yard, sweep the house, cook the midday meal, do the washing, then go to the shed and sort out the mildewed corn from the good seed. Make sure you have everything done by the time I get back. Otherwise I shall eat you.'

"A little while later the sorceress fell snoring into bed. Wassalissa offered her doll her crust of bread and told her about the work she had to do the next day. The doll said, 'Eat the crust yourself, and go to sleep. All will be well. Morning is wiser than night. Everything looks different in the light of day.'

"The next morning the white rider rode past, and it was day. Baba Yaga whistled, and her mortar, pestle, and broom flew up to the door. She stepped into her mortar and was gone. The red rider rode past, and the sun rose.

"Wassalissa was about to start her work, but it was already done. The doll had completed the work for her while she was sleeping. The only task left was to make dinner.

"When Baba Yaga came home, she inspected every inch of the house, the yard, the grain shed, pleased and yet furious that she could find no fault in Wassalissa's work. 'You did well,' she growled. Then she called on her servants to come and grind her corn. Three pairs of hands appeared out of nowhere and did their task. Baba Yaga made bread from the ground corn. She stuffed herself with that and with the food Wassalissa had cooked for her. This time she left nothing for the girl to eat.

"'Tomorrow you must do the same chores as today, but you must also go to the granary. There you will find a pile of dirty poppy seeds. You must sort the poppy seeds from the dirt and divide them into two separate piles. If you don't succeed, I will feast on you and suck the marrow from your bones.'

"Wassalissa began to tremble, but her doll whispered, 'Sleep. All will be well. Have you already forgotten your mother's blessing?'

"By the time Baba Yaga had left the next morning, everything was done. When Baba Yaga returned, she was even more livid to find Wassalissa's work faultless. She clapped, and the three pairs of hands appeared to press the oil out of the poppy seeds. She drank down the oil and ate her dinner. Wassalissa stood beside her without making any noise.

"'What's the matter with you?' asked the sorceress. 'Can't you speak?'

"'If you will allow, Lady, I would like to ask you some questions.'

"'Ask what you like,' said Baba Yaga. 'But remember, too much knowledge makes a person old.'

"'I only want to know about the riders,' said Wassalissa.

"'Why, that's simple,' said the sorceress. 'The white rider is my day. The red rider is my sun. The black rider is my night.' Wassalissa nodded but kept silent. 'Don't you want to ask anything more?' asked Baba Yaga.

"'No, Lady. You yourself said that knowing too much makes you old before your time.'

"'A wise answer, my dear. Well, now I shall ask you some questions. How did you manage to do all that work?'

"'I have my mother's blessing,' said Wassalissa.

"'Get out right away!' sputtered the hag. 'I will have no blessings in this house.' She chased Wassalissa out the door, took a flaming skull down from her hedge, stuck it on a stick, and thrust it into Wassalissa's hand. 'Here is your fire. Now, go! Right away! Before I change my mind and eat you!' So Wassalissa rushed off through the forest, her doll pointing out the way."

I was that girl, and I was running. I could feel the hard pumping of my lungs, the sparks glancing off my face. I was holding the fire in my hand.

"She arrived home by evening the next day. The flaming skull looked so fearsome, she wanted to bury it in the snow, but the doll whispered, 'Keep it!' So she went into the dark house and gave the fire to her stepmother. The woman used the skull to light the hearth. Then she tried to extinguish the skull itself, but it would not go out. It burned and burned, its eyes boring into Wassalissa's stepmother and stepsister the whole night through. By morning they were burnt to cinders. When day came, Wassalissa buried the skull. But that is not the end of her story."

Mrs. Waverly paused for at least a minute. I sat very still in my chair and waited for her to go on.

"Orphaned again, Wassalissa walked into town to look for shelter. A kind old seamstress took her in. Wassalissa spun thread for her new mistress, and the thread she spun was fine and soft as human hair. It was too fine to weave, but the doll gave her a magical machine in place of a loom. This machine produced the finest cloth there ever was. Wassalissa gave it to the old woman and told her to sell it and keep the money. The seamstress brought it to the royal court and showed it to the king. When he asked how much she wanted for it, she told him it was a gift. It was priceless! No money on earth could pay for such exquisite handiwork. The king thanked her, gave her gifts in return, and sent her on her way. He wanted to have a shirt made from the cloth, but there wasn't a tailor in the realm who could cut and sew such marvelous fabric without ruining it. Finally he went to the seamstress' house. 'Old woman, since you have woven such fine cloth, you alone can sew it.' But the seamstress told him that the cloth was the work of a beautiful young girl. 'Then let her make me a shirt,' said the king.

"Wassalissa didn't make one shirt. She made a dozen, which she gave to the old woman to present to the royal court. When the old woman returned from her errand, she told Wassalissa to comb her hair, put on her best dress, and wait by the window. The king was very curious to meet the young woman who wove such beautiful cloth. He sent a servant to bring her to the palace, and as soon as he laid eyes on her, he fell in love."

Mrs. Waverly's voice was strangely cool and ironic as she said this.

"He took her hands, set her on the throne, and made her his wife. Wassalissa's father came back from his long journey in time for their wedding. Wassalissa was married in the grandest style, with silk and jewels, but that is not the end of her story."

Mrs. Waverly paused for at least two minutes, sipping from her wine glass and resting her voice.

"*Wassalissa,*" she said softly, pronouncing each syllable like a separate word. Waa-saa-liss-saa. "Wassalissa was a good and loyal wife. She bore her husband seven sons and seven daughters. She lived long, outliving her husband, but through her years of marriage and her years of widowhood, she kept her doll with her, treasured in secret."

Her voice rose a little when she said the word *secret.*

"She kept her doll until she was a white-haired crone. She kept her doll and her secret of fetching fire on the darkest night with her until the end of her days."

Her tale finished, she drained her glass of wine. I drank down the last few swallows of mine. That night the wine was red. Red wine grown cold in the darkness. I shivered. My blouse was too thin, and

I'd left my cardigan upstairs in my room. I could tell that she was chilly, too, in her white muslin dress. She kept rubbing her arms to keep warm. *We should go inside now,* I thought. It was late, and tomorrow was an early day. We usually got up at six, had breakfast at six-thirty. Yet neither of us could move. I stared at the gibbous moon, emerging from the inky clouds the wind was pushing across the sky, the wind that made the trees creak like dancing skeletons.

Then I opened my mouth, and the most incongruous sentence came out. "Mrs. Waverly, why do you like fairy tales so much? They are for children."

It took her a while to come up with an answer. In the darkness I could not see the expression on her face, had no way of knowing whether I had offended her or not. I was mortified for having spoken so carelessly. *It was the wine.* I should never be allowed to drink another drop. As I was about to apologize, she spoke.

"Come up to the study, Kathrin. I have something to show you."

☞ On one of the windowsills in her study was a Russian doll made of brightly painted wood, cylindrical in shape, scarlet and gold, with a white face, black eyes and hair. "Here, Kathrin." She placed the doll in my hands. "Open her up and see what's inside."

I pulled the doll apart to find a smaller, slightly different doll. This opened to a smaller doll and a smaller doll still, a progression of ever-shrinking dolls, until I came to the core, holding the ninth doll, no larger than a glass marble, in the palm of my hand.

"When you look at her on the outside, you think she's simple and crude. But she's not. It's the same with fairy tales."

"Were these your great-grandmother's?" I began to put the dolls back together again, one inside the other.

"Yes. One of the few things she brought with her when she came to this country." Mrs. Waverly wandered to the window. "When I'm old, I'll pass them on to my eldest niece, and she'll pass them on to her children." By the time I had finished putting the dolls back together, she was looking out the window at the darkness.

"Where should I put them, Mrs. Waverly?"

She turned away from the window to face me. "Shall we end this Mrs. Waverly business? I call you by your first name. Why don't you call me Violet?"

I couldn't believe what she was saying. In Germany I would have never been invited to address a professor's widow by her first name. It simply wasn't done. It seemed like a travesty, defying my deepest notions of familiarity and distance, yet it was not my place to refuse. *This is America,* I had to remind myself. *They do everything differently here. And now you are an American, too.*

"Here, Violet," I murmured, fumbling over the syllables of her first name as if I were pronouncing a word in some completely foreign language: Greek or Japanese. She took the dolls from my hand and set them gently back on the windowsill.

That night I dreamt of the dolls, dreamt that my skin was also made of brightly painted wood, falling off in layers and layers until I had a different body, a different face from the one I had always known. I dreamt of the Virgin Czaress who sleeps in a garden guarded by lions. Her soft black hair is as long as a river, and under her red silk pillow is a vial of the water of life. The tales enveloped me like a cloak, and I entered them, a little farther, a little deeper each day. They became a part of me, layers and layers inside me. What I would take with me when I left this house was far more precious than the ability to type. The tales would become my secret treasure, the heirloom I could pass on to my little girl. I knew I was living under a spell but no longer resisted it. It covered me like a wave, sweeping me off the shore and drawing me deep into the ocean.

7 ⬧ On Saturday visitors shattered our idyll. Violet had invited her siblings and their families for dinner. "They live in the suburbs," she told me, "so they can have big yards and their children can have ponies and dogs, but when we have a party, they come to me. Seeing as they have such big families," she added wryly, "and I have such a big empty house."

The dining room table where I had spent the whole week translating and learning to type was covered now in lace and embroidered linen, decked with silver, crystal, china, and massive bouquets of lilies and irises. The guests began arriving around six o'clock, while I was still in my room, changing into my muslin dress and pinning up my freshly washed hair. I could hear the doorbell ringing, Violet's cries of welcome, and male laughter booming up the stairwell. That was the most jarring thing. In the two weeks I had been here, there hadn't been a single man in the house.

Coming out of my room, I nearly tripped over one of Violet's little nephews, who was chasing his cousins through the hallways. The children were opening the doors of the rooms I had never seen opened. They were running around the Professor's old smoking room, crawling under his billiard table, rolling on the dusty Persian rug like puppies, shrieking their delight and wriggling out of the grasp of their older brothers, who were trying to keep them from breaking the glass lampshades and the porcelain stallions on the mantelpiece. This house was as magical to the children as it was to me.

I walked down the stairway and followed the trail of laughter and noise, the burst of piano music. Turning off the front hall, I came to a set of double doors, wide open for the first time, revealing a spacious room with an eighteen-foot ceiling and blue Oriental rugs on a parquet floor that looked like an intricate puzzle made of dark and blond wood woven together. Huge mullioned windows let in the evening light, which glanced off the watered silk upholstery of the armchairs and sofas. On the far end of the room stood a pink-veined marble fireplace with an oil portrait of the Professor hanging over it. The adults gathered in a loose circle in front of that unlit hearth. Violet and Franny passed around glasses of champagne.

In the corner near the door was a grand piano with seven girls around it. They looked like sisters. The eldest was my age, the youngest about ten. In their white silk dresses, they were as lovely as porcelain dolls, with pink tea roses pinned in their dark hair, but they weren't acting very ladylike. Fighting for a place on the piano bench, four of the seven girls managed to squeeze on, their bottoms wedged tightly together. I thought the bench would snap under their weight. The oldest girl, sandwiched between her sisters, hammered out one of those loud American ballads while her sisters sang along in harmony. The song was about a woman named Clementine who had big feet but was lost and gone forever. I couldn't decide if the song was supposed to be funny or sad.

The girls didn't see me watching them. I felt invisible, like a spy. Then Violet caught sight of me and swept across the parquet floor, her skirt of lilac silk rustling around her. "Kathrin! There you are. Let me introduce you to my family." I followed her, trying to keep pace without tripping over the fringes of the Oriental rugs.

"Here we are," she said brightly, though her voice sounded strained. A bit too bright. "This is my family." Two balding, mustached men and two women, deep bosomed and full in the hips, dressed in glittering brocade. They smiled at me over their champagne glasses. I smiled back, wondering whether I should curtsy.

"This is Edward," said Violet, briefly linking arms with the older of the two men. "And this is Robert," she said, touching her other brother's elbow. "Robert and Edward, this is Miss Kathrin Albrecht, who has been working so hard on the translations." They each shook my hand.

"It's good to know my sister has finally found someone to keep her company," said Edward. "We were afraid she was turning into a hermit." There was affection in his voice, but also a hint of condescension. That puzzled me. What did he mean by that?

"And these are my sisters-in-law, Mamie and Caroline," said Violet, ignoring her brother's remark. I shook their perfumed hands, my fingers brushing their diamond wedding rings. They beamed at me in a patronizing way, like the charity ladies who used to come to the mill, but then everyone looked up as another woman entered the room. The girls stopped singing. The woman said something to them in a low voice, her thin arms folded in front of her. All the girls but the oldest got up from the piano bench and smoothed out their skirts. Then the oldest girl started playing a restrained minuet.

"This is my sister Margaret," said Violet when the woman joined us. Her lips stiffened when she said her sister's name, but her voice was as bright as before. "Unfortunately Margaret's husband couldn't be with us tonight."

"He's in Chicago on business," said Margaret. Her voice was like a steel wheel on gravel.

"Margaret, this is Kathrin Albrecht."

I offered her my hand to shake, but she just nodded at me without speaking or smiling. She looked older than the brothers, though I later found out she was younger, thirty-nine, only three years older than Violet. She shared her sister's waving dark hair and gray eyes. Once she, too, had been beautiful, but the years had not been kind to her. Whatever spark of vitality she'd had she had expended giving birth to her seven daughters, those girls at the piano, passing her bloom on to them, leaving nothing for herself but a brittle shell. Her eyes were like February. The way she looked at me! It was like being turned inside out and inspected. I would have slunk out of the room that minute had Violet not pressed a glass of champagne into my hand. "Cheers, Kathrin." She and her sister exchanged an unreadable look.

As if picking up some imperceptible cue, her brothers began arguing about Thomas Van Lear, the socialist candidate who was running for mayor of Minneapolis. Margaret and their wives drifted away, but

Violet stood her ground, entering into the debate, holding up her opinions as sagaciously as any man. "No, I disagree. He can't be any worse than the dolt they have in now. If you ask me, he—"

She stopped in mid-sentence. The piano music trickled to a halt. Someone was marching across the room, the soles of his shoes squeaking on the parquet floor. A young man in a blue serge suit worn shiny at the elbows. A young man with a fistful of pink carnations. Everyone stared without speaking. Then Violet's nieces started giggling, all seven of them in unison, hiding their mouths behind their manicured hands. I dropped my glass of champagne, which shattered in brittle needles on the beautiful parquet. "John," I said. My voice was barely audible.

"I told you I was coming by tonight." His face was red with indignation. The tips of his ears were blazing.

My eyes were fixed on the puddle of champagne and broken glass at my feet. Violet's nieces poked each other and whispered. Violet's brothers laughed. "Get the young fellow a drink." But John just glared at me until Violet stepped forward and took the carnations from his hand. "Aren't they lovely? I'll put them in a vase." She came to me and touched my shoulder. "Go on, dear. I'll take care of the broken glass. Have a nice time." There seemed to be nothing left to do but follow John out the door.

"You forgot," he said as we stepped out into the cool evening, the fading sun.

"I'm sorry. I thought it was a joke. I did not think you would really come."

"You thought I was going to spend Saturday night with Jan?" He glanced back over his shoulder at Violet's mansion and laughed in disbelief. "So she supports the socialists," he said. "Now I've heard everything."

We walked to a dance hall on Selby, a place John had read about in the paper, a swank place full of tuxedoed men with slicked-back hair and women in evening gowns so tight, it looked as if they had painted them on their bodies. A black band from New Orleans was playing Scott Joplin's "Magnetic Rag," the most wonderful music I had ever heard. Just listening to that music, you had to dance—but I didn't know how. In the midst of the writhing dancers, I felt like a lame donkey, but John was all grace and agility, moving so fast that no one could notice how worn his suit was. He swung me around him in circles, like a trainer breaking in a yearling horse. It seemed the only way to avoid falling flat on my face was to *let* myself be flung, relinquishing all resistance. It was intoxicating, like the few sips of champagne I had taken before the glass had slipped from my hand and shattered. I could taste the unfamiliar pleasure of bubbles rising in my mouth as the ragtime pulsed through my brain. What pleased me most was the lack of intimacy. A waltz is a moving embrace, but this sort of dancing was pure acrobatics. Only our hands touched. My shyness wore off as I concentrated on the steps, the rhythm. It was fun, but a frightening sort of fun, like the time when I was thirteen and borrowed my uncle's bicycle without his permission, walking it up the steep road behind our house, then coasting down at full speed, forgetting that I didn't even know how the brakes worked. All I had been able to do was hang on and try not to crash into anything.

The women in their plunging evening dresses were looking at John, some covertly, others with heavy-lidded stares. They must have found him handsome, because they gave me withering glances that said I wasn't in his league. Compared to them, I looked like a schoolgirl. I tried to see what they saw when they looked at him. His smooth brown hair falling over his forehead, his eyes boring into me before he swung me to one side and twisted me around. He pulled me close, then sent me spinning away. It was dizzying, this dance, like being drawn down a whirlpool. Each time he gave me that intense hypnotic stare, it was like falling down a well.

❦ We left at ten so John could make the last streetcar. Passing the alley next to the dance hall, we saw couples leaning against the brick wall, kissing and groping each other. I looked away, feeling like a child.

After the heat and noise of the dance floor, the cool dark streets were disconcerting. John and I didn't speak, didn't even look at each other, because the sight would have been too ghostly, our faces washed pale under the yellow streetlights. John lit a cigarette, its red tip glowing in the darkness like a disembodied eye. *He won't come to call on me again.* I had disappointed him, forgetting our arrangement, making a fool of him in front of Violet's family. I couldn't even dance. What he really needed was one of those flashy women in the low-cut dresses.

"How is your uncle?" I asked when the silence had grown too oppressive.

"The same as ever." John exhaled smoke.

We stood on the sidewalk in front of the Waverly mansion. I had never seen the front of the house at night before. The windows were lit up. Suspended rectangles of gold interposed on the façade, which was so dark, it seemed to melt away into the night. Now it was a different house altogether. Not a beautiful mansion, but the sorceress' house. And I was Wassalissa, coming out of the dark and cold. What did that make John? The prince come to rescue me? The thought made me laugh.

"What's so funny?" John asked.

"Nothing." A silly thought. In the story of Wassalissa, there was no prince. She rescued herself and only married the king after her adventures were over.

"Why are you smiling like that, Kathrin? What are you thinking about?"

"Listen! They are playing the piano." As we walked through the gate, the music drifted out over the lawn and hedges. Some ditty about a boy declaring his love to his sweetheart. Violet's nieces sang loud and shrill, then burst into helpless laughter. I imagined them giggling at me the instant I stepped in the door, imagined their mother giving me that stinging look, like I was some vulgar little foreign chit who had no business in her sister's house. The light over the front door had been left on, presumably for me, but I shrank away into the shadows. Leaving John to follow, I made my way to the servant's entrance on the far corner of the house, the door that led to the back staircase. That way I could creep to my room without meeting a soul. "Good-night," I whispered. "Thank you for the dance."

Feeling for the lock, I jabbed my key inside and was about to disappear into the house when John pressed me up against the door and started kissing me. I had never been kissed before. It wasn't anything like the flowery love scenes in the dime novels I used to find in the board-inghouse lavatory. It was like being suffocated. His teeth kept knocking against mine. Just as I was gathering my strength to push him away, he held me against his chest, cradling my head and stroking my hair, which affected me far more than the kissing had. No one had touched my hair like that since my mother died. I was too stunned to speak or move.

"You're happy now, aren't you, Kathrin?"

All I could do was nod.

"You know, I was the one who got you this job. Stick by me, and you'll never have to work in the mills again." When he finally pulled away, I was trembling. Drained and weak. "Next Saturday I'll come by at seven," he said. "And don't forget."

Before I could think of what to say, he was gone. I was alone in the dark, twisting the key in the lock, letting myself in. I switched on the light, bolted the door behind me, and climbed the back stairs with unsteady legs. The blood deserted my inner organs to swim at the surface of my skin. I was red, I was burning, a cinder spit out of a furnace. *You are such a child,* Lotte always told me. *When are you ever going to grow up?* I supposed I should feel something extraordinary now. By Lotte's reckoning, that kind of kissing would be enough to turn me from a girl into a woman, but I felt lost. The ground was slipping out from under me, and the inside of my mouth tasted like John's cigarette. Laughter and piano music rang through the walls as I climbed the back staircase, finding my way to my room as unobtrusively as I could. The first thing I saw when I opened the door was a vase containing John's carnations. Violet had set it on my dresser.

I hung up my good dress and stripped down, washing myself with cold water until my body felt as if it belonged to me again. Then I put on my nightgown and let down my hair so it fell across my face. Brushing my hair calmed me like nothing else. Lotte said my hair was mousy, but now as the electric light shone through it, I saw the differ-ent shades up close. The darkest strands were the color of horse chest-nuts. Then came gradations of pale brown. The lightest color was dark gold, like a jar of forest honey held up to the sun. What did John see when he looked at me? The way he used to tease me when I was still a mill girl in that awful gingham dress. Without him, I wouldn't be here right now. I wouldn't even know that houses like Violet's existed. I would be back in the boardinghouse, in bed with my cousin, listening to her snore. Then again, maybe that was where I belonged. Lotte loved me in her own gruff way, or at least she had before I left her behind. Violet's family was so brittle and strange. The forced jocularity of her brothers and the unpardonable coldness of her sister. Something was amiss here. Something that no one spoke of directly, yet it hung heavy in the air, poisoning everything. Remembering the way they had laughed at John tonight, laughed at us both, my stomach filled with acid. As much as I admired Violet, I did not look forward to seeing her family again.

Leaving the lights on, I crawled into bed and pulled the covers up to my ears. *You are such a child. Yes, maybe I am still a child.* I stared at the stars on the ceiling and listened to the noise of the party until my eyes grew heavy and I drifted off to sleep.

A knock on the door woke me in the middle of a dream.

"Kathrin?" The door opened a crack. I stifled a cry, then opened my eyes to see Violet. "Oh, you were asleep," she said. "I didn't mean to wake you. Your light was still on. I didn't hear you come in. I was worried about you."

I had been dreaming about her family. Her nieces were talking wooden dolls. Her sister gave me a poisoned apple that made my good clothes melt on my body and turn to rags. Shaking my head clear, I lifted myself on one elbow, my hair falling in my face. I pushed it away. The house was silent; the guests had gone.

Violet looked at me resolutely. "Why didn't you come down to say good-night? I was so afraid something had happened. You know, in my day, girls weren't even allowed out unchaperoned. Not," she added hastily, "that I wish to police you."

"I'm sorry." My tongue was dry and stuck to the roof of my mouth.

"Is something the matter? You don't look like yourself. Why were you so shocked when John came by tonight? I thought you were going to faint."

"John?" I swallowed. "I do not know if I like him that way." *There, I had said it.*

Violet was quiet for a few seconds. "Take it slowly. That's about the best advice I can give. You have all the time in the world for these things. There's no need to rush in if you aren't sure." She smiled to show me she wasn't really cross. "I'll let you go back to sleep."

"How did you meet your husband?" I asked before she could depart. "How did you know he was the right one?" Straddling the border between waking and sleep, I lost all sense of propriety, of which questions were permissible and which were not. My query was rendered slightly less audacious by the lateness of the hour, the hushed stillness of the house. Violet blinked, the corners of her mouth twitching slightly. She stepped into the room, closing the door behind herself, and sat at the foot of my bed.

"That's a long story." She was wearing her dressing gown, a kimono of dark red silk. Red like red roses, like claret wine. "When I was your age, I had to be taken out of school, because I was ill with pneumonia. I was at a boarding school in Wisconsin. My parents had to come and collect me, take me home by train. I have little memory of that time, but they tell me I nearly died." She fell silent, tracing one of the oak bedposts. Her face was downcast, her brow wrinkled. Just when I thought she had decided not to say anything more, she began to speak again in a mesmerized voice, as if she were telling the story of someone else, someone she had known long ago and nearly forgotten.

"My parents didn't know what to do with me. The illness, you see, was . . ." She closed her eyes, spoke slowly and deliberately. "Was preceded by a disappointment. There was a sadness in my youth, a grave setback I won't bore you with. It was a sadness of the heart. There's no cure for such things. That's when I met Arthur. He was a friend of my father's. He'd just come back from Africa and was full of tales of walking ghosts. In Africa, white is the color of death. That's how I must have appeared to him, dead pale in my dressing gown. I didn't tell Arthur of my disappointment, but my father did. So Arthur knew, but I didn't *know* that he knew until much later. We never spoke of my sadness. He didn't come to me with pity or sermons. He just sat in a chair in the corner of my room and told me stories, fairy tales, the way my great-grandmother used to. She died the year before, and I was still mourning her. I'm not a religious person, but when he kept coming day after day to tell me those stories, I thought he had been sent to take her place, to be for me what she had been."

Violet glanced up, smiling ruefully. "Do you know the story of Orpheus and Eurydice, Kathrin? The poet who calls his lady back from the land of the shades? That's what Arthur did for me. I was nearly dead, and he brought me back with his stories. He told me about Africa. In Africa, day and night are reversed. We see night as dangerous and evil, but there they revere it. It's a blessed time, when the heat of the day falls away, and you can see all the stars. For them noon is the evil time, because the shadows disappear, and people and animals have to hide from the burning sun. That's when the ghosts walk the earth."

She looked away. Her eyes were veiled. "One day he brought an atlas with him and showed me the places he had traveled. He told me he would take me to Europe, take me to St. Petersburg, my great-grandmother's city. If I would marry him, if I would have him. We were married on my nineteenth birthday. I don't think I could have accepted a proposal from any other man. After what happened, I . . . "

She stopped herself short. "If it hadn't been for Arthur, I would have never married. Arthur didn't just bring me back, he gave me my liberty. I never had a chance to go to the university as I longed to, but I learned so much from him, helping him with his research. It was Arthur who encouraged me to learn Russian properly, with a real teacher. My great-granny always spoke it to me, but that's when I learned to read and write it. On our second anniversary, we sailed to Europe. He took me across the Continent, then all the way through Russia on the Siberian Express. We sailed home by way of Japan, Hawaii, and California. We were traveling for over a year. That was probably the high point of my life."

I thought of the globe in her study and imagined tracing a circle around it.

"It's late," said Violet, rising from the bed. "Now get some sleep, and don't worry too much about John." On her way to the door, she gave me a sisterly pat on the shoulder. I wished I were her sister. I would show her far more affection than the frosty sister she had.

≈ I couldn't sleep after she left. My head was too full of questions. Not about John. She had managed to distract me from John, distract me from that kiss. All I could think about was the story she had told me. I tried to picture her as a girl of eighteen, my age. I imagined her growing up in that brittle family. Her portrait in the study had a wan, uncertain face. Now I knew why. Her "disappointment." What kind of disappointment would bring on a near-fatal case of pneumonia? It was none of my business. She would certainly never reveal it to me. She had been embarrassed by telling me as much as she had.

I closed my eyes and tried to sleep, but I kept seeing an invalid girl in an upstairs room, the curtains drawn to shut out the sun. The pallor of her face and the bleached white sheets glowed like snow in the semidarkness. Her black hair was bound in a single braid, making her look even younger than the schoolgirl she was. This was the young woman the Professor had fallen in love with. Even in her sick and wasted state, he had seen the beauty in her, the beauty that comes from inside, which illness cannot steal away. I could see him lowering his broad body into a flimsy white rockingchair designed to bear the weight of a young girl. I could hear him telling her stories of Africa, without any sort of introduction, leaping right in, drawing her spirit back into her body, back into this world.

What was it like to be brought back from the edge of death? I thought of her wedding portrait on the dining room mantelpiece. A bride of nineteen, her face still thin and hollow-looking from her long convalescence, one shy hand resting on her husband's shoulder.

Like Wassalissa, she had married a king.

≈ When I opened my eyes the next morning, the full flood of morning sunlight was streaming through the lace curtains. I didn't need to look at the clock to know I had overslept and missed church. *Just as well,* I told myself after the prickling of guilt had subsided. I felt too confused about everything that had happened to face either Lotte or the Jelineks. First I had to let the events of last night settle down. Opening my wardrobe, I reached for my muslin dress, but it smelled of stale smoke and sweat from the dance hall. I would have to wash it before wearing it again. Instead I put on Lotte's old green taffeta, the same dress I had worn to the interview. It fit more snugly around the waist than I remembered. I was filling out, putting on weight. After two weeks in Violet's house, I was already beginning to lose that hungry haunted look that had made Lotte call me a child. I looked at myself in the mirror, inspecting my reflection from different angles. My cheeks were full and firm, glowing as if I'd rubbed them with snow.

I found Violet on the back porch having her breakfast. An extra place had been set. "I thought you'd be coming down," she said, drawing out a chair for me. "I didn't hear you leaving for church." She poured me a cup of strong black coffee. Neither of us said much. We were still sleepy, trying to hide our yawns. She had shadows under her eyes. I wondered if she'd also had trouble falling asleep after our conversation last night, if she regretted having told me so much, but when I looked across the table and caught her eye, she smiled. "Skipping church, Kathrin! I'm surprised at you. You're turning into a heathen like me." I laughed. Then we gazed out at the laburnum, the gold rain tree, which had reached the zenith of its blossoming.

After breakfast we walked across the unmown lawn, the ankle-length grass thick and frothy in places with a creeping flower the same pale blue as my muslin dress. "In German we call this flower Männer-treu, because the flowers only last as long as a man's love." I meant it as a joke, but Violet looked at me sadly.

"Everything in this season is ephemeral, Kathrin. It has nothing in particular to do with men."

I had no idea what ephemeral meant.

"Do you want to cut some flowers for your room?" Violet led me to the far corner of the yard, where a bed of lily of the valley was growing in the shadow of the ivied wall, white as a snowdrift. "Smell them, Kathrin." Violet gathered up her skirt and knelt in the grass, closing her eyes as she inhaled. I knelt beside her. How odd we must have looked, two grown women kneeling before a flower bed as if it were a shrine. The scent of the flowers was so sweet. I inhaled as deeply as I could, filling my lungs with it.

"They only come once a year," said Violet. "We have to enjoy them while we can. I'll be right back." She walked off toward the house, leaving me on my knees in front of the flowers. I didn't want to move from this spot in the cushiony grass. *I want to spend the rest of my life here in this garden. Live here forever, quiet and cloistered as a nun.* Lotte said I was so backward with men, I'd wind up a nun anyway. That's when the memory of John's kiss came back, his tongue on my teeth, but I pushed it away into the furthest corner of my mind. *Later. I'll think about it later.*

Footsteps on the lawn. Violet lowered herself onto the grass beside me, balancing on her heels. She handed me a small green vase filled with water, then reached into the flower bed and cut me a thick bouquet with a pair of garden shears. I longed to bury my face in them, but I would have felt too foolish doing that in front of her. So I just let the tips of the bell-shaped flowers brush my lips. "Be careful," she said. "They're poisonous."

"What does ephemeral mean?"

"Fleeting," said Violet. "Something that passes quickly." She rose and shook out her skirt. "Do you want to go for a walk?"

I went in the house to put the vase of flowers on my bedside table before joining Violet at the front door. We walked down the long hill that sloped behind Summit Avenue. A cobbled road leading past the servants' quarters, old stables, and new garages. Down the hill to Fort Road and past the Irish taverns. Heading toward the river. We talked about everything in the world, everything except John Jelinek. Violet made John seem unreal, like an improbable enigma, something I had invented in my head. Just as in the coming weeks and months, when he came to fetch me, invading Violet's house like a thunderstorm or a wildfire, the confidences I shared with her would be swept away. And this was how my life began to split in two, like a river forking into separate but parallel streams, one roaring with rapids and waterfalls, the other deceptively placid.

8 ⚬ Sitting on the streetcar to Jelinek's, I smoothed my new linen skirt with the ivory and willow-green stripes. The skirt was Violet's. "I don't wear it anymore," she had told me. "The colors don't suit me, but it would look lovely on you. I hate to see something perfectly good going to waste." Not only did I live in her house, I wore her clothes now, too. It was almost like stepping inside her skin and trying to become her. Her skirt would give me special powers. She had sent me to Jelinek's to pick up an order of books that had come in, and at the bookstore, I was sure to see John. I had no idea what to say to him. When I thought of him, my cheeks began to burn as if they'd just been slapped. I wanted the old John back, the boy who had teased me like a brother.

Getting off the streetcar and walking to their shop, I tried to make myself feel as she must have felt that evening I had first seen her, when she had come into the bookstore in her pale blue suit. I didn't want to be a child anymore, didn't want to be pushed or led around. I wanted to be as poised as she was. When I saw him today, I wouldn't shrink. I would hold my head up.

When I stepped inside the store, however, there was only Mr. Jelinek, who greeted me as he always had, like a kinsman, as if nothing had changed. He admired my new skirt. "Each time I see you, you look more like a lady. I knew Mrs. Waverly would treat you well." He already had Violet's books wrapped up in brown paper, tied together with packing string so they would be easy to carry back on the streetcar. I got the money out of my purse, the crisp new bills Violet had given me that morning. The total came to $7.36. Probably the biggest order they had seen that month.

"You don't have to rush off now, do you?" Mr. Jelinek asked me. "Stay a while and keep me company. That boy's downtown today." There was a sour note in his voice when he said the word *downtown*. "It's nice when you come by." He got a chair from behind the front counter, so I sat down and told him about my week. For the first time I grasped how lonely he was.

"What is John doing downtown?" I asked.

"Looking for another job." Mr. Jelinek grimaced. "An office job. Working for strangers, Kathrin. He knows I'll pass the shop on to him one day, but he's too impatient to wait. That boy has two sides. One day he has big plans for advertising the store and turning it into a thriving business. The next day he can't wait to see the last of these books." The old man looked at me pensively, his eyes moving over my face as if he were studying a painting. "I can't get over how much you look like his mother."

I remembered the old photograph, that heart-shaped face and those downcast eyes. "How old was John when she—"

"Four," he said. "He can hardly remember her."

Losing his mother when he was four years old. Not since he was four had he known a woman's tenderness. I felt something loosening in my stomach, remembering Saturday night, the way he had held me against him, stroking my hair. The warmth of his body rising through his shirt to touch my cheek. I tried to focus on Mr. Jelinek's face so I wouldn't see John's.

"At least he has you," I said shyly.

"I tried my best to raise him right." Once he started talking about his nephew, he couldn't seem to stop. I think this story was something he had been longing to get off his chest for years, but until now he hadn't found anyone who would listen. He was telling me, because I sat so still and attentive, and maybe also because he thought I looked like Nadja. Maybe this was his way of trying to explain it to her. "I don't know if I succeeded. He didn't have an easy time, that boy. Losing his mother so young. I keep thinking how different he would have turned out if she had lived."

"What was she like?"

"She was a music teacher, Kathrin." When he spoke of her, he looked younger, the lines in his face softening. "She played the piano like a maestro, even though she didn't have that much conservatory training. None of us came from well-off families." He lifted his hands to indicate the shabby bookstore, the lack of customers. He stared out the window at the students walking past. "I lost my heart to her. She was twenty-two. I was thirty-six, just the age for settling down and having a family, but then she met my brother, who was ten years younger than me and twice as handsome. Guess which one of us she chose." He gave me a pained look. "I set sail for America the day after their wedding. Do you know anything of unrequited love?" He waited for me to shake my head before continuing.

"Remember this, my dear. It's our tragedies that shape us, but we don't know it at the time. We just muddle on the best we can. My brother was a printer, and a poor one at that. There was no work in our town, so he took Nadja to Vienna to look for something better. I sent them what I could spare. I thought if they didn't have money, at least they had each other. At least they had love. I'd been living here twelve years when I got the news that Nadja had died. Then my brother crossed the ocean with their son Jan. Did you know his mother named him after me? When he started school, he changed it to John. That boy can't stand having people think he's foreign, but you should have seen him when he first came here. Four years old and crying his eyes out for his mother every night. I cried with him. He gave me that excuse. And his father? He was my brother, Kathrin, my flesh and blood, but I tell you, the man was no good. Not for Nadja, not for that boy. Do you know he took his fists to both of them? His own wife and son. Some people have something broken inside them, Kathrin. Some people cannot love. He loved drink, but that was all he loved. You notice I don't say his name. His name will never be spoken in this house. He hadn't been a year in this country when he died a drunkard's death, leaving me alone with that motherless boy."

Mr. Jelinek started flipping through the ledger book. His hands were shaking. If I really were his kinswoman, I would have gone up and embraced him. I thought of the woman in the old photograph, then of John when he was four years old. Half sick from too much crying. Crossing the ocean with a violent man, a drunk.

"I have high hopes for John, though," said Mr. Jelinek. "He'll get on well in this country, because he has something I never had. He has ambition, Kathrin. An ambitious young man can go far here. His way is not my way, but I know he'll succeed." He was silent for a moment. "I know he cares for you, my dear. He's a good-looking young man, don't you think? He's not as rough as he seems on the surface."

What he said left me speechless. Looking at the old porcelain-faced clock, I saw it was almost three. We had been talking so long, I'd lost track of the time. *I must go now,* I was about to say, but I couldn't. Talking about John's parents had made him so sad. I got up from my chair and hung close to the cash register, chatting with him about nothing in particular, about whatever popped into my head, until the shop door opened. Thinking it was a customer, I picked up my parcel and was about to leave, but it was John. The awkwardness of Saturday night came back to me, but now it was different. I knew his story.

"Kathrin! What brings you here?" He kissed me in front of his uncle, who withdrew into the storeroom, leaving us alone.

"I came to pick up Mrs. Waverly's order. I must go now."

"You don't have time for a walk? You used to like going around the university and looking at the buildings."

"A short walk," I said.

≈ I still didn't know what I should be feeling. I kept looking at him with that double vision, the story his uncle had told me interposed on his every word and facial expression. He was in a good mood, punctuating every sentence with a laugh, but his laughter only sharpened the picture I had of that hurt little boy. I listened to him poking fun at the college students in their knickerbockers and argyle socks.

"A bunch of overdressed ninnies." We watched a group of young men going up the steps of Walter Library. "They used to come in the shop to look at the books without buying, but not the way you did, Kathrin. They barged in and messed up the shelves. They were looking through the books for dirty pictures. When Jan told them to leave, they just laughed at him. I had to wait until I was big enough to take them by the collar and march them out the door. I never let anyone get away with that again."

"How terrible," I said, "for your uncle."

He kept staring at the students going in and out of the library doors. "Never had to work or struggle for anything. Life just gets handed to them. The people who earn my respect are the people who have to work for what they have. Like you, Kathrin."

I was stunned. Here I was in Violet's skirt, and what he liked best about me was that I had worked in the mills? Too embarrassed to think what else to say, I pointed at the library and told him, "Once I went inside. When I was still working at the mill. I came in the evening when no one was there. I was so afraid, but I had to see what the inside was like. The ceiling is so beautiful."

"Let's take a look," he said, tugging my hand, but I balked like a horse.

"We cannot go in there *now*. There are too many people. They will see us."

"What are you afraid of? Do you think the police are going to arrest you for going into a library?"

"It is not for us," I said dourly. "They will know we are not students."

He laughed at me. "Kathrin, you and I are just as good as anyone else. Come on." He took my hand, and together we walked up those steps and into that gorgeous lobby. "You're right," said John as we craned our necks to stare at the ceiling. "That's really something." He squeezed my hand. "Somebody *made* all that. Somebody carved those beams. Somebody had to go up on a scaffold to do all that plasterwork and paint it in those different colors. I wonder how long that took?"

Meanwhile the students streamed around us with their books and satchels under their arms. They strode through the library with careless assurance, as if they owned it. Anonymous hands had carved and painted this ceiling for the students' edification and delight, but they didn't even bother to stop and look at it. But they looked at us. Since we were standing in the middle of the lobby, they could hardly ignore us. Even

as I gazed at the ceiling, I could feel their scrutiny. John and I were tres-
passers in their world. But John stood so squarely on that marble floor
and held my hand so adamantly that I had to stand as firmly rooted as
he did. We were taking this small space and making it ours in utter
defiance of the looks we were getting.

One particularly thick-necked young man sauntered up to us. With
his broad shoulders and square jaw, he looked bigger and tougher than
John. I tugged at John's hand to signal that we should be on our way,
but John just smiled at me cryptically before turning to address him.
"Would you take a look at that," said John, pointing upward with such
authority that the student even obeyed. "Isn't that a remarkable ceiling? I bet you never even noticed." Then John spoke to me in a voice
loud enough for every passerby to hear. "Did I tell you that I'm going
to start taking classes, too?"

I gaped at him. Was he putting on an act?

"I'm starting night school," he announced, as proudly as if he were
enrolling in the university. "A course in accounting. I signed up today."
At that, he took my arm and led me back out the doors. We left the
thick-necked student gawking open-mouthed at the ceiling and
pointing so that the others would look up, too. John was laughing
under his breath. I joined in. When we were back outside, we laughed
ourselves silly.

As John walked me back to my streetcar stop, I decided that his
uncle was right—John would go far in this country. I knew he would
be at the head of his class, just as I had been first in my English class.
John would go farther than any of those college boys. And he wanted
to take me with him.

⟶ I was back at Violet's house at six, two hours later than I had
promised. "Violet!" I cried, running up the stairs two at a time with
the parcel of books pressed tight to my chest. I burst through the study
door after a hasty knock. "Violet, I—"

The words froze on my tongue. She was not alone. She and her sister were sitting in the chintz armchairs in the alcove, the same place
she had sat with me during the interview. Margaret glared, and Violet

turned to me with tired eyes. "Do you have the books? Could you put them on my desk, please? Thank you, Kathrin."

"And here's your change," I murmured, leaving the handful of coins next to the books and ducking out the door. I heard Margaret raising her voice. *"That was your skirt she was wearing!"* I bolted down the stairs to the kitchen before I could hear anything more. Franny sat at the kitchen table, gutting trout, scooping the innards on an old newspaper.

"Is she staying for dinner?" I asked.

Franny nodded and rolled her eyes.

After a quick nod to her, I stepped into the pantry to take a heel of yesterday's bread. I was so hungry, even the raw fish looked appealing. How many fish were there, two or three? It occurred to me that if Margaret were staying for dinner, I might not be welcome to join them. Gnawing the bread, I climbed the stairs to my room. Somewhere on the other end of the house, muffled by walls and closed doors, I heard angry voices. I remembered how Mr. Jelinek had cursed his brother. When men are angry, they are hot, like pots of water boiling over. But when Violet and her sister were angry, they were cold, freezing. Icicles stuck to a drainpipe. I lay on my bed, my hands folded over my grumbling stomach.

Just as I was gathering the energy to get up and make another trip to the pantry, I heard footsteps coming down the hall, a knock on my door. Lurching off the bed, I brushed out the wrinkles in my skirt. *Violet's skirt.* "Come in!"

"There you are," said Violet. "I thought you were in the garden at first." Her voice was the same as always, but her face was drawn, and the skin around her eyes was red. "Did you have a nice chat with the Jelineks?" She didn't seem the least bit angry about my coming back late.

"Yes."

"I hope you're hungry. We have a sumptuous feast prepared. Three trout and only two to eat it."

"Your sister, I thought she—"

"She's gone." Violet sounded positively arctic.

Neither of us made any reference to Margaret as we sat down to our plates of trout amandine. Violet spoke of traveling instead. "When I finish Arthur's last project, I'll go abroad. Get the house off my hands, and jump on the first train heading south."

I put down my fork. "You will leave this house?" I tried to keep the tremor out of my voice. *Don't get too used to the soft life,* Lotte had told me. Of course, I knew I wouldn't stay with her in this house forever, only until the end of summer, but I never thought that she could just pick up and leave.

"It's far too big for me, Kathrin. You must have made that observation yourself. I've wanted to sell it for years."

"It is so beautiful. To me it is like a castle." The way I was talking, I sounded like a child. Staring at the dead fish on my plate, the hunger inside me died.

"Yes, it's beautiful, but full of ghosts." Violet passed me the French beans. I set the bowl in the middle of the table without taking anything. How could she even think of leaving such a splendid house? And where would I be when she left?

"Where will you go?"

"South America this time." Now Violet was animated, her hands moving as she spoke. "I've never been there, but I've read that in Quito, Ecuador, there's a cathedral built directly on the site of an ancient Incan temple. They say Quito itself was the site of El Dorado, the city of gold."

Quito, Ecuador? I had never heard of the place.

"I've never traveled on my own before, only with Arthur. But just once I'd like to go off on my own, just to prove . . . I don't know. Just to prove I can. That's your doing."

I looked up from my water glass.

"You came here on your own, making a new life for yourself in another country." She stared at my untouched plate. "Aren't you hungry tonight? You're not brooding about John, are you?"

"No." I started eating again, moving my fork from my plate to my mouth, but I tasted nothing. Violet sank back in her chair, a distracted look in her eyes. *Too full of ghosts?* What ghosts, I wanted to ask, but the question stuck in my throat, trapped there like a fish bone. Who was this woman sitting across from me? A rich woman who supported the socialists, who had a sister she only quarreled with, who had a beautiful house filled with beautiful things that she would just as soon abandon to go off traipsing God knows where?

≈ When John showed up on Saturday night, I was prepared, my blue muslin dress freshly washed and ironed. In the dance hall, I managed to move my body around the floor without crashing into anyone or twisting my ankles. This time I let myself surrender to the pleasure of it. John was Mr. Jelinek's nephew. We had the old man's blessing. With John, I didn't have to feel inferior or put on an act; he respected me for exactly who I was. Even if Violet sold the house and went off to South America, I would have John and his uncle. *These are my people,* I kept thinking. Plain and humble. They would stick by me until the end.

Nothing to fear, I told myself when we left the dance hall for the dark streets. When John took my hand, I tried to get used to its texture and heat, his long fingers interlacing with mine. A block away, we still heard the music of the dance hall, tinny sounding from this distance. The street lamps were shining globes of yellow-white, each with its attending cloud of moths. If I jumped as high as I could, I would touch their powdery rasping wings. John let go of my hand and dug into his pocket for a cigarette. As he struck a match, the flame illuminated his face. He was too busy lighting his cigarette to notice me studying the lines of his cheekbones, his sloping jaw and narrow chin, his thick eyebrows. I was searching his face for some resemblance to Nadja. *His mouth,* I thought, *and his eyes.* His eyes were hazel like mine. No wonder I used to pretend he was my brother. John dropped the match and stepped on it. Darkness settled around us again.

"Do you remember your mother?" I asked him.

"You've been talking to Jan." He exhaled a ribbon of smoke. "The past was nothing but misery, and he keeps bringing it back."

"Do you remember her?" I persisted. "For me it is hard to remember my mother. I was sixteen when she died. That is not so young, but I cannot remember her face. Her voice, yes. The things she used to say and do, yes. But not what she looked like."

"I remember her singing while she did her piecework." John spoke hesitantly. "Jan told you she was musical, didn't he?"

I nodded.

"She did piecework at home. Sewing. I can't remember what. We must have needed the money. My father drank his wages away, but I suppose Jan told you all that, too."

"Do you remember Vienna? Your uncle said that is where your parents lived."

He laughed, but in a constricted way. "I remember being cold and hungry mostly. We lived in an attic apartment. I remember my father banging his head on the slanting ceiling, and I can remember coming over on the boat after my mother died. The strange women on the ship had to take care of me, because my father wasn't much good for that. Then we came over here, and Jan fussed over me night and day, trying to make everything all right. You know how he is. It's strange." He paused for a second. "What memories I have . . . I'm not sure if they're really mine, or if they come from Jan's stories. I've heard those stories so many times."

He yelped. His cigarette, which had burned itself all the way down, had begun to burn his hand. Dropping it into the gutter, he turned to me, threading his fingers in my hair and kissing me. His rough stubble rubbed against my lips. We kissed until my skin was raw. "You will miss your streetcar," I whispered finally.

He laughed. This time his laughter sounded happy. He put his arm around my waist, and that's how we walked the rest of the way to Violet's. His arm pulling me close, my arm around him. The most intimate I had ever been with a man. Neither of us spoke until we passed through Violet's front gate. On the front step, under the light Violet had left on for us, we said good-night and kissed again, but only briefly. You couldn't lose yourself in a kiss in that flood of light. "Next week," John said before he departed, running out the gate to make the last streetcar.

Slowly, I told myself as I opened the front door and locked it behind me. Violet said to take things slowly. I walked up the stairs more slowly than I ever had, trying to plant each foot firmly on the ground before lifting it again. When I reached the second-floor hallway, I noticed the bar of light beneath the door of Violet's study. I knocked.

"Kathrin, is that you? Come in."

She was sitting at her desk and writing in a rose-colored notebook, which she closed as I came in. She was wearing her red kimono. Her hair was bound loose at the nape of her neck. She looked younger that way. She also looked sleepy. I wondered if she had been waiting up for me. "You had a nice time," she said. It was a statement, not a question. Could she read my moods so easily?

"Yes," I said. "You would like it, too." She smiled as I said that, waiting for me to elaborate, so I did. The late hour invited such confidences. I talked on and on, much more freely than I ever had with her, describing the whole scene, from the ragtime music to the women in their sleek dresses and the dances themselves. It was rather embarrassing, the way I gushed. I couldn't help it. I was giddy as if I'd been drinking wine, but I'd only had a paper cup of lemonade. "There is a dance called the hula hula and another dance called the turkey trot."

"I see I was born too early," she said. "In my day we only waltzed. It was so tedious, Kathrin. You can't imagine. At my school, there were all these cotillions and balls. I told you I went to that girls' school in Wisconsin. Well, we were right next door to a military academy. The idea was to match us up, but everything was under strict control, with chaperons everywhere. It was deadly."

Deadly? It sounded charming enough to me. Schoolgirls and young cadets, whirling away to old-fashioned waltz music. Like a scene in a romantic novel.

"We had these little cards and pencils tied to our wrists. We were supposed to write our partners' names in the boxes. The object was to dance with as many different boys as possible. I thought it was like a slave auction."

How could she sound so bitter about something as innocent as a school ball?

"One of the best things about leaving school and getting married was that I wasn't expected to go to any more dances. Arthur hated dancing as much as I did."

Yes, I thought. *An intellectual man would never have the patience for something as frivolous as dancing.* Try as I might, I could not picture Violet and the Professor dancing together.

"My mother told me a girl's dancing days end when she gets married," I said. "We say that a girl's wedding dance is her last dance. After that she is too busy having babies." I smiled at my own joke, meeting Violet's gaze. Only then did I realize what I'd said. It was too late to take it back.

She nodded soberly. "I suppose you think it's strange that I never had any."

"No. I did not mean it like that." I was heated up and flustered, but she was perfectly composed.

"We wanted to have children, you know." She looked at me without blinking. I never thought a lady like her could be so blunt and unashamed about something so private. "That's why Arthur bought this big house. We wanted to fill these rooms with children. But we weren't lucky that way." She folded her hands over her stomach, her womb, flat as a young girl's.

"I'm sorry." What else could I say?

"There's no need to be," she said. "It's water under the bridge. My brothers and my sister had more than enough to make up for me. I think I'm a better aunt for being childless. My nieces always come running to me when they have a fight with their mother."

I was at a loss, wondering how I could say good-night and creep off to bed without seeming rude.

"Kathrin," she said, drawing her hands absently over the closed notebook. She paused for at least half a minute, searching for words. I just stood there shifting my weight from one foot to the other, wondering what she was going to say and why she was suddenly so tongue-tied.

She took a deep breath. "You mustn't take this the wrong way."

I closed my eyes. *She's found fault in me. I did something wrong.*

"I don't want to say anything bad . . . " Her voice trailed off. Then she started over again, speaking quickly, her eyes on her notebook. "I don't want to say anything bad about John, but I'd be on the cautious side if I were you." She glanced up at me. "Remember our conversation last week? About taking things slowly and keeping your head? It's no good being too starry-eyed and naive about these things."

Starry-eyed and naive? What was she talking about? Then I caught sight of myself in the mirror on the study wall and saw what she must have seen. Me in my blue muslin dress, my hair mussed up, coming down in frantic disarray from the tight careful knot I had bound it in. A girl with her hair messed up from dancing and kissing. My lips and the skin around them were flushed and inflamed from John's stubble. *She can see right inside me.* Trying to smooth my hair back into place, I turned away from her and paced up and down along her bookshelves.

"I'm sure he's a perfectly decent young man," she said, "but I don't know that he's the one you should be hanging all your hopes on."

"You do not like John?" I traced the edge of the bookshelf, the thin film of dust Franny had missed.

I heard her suck in her breath. "I'm not saying I don't *like* him. I've only spoken to him a few times, but he seems . . ." She couldn't finish her sentence. "His uncle is a *very* dear man. You should see Mr. Jelinek's face light up when he talks about you. He adores you."

I stared at the gold stamped letters on the row of leather spines and inhaled the smell of book leather—what the Professor must have smelled like.

"Kathrin," she said. "I feel responsible for you. Seeing as you don't have a mother anymore."

Something inside me came undone when she said that. Something welled up, threatening to spill out. A burning arrow ran through me at my weakest point. I clenched my teeth to make my jaw firm and unmoving.

"There's real love, and then there's infatuation. It pays to know the difference. Of course, you should go to dances and have a nice time. You're young, and you should enjoy your youth. But remember, once you step over a certain line . . . " Here she had to stop for breath. "Once you marry, everything changes. Don't throw away your youth too quickly. Once you lose it, it's hard to get it back."

She sounded like the priest at St. Francis in my old neighborhood. *Purity is the crown of womanhood.* And this from a woman who never went to church.

"It is only our second dance," I managed.

"Yes, I know," she said, more softly now. "I wasn't accusing you of anything, Kathrin. It's just that I've seen too many girls your age make the wrong choice only to discover their mistake too late, that's all."

I finally turned around to face her, about to say good-night and go to my room, when she started speaking again.

"I married too young." Now she wasn't talking to me like an older woman lecturing a girl, but like a friend making a confession. "Of course, it was different in my day. That's what young girls *did*. Every mother wanted to get her daughters married off as quickly as possible. I told you the circumstances surrounding my marriage. There wasn't much else I could do, but nowadays girls have more opportunities. My eldest niece says she won't get married until she's at least twenty-five. She wants to learn a profession first. She and my sister are always locking horns about that."

Violet broke off. "I hope I haven't made you cross by saying all this."

"No," I said, but I couldn't look her in the eye.

She bowed her head, her hands knit in her lap. "Just think a little about what I've said."

"Yes," I murmured, turning to leave. "Good-night."

"Say you aren't cross," she said before I could make it to the door.

"I am not cross."

"Good-night, Kathrin."

⁓ But I was cross. Walking down the hall to my room, I was fuming as I used to after a bad day at the mill. *How dare she spoil my hopes for John? Who was she to say he was no good?* Of course, she hadn't said it in so many words, but she had certainly implied it. What *right* did she have talking to me that way, as if she were my mother? Only five days ago, she'd been talking about running off to South America.

When I reached my room, I was nearly in tears.

Kathrin, you are such a child. Grow up. She's not your mother or anything close. I shook the pins out of my hair and started brushing it so roughly, it hurt. Violet was my employer, a kind and generous employer, but she would never be anything more. At the end of the summer, my work in her house would be done, and then she would send me back out into the cold. *With a reference,* I reminded myself. *And typing skills.* She had promised to help me find another job. Nevertheless I would be on my own again, surviving on my own wits and my own skills. While she was off traveling in distant countries, I would spend my days typing some businessman's letters. No doubt she had meant well in giving me that advice, but she and I did not inhabit the same universe.

My time in her house was just a brief interlude. How foolish I'd been in trying to fashion her into something larger than life—a sorceress, or another mother. Looking at it with cold practicality, the part I played in *her* life was very minor. *Of course I was hanging my hopes on John.* I didn't want to be alone in the world. Hadn't he helped me get this job? Hadn't he promised that if I stuck by him, I'd never have to go back to the mills? I needed a friend who would endure. He and I breathed the same air. What did Violet Waverly know about being adrift in another country with no family or home?

When I came downstairs the next morning, she was sitting at the wicker table on the back porch. I saw her through the screen door, but she didn't see me. She was staring out across the lawn at the laburnum tree. The brilliant gold flowers were fading now, shriveling up and closing on themselves, turning into seed pods, yet she was looking at that tree as if it were the most beautiful thing in the world. Suddenly my grudge against her seemed petty. I stepped out onto the porch and joined her at the table. We ate our breakfast, just as we always did. Neither of us mentioned John, but he was there, the invisible rock our conversation flowed around.

The next weeks passed quickly, a blur in my memory. A blur of dancing until my feet ached, of kissing till I ached all over. There were two Kathrins. One only came into her own after dark, with John, bound up in his penetrating stares in the half-light of the dance hall and his conjuring of our future as he walked me home. When he kissed me in the dark streets, it was like falling down a long well, the moths all around us, brushing up against my skirt. When I thought of the couples who groped each other in the alley, I felt a wave of dread and disgust. John and I weren't like that. He knew it was kisses I wanted, and tenderness, not some vulgar scrape in the bushes. But sometimes I wondered what would happen if he didn't have a streetcar to catch. Sometimes I was frightened of my night self.

The purity and solitude of my working week and my life with Violet seemed to lift me to another plane, absolving me of my Saturday night transgressions. By day I was a different person, the girl who wore white blouses and sat in Violet's dining room translating and typing story after story. The tale of the young girl who fell into a lake and was adopted by swan women, living with them in their underwater palace. And the story of the miller who chopped his daughter's arms off and sold her to the devil.

On Sunday mornings, not so many hours after saying good-night to John, I went to mass, not in my old neighborhood, but down the street at the St. Paul Cathedral, where no one knew me. I could sit discretely in back and stare at the beautiful ceiling when the sermon grew too boring. Kneeling before the altar and taking the wafer in my mouth, I felt safe again, protected. I was afraid to know what would happen if I strayed too far beyond the boundaries that had once circumscribed my life.

Spring was fading. Summer ripened. The last irises wilted into brittle wasted stalks, replaced by roses, bloodred and milk white. The second half of June brought a heat wave, hot humid nights when the only relief was to sit outside by candlelight, listening to the breeze rustle the trees. Those nights Violet played nocturnes by Chopin on her phonograph, the piano music rippling like rain down a windowpane.

When I look back, I want to remember John as he was in those weeks of early summer, on those nights when it was too hot to dance, when we just walked the dark streets from Summit to Crocus Hill and back again, the mansions like silent witnesses. Those were the nights that he told me his plans. He wanted to fix up the store, turn it into something prosperous. His evening classes filled his head with dreams. Those nights he talked like a magician, an alchemist who had the power to take a crumbling old storefront and turn it into gold.

We caught glimpses into the mansions, their lit-up windows revealing lush interiors, silver candlesticks and tufted velvet armchairs. He took it in with such hunger, hunger that was just the same as longing. He was biding his time, planning to make such things *his*. Or *ours*, as he kept saying. "Look at those mansions! They're built to look like palaces. People came over here to escape those kings and emperors, then you see the people who made their fortunes off the backs of the poor and set themselves up like royalty. My parents—what did they live for? And Jan? And that cousin of yours who's still sewing flour bags? They think they can grind people like us into the ground. Well, nobody's going grind me down. They're too complacent, those rich people. They're going nowhere. The future belongs to people like you and me." He talked and talked. I listened. There is infatuation and then there is love. I kept asking myself if this faith I had in him was the beginning of real love.

⤫ We started going down to the river on Saturday nights and Sunday afternoons. The wooded banks gave us the privacy we wanted. "The only thing I miss from home is the forest," I told him as he pressed me up against the rough bark of an oak. Clouds of mosquitoes danced around us. Fireflies lit up the sumac as he pulled down my hair, taking out the pins and combs, running his hands through it, smoothing it over the front of my blouse and burying his face in it, holding me as if he would never let go. *This is like falling*, I thought, my arms around his neck. *Like flying*. The blood rushing beneath my skin, heating the surface, pounding in my ears, like St. Anthony Falls used to in my days at the mill. *Slowly, slowly*. I ran my fingers over the nape of his neck, the hollow between the tendons, so exposed and vulnerable. I wanted this summer to go slow and sweet, like honey dripping off a spoon. I had already forgotten the sadness in Violet's voice when she had said the word *ephemeral*.

⤫ At the end of June, John left his uncle's shop to work for Paramount Office Supply in downtown Minneapolis. He started as a clerk, helping with the paperwork and bookkeeping, the same things he had done for his uncle ever since he was fourteen, except now he got paid twelve dollars a week for it. "We need the money," he told me. "Jan can barely keep the bookstore afloat."

Mr. Jelinek regarded his nephew's defection from the store as a betrayal. "At least you love these books," he told me when I came to pick up Violet's next order. Again I was the only customer. I was beginning to suspect that Violet was ordering these books not because she needed them, but because she knew Mr. Jelinek would go out of business otherwise. 'You can't make money selling old books,' he keeps telling me. He has all these new ideas about how to turn the business around, how he's going to make us all proud, but that means selling something that goes fast, off the shelves in one day. I'm afraid he'll want to start peddling hair oil and bicycle chains." I couldn't tell if Mr. Jelinek was more angry or wounded. "Between you and me, you're the one thing that gives me hope. You love these books as much as I do. What I told John . . . "

Mr. Jelinek cleared his throat, looked at me, then looked away. "What I told John is that I will hand the business over to him the day he marries you."

I blinked and gazed out the window at the sidewalks, deserted now in the summer with the students gone. Just a swaybacked mare hitched to a coal cart, her skin twitching as she shook off flies. I felt the old man's hand on my elbow.

"It won't happen tomorrow, you know, but one day. Next year he'll be twenty-four, and that's as good an age as any to settle down. You don't think I'd let him go with you unless his intentions were honorable?"

Slowly. Slow as grass growing. While Mr. Jelinek busied himself with the electricity bills, I paced the aisles. *Slowly.* But my pulse was racing. For one moment I allowed myself the fantasy of being John's wife. Part of a family again. The Jelineks *needed* me, needed a woman in their household to make it a home. I could be the peacemaker, bringing harmony between the two men. John could go off and work wherever he wanted, bringing a steady income into the house, while I helped his uncle in the book shop. Wasn't that what I had wanted all along? Living in this forest of books, the sun shining through the

Bohemian glass. Having a husband and children. Safe and protected for the rest of my life.

☞ I stayed in the store until John came home from work, wearing the new suit he had bought with his first week's wages. His old suit had been too big for him, giving him the air of a boy in his father's clothes, but now he looked like a man, the dark gray gabardine hugging the long lean lines of his body. He had never been more handsome to me than he was that day, whistling a dance hall tune and carrying the newspaper under his arm. "For you," he said, handing it to his uncle, kissing me when the old man's face was hidden in the paper. "Just look at the headline," he said cheerfully. "Some hothead shot the Austrian archduke."

9 ∜ By the middle of July, the German translations were nearly finished, but Violet still found work for me. As my typing improved, I became her secretary. Every morning she gave me a stack of her neatly penned manuscripts to type. Some were her translations of the Russian fairy tales. Others were introductions, explanations, and treatises. Many of the passages seemed curious, though I didn't think about them too deeply at the time. I was concentrating on typing as quickly and accurately as I could, following the stream of her handwriting. The words and sentences themselves went through me like a glass of lemonade you drink on a hot day without even tasting, but their flavor lingered, like the sweetness on the tongue after the lemonade is swallowed. Later, after my daughter was born and everything in my life seemed fixed as if it were set in stone, they would return to me in fragments, like remembered dreams.

> All the real heroines are maidens. After marriage their magic wanes. They become mundane. They lose some vital essence, like a flower plucked from its roots in the midst of its unfolding. It is not the knowledge of the body or the piercing of the hymen that initiates this loss. When I say "maiden," it is not the hymen intacta state I am referring to, but an archetypal state: the idea of endless freedom and the wealth of unexplored possibilities. The Virgin Czaress in Russian legend who is queen of her own country in her own right, not through her father or her consort.
>
> Once the maiden relinquishes her independence to marry, she goes through a long period of dormancy and incubation. Her powers only return to her when she is old and solitary:

after the death of her husband and the leave-taking of her children. Sometimes she appears as a wise woman, other times as a sharp-tongued witch like Baba Yaga, and it is to this fearsome hag that the young girls go to solve their riddles, to get some healing potion, to learn the secret that will save them. The maiden and the witch are opposite ends of the same pole. The yawning gulf which separates them is the domain of marriage and motherhood.

I checked the passage for mistakes before rolling a new sheet of paper into the typewriter and continuing.

The maiden represents all the hopes of the world. She sits spinning at the fountain and pricks her finger, a well of red blood. She leaps through the fountain, entering into a different world entirely.

~ That week I typed the tales of maidens, resourceful and unresourceful, lost and lucky. Saturday nights and Sunday afternoons I spent on the riverbanks with John. We stopped going to the dance hall. It wasn't just the heat that kept us away but the money. John's new job just paid the bills and his night school tuition. The bookstore was so deep in debt that John was saying his uncle would have to finally give in and put it up for sale before they went bankrupt. "I'm afraid it will break Jan's heart," he said. "For him it wasn't just a business; it was our home. In the old days, he did all right. At least he could pay the bills. The customers were his friends, mostly. They'd spend hours talking with Jan and maybe buy a few books before they went home, but those friends are either dead or gone by now. It's sad to see it coming down to this."

We took to having picnics by the river. It was the cheapest and most satisfying outing I could think of. Violet lent me a basket she never used, one of those huge American picnic hampers equipped with flowery blue plates and real silverware. There was plenty of food in her kitchen to take along. Fresh baked bread, cold chicken, cucumbers and radishes from the garden. Fresh cherries and the first raspberries. Ripe melon. Plum cobbler. Violet gave us so much, the basket nearly burst from it. Even John had a hard time carrying it to the riverbanks.

Those days in July, he reminded me of Atlas, his shoulders and back straining from the weight he had to bear. During our picnics, it astounded me how much he could eat, yet he was thin as a sapling and never seemed to get enough. The only time he put down his burdens was when we embraced. He liked to push me down on the picnic cloth, his groin rubbing against the soft part of my thigh. That's as far as I would let him go. I wouldn't let him push my skirt up or open my blouse, but when he lay on top of me, I felt his weight, his hunger grinding me into the earth. Those evenings by the river ended with both of us breathless and sore. "One day I'll miss the last streetcar," he told me. "You'll have to sneak me up into your room with you. That house is so big, she'll never even notice. I'll sleep in your arms the whole night."

⁕ On a sweltering Sunday like any other in late July, we had our first fight. We had just finished our picnic of cold chicken and cucumber sandwiches, the only things I could imagine eating in that heat. The air was heavy as a velvet curtain and humid, with no discernible breeze, but down in the shade by the river, it was almost bearable. I was leaning against one of the boulders at the water's edge and picking the last bit of meat off the wishbone. John was throwing stones across the glassy green river. I counted how many times they skipped before they sank. His record was five.

"I started working in that store when I was fourteen," he was saying, his back turned to me. "I *know* I could run it better than him. He's so stuck in the old ways. I'm the only thing standing between him and bankruptcy, and I have nothing to say about how he runs the place. Nothing! He expects me to stand there and bite my tongue."

"He is old," I said. "You should be patient."

"Patient!" He grabbed at a low hanging branch, pulling it down and then releasing it so it bounced upward again. "If things don't change soon, there'll be no more store to pass on. We'll have to sell it to strangers. I go out to work every day and bring home twelve dollars a week, and it's still not enough to cover *his debts.*"

I bowed my head, at a loss for words. He threw another stone in the water.

"If he just auctioned off those books, we could start over again."

"You said it would break his heart."

He was silent for a moment, and then laughed sharply, his words rushing out in an angry staccato. "If I could find a way to make money off those books, I'd do that for the rest of my life, but we've been losing money for years. The trouble with Jan is that he sees things either as a romance or a tragedy, but never as they really are. He can't face up to the plain truth.

"I grew up with those books. They were always there. I was proud of them. They're beautiful." As he said *beautiful*, he turned around to face me, his skin stretched so tightly over his skull that I couldn't bear to look at him. "Beautiful books are for the parlor, but they don't pay the rent. The only problem is that Jan and I don't have a parlor. *People like us don't have parlors, Kathrin!*" He had never spoken harshly to me before, but now I felt the full force of his temper. "Or have you been living so long in that woman's house that you've forgotten what it's like for the rest of us?"

With sweaty, shaking hands, I started putting the dirty dishes back into the hamper.

"I think you had better take me home." I lowered the hamper lid and strapped it shut. A mosquito landed on my wrist. I slapped it, then wiped the red stain away with a handful of grass.

"Home?" he echoed. "So that's your home? On Summit Avenue?"

Struggling to my feet, I hoisted the picnic basket with both hands and started up the path.

"I'd be awfully careful about calling that place your home," he said, following close behind. "Just because some rich woman wanted to play philanthropist to a mill girl doesn't mean you belong there."

"Stop it, John!" As I swung around to face him, the basket of china dishes rattled like a sack of bones against my hip. For a moment, I thought I had broken her beautiful plates. "Just stop it!" I realized I was screaming at him and sobbing like a slapped child.

"Kathrin, don't. I'm sorry." He reddened, his jaw loosening. He took the picnic basket from me, set it on the ground, and held me until I stopped crying. "I'm sorry I made you cry, and I didn't mean to talk badly of Jan, but I don't know what I'm going to do." He sounded frightened. "The way things are going now, I'll have to quit night school. I don't even know how I'm going to pay for the coal in winter."

I took his hand and held it against my cheek. "Can I help? You helped me get this job. Maybe I can help you."

He shook his head. "We're far beyond your help. Let's get you home," he said gently, "before it gets dark."

"I do not *have* a home. You said so yourself."

"Kathrin." He cradled my head against his chest. "I'm sorry I said that, but I worry about you. You're so much like Jan; you're good-hearted but maybe a little too sentimental sometimes. You shouldn't expect too much from that woman. She saw a bright girl who was very poor, and she pitied you and wanted to be kind, but don't go thinking she's your friend. Come on now, Kathrin. Don't be sad anymore." He picked up the picnic basket, and we walked up the path to the road.

〜 I let myself in the house and went straight to the scullery to unpack the picnic basket. Thankfully, nothing was broken. Making as little noise as possible, I washed and dried the dishes, packed them away inside the basket again, and put the used napkins in the laundry bag. Through the screen door I could hear phonograph music from the back porch, enough noise to cover my footsteps as I made my way through the kitchen and up the stairs to my room. I couldn't face Violet tonight. She would take one look at me and see that I had been crying. She would ask me why, and that would set me off again.

〜 Getting up early the next day, I rehearsed various excuses for my antisocial behavior the night before. Violet was sitting at the breakfast table on the back porch, but her plate and coffee cup were empty. She was reading the morning paper. When I sat down beside her, she didn't say a word, just went on reading as if I weren't there. *She is angry,* I thought, until she finally looked up and I saw her bloodless face. "Look at this, Kathrin." She passed the paper to me, and I squinted at the black letters swimming over the front page. War had broken out in Europe.

❧ That August I think everyone went around in a daze of shock and bewilderment. We had never seen a war like this—a dirty cesspool, sucking in nearly every nation in Europe, sucking in Canada and Australia, too. The series of battles and alliances resembled some horrible game of chess. The barrage of headlines screamed day after day. The speed at which it unfolded was the most gruesome thing. Three days after the declaration of war, the Germans marched into neutral Belgium. By the seventh of August, they had taken Liége, were making headway across Flanders, sweeping toward France. One city fell after another. The Belgians were forced to live under military rule. By the end of August, the first reports of starving civilians started cropping up. Too frightful to believe, but it was there in the paper. The picture of German recruits, none of them older than I, hanging out of a railway car with the slogan AUF GEHT'S NACH PARIS written in chalk under the train window. *A trip to Paris.* They thought they were going on a short vacation. The papers said the war wouldn't last more than a few months.

My uncle had told me there would be no more war in our lifetime, that the world had grown too civilized for such things. But when I saw those pictures of my countrymen, I thought the age of barbarism had returned. Sometimes I wondered if my uncle had possessed the gift of prophecy. That despite his idealism, his talk of no more war, he had known the truth. Had he sent me across the ocean, because, already in 1911, he had seen the storm clouds coming? I wrote him a long letter, wondering if it would even get through to him now.

❧ John and I forgot our shouting match by the river. The war overshadowed everything else. Even though it was on the other side of the ocean, it was already driving up the price of coal and flour over here. John had an even heavier burden to bear. "Just be glad you are here," I kept telling him. "Over there they would make you fight."

❧ Mr. Jelinek took the news very hard. The next time I visited the store, he was stooped over sweeping, and looked older and more frail than I had ever seen him. "Each time I look at the paper," he said, "I think I've lived too long."

I wandered up and down the aisles, trying to take comfort in the books as I had in the old days at the mill. Here was the book on etiquette I had been reading in May, the night I had first seen Violet. And over there was the book of fairy tales she had been reading. I knew its position on the shelf by heart, could find it by touch with my eyes closed. For some reason this book soothed me like no other. Everything in my world was crumbling; no solid ground remained anywhere; I had nothing to hold on to but these tales. Taking the book from the shelf, I began to page through it until I found the picture of the woman with the wand. I imagined showing it to Violet. *"When I first saw you, this is what I thought you were like."* Gently I closed the book and carried it to the cash register.

"That's a lovely old book," said Mr. Jelinek.

"It is a present for Mrs. Waverly," I told him. Even if she were only my employer and not my friend, she had shown me kindness, and I didn't want my time at her house to end without giving her some token in return.

I didn't give her the book right away. I was waiting for the right occasion. She seemed to have a lot on her mind those days, though I had no idea if it was the world she was troubled about or something more personal. Those days she was opaque as clouded water.

On the last day of August, she shoved the morning paper into the kitchen stove before I could even see the front page. "I've had enough of this," she said. "I used to despise people who were apathetic about world affairs, but now I just want to stick my head in the sand."

"It was something terrible about Germany," I said, but Violet was in no mood to discuss it. She was too restless to work on the manuscript.

"Will you come downtown with me, Kathrin? I have a lot of little things to buy. Cleaning things. I want to give the house a top-to-bottom clean. I'm helping Franny. It's too much work for one person to do alone. If you came along to the shops with me, it would be very nice. I could use an extra set of arms to help carry."

"Yes, of course I will come."

"I'm having a party next week," she said. "At first I thought I'd call the whole thing off. How can you have a party with a war going on? But now I think a party would do us good."

"A dinner party?"

"A birthday party." Her voice was distant.

"For your sister?" I asked, reading her tone.

"No." She looked at me, reddening. "For myself. It's not meant as self-indulgence," she added quickly. "Just an excuse to invite the family over again. It's been weeks since I've seen my nieces."

"Your birthday?" I smiled. I already had her present.

After breakfast we started off down the hill, heading downtown. It was the end of summer, a blinding blue and gold day, and a few of the leaves on the avenue were already beginning to turn. "Fall's my favorite season," said Violet. "Most people like spring or summer best, but I like fall. The bright leaves and the early twilight." Even as she said this, I knew her mind was somewhere else, chewing on tougher thoughts. We walked a few minutes in silence before she spoke again. "You know, Kathrin, we're nearly finished with the book. I just need to make some corrections and have you type a few more chapters, then it will be out of our hands." She glanced at me sideways. "Have you given any thought to your future?"

I balled my hands up, pressing my fingernails into my palms. This was no surprise. From our first interview I'd known this day would come. "I can type now. I will start looking for a job in an office."

"Is that what you really want, Kathrin? To be a typist?"

Her question left me speechless and infuriated. Who else but a wealthy person could ask such a thing? What other choice did I have if I didn't want to go back to the mill? But then I blurted out an answer that shocked us both. "John and I are thinking of getting married."

"That seems awfully hasty." She picked her words carefully. "Of course, it's none of my business, but surely you'd want to wait a bit." She paused, slowing her pace and looking me in the eye. Giving me that same look she had during our previous woman-to-woman talk, as if she could see straight into my soul. "Not that I mean to pry, but you and he seem to be getting rather intimate lately."

I nearly tripped when she said that. I knew she was referring to our late nights on the riverbanks. Naive as it sounds, I had hoped to keep those trysts secret from her, to keep my days with her and my evenings with John strictly separated, with an impenetrable wall between them.

"I'm not going to bore you with another sermon," she said. "I'd just hate to see you getting yourself in . . . " *In trouble.* She had almost said *in trouble.* "In a situation you might later regret."

"We will get married." I was talking too fast to know what I was saying. "We are not rushing into anything. We will not marry tomorrow, but in a year or so."

"In a year? You're eighteen! I was thinking more of four years." I could feel her eyes on me but could not bring myself to meet them. "I was thinking of college."

At first I thought my ears were playing tricks on me. I looked at her and shook my head. "That is not for someone like me." Not even my uncle had been to a university. That was for rich people.

"You're a very gifted young person. If you applied for a full scholarship, you would probably get one. It's too late for this term, but maybe in winter, after the holidays." She looked at me steadily. "You're far too bright to be someone's typist, Kathrin."

Everything blurred. I stepped down from the curb directly into the path of a delivery wagon. Violet grabbed my arm and pulled me back to the sidewalk. "Watch yourself, dear." Her eyes moved over my face. "Think about what I've said. When we're finished with the project, we'll go to the university together and get you the right forms to fill out. If anyone deserves a scholarship, it's someone who has worked her way up from nothing like you."

I tried to picture myself sweeping into Walter Library with a bundle of books in my arms.

"John will wait for you," she said. "If I were in his shoes, I'd certainly consider you worth waiting for. Besides, a long engagement would be good for him, too. That would give him a chance to pay off his debts." Violet knew as well as I how close the bookstore was to bankruptcy. She had nearly offered the Jelineks a loan but was afraid of offending their pride. "If you gave him four years," she said, "he could really get a foothold in life."

There was a gap in the traffic. Violet took my arm and guided me across the street as if I were a blind person. At that moment I was blinded by everything. The turquoise sky, the rust-colored brick ware-houses and departments stores, the team of blood bay horses pulling a green milk wagon, the sun flashing off the black hood of a brand new Ford. My head was bursting with it all. If Violet had let go of my arm, I would have floated off into space.

"There's something I've been wanting to say for a long time," she said when we reached the other side. "I never quite knew when or where to start. I'm afraid I came across far too heavy-handed during our last talk, but I have to tell you anyway."

"It is about John," I said.

"No, Kathrin. It's about me." This time she was the one who couldn't look me in the eye. "I think I told you about my disappoint-ment. Well, it was more than a disappointment. I did something scan-dalous that disgraced my whole family. Apart from my sister, they've forgiven, but they've never forgotten. It happened when I was your age. More than anything in the world, I wanted to go to college, but I couldn't, because I never even managed to finish high school with my pneumonia and the whole fiasco.

"I married so young, because that was the only way I could leave my family and my scandal behind and have a life of my own. To this day my sister thinks I married Arthur for his money. That's nonsense. I would have married him even if he were poor. He was the only one in the world who didn't despise me."

What could Violet have possibly done that was so shameful? Then, catch-ing a glance at her flushed cheeks and downcast face, I knew. It must have been a lover. Violet must have fallen in love and gotten herself in trouble. Her lover had abandoned her. That was a proper scandal. *And the pneumonia,* I thought. That could be a euphemism for something else. She had made herself ill from trying to abort. It happened all the time. Young women swallowed lye, drank bottles of gin and stepped into searing hot baths, scraped out their insides with knitting needles. That's why Violet and her husband could never have children; why she didn't remarry; why she had warned me to keep my head with John; why her sister still hated her.

She turned to me. "What I've just said. Did it shock you?"

I looked into her eyes. They were like stars. If we were closer in age, I would have given her an impulsive hug. I thought of how beautiful she must have been as a young girl. Who could just seduce her, then abandon her? How evil. "Everyone has secrets," I said. It was the only comforting thing I could think to say. As we walked through the city streets, I kept glancing at Violet out of the corner of my eye. Nothing had changed between us, yet everything was different. From that minute onward, I stopped thinking of her as a benevolent employer and started thinking of her as a confidante, someone I shared a secret with.

❧ On our way back from the stores, our arms laden down with parcels of beeswax, Sunlight Soap, and silver polish, we saw a uniformed Red Cross nurse collecting money for the war relief in Belgium. Violet gave her five dollars. I gave her fifty cents, all the spare change I had with me. It seemed the least I could do. In the next few days I would find out why Violet had been hiding the paper from me. The first caricatures of spike-helmeted Huns were coming out. Huns trampling dead women and bayoneting babies.

Although Violet told me I didn't have to, I joined her and Franny in the cleaning. If nothing else, it helped rid my mind of those ugly pictures. Since I was the youngest, I volunteered to drag the Persian rugs out to the clothesline and beat the dirt out of them. I swung the carpet beater back and forth until my eyes ran from the dust, until my back and shoulders were aching. I was so angry, I thought I would burst. I didn't know what to think of Germany anymore. You could never afford to take caricatures too seriously, but I believed the stories of hunger in Belgium. It's the innocent who suffer the most in any war. That's why my uncle was a pacifist. I wished he could have been with me, explaining this to me in a way I could understand.

When I'd finished with the rugs, I joined in the furniture polishing. This was lighter work. It calmed me. Housework wasn't so bad if you did it together with other women. It turned into a contest, a race against time. How clean could three women make the house in the four days left before the party? I climbed to the top of the wobbly stepladder to take down the curtains for Franny to wash and iron. I cleaned the ceilings with soft chamois, polished the chandeliers until they sparkled like icicles. Violet washed the windows and polished the silverware. We sang while we worked. It was a mad week. *Besides,* I was thinking, *a week of helping with the housework meant missing a week of typing.* I would have to spend at least one week longer in Violet's house before the project could be finished. I did not want to leave this place. Violet's talk of college seemed unreal and shadowy compared to this house I loved, its closed-up rooms hiding secrets and ghosts. I went into Professor Waverly's smoking room, still redolent of pipes and cigars, and sat in one of the old oxblood leather chairs. I could feel the Professor's presence, like a guardian spirit, lingering over the house and everyone who lived here. Maybe that's why Violet wanted to leave. The air was just too heavy, full of numens, spirits, and portents.

≈ On the day before the party, Violet decided that I had done enough of the heavy work and gave me the task of sorting through a box of papers. "Anything that you've already typed, you can throw away." I sat alone on the freshly beaten Persian carpet on her study floor with the papers spread around me. In the pile of handwritten pages, I found an old photograph of a delicate-looking girl in a white blouse with a black ribbon at the collar. Her straw boater left her face half in shadow. She had high, finely sculpted cheekbones, a graceful neck. Her hair was pale blond, silvery in the old photograph, framing her face in fine ringlets. She would have almost looked angelic if it hadn't been for her eyes, which were surprisingly dark for her coloring. Fiery and stubborn. Running across the bottom of her white blouse was a message in black ink. *Dear Vi yours forever XXXX Lynnette.* I set the photograph on Violet's desk and continued sorting through the papers. When Violet came to call me for lunch, I showed her the photograph. She went white around the mouth. "This was in that box? I've been looking for it for years. I thought that I'd lost it. Strange." She set the photograph on the mantelpiece. "Strange how one misplaces things."

"She was your friend?"

Violet nodded absently. "My best friend."

"Do you still write to her?" I thought guiltily of Lotte. I must really send her a card and arrange to meet her again. I wanted to know what Lotte thought of this war. My cousin didn't care two figs about Kaisers or politics. Right now I would welcome her earthiness, her belligerent common sense.

"She's dead." Violet lowered herself on the arm of one of the chintz chairs.

"Your friend? I'm sorry."

Violet tugged off the scarf she had tied over her hair to keep the dust out. "She died in childbirth. Her first-born. She shouldn't have been allowed to have children in the first place. Her hips were so narrow. The baby died with her. Six months later her husband married again."

I thought of Mr. Jelinek and his photographs of John's mother. "She was very pretty."

Violet kneaded the kerchief in her hands. "She was exquisite, Kathrin. The most beautiful person. That picture doesn't do her justice."

10 ✒ On the day of the party, it was unseasonably warm, as if summer had returned. I washed my hair, then combed it out on the back porch, letting it dry in the sun. I was going to do my hair in a completely new way tonight, weaving pale blue satin ribbons through it, ribbons that matched my muslin dress. *Mermaid's hair.* What would John say when he saw me tonight? I imagined him pulling me against him, kissing me with all his hunger. "Pretty, pretty girl," he called me. What is beauty anyway but a woman's face made incandescent by love?

Upstairs on my bureau was my present for Violet. While cleaning out the closets, I'd come across a roll of red marbled paper to wrap it in, a length of silver ribbon to tie around it. Violet probably wasn't even expecting a gift from me, so it was sure to be a surprise. I hoped she would open her presents before John came to fetch me tonight.

Running the comb through my damp hair, I looked out toward the garden, where she was gathering flowers. So far she had picked asters for the front hall, snapdragons for the study, and roses for the dining room, but now I saw her coming toward the porch with an armful of gold chrysanthemums. It had to be some mistake. Gold chrysanthemums, the same flowers I had laid on my mother's grave. *November flowers, graveyard flowers, flowers of the dead.* At home we used chrysanthemums for decorating tombs. I watched Violet carrying them into the house. Bending her face to the golden flowers, she inhaled their spicy fragrance. She was singing to herself. Singing under her breath.

✒ I was apprehensive about seeing her family again. The memory of their laughter still burned in my ears, and the thought of Margaret left me frozen. When they came in the front door, I sat high up the staircase and watched them through the balustrade. The seven nieces flitted in one by one, each wearing a silk gown. Their dresses weren't white this time, but different shades of rose, ranging from palest pink for the youngest sister to a deep fuschia for the oldest. Seeing them spin around in circles, modeling their new dresses for Violet and the uncles, I remembered my dream of the talking Russian dolls.

"These are their last good dresses for the year," said Margaret. "The war is driving up the price of silk."

Violet wore a silvery evening gown that left her shoulders bare. It suited her perfectly. If she stepped outside at midnight, she would shine like the moon. I watched her nieces gathering around her, exclaiming about her beautiful dress, the silver corona in her hair. Any casual observer would think they were Violet's daughters. They resembled her more than their mother—especially Emily, the oldest girl. She looked just like Violet's portrait in the study, looked like Violet when she was my age. When Emily and Violet stood face to face, they looked like images in a mirror. A girl in her youth and a woman in her prime. Emily touched Violet's hand and whispered something in her ear. She came to Violet to tell her secrets. No wonder Margaret was so rancorous and jealous. I knew Margaret's type. There had been plenty of women like her in my old village. A woman like Margaret would never forgive Violet for her girlhood scandal. She would expect Violet to be punished for her sin. *Spiteful harpy.*

I thought I was hidden from view, but just then, as if reading my mind, Margaret looked up and caught me in the act of staring at her through the balustrade. I stood up at once and acted as if I had been sitting on the steps to tie my shoelaces. Turning around, I was about to go upstairs when Violet called me. "You all remember Miss Albrecht," she said as I reluctantly came down the staircase. Emily gawked, but at least she and her sisters didn't laugh.

At Violet's bidding, everyone filed into the drawing room. Out of politeness, I joined in. John would be coming any minute, and then I could escape. Emily seized Violet's arm and led her aside. She was agitated about something. Sitting with her aunt on one of the settees, she was soon locked in an intense discussion with Violet. Ignoring them, Margaret rested her eyes on me. "Miss Albrecht," she said in her gravelly voice, "you look very nice this evening." What she said was a compliment, but it chilled me. I knew there was some hidden message here, but I didn't have any desire to find out what it was. "Thank you, ma'am," I murmured, retreating to the other side of the room where the men were discussing the war. "The outcome of a battle used to depend on a group of brave, well-trained men," said Edward. "But nowadays three men and a machine gun can mow down a whole battalion."

Mow down? At first I thought I had misunderstood. Could human beings be mowed down like grass? An image came to me of a field of men lying facedown in their own blood.

I ran to the kitchen to see if I could help Franny. "Go to the cellar and bring up some wine," she said. "They tell me they don't like the punch." She was in a bad temper, hovering over a steaming pot of purple cabbage leaves that she fished out, one by one, with a pair of silver tongs. The boiling cabbage made Violet's kitchen smell like my old boardinghouse. Opening the cellar door, I switched on the electric light and descended into the gloom and damp. Hardly any jars of preserves on the shelves, just lots of dusty wine bottles. I had no idea which to choose. Drawing out one after another, I puzzled over the French words on the labels. Like the names of battlefields. A few minutes later Violet came down the stairs. "Kathrin! What are you doing down here?"

"Franny told me to get wine, but I do not know what kind."

"Franny has too much work. I should have hired in some extra help tonight." She examined the bottle I was holding. "No, dear, that's a dessert wine. Let's see." She put that bottle back and pulled out two others. "You can carry two, and I'll carry two." As she handed me the bottles, she lowered her voice to a whisper. "Emily was telling me she wants to train as a Red Cross nurse. She wants to go to Serbia! Imagine! Margaret would explode if she knew."

"Your sister does not like me," I whispered back. "Do you know why? Did I do something wrong?"

Violet looked away. "Kathrin, don't take anything Margaret says or does to heart. She is the way she is, and I don't think there's anything that can be done about it. But it's nothing *you* did. It's far more to do with her and me. Let's go back upstairs." Following her up the cellar steps, I watched her glittering silver hem brush up against her black silk stockings. Even her shoes were silver.

"When's John coming?" She set the wine bottles on the kitchen table and wiped the dust off with a wet dishcloth.

"He should be here now."

"You can drink some wine with us while you wait for him. Your hair looks gorgeous, by the way. You look very pretty tonight."

⬿ The wine was older than I was, heavy on the tongue, and so dark, it was nearly black. I sipped from my glass sparingly. I didn't want to be drunk when John came. I kept glancing at the gilded hands of the clock. Eight-thirty. Eight-forty-five. He'd said he would be here at eight, but sometimes the streetcars ran late on Saturday night.

At nine we sat down to dinner. It had not been my intention to join Violet's family at the table, but now there was no polite way out. I kept praying John would burst into the dining room as abruptly as he had burst in last time, but the food was laid out, and still he did not come. Violet had decided on a menu of Russian peasant food, which accounted for the cabbage. There was borscht, black bread, stuffed cabbage, and blintzes, the food her family's ancestors had eaten long ago. The food was good but heavy. Each bite seemed to weigh me down in my chair until I thought I would never rise again. For dessert there was a pie of apples and poppy seeds. If Violet and I had been alone, I would have told her that my mother used to bake apple and poppy seed pie, too, but each time I looked up from my plate and saw Margaret, I was struck dumb. The black poppy seeds wedged themselves between my teeth and under my tongue. Where was John? It was nearly ten. Maybe his streetcar had broken down. Or worse. I could not stop blaming the chrysanthemums. Graveyard flowers are a bad omen. I was haunted by an image of him being hit by a truck, his bones crushed under heavy tires.

"But pacifism is just plain naive," Edward was saying. "You have to defend your country."

"Precisely," said Robert. "But that doesn't mean sending our boys over there to fight in someone else's war. Let them fight their own wars."

"Have you heard that some are running off to Winnipeg to enlist in the Canadian army?" Robert's oldest son asked. He looked about fifteen.

"That's the most idiotic thing I ever heard of," his father snapped. "This is supposed to be a free country, and then you get half-baked boys running off to fight for the King of England. It's a disgrace."

Edward was amused. "We should get Pershing out of Mexico and send him over there. He'd have the Kaiser on his knees in no time."

For once Violet did not join in. Like the other women at the table, she was silent, her eyes moving back and forth as she followed her brothers' dispute.

She waited until after the dishes were cleared away before opening her presents. Margaret gave her a cookbook big enough to use as a doorstop. *A cookbook for a woman who never cooks,* I thought. Edward gave her a silver fountain pen, which she waved in the air like a baton. Robert gave her a burlap bag of crocus and hyacinth bulbs, which seemed to please her most. Finally I stepped forward and gave her the brightly wrapped book. "Kathrin," she said sternly. "You should be saving for your future and not buying presents for me." But her face softened when she opened it. "This is the fairy tale book from Jelinek's. Kathrin, you're a dear." She kissed my cheek, and I smelled her perfume, which made me think of dark spicy roses.

The men adjourned to the Professor's smoking room, while the women went back to the drawing room. It was eleven o'clock. The streetcars stopped at eleven. John would not be coming. The heavy food and wine curdled in my stomach. Margaret stared at me in cold appraisal, not even hiding it. Violet was too busy chatting with her nieces to notice. I got up and left the room, running out the back door and into the yard. Enclosed by darkness, I began to cry. Where was John? How could he just not show up?

The day had been warm, but the night was so cold. I wandered up and down the lawn, the damp grass soaking my shoes and stockings, a chill that sank into my bones. I found myself under the laburnum, the gold rain tree. Once it had been covered in shining golden flowers. What remained were black seed pods that rattled in the wind like skeleton hands. How could he stop caring for me from one day to the next? I went through each evening we had spent together in the past four months. Only now did it occur to me that he had never once come out and said that he cared for me. He had never once said *I love you.* He had told me I was pretty. Once he'd even told me I was beautiful. He had kissed and held me, pressed his head against my breasts and said that if he died there, he would die happy, but he had never called me by any endearments. Even Violet and Mr. Jelinek called me *dear* from time to time. That's what I wanted to be. Dear to him.

It's useless. You have deluded yourself. He was a handsome young man. He could be very charming when he wanted. He certainly knew how to kiss, but he would never really love me. He had too many burdens weighing him down. He might come to me for certain comforts, but no matter what his uncle might have said, he had never showed any intention of declaring his love outright, of asking for my hand.

There you go, I told myself. My job at Violet's would end soon. Violet would be going off to South America next month, for all I knew. The talk of college seemed too unreal to consider. John had cast me off, and the world was at war. Most of the boys I'd grown up with were marching off to one of the fronts to shoot at other boys from neighboring countries. Mowing each other down with machine guns. I wondered if any of them could say what they were fighting for. What was my uncle doing now? He would never volunteer. Never. But if they conscripted him? Graveyard flowers. This was a season of graveyard flowers.

When I couldn't stand the cold anymore, I went inside, heading straight to the washroom to scrub my face until it looked normal again, no trace of tearfulness. Then I returned to the drawing room. Violet looked up at once. "Is everything all right, Kathrin?"

"Yes. I am just tired. Good-night."

The room of women and girls echoed good-night to me. I turned and climbed the stairs to my room.

⮑ Mama kept a big kitchen garden, but the chickens always got in and pecked at what they weren't supposed to. My brother's consumption had returned. He was coughing up blood every night. Mama laid poultices of coltsfoot on his chest. We couldn't afford to get the doctor. Father went out to shoot deer. I hated him for it, but I ate the venison just the same. I was so hungry, never any end to my hunger. In the old days, they said our valley was cursed, full of evil spirits. A narrow valley with so little sunlight. A girl once drowned herself in the mill stream. She was pregnant, and her father turned her out of the house. Her ghost still haunts the valley, a hungry phantom scratching her papery skin until the blood begins to flow, staining the water red. It is not water that turns the mill wheel but blood. Thick coagulating blood like the kind you make sausage from. Bright pulsing blood from an opened artery. The smell of it like freshly slaughtered venison. My brother coughing up his lungs until his face turned blue. Every spring the river flooded, washing up drowned water rats, white-bellied fish. Now the blood rose, filling the valley. The only thing to do was rush up the hill, run until your lungs were bursting, seek higher ground.

Our house was so old, the timber was black. Crooked green shutters that flew off in winter storms. The back door was ajar. I was coming in from the garden, calling Mama, disobeying her wishes, bringing graveyard flowers into the house. "Mama?" I was frightened. I drew back the quilt to see her face. Just one more time before she died, I had to see her face.

It was a skull I saw, a never-ending river of blood.

⮑ *"Kathrin!"* Violet's hand was on my shoulder. I opened my eyes and saw her face, golden in the lamplight, her hair loose over her shoulders. She was wearing her dark red kimono. The skin beneath her throat rose and fell sharply with each breath. "Kathrin, you were screaming the whole house down. It's just a dream."

I sat up and clenched the edge of the sheet to anchor myself.

"You're shaking all over. It must have been an awful dream. Or is it John you're upset about?" Violet touched my wrist. Her fingers were warm and smooth. I opened my mouth, then closed it. Nothing was real. I had no idea what was real anymore. I had to bite down on my lip to keep myself from crying in front of her.

"You look like you've seen a ghost. Why don't you come down to the kitchen? I'll make you some tea. It's all right, Kathrin. We all have nightmares sometimes."

I turned to her. Her face was so clearly illuminated by the lamplight. "I thought a mare was a horse."

"A long time ago people believed that the nightmare was a horse. A horse that brought bad dreams." It was calming to hear her talk so authoritatively. She handed me my slippers, the old woolen ones I had worn last winter in the boardinghouse. "Do you have a dressing gown?"

"No."

Violet opened the wardrobe and found a cardigan for me. "It gets cold now at night."

"Is it late?" I could not escape the horror of my dream. It lingered on me like an unwelcome piece of clothing. Unheimlich.

"Two o'clock. I was getting ready for bed when I heard you screaming."

I followed Violet through the maze of hallways to the kitchen. "I'll make you tea with chamomile and hops. That's best for sleeping." She moved around the kitchen as briskly as if it were daylight. As she filled the tea kettle with rushing water from the tap, I thought of the river of blood in my dreams.

"My mother," I said. "She grew chamomile and hops in her garden." And then it happened. I burst into tears as noisily and gracelessly as a toddler. Ashamed, I hid my face from her. I would have run out of the room if she hadn't stepped in my path and taken me in her arms. My whole body was heaving, out of control. How could Violet even bear to be in the same room with me? I felt her stroking my hair, much differently from the way John had, more delicately, more like a mother. I clamped my mouth shut, commanding myself to stop crying at once, but now that I had started, there was no stopping it. I clung to her so tightly, I felt her collarbone jutting into my forehead.

"Is it John? Maybe he was sick tonight. The stomach flu's been going around. Maybe you'll get a card from him on Monday morning explaining everything."

"He will never love me."

"If that's the case, then you're better off without him. Do you want to talk about your dream?"

"No, it is too terrible."

"The food tonight was heavy. It's common, you know, to have bad dreams after a meal like that. Why don't you sit down, and I'll make you your tea."

"Why are you so good to me?"

"Why?" Violet drew away from me. "Do I need a reason?"

"John says you are only kind because you pity me."

"Pity!" She looked at me testily. "Is that what you think, Kathrin? In all the time you've known me, have I ever once treated you like one treats people one pities?"

I could not speak.

"He *said* that to you?"

"Yes."

"Then you *are* better off without him. I've always had my doubts about John." She walked across the kitchen and came back with a clean dish towel. "Here, Kathrin. Dry your eyes." I obeyed her, trying my best to compose myself, but it was useless. I couldn't stop crying. I was a ridiculous child. Violet would throw me out tomorrow. I thought of my future without her, without John. No home to go to. Home was a myth that did not apply to me. The place I had come from was a graveyard. I was rootless, an orphan. I belonged nowhere. I had estranged myself from my own cousin. I didn't have a single friend, unless you counted Mr. Jelinek, but I could hardly go on visiting him if I was no longer seeing John.

Violet laid her palms on my shoulders. "Tell me, dear. I can't help unless you tell me."

"My mother," I said at last. "I can't remember her face!" I was really behaving like the worst sort of child. If I had carried on this way at home, my father would have strapped me.

"You don't have a photograph?"

I shook my head.

"Do you remember Lynnette, my old school friend? The one whose photograph you found?"

"Yes."

"When she died, part of me died, too. There was a time when I couldn't remember her face, either. I have no easy answers for you, Kathrin. There's no cure for love or death."

"When will you go to South America?"

"South America?" Violet's face was a blank.

"You said you would go there."

"Oh, Kathrin." She laughed and shook her head. "That was just something I said when I was angry with my sister. Did you really think I was going to run off like that?" She smoothed my hair away from my face. "Yes, that's precisely what you thought. I can read it in your eyes. Kathrin, I don't believe this. Only on Monday I was talking about your going to college. Don't you remember that?" She took the dish towel and began to dry my eyes. "Do you honestly think I'd just run off and leave you?" She touched my face. "Listen, dear. I can't bring your mother back, but I'll never ever leave you in the lurch. In fact, if I do go traveling, I might even take you with me. It's more interesting with a companion, and you're the most amiable companion I can think of. Can you imagine me riding donkeyback through the Andes with Margaret?"

The image was so comical, I had to laugh.

"You've been an excellent secretary and assistant to me. If I talked about sending you away to college, it was only because I wanted the best for you. Nothing would make me happier than seeing you go to the university and making something of your life. You're a wonderful secretary, but I think you could do much more. And don't you dare think I'm saying this because I pity you."

"No." I couldn't look at her. If I looked in the face of that much goodness, I would break down again.

"Do you still want that tea?"

"No, thank you."

"Why don't you go back to bed and try to get some sleep?"

"You go on," I said. "I will just sit here a while. Thank you," I added, sitting on one of the kitchen chairs. I put my hands on the edge of the table, gripping the dense oak as hard as I could, trying to bring myself back to earth. I expected Violet to leave the room, but she stood in the doorway with her arms crossed in front of her. "Kathrin, you are completely out of sorts." She pulled out a chair and sat beside me. "You don't have any color in your face. Was your dream so bad?"

"Yes."

"You dreamt of your mother."

I closed my eyes. "I could not see her face, just, how do you say, the bones, the skull."

"It's this talk of war."

"It is terrible. I am ashamed."

"What's happening over there has nothing to do with you." Violet paused. "You're afraid to go back to sleep, because you think the dream will come back."

I nodded miserably.

"Well, come along with me, then. You won't be so frightened." She took my hand, drawing me up from the chair. "Come on, dear. You can't stay in the kitchen all night."

≈ Stepping into her room was like entering a forest. The walls were papered in dark green, a pattern of densely woven leaves. The furniture was carved oak. The bed was a vast thing with a massive oak headboard, very old. Violet drew back the covers for me. "Good-night, Kathrin. Remember, only nice dreams."

I stepped out of my slippers, folded my cardigan, and set it neatly on the chair beside the bed. Then I lay down, pulling the covers over myself and arranging my limbs on the unfamiliar topography of the old mattress, its hills and valleys. This was her marriage bed, where she had once lain with the Professor. I tried to imagine her as a young woman in the arms of an old man, but I could not.

The lamplight penetrated my closed eyelids, making things orangey, warm. I heard Violet going into the adjacent bathroom. The noise of a toilet flushing, water running. *Water,* I told myself, *pure clear water and not blood.* I touched my belly. It was swollen and tight. My breasts hurt. My back ached. Tomorrow my period would come. *See,* I told myself, *that explains everything.* The dream of blood, my weeping fit. If I looked at it with a clear head, the whole thing was humiliatingly banal.

The bathroom door opened, and I could hear footsteps approaching the bed. I opened my eyes. Violet had taken off her kimono. She was wearing a thin cotton nightgown that left her arms bare. Her hair was loose around her face. Like this, she looked much younger, not like a professor's widow. I watched her pulling back the covers on the other side of the bed and climbing in.

"Good-night," I said.

Violet smiled and drew the covers to her chin. She smelled of lavender soap and rose water. "Good-night, Kathrin. Now get some sleep." She shut off the lamp.

Darkness again, but not pitch darkness. The streetlights and moonlight crept around the corners of the shades and curtains. I listened to the wind tossing the elm branches against the window pane. I could hear her breathing, deep and even. She was asleep already. I closed my eyes and buried my face in the linens, which smelled faintly of her rose water.

The dream kept coming back. The staring skull, the graveyard flowers, the drowned girl, the river of blood. Each time I emerged sobbing, covering my head with the pillow, trying not to wake Violet, but in the end I did.

She turned on the lamp. "Another nightmare? Come, dear. Come to me." She held up the covers so I could roll toward her. She leaned over me, wiping my tears with the edge of the sheet. Her hair was falling around my face as she bent to kiss me. It wasn't like John's kisses. It was soft. Like a mother's touch. It broke the spell. The horror of my dream melted away. I looked up into her eyes, gray like the ocean I had crossed to get here. She kissed me again, half on my cheek, half on my mouth. Then she reached over to shut off the lamp.

Nestled in darkness, her arms wrapped securely around me, her hair against my closed eyelids. These were the last things I remembered before I fell into a dreamless sleep.

⮑ Nothing had changed. Everything was different. When I woke the next morning, Violet was sitting in front of her vanity in her red kimono, brushing her hair. I sat up in bed. Our eyes met in the mirror. "I didn't want to wake you," she said. "You looked so peaceful." Her face was shining, flushed from sleep.

I was afraid to look at my reflection, at my eyelids swollen from all that crying. Throwing off the covers, I got up, stepped into my slippers, put on my cardigan, making myself decent. Then, without saying anything, I walked up behind her, took the brush from her hand and started brushing her hair. My throat was too full to speak. This was the only gesture I could think of to thank her for her kindness. If I tried to put it into words, I would just get weepy. As I moved the brush in gentle, even strokes, she submitted without a word. Our eyes met in the mirror again. She smiled. When I had brushed through the tangles, I arranged her hair in a loose chignon. She handed me the pins and combs.

"Now it's your turn," she said, taking the brush from me. We traded places. The morning sun poured through the window, catching my face in a golden bar and glancing off my hair. "It's like spun gold in a fairy tale." She drew up a long lock with the brush, then let it fall. "With your hair down, you look like Eve. Or Gretchen in *Faust.*"

In the old days Lotte and I used to take turns brushing each other's hair, but there was never enough time to enjoy it. We had to rush off to the mill or to mass on Sundays. It was never this luxurious. Now I dared to look at my reflection. It was as if Violet had waved a wand over me. I was beautiful. Something had shifted inside me, something I had no name for.

"Are you going to church?" she asked me.

I glanced at the clock on the bureau. It was 9:30. I would have to get dressed right away and run out the door to make it on time for ten o'clock mass. "No," I said, settling myself even more comfortably, closing my eyes and feeling her move the brush through my hair.

We breakfasted in Violet's study. Having eaten such heavy food the night before, I thought I would never eat again, but I was ravenous, devouring so much of the leftover black bread that Violet laughed. "It's such a pleasure watching you eat. You enjoy your food more than anyone I know." We spent at least an hour drinking our coffee. It was Sunday. No work to do, the whole day stretched before us like a gift. I heard the cathedral bells ringing down the avenue, but any guilt was banished by the comfort I felt. Neither of us talked about what had happened the night before. Neither of us mentioned John. I was content to let him go his way without grudge or recrimination.

As we drank our coffee, I noticed the book of fairy tales I had given Violet. It was sitting on the mantelpiece next to the Russian dolls and the photograph of her old school friend. I went over and took the book down, opening it to the illustration of the woman with the wand. "When I first saw you," I said, handing it to her, "this is what I thought you were like."

She studied the picture for a few seconds. "I'm sure you overestimate me." Her eyes darted up to mine. "But it's very sweet of you. Shall we go for a walk?"

We glanced at the newspaper before setting out. The Germans had finally been stopped at the Marne. It looked as if they wouldn't be reaching Paris. Maybe that's all they needed, one serious defeat to realize it was a mistake. Then they would swallow their hubris, turn around, and go home. The world would go back to what it was like before the war.

While Violet went to her room to get her walking shoes, I sneaked down to the drawing room, took the chrysanthemums out of their vase, ran out the door with them, and flung them into the compost barrel behind the garden shed. *No more graveyard flowers,* I thought, as I walked with Violet down the hill to the river.

11 ✒ When I was thirteen, my brother died, and I had to take on his old chores. When I was fifteen, my father died. My mother and I split the men's work between us. When I was sixteen, my mother died, taking what I thought was left of my girlhood with her. Yet I look back to my time in Violet's house as a belated youth, my brief season of unfolding and flowering, during which I was as pure and strong as the waxing moon. It was my supreme season of happiness, when I thought that even the war was something that could be swiftly stopped and healed.

During those mornings we spent brushing each other's hair, we dropped all pretense of being employer and assistant. We were friends. There was nothing dramatic in this change. No fireworks or explosions. It was quite different from what I had experienced with John. It was just a subtle alteration, a blossoming of what had been planted and had taken root that May evening when we first met in the bookstore, hardly perceptible to the outside eye.

Our solitary hours of work were framed by shared meals, the same as before, except now we spent even longer over our morning coffee and broke off work in the late afternoons so we could go for walks together before it got dark. We sat up past midnight, talking and drinking tea. When we finally fell asleep, it hardly seemed to matter if I slept in my bed or Violet's. Back in the boardinghouse, Lotte and I had shared a bed for nearly two years. The difference was that Violet and I cared for each other a lot more. This closeness was like nothing I had ever known. Still I had no label other than *friendship* to describe what we shared. Violet was my dear, dear friend.

⌇ During the early frost that September, we made dresses. My summer things were too flimsy for the cool weather, and none of my old clothes from last winter fit me anymore. Since coming to Violet's, I had gained fifteen pounds. Violet took me downtown, and I bought yards and yards of wool and flannel. At the mill I had hated sewing, but during those weeks I learned to love it again. Violet had a machine, but my time at the mill had turned me against machines. Sewing by hand, I savored each stitch. I sewed in her study, in one of the chintz armchairs by the window, while she sat at her desk and proofread the manuscript. The following week she was supposed to deliver it to the university, yet she seemed reluctant, as I was, to let it go. I think she was glad each time she ran across a spelling mistake or typing error. I put down my sewing, ran to the dining room, and typed the page over for her as many times as she asked. Neither of us wanted this project or this season to end.

Sometimes she just stuck the manuscript in a drawer, sat in the other armchair, and chatted with me as I sewed. She admired my work but thought the colors I had chosen for myself were too dull. "Dark blue, Kathrin! Gray! You're young. You can carry bright colors." She left the study, returning five minutes later with a folded length of red velvet. Red like garnets. A few shades darker than her kimono. She held it out so I could stroke it. I had never touched velvet before.

"My nieces gave it to me last year. I used to love sewing." Violet cleared the books off her desk and began to unfold the heavy cloth. "Six yards," she said. "Just enough for a proper evening gown."

I thought how lovely she would look in it, the red velvet against her milky skin and black hair. "It will be even nicer," I said, "than your silver dress."

"It's not going to be for me, Kathrin. It's going to be for you."

I stopped sewing and shook my head. "It is much too fine for me. Where would I wear such a dress?" Lately our conversations had taken on a teasing, bantering tone. Like two sisters, like mother and daughter.

"I'm sure we'll go to the theater this winter. And once you start college, you'll need a few nice things. Every young woman should have an evening gown."

Going to the theater? That was for rich people, but now I let myself dream of curtains opening to an elaborate set. A play by Shakespeare, the actors and actresses talking to each other in that fantastically unintelligible old-fashioned English, each sentence like a poem. Sitting beside Violet in one of the front rows. She would be wearing her silver dress. In the red velvet, I would look elegant enough to accompany her.

"I already have a pattern in mind," she told me. "Very simple. A V-neck and a princess waist with a satin ribbon. Otherwise no ornamentation." She came to the armchair where I sat sewing and held the folded velvet against my shoulder. "Red is your color." There was a note of triumph in her voice. "I have just the thing to go with it. A beautiful silk shawl I haven't worn in years. Come upstairs. I'll show you."

Putting aside my half-finished blouse, I followed her to her room. She knelt in front of the oak chest at the foot of her bed and pulled out a soft bundle swathed in many layers of yellowing tissue paper. I sat on her vanity chair and watched her unwrap it, watched her unfold an immense silk shawl with a trailing fringe. Bloodred patterned with gold, silver, and deep blue. Violet shook it out gently, releasing the bit of dust that had made its way through the tissue paper. Then she turned me around in the vanity seat so I was facing the mirror and wrapped the shawl around my shoulders. I could feel the silk against my throat. Soft, like freshly washed hair. I had never worn silk. It made me look different, exotic. An actress or an opera singer.

"This is so beautiful. It looks Russian. Did you get it there?" I imagined the Professor buying it for her on their travels.

Violet smoothed the silk over my shoulders. "No. Lynnette gave it to me."

"Your friend from school?"

"Yes. For my sixteenth birthday."

"You never wear it."

Her hands fell to her sides. "It's a shawl for a young woman. It looks much nicer on you."

I thought about her friend who had died. "Did you like boarding school?" I only knew about boarding schools from the snatches of *Jane*

Eyre that I'd read at Jelinek's. They were supposed to be horrible places, nothing but gruel to eat, yet Violet's family had sent her to one. I wanted to piece together her life: not just Violet as she was now in her mansion, but the girl she had been when she was my age.

"Kathrin, it was a whole other world. Only girls. The teachers were nearly all female. Spinsters with lofty ideas. It was strange getting used to it, at first. Lynnette took me under her wing." Violet closed the chest and sat down on it. "Of course, there were lots of silly things like deportment lessons. We spent hours practicing how to curtsy. I would have rather learned algebra or chemistry like my brothers. And I told you about those dances."

I turned around in the vanity seat to see her rolling her eyes.

"Waltzing the whole night with pimply cadets, Kathrin! It's not like going with a boy of your own choosing. Everything was stiff and forced."

There was such acrimony in her voice, I wondered if one of those cadets had been responsible for her disgrace, her "pneumonia."

"Lynnette hated it as much as I did. We'd sneak off together, hide out on the school roof, and drink white rum that she smuggled into school in an old cologne bottle. They would have thrown us out if we'd been caught."

"Your friend," I said. "Did she come to your wedding?" What I really wanted to know was if her friend had stuck by her through her scandal.

Violet stood up and began to pace like a cat. "No. We were no longer friends by then. She got engaged during our last year in school. A boy from her hometown, someone her parents picked for her. He came up for one of the dances and decided he didn't like me. He told her to break off our friendship, and that's what she did."

I had never heard of such a thing.

"She was so infatuated with him, she would have crawled on all fours and barked like a dog if he'd asked her to. I would have forgiven her for everything if I'd seen anything *admirable* in him, but I knew from the start that he was going to make her terribly unhappy. And you see, I was right. I'm afraid I didn't behave very well after that. I made a wretched fool of myself."

Betrayed by her best friend. Violet would have succumbed to any young man who offered her a sliver of kindness. *That's when it happened,* I thought. *Her seduction.* I wanted to go to her and take her hand, but I didn't. Something about her sorrow demanded privacy, distance. Fingering the shawl, I listened to her voice, which sounded as if it were coming from far away, like the sound of waves in a seashell you hold against your ear.

"I'd been married a little over a month when I got word that she died having that bastard's baby." That was the first and only time I heard her using vulgar language. She turned away from me. I couldn't see her face, but I heard the trembling in her voice and wondered if she was crying or about to. "In the end, she came to regret her choice. She wrote a letter begging me to forgive her, but by the time it reached me, she was dead. She died thinking I hated her."

A minute or so passed in silence. I could hear the ticking of the brass alarm clock on her bureau. Then I got up from the vanity seat, and she turned to me. She was smoothing her face with her hands, coming back to herself. We sat together on the bed. She rearranged the shawl around my shoulders. "Like this, you look like a princess in a Russian fairy tale. I want you to keep it. It's a crime to hoard away something so beautiful." She spoke too quickly and firmly for me to protest. "Your birthday's in November, isn't it? This will be my present to you. This and the velvet dress."

I didn't know what to say. That she would give me something that was so dear to her. All the things she had given me. No words of mine would be good enough to thank her for them.

"The scandal," she said, looking into my eyes. "I haven't spelled it out to you by letter, but I think by now you must know."

I nodded, assuming she had been trying to tell me about a pregnancy followed by an abortion.

"And you still care for me, Kathrin?"

"*Yes,*" I said with so much emotion that she put her arm around me. "What did you think? That I would hate you?"

"Margaret does," she said calmly. "Because of that."

"*She is terrible.*" My loyalty was the one thing I could give her in

return for everything she had given me. I offered it up unquestion-
ingly. She smiled at me a bit brokenly and ran her hand over my hair.
In spite of everything she had just told me, I still believed a man had
brought about her downfall.

      Nothing changed. I spent my days typing and sewing. Violet took my
measurements for the velvet dress. I helped her cut out the pattern.
The dining room table became our work bench. It was the only surface in the whole house that was big enough for all that velvet. I stood
on a chair while she knelt on the floor and pinned up the hem. "You'll
need silk stockings to wear with this. And high-heeled shoes." She was
turning me into a lady.

    She used the machine and worked fast. Within a week the dress was
finished. I modeled it in front of the full-length mirror on her closet
door. She placed the shawl around my shoulders. I couldn't stop looking at my reflection. It was just as she had said. Red was my color. Red
made me glow, made my hair look burnished. Dark honey gold, not
mousy. I turned round and round in front of the mirror, watching the
skirt fly out to reveal the black silk stockings she had lent me. I was
barefoot. None of the shoes I owned would do this dress justice. I
couldn't stop laughing. Violet got out her silver shoes that she had
worn with her silver dress.

    "I don't think these will fit," she said, "but try them anyway."

    I stepped into her shoes. It was the first time I had ever worn high
heels. Tottering like I'd had too much wine, I grabbed her arm to
steady myself. In the mirror I saw a stranger reflected. A stranger in
velvet and silk, in red and gold and silver.

    "Next week," she said, "we'll go to the theater. They're playing *The
Lady from the Sea* by Ibsen." And I thought of the mermaid in the book
of fairy tales.

      A few days later she went to the university to hand over the manu-
script. "I have to look as respectable as possible. These professors were
Arthur's friends and colleagues." I brushed her hair and watched her pin
it up into a matronly French roll that made her look like Margaret. Then

she put on a somber navy blue suit and a matching hat with a blue-black veil that cast a shadow on her face. I sat on the edge of her bed as she opened her jewelry box and extracted a string of jet beads and her gold wedding band, the only time I saw her wear it. For the first time since I met her, she looked like a real widow. She put the manuscript in a black leather briefcase, one that was so slim and ladylike, it looked like a handbag. Outside on the street, the cab honked for her. Franny shouted up the stairwell. "Wish me luck," she said, sweeping out of the room. I followed her down the stairs. "The next time I go to the university," she said, "I'll take you along." Then she rushed out the door and into the waiting cab.

I went to the study and opened my sewing basket. Since there was no real work left for me to do, I sewed a taffeta lining into my new skirt of dark gray wool. The color Violet thought was too drab for me. The sun poured through the window, spilling into my lap, making it warm. The newspaper was lying on her desk, but I didn't bother looking at the headlines. I was too warm, too comfortable, the wool heavy in my lap like a purring cat. When I closed my eyes in the stream of sunlight, I saw gold and then red.

I'd been sewing for an hour when I heard the doorbell ring, then Franny calling me. "Miss! It's for you." When I came down the stairs, she was holding an oblong cardboard box. "It has your name on it," she said as she handed it to me. My name in John's handwriting.

After Franny had returned to the kitchen, I sank down on the bottom step, numbly undid the cellophane seal, and opened the box. I saw red, red roses, a dozen of them, crackling like flames at the top of their prickly stems. Lifting them out of the box, I scratched my fingers on the thorns. I lifted them to my nose and lips, but they were hothouse flowers. They had no fragrance. I was hot, then cold, then hot again. *Three weeks.* After three weeks of silence, how could he just send me roses? *Red roses.* At home, they were a symbol of undying love. You only gave them to the girl you wanted to marry. He had been born in Vienna, he must know these things from his uncle.

Red roses. *How could he?* If Violet were there, I would have asked her, but she wasn't, so I sat on the bottom step, rocking myself back and forth, holding the roses to my breast like a thorny child. Then I saw the envelope at the bottom of the box. I took it out and let the roses fall in my lap. Ripping it open, I nearly tore the card inside.

> Dear Cathrin,
>
> I'm so sorry about the other Saturday. My uncle and I both had the flu, and everything was upside down. I'll come this Saturday next and make it up to you.
>
> Love, John

My head vibrated like a church tower on Sunday morning. He had signed his card with "love." Did he mean it? Did he really love me? Red roses. They must have cost a fortune. Money he couldn't afford. The flu. You could die from a bad case of flu, especially if you were old and frail, like Mr. Jelinek. Why hadn't he told me they were sick? If he had just sent a card, I would have brought them oranges. I would have made them coltsfoot tea and chicken broth and hot rum with lemon juice and honey.

These were the thoughts that ran through my head as I carried the flowers up to my room. Then I realized I didn't have a vase for them. Leaving the roses on my bed, I ran down to the kitchen. Somehow I had to run instead of walk. When I burst through the kitchen door, I was panting.

"Something the matter?" Franny frowned as I hunted through the cupboards for a vase that was big enough to hold a dozen long-stemmed roses.

I shook my head.

I arranged the roses on my windowsill. They were the same red as the Virginia creeper outside my window, the same red as the shawl and the velvet dress. I set the little card beside the vase. Everything was churning up inside me. Once I had thought we would marry. Then I had thought he would never really care for me, that I was better off forgetting him. Now I didn't know anything. I had no idea what I felt. I imagined him sick in bed with no one to look after him. *Upside down,* he had written. That was it exactly. Everything was upside down. What would I do when I saw him on Saturday? Just continue as we had left off, like nothing had changed?

Today was Tuesday. I counted the days off on my fingers. I could think about it until Saturday night. I needed the time to sort everything out. I brooded about John and the odorless roses until I heard the front door open. Violet was back. "Kathrin!" she called, her voice brimming with excitement. Before going down to meet her, I closed the curtains, concealing the roses on the broad windowsill behind them. Now they were hidden from everyone but me. If Violet came into my room, she would never even know. I couldn't explain *why* I wanted to hide the roses from her. Maybe because I knew she disliked John, that she didn't think he was good for me. I didn't want to talk about him with her or anyone until I saw him again and knew how things stood.

"It's out of our hands," she cried, when I came down the stairs. "They were very, very pleased with it."

Even in her dark clothes, she looked radiant, like a new mother. Her happiness was so infectious, I hugged her, breathing in her perfume, her smooth cheek against mine, banishing thoughts of John for the moment. Brooding about him wouldn't solve anything. *Give it time. Time will tell. You're going to college. You have four years to make up your mind about him.* That's the advice she would have given me if I had asked her.

"Your name will be on the frontispiece with mine," she said. "I wouldn't have been able to finish it in less than a year if it hadn't been for you." She took off her hat. Her hair was coming loose. She looked like a girl, like a woman who had gotten her youth back. I thought of the Firebird in the Russian fairy tales who guards the water of youth and the water of life. "I'm so happy, Kathrin! We have to celebrate. Let's open a bottle of wine."

⮑ Dark red claret—we drank it in front of the fireplace in her study, a plate of bread and cheese and pears between us. By late afternoon, the light was fading, but the fire bathed her face. She had taken off her dark suit, put on a dress of light blue cashmere that made her eyes

shine like stars. If red was my color, blue and white and silver were
hers. Curled on the Persian rug, she was a different person from the
one who had set out this morning in the jet beads and veiled hat.

"I can't tell you what a relief this is. Ever since Arthur's death, I've had
this *weight* on my back. But it's over, all the unfinished business. I can
send his old manuscripts to the university archives." She took a long sip
of wine and hugged her knees to her chest. "The slate is clean, Kathrin.
It's like starting over again. I could go anywhere or do anything."

"Will you go to South America?" Now I could tease her about it.

"Not right away," she said in the same facetious tone. "First I have
to sell the house."

"Will you really sell it?"

"Yes. That's the next logical step. It was always Arthur's house more
than it was mine. I think I'd like to move to our old summer house. It's
just a cabin, up near the St. Croix River, but so pretty, Kathrin. Nothing
but forest. There are still some wolves up there. In winter you can hear
them howling." She bit into a pear.

I lay on my back and stared at the molded ceiling, the pattern of
grapevines and roses. "I love this house."

"I'm not selling it next week. It takes months, sometimes years to
find a buyer for a house this size." She got up to put another log on the
fire. I rolled over and watched the sparks flying out, lighting on her
sleeve, but she brushed them away and put the screen back in place.
"When you start college," she said, staring into the hearth, "they'll want
you to live on campus, at least for the first year. It's probably best. That
way you'll meet other girls your age."

"I would not live here anymore?"

"You can visit me on the weekends and tell me everything you've
learned. In the summer we can travel together." Her face was red. I
couldn't tell if she was blushing or if it was just the heat of the fire.
"Tomorrow we'll go to the university and get you the forms to fill
out. I can show you Arthur's old office. We'll drink sherry in the fac-
ulty lounge, and I'll introduce you to the professors and deans." She
picked up her wine glass again. "Next week we'll go to the theater.
And then we can go up north. I'll show you the cabin." She stretched

out her legs. "You'll like it up there. By this time of year, the mosquitoes will be dead."

"My mother's house," I told her, "was a cabin in the woods."

~ Since we were going to the university in the morning, I decided to
bathe and wash my hair that night. Beside the tub was a wicker table
with her oils, soaps, and unguents on it. I knew she wouldn't mind my
using them, so I opened the amber and cobalt bottles one by one,
inhaling their contents, sprinkling rosemary and sweet orange oil into
the bathwater, making everything smell like summer. I scrubbed my
skin with lavender soap, washed my hair with elder flower shampoo.
The wine made me dreamy, languorous, and slow. I didn't want to
think about John, didn't want to think about leaving Violet's house. I
wanted everything to remain exactly as it was, like a delicate insect
caught in amber. Preserved forever. I would keep it like a jewel.

Rising from the bath, I rubbed rose oil into my skin, which made
it glow as if it were polished. I dabbed rose water on my face and neck.
My flannel nightgown and my old cardigan were on the chair next to
the sink, but something made me reach instead for Violet's kimono,
which hung on the door and smelled of her perfume. The dark red
silk felt like rose petals against my bare skin. The sensation rooted me
in place, made me forget the past and the future. Feeling the silk
against my skin, all I could think of was the present, my life with Violet
in this house.

I wanted to see what I looked like in her kimono, but the mirror
was too steamy. I stepped into my woolen slippers, worn thin at the
soles, and walked down the hall to my room, switched on the electric
light. It glanced off the silk like sunshine. I stood in front of the mirror with my damp hair trailing. A bloodred mermaid. When my hair
was wet, it looked dark, almost as dark as Violet's. I gazed into the mirror to see what I would look like if my hair were the same color as
hers, but I had forgotten to belt the robe. As I raised my arms to comb
my hair, the kimono opened like a curtain, and I saw my nakedness
reflected. My skin shining from the bath and the rose oil. My skin was
golden. Staring into the mirror, I combed my hair until it was smooth.

And then I went to the window, opened the curtains, took the vase of roses from the sill, and closed the curtains again. I pressed the tight red buds against my throat. They would open slowly, unfurling to reveal their deep scarlet centers. When I was a child, my uncle taught me to slice flowers in half to find the stamen and pistil. "Male and female," he told me. "People and animals are either male or female, but plants are both at once." I put the vase of roses on the dresser and opened the robe completely, looking at my body, my whole naked body deliberately for the first time, at the unknown woman in the mirror. The woman in the glass had never been a hungry mill girl, her breasts were too heavy and full. I weighed them in my hands, then let my hands glide down my rib cage until they touched my belly, smoothly rounded like the bellies of the marble goddesses I had seen in books. Except it wasn't cold stone but silky and warm, downy like peach skin. Then I reached the triangle of hair just an inch below my fingers. I didn't dare touch myself there. Mother said it made you mad, made you go blind. I didn't touch myself, but I opened my legs to see the pink flesh parting. There are sins of deed and sins of thought. At that moment, I believe I cast my maidenhood aside. I became a woman.

I went to the windowsill to get John's card, reached blindly through the crack in the curtains, but then I heard footsteps down the hall, a knock on my door. The card fell behind the radiator. I had just enough time to cinch the kimono before the door opened. Violet was holding my nightgown and cardigan. "You left these in the bathroom," she said, but then she saw me in her kimono. Her face went as red as the silk. I could tell by the way she averted her eyes that she knew I was naked underneath. She looked past me to the roses on the dresser. I squeezed my eyes shut, wondering how I could possibly explain.

"They're gorgeous," she said. "Did you pick them today?"

I could only look at her, slack-jawed and mute.

"It's good," she said, "that you picked the last roses before the frost could kill them."

A noise welled up from the bottom of my throat, an animal noise that made me ashamed. She crossed the room and came to me. "Kathrin."

Catherine wheels rolling down from the highest hill. All the way down they burn.

A strand of wet hair was stuck to my collarbone. She moved it aside. Her fingers rested on the place where the edge of the kimono met my bare skin. She looked at the roses and then at me.

She didn't know about chrysanthemums, but she knew about red roses.

The look she gave me was not the look of a sister or a friend, but a sorceress. Even as it burned me, it held me in thrall. She put her hands on my shoulders. Her grip was gentle, yet surprisingly strong. She kissed my lips and pushed me back slowly, carefully, so I fell on the bed. She unknotted the cord of the kimono and parted the silk. Her hair was soft against my throat as she leaned over me, stroking my breasts and then kissing them, suckling me like a child. In a rush of air, I inhaled and stared at the stars on the ceiling. Her head slid down my belly, and she kissed me there, too. And then she pushed my thighs open, and I felt her mouth and tongue in the place where I didn't even dare to touch myself, where I had never let John come near. She opened me like a Russian doll, taking me apart until she found the center.

The stars were flung in patterns that were beginning to speak to me. There were the Twins, there was the Lion. And there was the Virgin. I was rising to meet those stars. The night sky is a woman's body, a goddess made of stars, arching over the earth. Stars fell on my body like gold rain. Waves of heat shot through me. Gasping and writhing, sobbing out loud, I stuck my fist in my mouth so Franny wouldn't hear. And then my body was still again. I felt her cheek resting on my damp thigh, her hand on my belly. My hand touched hers. When I tried to speak, all I could say was her name. She held me and brushed away my tears with her hands. She wept herself, kissing my neck, burying her face in my wet hair. Her words, spoken into my hair, reached my ear like a voice in a dream. "I love you, darling. If you only knew how much." She stroked my hair until I started crying again, then kissed me, holding me until I stopped.

She opened her bodice and chemise, took my hand and cupped it against her breast, a tight bud against my palm. I helped her out of the rest of her clothes and stroked her, kissed her. She was so fine-boned and slender. Old enough to be my mother, yet her breasts were more like a girl's than mine. She let her hair down, let her hair fall over me, around our faces like a veil. Our hair tangling together, damp and dry, dark and light. I began to shiver.

"It's cold," she whispered. "Get under the covers." She got up naked to shut off the light. Then she crawled in beside me, her arm around my waist. The bed was so narrow, we slept nestled like two spoons.

Everything had changed. Nothing could ever be the same again. I awoke to rain against the windows, Violet's hand tracing the curve of my hip, her lips tracing the nape of my neck. She pulled me around so we were lying face to face. The way she looked at me, her eyes full of longing like the eyes of a saint, like Sebastian, naked and bound, pierced by a thousand arrows. She kissed me. On the dresser the roses bloomed as if it were the middle of June, the buds unfolding in red velvet.

Violet got out of bed and dressed slowly, as if in trance. I saw the silver rainy light on the planes of her body. She handed me the red kimono. I rose from the bed, my back to her, and covered myself. She took my arm, drew me out of the room and into the hall. We passed Franny. "Good morning," Violet said, as calmly as ever, but Franny looked the other way as if she didn't see us. I thought I would never be able to look Franny in the eye again. Violet led me into her room, where we brushed each other's hair, the same as always, except everything was different, irrevocably different.

I looked out the window at the rain coming down, the wind ripping through the birch trees, tearing off boughs. "Such weather," said Violet. "Maybe it's better if we put off the university until tomorrow."

"It is better to wait," I agreed. My voice was the voice of a stranger. My reflection in the mirror was the face of a woman I did not know. A young woman in a red, red robe. The outline of her breasts beneath the silk, falling and rising with each breath. As soon as Violet had pinned my hair into place, I went to my room to dress. A black wool skirt and a plain white blouse buttoned all the way up. Black and white, like a schoolgirl or a nun. Fishing John's card out from under the radiator, I read it again, crumpled it in my fist, then smoothed it out and stuck it in my pocket.

We had breakfast in the study, the same as the day before and the day before that. The fire in the hearth spit out sparks, but I shivered, warming my hands on my coffee cup. Each look she gave me made me remember the feel of her mouth and hands on my body.

"You're so pale," said Violet. "Is everything all right?" Her eyes were so full of tenderness, I could neither meet them nor look away. Focusing on her throat and her lips, I smiled and nodded, saw the worry around her mouth easing, her lips curving as she smiled back. She looked so young that morning. Soft, like a woman who had made herself new again, a grown woman who had stumbled on a second youth. So beautiful, the flames in the hearth glancing off her hair. Downstairs the doorbell rang. Violet put down her coffee cup. "In this weather! Who could it be?"

We heard Franny open the door. Women's voices. Margaret's voice. Violet's face went papery. "Excuse me." She marched out of the study, down the stairs. Margaret's voice was knifelike as ever. She had her daughters with her. I heard Emily, shrill and happy. "I'm going to nursing school! We came in the rain to tell you."

Margaret interrupted. "I'm not letting her go off to Serbia, you know, but nursing is a respectable profession for a young lady. I see no harm in it."

The nieces all talked at once. Violet's voice broke through. "Emily, I'm so happy for you. Kathrin's starting college next term, too." Her voice was transparent with joy. "Kathrin!"

I put my hands on the armrests, pushed myself up from the chair. But I stopped halfway down the stairway, afraid to join the knot of women and girls at the bottom. Afraid to come anywhere near Margaret. Now I knew why she hated me. "That German girl's still here?" I heard her asking. "You said the translations were finished."

"Mother!" one of the girls hissed.

"Emily will be starting nursing school," Violet told me.

"Congratulations," I said. My face heated up when I looked at Emily. Passionate and willful, like Violet in her youth. I thought of

Lynnette, the dead girl in the photograph. Pneumonia borne of spurned love. Clutching the banister, I smiled as if nothing had changed.

"We're going out to celebrate," said Violet. "You're invited, too."

"There's no room for her in the cab," said Margaret.

"Come on, Kathrin," said Violet.

"You go on," I said.

Violet looked up the stairs at me, her smile faltering.

"It is a family occasion," I said, astonished at how evenly I could speak. "Have a nice time."

Violet's nieces pulled her out the door. I watched it close behind them. I went up to the landing and looked out the window, saw them piling into the cab. The nieces had to sit in each other's laps. Their mouths wide with laughter. Violet kept looking back, but I don't think she saw me. The outside light reflected off the window glass, making it opaque. I let the curtain fall back into place.

I went to my room, picked up the crystal vase of red roses in both hands, and nearly hurled it into the mirror but stopped just in time. I couldn't bring myself to break anything of hers. Instead I hammered the walls with the flat of my hands, crying aloud in hoarse gulps, hoping Franny wouldn't hear. *What a stupid, stupid child I was, unforgivably stupid and naive.* Something like this could never happen to Lotte or the other mill girls. It could only happen to me.

The things that pass in secret behind respectable doors and windows. How long had she cared for me in that way? When had it started? When she made me the velvet dress, when she gave me the shawl? With the first kiss on the night of my bad dreams? No, with the first look she had given me in the bookstore in May. She had cared for me even when I was a mill girl in a hideous gingham dress. I fell to the floor and covered my face. I was not innocent. *I* was the one who had started it, gawking shamelessly at a strange woman in a bookstore. Sneaking up on her in the garden, throwing myself in her arms after my nightmare. Coming to her bed. Giving her the book of fairy tales, showing her the picture of the woman with the wand. Every act an overture, an invitation. Wearing her robe with nothing underneath, scenting my body with her perfume. I hid my face in my hands so I wouldn't see the bed, but I smelled it. The smell of the rose oil and the smell of what we had done. John's roses had no odor, but the bed was a blooming garden.

I pulled my suitcase down from the top of the wardrobe, opened the wardrobe, and packed my clothes—only the clothes I had bought or made myself. I kept nothing she had given me. Not the velvet dress and not the shawl. Kept woman, Lotte had called me. *You look like a kept woman.*

I packed my comb and hairbrush, remembering how we had brushed each other's hair, the stories we had told each other on the porch at night, the way she had held me when I was frightened and lost, the comfort I had felt, rooted in place, in her arms. I could have gone on like that with her forever had we not done what we did last night. Now I was marked, branded, naked to Margaret's stings. I'd been cast out of the garden. I had tasted the apple. I could never again call what we had shared simple friendship. What we'd shared had been love.

Burning wheels plummeting into the millstream. Consummation.

I threw my suitcase down and ran to her study.

The smoke that rises when the flaming wheel descends into the water's embrace.

I looked at her portrait over the mantelpiece. She was so lovely. When she had been my age, she had nearly died for love. I thought of deliverance. Religious words. *Redemption, salvation.* I sat at her desk and ran my hands over her books. Under a paperweight of flame-red glass, I found a tooled leather notebook. Rose-colored leather. The same notebook she had been writing in when I had come to say good-night after my second dance with John, the night she had told me not to hang my hopes on him. I opened it. Pages and pages of her handwriting. From the typing I had done for her, I could read her handwriting as well as my own. There it was. My name. Over and over again. And here was the passage dated the morning after the night I had first slept in her bed.

> Kathrin is like the tree she calls Gold Rain. Shimmering and quaking. She is elemental, like fire and sunlight and a moonless night woven together. She has no idea how beautiful she is.

I closed the book and murmured a silent apology for having opened it in the first place. I put it back under the ball of fiery glass. I was the most desolate of moonless nights. I had plucked the fruit from the forbidden tree. I had let the serpent twine around my body, whisper into my ear. She had given me her fire, and it had scorched me through. My old self was burnt to cinders. Still the fire wouldn't go out. It licked me, consumed me. I was blazing. I could never be the same again.

I went to my room and picked up my suitcase, went down the back stairs to avoid meeting Franny on my way out. I left through the side door, the back garden gate, the alleyway, so I wouldn't meet Violet if she came back early. I knew that if I saw her, if she called my name and gave me one kind look, I would come undone. I would fall weeping and lost and furious at her feet. I would bury my head in her lap and let her stroke my hair and comfort me. I would never be able to leave her again.

Fire feeds on air. The faster I ran, the hotter and more blinding that flame grew, that fire that would follow me always, just like the tales.

Book Two

WOMAN: THE WELL

1 ∞ By the time I got off the streetcar in Minneapolis, it was dark. I welcomed the darkness. I pulled my coat collar up around my neck, tilting my hat low over my forehead, so no one could see my face. I shrank from the streetlights, shrank into the shadows. Somehow or other, I found my way into a narrow alley smelling of coal. It was so dark, I nearly had to put my suitcase down and feel my way along the brick walls. I was looking for Jelinek's, for their back door. Not their front door—I couldn't face Mr. Jelinek. I had to see John before I did anything else.

He did not sleep in the same upstairs apartment as his uncle, but in the room behind the bookstore. The light was on in his window, and I could hear the phonograph music he was playing, "The American Beauty Rag," which brought back memories of the dances we had gone to, that lost summer I would never be able to bring back, no matter how hard I tried. Going to the rain-splattered window, I tapped the glass with my fingernails, scratching like a mouse. Nothing happened. I rapped the glass with my knuckles. Holding my breath. He came to the window. I saw his face, his eyes squinting to pierce the darkness, his brow rumpling in surprise and confusion when he saw it was me. He pointed to the door. I hauled my suitcase to the stoop and waited. He opened the door, his tall frame silhouetted in the yellow lamplight. *He really has been sick,* I thought. He was so thin, his cheekbones stuck out like towel bars.

"Kathrin," he said. How alien his voice sounded after three weeks. I had hardly heard a male voice in all that time. "Kathrin, what happened?" His voice was so loud, I was afraid his uncle in the upstairs apartment would hear.

"Shh!" I put my finger to my lips, stepped over the threshold into his room, stopped a few inches in front of him. I wanted him to clasp me in his arms, wanted everything to be as it had been before.

"Kathrin?" He saw my suitcase. "Kathrin, what on earth—"

"Shh!"

"Don't tell me she fired you."

I was silent.

"Oh, Kathrin," he said sadly. "I was always afraid something like this would happen."

"You *what?*" I stared at him in dazed horror, shaking my head.

"She's not your friend," he said. "I told you that before."

"No." I turned away so he wouldn't see my tears. "She is not my *friend.*"

"I was always afraid you'd find out the hard way," he said, "that she wasn't as nice as you made her out to be. People like her are never friends to people like us."

I looked around his room, even bleaker than my old room at the boardinghouse. Cracking plaster on the walls, yellow from cigarette smoke and coal fumes. A broken-down wardrobe and dresser, an unlit potbellied stove. Green linoleum worn through in places, exposing the floorboards. The smell of damp and rotting wood. The peeling gray paint on the other door that led to the shop. The unmade bed in the corner. I fixed my eyes on the gramophone, the only object in the room that wasn't falling apart.

He came up behind me and put his arm around my shoulder. "Tell me what happened."

I turned around and looked straight into his eyes. "Do you love me, John?" The question the woman is never allowed to ask, only the man. He blinked. "You sent me roses." I had to struggle to keep from shouting. "You sent me *red* roses. What did you mean by that, John?" I went over to the phonograph and wound it up, put the needle on the record. Bright tinny dance music to swallow our voices so Mr. Jelinek wouldn't hear. My eyes were blurring. If he hadn't sent me those flowers, if Violet hadn't seen those flowers in my room, I wouldn't be here, having to explain myself. I would be back with her. Still innocent, ignorant, and perfectly happy.

"Kathrin." He stepped forward and embraced me. I began to cry, began to pound his chest until he took hold of my wrists.

"Three weeks," I said. "I thought you forgot about me. I thought you found another girl." *Please let him say it. The thing she said to me last night, her mouth in my hair.*

"Kathrin, I was sick as a dog. I couldn't eat for five days." He spoke so loudly, I covered his mouth. He kissed my palm. "Katie, how can you say those things?" That was the first time he called me *Katie*. "Of course, I love you. I thought of you the whole time."

He kissed me, and I kissed him back with all my bewilderment and all my pain. I grabbed hold of his collar and kissed him more passionately than I ever had, clinging to him as a drowning woman would cling to a raft. He took off my hat, still wet from the rain, and threw it on the bed. He pulled the pins out of my hair and ran his hands through it, kissing me so hard, I thought he would steal the breath from my lungs. The stubble on his chin rubbed me raw. I let him kiss me until my mouth was swollen and red, because he kept saying over and over, "Katie, I love you." The effect it had on me was like a magic spell.

I let him push me down on the bed. I don't know whether he was more alarmed or amazed that I didn't resist him; that I didn't say *No, stop;* that I let him draw me out of my clothes, let him still my shivering with his naked body on top of mine, his weight grinding me into the sagging mattress. I let him push my thighs apart. I let him enter me. I let him, because I thought this could undo what Violet and I had done. Erase it. It hurt so much, I had to bite his shoulder to keep from screaming, but I not only let him, I returned his embraces fiercely, shamelessly, as if my life depended on them. For an instant I thought of my mother, and it was all I could do to keep from sobbing aloud. But how vital he was, how he filled me, his heat, his life piercing me wide open, splitting me in two. I was falling down a long dark well, falling into a dark wet place where I wouldn't have to explain myself, to the bottom of the sea. No longer a creature of earth, I was a mermaid who lived on brine, who drank down the salt of her tears.

"Don't cry, Katie." He pressed his face between my breasts. I cradled him, running my hands through his hair, over the muscles of his back.

The vulnerable skin on the nape of his neck was as soft as a woman's skin, as soft as my own. My heart was thudding, thudding, loose inside my rib cage. This was what men and women *did*. I had lost my innocence but also my ignorance. I was a real woman, naked in the arms of the man who loved me. There was blood on my thighs, that christening of blood. *Pricking my finger on the spindle*. This made me real. No one could tell me I wasn't a real woman.

When I awoke the next morning, I couldn't remember where I was. The gritty sheets on my bare skin, the heat of the naked body next to mine. I thought I was dreaming. The room was filled with the gray half-light that comes just before sunrise, but the sun rises late at the end of September. Already there were footsteps overhead, footsteps that made the ceiling vibrate like the skin of a drum—Mr. Jelinek stumbling into the kitchen to light the stove and make breakfast. Then I remembered everything. Then I knew exactly where I was.

As quietly as I could, I got up, my bare feet hitting the freezing linoleum. My bladder was ready to burst, but there was nowhere to empty it. The bathroom was in the apartment upstairs. I stepped into yesterday's underwear. It still hurt down there, but I didn't have time to think about that. I bent to pick my clothes off the floor. My skirt and black wool stockings were clammy from yesterday's rain. Without waking John, I made myself as decent as I could with no washstand, no mirror. I got my brush out of my suitcase and did my hair by touch, the way I used to at the boardinghouse when the electricity wasn't working. I had to look respectable. Today I would go downtown to look for work. An office job. Didn't I know how to type? Putting the brush back into my suitcase, I closed it and shoved it as far under John's bed as it would go. I could hardly drag it around the city. I smoothed out my battered hat and laced my shoes. I was a neat, proper girl like any other, except I wasn't a girl anymore. I was a woman.

I leaned over the bed and kissed him awake. He jerked and groaned. I covered his mouth and kissed his eyelids, still gummy with sleep. "I must go."

"Kathrin." He said my name as if he still couldn't grasp what we had done. I found myself wondering who washed the sheets. What would his uncle think if he saw the blood stains?

"Where will you go?" he asked.

"Downtown. To find a typing job."

He squeezed my arm and kissed me. "You'll come by again tonight, won't you, Katie?"

I nodded.

On my way down the alley, I found an outhouse with an unlocked door. In my time at Violet's, I had nearly forgotten how much outhouses stank, but I made grateful use of it just the same. The seat was too filthy to sit on. I lifted my skirt, pulled down my underwear, and straddled the reeking hole. *Don't get too used to the soft life.* The soft life was over. The soft life would never be mine again. But my new life was just beginning—not as a kept woman, but as my own woman.

≈ I walked downtown, saving myself the nickel for the streetcar fare. In the shop windows I passed, I caught glimpses of my reflection— a young woman in a black skirt, a high-necked white blouse, a camel-colored overcoat. I looked like any other young woman going around the city to look for work. If John could find a job just by asking around, so could I. I was nearly nineteen. I spoke good English and dressed well for my station. No longer a pitiful mill girl. I could take care of myself.

The first place I went was the Minneapolis Grain Exchange. *They must be doing good business,* I thought, *with the war driving up the price of flour.* They could afford to hire some extra typists. Smiling blindingly like the posters of Mary Pickford I'd seen outside the motion picture houses, I walked up to the man at the main desk and said I'd come by to ask if they needed any office help. The gray-faced man wrote down a number on a yellow slip of paper. "Room 304. Talk to Mr. Anderson."

I ascended to the third floor in a glass-walled elevator. For the first time in years, I began to pray earnestly. *Please, oh please.* I wanted to return to John with good news.

"Good morning," I said to the man behind the walnut desk in Room 304. "I have come here to apply for a typing job." Trying to

sound brisk and efficient, as American as possible, not like some immigrant who had stepped off the boat two-and-a-half years ago, or
someone who had once slaved away sewing flour bags. I folded my
hands neatly in my lap as he looked me over. My nails were trim, no
dirt under them. I had nothing to hide.

"Do you have any experience working in an office, miss?"

"Yes," I said, lifting my chin. "For the past five months, I worked as
a private secretary for a lady on Summit Avenue."

"Private secretary." He shook his head. "You didn't work in an
office."

"No, but I typed every day, eight hours. Six days a week."

"What kind of things did you type? Private letters? Accounts?"

"She was writing a book on folklore." I couldn't really bear to talk
about her. Breaking into a sweat, I clasped my hands together to keep
them from shaking.

"Did this person write a reference for you when you left her
employment?"

"No. No, sir."

"Did you ever go to secretarial school?"

"No, sir."

"Do you know shorthand? Stenography?"

"No, but—"

"Do you have a diploma from an American high school?"

"No."

He took a piece of notepaper and a pencil, pushed them across the
desk to me. "Can you write down the name and address of your previous employer?"

"Sir?" The smile was frozen on my face, but now it was more like
a mask, a grimace.

"Anybody can come in claiming they worked as so-and-so's private secretary. We would need to hear from the lady herself."

"She has gone abroad," I said, but it didn't sound convincing, even
to me.

Mr. Anderson looked me up and down and laughed. "Young lady,
I don't know what it's like where you're from, but around here, you

need a reference to get a job. Why don't you write a letter to this woman and ask her for one? Once you have a reference, we can talk again." He showed me to the door.

It was the same story everywhere I went. Even the worst-paid typing pools demanded a reference or a certificate from a secretarial school. By noon I couldn't go on anymore. I hadn't eaten anything since breakfast yesterday morning. Twenty-four hours after leaving her, and I was just as hungry as before I had met her.

I went into the first café I could find and laid down twenty-five cents for a hot lunch and a cup of weak coffee. Stuffing myself like a farmhand, I didn't care who saw. A plate of roast beef and mashed potatoes, green peas from a can, everything drenched in runny brown gravy. I ate as if it were my last meal, sitting at the zinc counter, in front of me a red silk rosebud in a white vase. Surrounding me were office girls with pinched little faces, trying to look ladylike and delicate as they shoveled down their mashed potatoes and gravy. Squeaky voices, rabbity eyes, sallow skin. They didn't look a whole lot different from mill girls. They were just American and better dressed.

After lunch I went to the Lumber Exchange, to Minnesota Mining and Manufacturing. The interviews went the same as before. Finally one of the office managers gave me a little pink card. "If you're really hard up, sweetheart, you might want to try these people."

Eaton's Domestic Help Agency
Maids, Cooks, Charwomen
Serving the Best Households in Minneapolis and Saint Paul
Since 1883

I returned to John's room hungry and sore. He was waiting with a pot of tea and a cheese sandwich like the one he had given me last spring when I was a skinny mill girl. I took all the comfort he had to offer, yet I was afraid of appearing needy. John had enough troubles of his own. I didn't want to drag him down. I wanted to make my own way, make him proud of me.

"Did you find anything?"

I took a while to reply, chewing methodically and stalling for time. How could I tell him the truth without sounding desperate? Finally I just spat it out.

"Everyone wanted a reference, but I do not have one."

"She turned you out without a reference? What kind of a high and mighty bitch—"

"John, please!" When he spoke of her in that cutting voice, I felt a queasiness inside me, like strong coffee on an empty stomach, eating away at my insides. Whenever I closed my eyes and allowed my mind to wander, I saw her face arching over mine, her soft black hair falling over my brow. Her eyes full of love. She would have given me anything I asked for. She would have sent me to college.

"What are you going to do?"

"I have some money I saved this summer. I will put it in the bank. Then I will find some sort of work. Any work. There must be some job I can get without a reference."

"Cleaning toilets," he said sarcastically. "Or do you want to go back to the mill?"

"There is nothing wrong with working in a mill. Maybe I can get a typing job there. They know me at the mill. They know who I am."

John looked at me as if I were a half-wit. "You said before they nearly fired you."

"I was very young when that happened. It is different now."

"You're going back to her," he said, "and asking for a reference."

"I cannot."

"If you don't go back there, I will. I have a thing or two to say to that woman." His eyes were molten. He meant every word.

"No, John. If you do, I will never speak to you again."

"Kathrin!" He grabbed hold of my arms. A look passed over his face as if he were trying to decide whether to embrace me or shake me until my bones rattled. "What's wrong with you? You'd rather take some rotten job than go back and ask her for what she should have given you in the first place?"

"I will never go back there. I cannot face her anymore."

"And why not?"

I was silent, my lips clamped shut. He let go of my arms. "You're the most stubborn girl I ever met. You'd really go back to the mill?"

"If they offer me something good. Tomorrow I will talk to my cousin." I sat on the edge of his bed, picked up my cup from the floor, and drained my cup of lukewarm tea. Upstairs I heard Mr. Jelinek's footsteps as clearly as if he were in the same room. The walls in that building were so thin. "Do you think he knows I am here with you?" I whispered, but John didn't answer. He had disappeared through the door into the shop. At first I thought he had walked away from me to clear his head, but then I heard the faint noise of typing. "John?" I went through the open door, through the darkened maze of book-cases, until I found him at the counter. Under the light of a goose-necked brass lamp, he was pecking at the keys with two fingers. "John?" My voice rose, small and uncertain, but he ignored me until he was finished. Then he pulled the sheet out of the typewriter, dug a fountain pen out of the drawer, and scrawled something at the bottom. "Here, Kathrin." He handed it to me. "Here's your reference."

> John Jelinek, Proprietor
> Jelinek's Antiquarian Bookstore
> 518 12th Avenue
> South-East Minneapolis
>
> September 30, 1914
>
> Dear Sir,
>
> I have employed Miss Catherine Albrecht as a secretary at my establishment since January 5, 1912. Her duties included typing, filing, and light bookkeeping. She was a dedicated employee and never missed a day's work. It is only due to declining business that I must let her go. Miss Albrecht would be a welcome addition to any business or firm. I will gladly stand by her and vouch for her performance. I recommend her wholeheartedly.
>
> Sincerely yours,
> John Jelinek

He was a magician. He could conjure up something from nothing. He would always find a way, but as I read it, I shook my head. "None of this is true." I didn't want to be ungrateful, but I didn't like lies. "You are not the proprietor. What if they check?"

"My name's the same as my uncle's. If they contact us, I'll do the talking. Don't you worry about that."

"But I was not even in America in January, 1912. I only came over in March."

"Who's going to know, Kathrin? Do you think anyone out there gives a damn? You just have to get your foot in the door somewhere and get a job. That's the only thing that counts."

"But it is all lies."

"It'll have to do. Or would you rather spend your life sewing flour bags?" He took my arm and led me back into his room. "Think of your future," he said. "Think of *our* future." He took the reference from me and set it on his dresser. Then he took my face in his hands so I had to look into his eyes. "You'll go out and get yourself a job tomorrow. Something you can stick to. A year or two down the line, we'll get married. When we've saved enough."

I closed my eyes and kissed him, everything welling up in my throat. It wasn't exactly the proposal I had imagined, red roses and an engagement ring, but it was a promise just the same. My future was settled. All I had to do was step forward, find a job, work hard, and love him. We shut off the lamp and fell into his bed. This time he stroked me everywhere, trying to inflame me. I threw my arms around his neck and whispered his name. It didn't hurt as much as before. The place between my legs felt less like a wound. At the crucial moment, he pulled out of me. "So we won't have any accidents," he said, wiping the semen off my belly with his handkerchief.

Everything will be fine. Once I had a job, I'd find a respectable place to live. Then I could face Mr. Jelinek again and Violet, too. She and I would meet in some downtown café. I would pay for her coffee. I would look her in the eye and explain myself. No longer a frightened girl in thrall of a sorceress, but her equal.

That next morning, as John and I took the streetcar downtown, I thought of the story in the Bible about the birds and the lilies in the field. I wanted to create myself anew. After seeing John off to Paramount Office Supply, I bought a newspaper and studied the want ads. The most promising ad was for Barker Metals. They needed an office girl as soon as possible. They paid eight dollars a week.

Mr. Barker himself interviewed me. I later found out that he came from an old, established Minneapolis family. He lived with his wife and four sons on Lake of the Isles, in a mansion even grander than Violet Waverly's. He was rich enough as it was, but in the coming years, he would grow even richer, making his fortune as a war profiteer. Of course, I had no way of knowing that at the time.

To be honest, I don't remember much of the interview. My memory is blurred by everything that happened afterwards. I remember the opulence of his office. The dark paneled walls, the maroon carpets, the smell of stale cigars and expensive brandy in glass decanters, the mahogany desk that reminded me of Violet's, the green shaded lamps, the stiff little visitor's chair I sat on, my spine perfectly erect. I remember him putting on a pince-nez to peer over my false reference.

"Your former employer was very fond of you." I think that's what he said, viewing me through his pince-nez. The lenses magnified and distorted his pale watery eyes. "Personal testimony says more than anything else." The thing I remember most distinctly was the way he enunciated the words *personal testimony*. He was so impressed by John's forgery that he didn't even make me take a typing test. "Tomorrow's Friday," he said. "There's no sense starting a new job on Friday. Come in on Monday. Eight sharp."

I remember running down the sidewalks, my lungs bursting with happiness, straight to the YWCA. The sound of my heels across the tile floor in the lobby as I rushed to the front desk to book a bed in the dormitory. It was the cheapest, most respectable downtown lodgings I could think of. I remember making up my bunk bed with the regulation red-and-white gingham sheets and gray blankets. The cacophony of female voices in the slope-ceilinged dormitory. Big-boned Finnish girls down from the Iron Range who spoke American and swore like lumberjacks. Swedish girls up from their families' South Dakota farms. They clung to each other and whispered, viewing this alien city with fearful eyes. Croatian girls who had crossed the ocean to flee the war and work in the flour mills. I remember smiling at the circle of faces, trying to flash my goodwill.

I got a towel from the receptionist and took a bath, my first since leaving Violet's house. I scrubbed my whole body with institutional pink soap, scrubbing away the last traces of her perfumes and unguents, of what we had done together, of what I had done with John. Stepping out of the bath, I dried myself, rubbing the towel across my skin until it glowed pink and tender, pure as a baby's. *My own again. My body was my own.* In an hour, my hair would be dry. Then I'd meet John when he got off work and tell him my news.

2 ∾ "Katie, I knew you could do it!" he cried, hugging me so fiercely, right there on the sidewalk in front of Paramount Office Supply. Everyone was looking. The black men who swept the litter from the streets were pointing and laughing uproariously. I thought the whole world was happy for us. We couldn't stop kissing, not even when we boarded the streetcar to his room.

"This is just the beginning," he told me. There weren't any free seats, so we stood in the aisle with our arms around each other. "If we both save for two years, we'll do fine. We'll buy a house with a big yard." The power in his voice convinced me that he was truly a magician, conjuring up a future full of brand-new furniture and factory-woven rugs, a Ford parked in front of a freshly painted clapboard house, happy children playing on the lawn. I could see it as clearly as a colored illustration in a magazine. "On Sunday, you'll come over for a meal at our place. Then we'll tell Jan we're engaged. He's been kind of temperamental lately. Give me a few days to get him ready for it."

We got off one stop early, so Mr. Jelinek wouldn't see us from the bookstore window. I waited at the corner while John went off to get my suitcase. Then we got on the next streetcar going downtown. After delivering my suitcase to the Y, we went dancing for the first time in months. I loved the way he looked at me, his eyes burning with pride. I felt like a heroine of Shakespeare's, living on love! With his magic and his ambition, his hunger wedded to mine, we could do anything.

Unfortunately we couldn't dance for long. I had to get back to the Y in time for the 9:30 curfew. That night I dreamt of white clapboard houses and of having a little boy who looked just like him. I couldn't wait until we told Mr. Jelinek. I wanted his blessing so badly. When we married, he would live with us. A whole room in our house would be reserved for him and his books. He could spend the last years of his life in ease, enjoying the fruits of our success, playing with our children. He could put his old photographs on our mantelpiece. A home. And when we had enough money saved, I could send for my Uncle Peter to come and join us. I would take him away from the Höllental and the war.

～ On Saturday, John took me to Lake Calhoun. We walked around it slowly. It was raining, but that didn't matter. We huddled under his black umbrella. He went home early that night to prepare his uncle for Sunday, when I would come and we would announce our plans. I was so excited, I could hardly sit still. Not knowing what else to do with myself, I washed my hair, brushing it out by the gas fire in the dormitory until it was dry.

Moving the brush through my hair, my vision of clapboard houses faded. Brushing my hair brought back memories I could not endure of red silk and gentle hands. I tried to clear my mind by concentrating on the activity around me, the young women jabbering and bickering in different languages. Would I make any friends here? These girls were more or less my age, but compared to them, I felt grown up. They seemed so innocent, like children, even the Finnish girls with their sharp tongues and the Croatian girls with their downcast eyes. I felt older than any of them. I was already a woman with a past, with secrets burning up inside me. The girls knotted together in pairs, in clusters, but I was alone.

～ On Sunday morning I got up early and walked to the Basilica of Mary for high mass. None of the other girls at the YWCA had the presumption to set foot in the Basilica. The Basilica was for rich people, but I didn't care. My time at Violet's had habituated me to beauty, and my longing for it was greater than before, greater than during my time at the mill. I needed that thundering bombastic organ music, those flickering wax tapers, the sunlight pouring through stained glass. I needed to lose myself in the clouds of frankincense rising from the silver thurible the altar boy swung back and forth in his soft freckled hands.

The sermon went through me like air. I hadn't come here for the sermon. And I couldn't look for too long at the image of Jesus on the crucifix. The sight repelled me, the naked male body, the eyes full of accusation and misery. I gazed instead at the statue of the Virgin, cloaked in her mantle of golden stars, the silver crescent moon at her feet, at the woman clothed in the sun. Looking at her face, I saw Violet's. I shut my eyes, resting my forehead on my clasped hands. My eyes were filling with salt. Hot salt was spilling through my lashes, wetting my face. Brushing the tears away with my fingers, I tried not to break down in the middle of mass. I took deep breaths while chanting the Latin, the lovely, jewellike words, so musical, I didn't care what they meant. I just chanted and chanted until the Latin filled my brain, drowning out everything else. Stella maris semper clara misterium mirabile . . .

✻ When mass was over, I hurried to the streetcar that would take me to John's. I commanded myself not to think of her, but her presence was so strong, I could almost believe she was sitting behind me. I even turned around in my seat to look, but it was just an old lady in a blowzy straw hat. Staring out the window, I tried to think of John, of our love, our future, but with each intake of breath, I felt something sharp and bitter like a cold blade in my stomach, a Judas blade. She had shown me nothing but kindness, and I had run away from her without a word. I could have at least left a note. Maybe she thought I hated her, that I had betrayed her as callously as her old school friend. That look she had given me the morning I woke up in her arms. Eyes full of passion like a saint's. I could never go back to the Basilica. Whenever I looked at the Madonna, I would see her instead. If I went on like this, I would go mad. I would have to order my life so that I had no time for introspection. Introspection was perilous.

✻ John was waiting for me at the streetcar stop. I arranged my face in a smile as I ran up to him, but something was wrong. He was angry and tense, taking short nervous drags on his cigarette.

"What happened?"

"We had a visitor last night," he said. "Guess who?"

"Visitor?"

"The Waverly woman. She came to ask if we'd seen you. She was sitting with Jan at the kitchen table when I came home last night."

I folded my arms tight over my stomach, over the cold Judas blade inside me. "Is she there now?" I couldn't face her, not yet. Later, in a few weeks, in a month. I would write her a letter, meet her in a café. I really would, but not now. I was too raw. I would take one look at her and fall to my knees, a bawling idiot.

"No," he said. "And she won't be back, either. I gave her a good talking-to. I don't think she'll show her face around here again."

"You *what?*" I grasped his wrist so hard, he flinched. "You were not rude to her, John?"

"Did you expect me to roll out the red carpet for her after what she did to you?"

I began to gulp for air. Audibly. Like a fish. "She did not do anything bad. She was good to me. You had no right. What did you *say* to her?"

"What's the matter with you? If she was so *good,* why did you run away?"

"What did you say to her?" I was practically screaming.

He gave me a hard look. "You answer my question first. Why did you run away?"

I cupped my hand to my mouth. I hadn't had breakfast that morning, just a cup of coffee. Something bitter inside me. I thought I was going to be sick. "I told you I cannot talk about it."

"Why not? If you're going to marry me, you better start telling me the truth."

"I never told you any lies." I took a deep breath, trying to steady my stomach. "Please, John. Tell me what you said to her."

"I told her off for turning you out the door without a reference. She got out a piece of paper and wrote one for you, then and there. On our kitchen table."

Oh, dear God.

"She said she owed you ten dollars for your last week's wages, and she gave the money to Jan for safekeeping. Ten dollars, Kathrin! Why didn't you ask her for the money before you left?"

I was beyond answering him. I was a mermaid trapped at the bottom of a well. Mermaids can't speak. They have no voice.

"She said she went to your old boardinghouse and talked to your cousin, but your cousin told her she hadn't seen you in months. She left a note for you and some application forms to fill out. She said she wanted to send you to college." He spoke contemptuously, as if it were a farce on her part, a cruel joke. I walked a few paces away from him. He was saying something else, but I couldn't listen anymore. After everything that had happened, she had given me the college forms. She still meant to help me. My skull was on fire. My brain was full of rushing water. Heat and steam. It was deafening.

"Kathrin?" I felt his hand on my shoulder.

I looked at him but did not see him. All I saw was empty space.

"Jan's waiting for us," he said. I thought he would be annoyed with me, but this time he spoke gently, taking my arm and steering me across the street. "I never liked her," he said. "She's a handsome woman, all right, but too full of herself. Too many airs." He paused, studying my face. "Why are you so sad, Kathrin? We're going to tell Jan our good news."

I smiled for him, but I felt false. Rotten and hollow.

❧ Mr. Jelinek was waiting for us at the kitchen table. This was the first time I had seen him in over a month. "Hello, Kathrin." His voice was weary and resigned. From the look he gave me, I knew that he knew I had been sleeping in John's room. He kept glancing from me to John, as if trying to decide which one of us had disappointed him more. I don't think he was angry as much as hurt and betrayed that we had carried on that way behind his back.

"Sit down, Kathrin."

He pulled out a chair for me. The noise it made as it scraped across the linoleum. I sat down with as much dignity as I could, wondering what I would say to him, but he just handed me a big brown envelope with my name in Violet's handwriting. It was not sealed but tied shut with a string. I undid the string as an excuse not to look at Mr. Jelinek. Sticking my hand blindly into the envelope, I drew out a crisp ten-dollar bill. I reached in again and touched paper, pulling out the college entrance forms and the impromptu reference she had written for me, four times longer than John's. I couldn't read it with Mr. Jelinek looking at me. There was one last thing in the envelope. A plain piece of notepaper, her handwriting running across it in short, precise lines. Not an intimate message, nothing I had to hide from John and his uncle. She had probably written it last night. Here at this table, under their gaze.

October 2, 1914

Dear Kathrin,

   Could you please contact me, either in person or in writing? I am very concerned about you. If you need to reach me after November 1, I will not be at my St. Paul house anymore but at my cabin. The address is #10 Hill Road, Larkin, Minnesota. Please let me hear from you.

Very sincerely,
Violet Waverly

   When I looked up from the note, I saw a dull gray cloud. John was talking to his uncle. I heard his voice as if it were coming from another room, muffled by a closed door. "Kathrin and I are engaged."

   "After all this," said Mr. Jelinek, "I certainly hope so."

That next week I was so nervous, I couldn't sit down for more than five minutes. If I let myself sit still and think, I would come unhinged. I hid Violet's note and the college application forms in my old English grammar book at the bottom of my dormitory locker. I put the ten dollars in the bank. On Monday I started my new job at Barker Metals and spent the first week trying to ingratiate myself, smiling like a chorus girl as I typed letters and filed papers. I even answered the telephone for the first time in my life, attempting to hide my ignorance and awe behind a mask of diligence. How strange it was talking to invisible people through that black mouthpiece, like the old woman in my village who said she could speak to dead spirits through a hollow bull's horn. All those disembodied voices haunted me.

I wasn't the only office girl at Barker Metals. There were three others, sullen Americans who whispered among themselves, looking me over and trying to figure out why Mr. Barker had hired me, someone with an accent who had never touched a telephone or filing cabinet before. I heard them discussing the girl who had worked my job before me, the girl they kept saying "had to leave." Why did she have to leave? I could hardly ask them outright. I just smiled like a wind-up doll, doing my work as best I could, so no one would find fault in me.

At night I attempted to write to her. *Dear Violet.* I kept getting stuck and crumpling the paper in a ball. What could I say to her? *Do not worry about me. I am fine. I have a good job and a decent place to live. I am engaged. It is for the best.* The sort of letter you write to your least-favorite aunt.

Violet, you were so good to me, far better than I deserved, but I had to leave after what happened. You must know I had to leave you. When I wrote that, I pressed the pencil so hard, the paper tore. *What we did together. I never knew such things existed. You were like a mother to me.*

My soul was bursting from my secret, like a rucksack full of stones, so heavy, I thought I would collapse under its weight. I had to tell someone, but who? Certainly not John. I would die if he knew. I nearly went to confession, but that would have been an even worse betrayal of Violet. *"Father, forgive me. I have sinned."* Whispering about what we had done through the dark screen to some strange priest, airing it like dirty underwear? If I told anyone, it would have to be a woman. At Barker Metals I had Saturdays as well as Sundays free. My first job with a full weekend. On Friday after work, I went walking with John. "I cannot meet you tomorrow night," I told him. "Tomorrow I must visit my cousin."

"You haven't seen her in half a year," he said. "What makes you want to see her now, all of a sudden?"

"It is her birthday." That was the first time I lied to him.

⌐ Late Saturday afternoon I bought a fancy chocolate cake at the Swedish bakery on Nicollet. I had the lady behind the counter put it in a pink cardboard box and tie it up with yellow ribbons. Then I took the streetcar to the Pillsbury Mill, positioning myself outside the main door, so Lotte would see me when she came out. It was getting dark earlier now. The sun was setting grandly over the West Bank, the sky turning gold and purple, but I kept my eyes glued on the stream of mill workers coming out the door. Those skinny girls with their limp dresses and drooping spines. Six months ago I had been one of them. But then I saw a woman more stalwart than the rest, adjusting her black straw hat with the silk poppies and cornflowers. I ran to her and caught her wrist. "Lotte!" I gave her an anxious little kiss on the cheek, breathing in her smell of lilac perfume and cigarettes, trying to rekindle our lost kinship. I took the tin lunch pail from her hand and pressed the cake box into her arms. "Chocolate cake, Lotte! Your favorite."

The look she gave me was incredulous, uncomprehending. I realized I had spoken English. I laughed. My laughter sounded forced. "Dei' Lieblingskeuche, Lotte. Schokolade." The German came out in a rusty sputter, like water from a pump that hadn't been used in months.

"Kathrin, that's *you?*" In my overcoat and gray wool skirt, I thought I was dressed plainly, modestly, but by mill standards I was a lady. "You're all grown up now." But then she eyed me critically, easing back into her old belligerence. "Well, what brings you to the mills? I see you left your rich lady. Any port in a storm, eh?"

"I missed you, Lotte."

She rolled her eyes and stuck a cigarette between her lips.

"Let's go somewhere and talk," I said.

"Can't. Sepp's waiting for me." He was standing a few yards away. I nodded in his direction as civilly as I could, but he did not recognize me in my new clothes.

"Lotte, please." I linked arms with her. "Bitte," I said. "Bitte, bitte, bitte," using my orphaned younger-cousin voice, which turned her to butter.

"Oh, all right." I watched her go over to negotiate with Sepp, listened to them bickering like an old married couple. She was even picking up some of his Bavarian dialect. Meanwhile the mill workers, male and female, looked me up and down before scurrying off. The way I was dressed, they must have thought I was a social worker or some brand of missionary. Lotte came back with a glowing cigarette in her mouth. "Let's go to the boardinghouse," she said, talking around the cigarette. "Alma's out tonight. We'll have the room to ourselves."

≈ We sat on the edge of her bed, two feet apart, a respectable distance. We each had a chipped blue saucer with a piece of cake on it. I was picking at my first piece, but Lotte was on her third, grumbling loudly to hide her pleasure. "Where did you buy this? At a *Swedish* bakery? What do *Swedes* know about baking cakes?"

"You have frosting on your mouth, Lotte." Bit by bit, I felt our tenuous kinship coming back.

"So," she said, wiping the chocolate off her lips, "you still haven't told me why you decided to grace me with a visit."

"Mrs. Waverly," I said quietly. "The lady I used to work for. I heard she came here and asked you about me."

"She walked and talked like an empress! But when I told her I hadn't seen you in God knows when and didn't have a clue where you were, she looked like she was going to start bawling right in front of me. Then she turned around and left."

I closed my eyes. She had been here, in this little room. Only a few days ago.

"Kathrin? *You're* not going to start crying on me, are you?"

I opened my eyes, still blessedly dry. "No."

"Good, because you know I could never stand it when you put on the waterworks." Lotte set her fork down and looked at me expectantly. "Well, are you going to tell me what happened?"

I told her. About Violet. Gazing at the threadbare carpet with the grimy yellow roses, I told her everything. Only when I had reached the end of my story did I lift my eyes to look at her. I was expecting a furious lecture, but for the first time in her life, Lotte was speechless. She stared at me, pale and unbelieving, as if she did not know me. I was not the same girl she had shared her bed with for two years. The silence and that look she gave me were unbearable, so I plowed straight ahead, telling her about John. This at least was something within her range of experience. This brought the color back to her face. By the time I had finished, she was boiling. "How could you be so *stupid?* Do you have cabbage for brains? What if you get yourself in trouble? Did you ever once think of that?"

"We were careful," I said.

"Careful!" she sputtered. "If you're careful, you don't do it in the first place."

Despite her reputation and her paint, Lotte was a virgin. That was not to say she was inexperienced. As I later found out, she and her lovers had done everything a man and woman could do together without doing *that*. In many ways, Lotte was much smarter than I was.

"John and I are engaged," I said.

"Where's the ring? I won't believe a word of it until I see a ring!"

"It's official without a ring. We told his uncle last Sunday."

"Well, well," she said grudgingly. "When you actually get around to the wedding, send me an invitation, but in the meantime keep your legs together. If you get yourself in trouble, you'd better not expect me to come and rescue you. You'll be on your own then."

I can't say how comforting it was to hear her scolding me as she used to, as if nothing between us had changed. The story about John seemed to have canceled out the story about Violet, wiping it completely from her memory, like a blow on the head.

"When are you and Sepp getting married?" I asked her this as gently as I could.

"When we have enough saved up for a proper white wedding. In a *church*. Not some justice-of-the-peace hush-hush quickie job like *some* people have to have." She picked up her cake again, eating so fast, the fork was a blur. "This man of yours," she said when she had scraped the last of the frosting off the saucer. "Will I ever get to meet him?"

I imagined introducing Lotte to John. "He's so skinny, he looks like a dressed-up broom," she'd say. "Why don't you just marry a telephone pole?" But she would never tell him about Violet, never betray me. Family counted for something. My secret was safe.

"Do you love him?" she asked.

"Yes! Of course. What do you think?"

"Then you have to forget that woman. Forget you ever met her." So it wasn't wiped from her memory. "You can't have her hunting the city for you. I don't want her coming here again."

"She won't," I said. "She wouldn't."

"Kathrin, listen to me. You can't leave something like that dangling. You have to write her a letter. Tell her you're getting married."

I looked at her uncertainly. Her jaw was as firm as cast iron.

"You're an engaged woman, Kathrin. You have to put that behind you."

On Monday morning, when no one was looking over my shoulder, when Mr. Barker was locked in his office and the other office girls locked in their whispering, I took a sheet of paper and rolled it into the typewriter—plain paper, not the Barker Metals stationery, nothing with a name or address on it. I closed my eyes and began to type by touch. When you type, you can't go backwards. You can't erase or cross out. It doesn't matter if your hands are sweaty or shaking. You just press one key after the other until you come to the end of the line. Then the bell rings, and you go to the next line. You go on until the whole thing is in front of you. Black-and-white and irrevocable.

October 10, 1914

Dear Violet,

I am so sorry I made you worry about me, but I can never see you again after what happened. I am engaged to be married. I think it would be best if you forgot about me. Thank you for your kindness.

Sincerely,
Kathrin Albrecht

When I signed my name at the bottom, the ink smeared and my signature was a blur, but I just folded the letter and stuck it in a plain white envelope. I wrote out her address as neatly as I could. Then I sealed it.

During my lunch break I took the envelope to the post office, bought a stamp for it, and dropped it through the brass mailing slot. As soon as the letter fell from my hand, I wanted to stick my arm in the slot and retrieve it, take it back, tear it up. I had to force myself away. If I had been a man, I would have headed straight for a saloon to buy myself a stiff drink. That's what I needed, some rotgut to burn all the way down my gullet, to make everything fuzzy and numb, to obliterate memory, obliterate the past.

That day was like a funeral for me, like closing a door or a coffin lid forever. What I did could not be undone. It was like boarding a ship and crossing the ocean to another country where I would have to speak another language and be a different person. There was no going back. The only direction was forward, into the future, one step in front of the other. I had already lost sight of the horizon I had left behind. *Human beings are capable of learning anything.* People learn to dance on tightropes and sing opera in Chinese. I would learn to forget.

3 ❧ During October and November, 1914, I taught myself to forget with all the energy and determination I had formerly reserved for learning English. If there were some teacher handing out gold stars for forgetting, I would have gotten a slew of them. I would have gotten a parchment diploma with my name in red ink.

Every Saturday night John took me dancing. I can no longer remember the tunes or the things we said to each other, but I remember his excitement. His evening classes had started again. They filled him with fire, with visions of the things he would do, of the things we would have. We lived in the future, he and I. The present was only an interlude.

He usually got me back to the Y before the curfew, but once, twice, we were too late. Then he took me to his room. We were in love. We were engaged. When John pressed me down in his bed, it was like falling into a well of forgetting. There was nothing in the whole world but his body rocking on top of mine, no past. And the present was hardly present, except when we were together, when he held me in his arms.

I took a Barker Metals cloth-bound desk calendar home with me. I didn't think anyone would miss it. It was nearly the end of the year, anyway, and it still hadn't been used. I hid it under my pillow. At night before going to sleep, I drew a big red X through each finished day. My life that fall was a march of red X's, counting off the days until the weekend, until Thanksgiving and Christmas. I thought it would be that simple. I thought it was a matter of persevering. I was trying to spin a life for myself, a future, working and saving, counting the days.

My life at this stage was perfectly suited for making myself over from scratch. I no longer had the leisure for memory or reflection. I no longer had the solitude. I was never alone, anywhere, not at the office, not in the dormitory. Even when I sat on the toilet, there was someone else on the other side of the wooden partition, girls squeezing their pimples or brushing their teeth. In the evenings when John was at his night class, I went to the YWCA reading room. Since the public library was closed by the time I finished work, I made do with the Y's sparse collection, which consisted mainly of slender novelettes about the moral dangers awaiting farm girls who came to the big city. Despite the fact that those novelettes were published by some Bible society, they reminded me of Lotte's dime novels. There were always two heroines, a good girl who got married in the end and a bad girl who suffered some horrible punishment. The only serious book was *Jane Eyre,* which I immediately borrowed, trying to read a chapter every evening, though I sometimes grew tired of the heroine's eternal primness and her homilies. There was also a ponderous-looking tome called *The Book of Nature.* One evening I took it down and read a page.

> You young women may at times be unavoidably compelled to hear a vulgar word spoken, or an indelicate allusion made: in every instance maintain a rigid insensibility. It is not enough that you cast down your eyes or turn your head, you must act as if you did not hear it; appear as if you did not comprehend it. You ought to receive no more impression from remarks or allusions of this character than a block of wood. Unless you maintain this standing, and preserve this high-toned purity of manner, you will be greatly depreciated in the opinion of all men whose opinion is worth having.

"You have a good figure aptitude, Catherine," Mr. Barker said one morning when handing me an invoice to type. Every time he handed me something, he made an excuse to touch me, his arm coiling around my waist like a tentacle. He always wore his pince-nez when addressing me, his colorless eyes peering through the round lenses like the eyes of a fish. "Figure aptitude, my dear." He pinched my waist. "Do you know what that means?" Because I had an accent, he spoke very slowly to me, overenunciating each word, as if I wouldn't be able to understand him otherwise. He called the other girls by their surnames. Miss Simons, Miss Carroll, and Miss Dupree, but he insisted on calling me by my first name. Not my real name, but the Americanized version John had written on my reference.

Of course, he took liberties with the other girls, too, brushing their backsides as they bent to get something out of the bottom drawer of the filing cabinet, then apologizing, as if it were an accident. "Pardon me, Miss Dupree," he was always saying in a singsong voice. But with them it was different. They weren't as vulnerable as I was. They had been there longer. They knew the ropes and banded together. They might have chosen to pull me into their protection, but they didn't. They avoided me, as if I were marked, singled out, as if they knew I was bad luck—a black cat or a woman scarred by smallpox. At least at the mill, I'd had Lotte. Here I was on my own.

I didn't tell anyone, didn't mention a word of it to John, but I dressed as uninvitingly as possible, making myself deliberately dowdy, with high-necked blouses and skirts so long they were unfashionable. I bought a bottle of musty lavender toilet water, the kind old ladies wore to church, and pulled my hair back severely from my face to make myself look formidable. I told myself everything would be fine if I just acted modestly and ignored Mr. Barker. It was like a head cold. It was harmless and would go away in time.

I believed it was simply a matter of making a red x through each used-up square on the calendar until two years had passed, and John and I had enough money to marry. But at the beginning of November, when I was approaching my nineteenth birthday and the anniversary of my mother's death, I stopped making the xs. The parade of crossed-out days began to frighten me. My period was over three weeks late. There it was in front of me, in red ink on white paper. The calendar was now tainted—I threw it away.

 I kept telling myself not to jump to conclusions, not to panic until I *knew.* It could have been anything. Sometimes I was irregular. It could have been the shock of changing my life around, the commotion of starting over. That's enough to disrupt a woman's cycle. After my mother's funeral, I'd gone for nearly two months without my period. I wasn't about to go to some doctor and lay down good money for a humiliating examination and a lecture on morals. At home I would have known what to do. There were special plants—Poleiminze and Gartenraute. When brewed together in a strong tea and taken early and often enough, they would bring back a tardy period. But how could I find these herbs in an American city in November? I didn't even know the English names for them. *Tomorrow,* I kept telling myself, *I'll worry about it tomorrow.* As long as I had a flat stomach and wasn't getting sick, I would try not to think too much about it. I would just go on, day by day, praying for my blood to come back.

John took me dancing for my birthday. He bought me a single red rose. I clung to his neck and kissed him so hard, he laughed. "Katie! Are you trying to eat me up?" We danced and danced, and I tried to lose myself in the wells of his eyes. I kept kissing him as if I would never let him go. I couldn't tell him. Of course, I couldn't. How could I tell him if I didn't even know for sure myself? If worse came to worse, he would marry me. He had promised. But I didn't want to worry him until I knew. I didn't want to harp or nag. It could be a false alarm. I didn't look the least bit pregnant. I was losing weight again. My skirts were getting so loose around the waist, I had to buy a belt.

I was good at forgetting. I was a master at it, a genius. December, 1914, is a blur in my memory, a dirty mirror that does not reflect. It's a dead place inside me, a scar. Even now I cannot bring up many details, only bits and pieces, like the first time I got sick in the morning. The other girls in the lavatory heard me, and I saw the way they looked at me when I announced I had the stomach flu. "It's been going around," said Sirppa, one of the Finnish girls, but I could tell she wasn't fooled. She knew about the two times I had missed curfew and stayed out all night.

I got dressed and went to work. I tried to think of what I would tell John. "It looks like I am in trouble now. We were not careful enough." After all, we were engaged. He would have to marry me. But there was the hitch. He would do it because he *had* to, out of duty. I was so afraid he would hate me for it. It was much too soon. He could barely support himself and his uncle. They couldn't even find a buyer for the book shop. With so many debts to pay off, how could he support a wife and child? The next time I saw him was Friday. The longer I put it off, the harder it would be. I really had to tell him.

At the bottom of my suitcase, sewn into a tiny muslin bag in the lining, was my mother's wedding ring. It wasn't fancy. It was plain, as her life had been. A thin silver band with no ornamentation, no stone. But it was real silver. I put it on my finger where an engagement ring would go, supposing I had an engagement ring. It just fit me. My mother hadn't been able to wear it in her later years. Her hands had gotten too rough, her fingers too swollen. I couldn't remember her face, but I remembered her red hands with the thick blue veins and tendons, the hard callused palms. They were the hands of an old woman, though she was only thirty-six when she died. I wore her ring to work, hoping it would protect me, like a charm, a talisman, like the golden hazel tree that watched over Cinderella in the fairy tale, the golden tree where her dead mother's ghost lived.

On Tuesday afternoon I got sick at work. Fortunately Mr. Barker was in his office, and didn't see me running to the washroom. I made it just in time, locking the door and spewing into the toilet. Everything gushed out of me. It was like being turned inside out. But I didn't cry, didn't let myself. I would have to grow a thicker skin. I would have to grow up.

I pulled the chain, flushed the toilet, turned on the tap, and held my hands under the cold water until my fingers were numb. I splashed my face, then put my mouth under the faucet to rinse out the bitterness. I drenched the bowl in lavender toilet water to hide the sour smell of vomit. When I looked in the mirror, I did not see a woman but a child, lost and wretched. My face was white as the belly of a washed-up fish. I pinched my cheeks to get the blood flowing. I pinched so hard, I nearly bruised myself. I touched my mother's ring for luck. It was hard, cool, unyielding.

I unlocked the washroom door and went to my desk. One by one, the girls looked up at me. "Are you all right?" asked Miss Simons.

I nodded, smiling like a fool.

〰 Half an hour later, Mr. Barker leaned over my desk to inspect the letter I was typing. When I had finished, he seized my hand.

"Catherine, what a lovely ring you have. Is it new?"

I pulled my hand away, rolled the letter out of the typewriter and gave it to him. I tried to keep myself from shaking. The way he looked at me through his pince-nez, I thought I was going to be sick again.

"It is an engagement ring. I am engaged to be married, sir."

"Indeed. And who is the lucky man?"

"You would not know him, sir."

"That skinny boy who meets you out front on Friday nights?"

"Yes, sir."

"I do notice that on Fridays you dress with a bit more dash than on most days. The blouse with the lace collar you wore last Friday, for instance. That set off your figure quite well. Particularly the front of your figure. Did you buy that just for him?"

The phone rang. I lunged across the room for it. "Barker Metals," I said, trying to sound brisk and alert.

"Hello? Hello?" A woman's voice. "Who is that I'm talking to?"

My head was an empty place of spinning stars. Was that Violet's voice, coming to me over the telephone line like the voice of a spirit? Everything wavered. For a second I thought I would drop the receiver. I thought I would faint.

"Ma'am?" My voice was so taut, I thought it would break. "What number were you dialing, ma'am? This is Barker Metals, Miss Albrecht speaking." The room grew dim around me.

"This isn't Dayton's?" the woman asked. Not Violet, some stranger. "I was trying to call the Fur Department at Dayton's Department Store."

"You dialed the wrong number, ma'am. This is Barker Metals."

She hung up. When I put the receiver back on the hook, Mr. Barker was standing beside me. He grabbed my hand. *"Such a stunning ring,"* he said, continuing where he had left off, as if there had been no interruption. "Your young man must be absolutely smitten with you, my dear." He turned my hand over and started stroking the inside of my wrist, giving me his fish look. I bit my bottom lip as hard as I could.

Miss Carroll, Miss Simons, and Miss Dupree came back from the filing room. Mr. Barker flashed them a watery smile, dropped my hand, and retreated to his office. I went to my desk, took the first handwritten invoice in the basket, stuck a sheet in the typewriter, and started typing. I could feel them looking at me. I couldn't look at them. If I had looked at anyone right then, I would have burst into tears. They were murmuring behind their hands. Then Miss Carroll crossed the room and sat on the edge of my desk. "If I were you," she said in a low voice, "I'd get out of here."

"You work here. You have worked here a long time." I kept typing steadily, my voice quiet and calm. "What makes you think I should leave if you do not?" Did she think I was from a well-to-do family, that I could just quit a job because I didn't like it?

"You know exactly what I mean," she said. "If I were you, I'd take my next paycheck and disappear. Before it's too late."

"Too late for *what?*" I couldn't snap at Mr. Barker, so I snapped at her.

"Before you end up like the other girl."

"What other girl?"

"The girl he fired before he hired you."

Before she could say anything else, the phone rang. She went to answer it. "Good afternoon, Barker Metals." When she talked on the phone, she sounded sweet. She looked sweet, too. Milky skin and glossy black hair. Almost like Violet's nieces, except her eyes were green, not gray, and her face was round, the bridge of her nose covered in dark freckles. She wore an engagement ring. A real one. A slender gold band with the smallest of diamonds, which glittered like a piece of broken glass.

〜 I looked the herbs up in the dictionary. *Poleiminze* is pennyroyal. *Gartenraute* is rue. *Rue,* I discovered, also means *bitter regret.* None of this helped me. It was December. There was a foot of snow on the ground. Where was I going to get herbs?

That night I lay awake in my bunk bed and tried to plan my future. No matter what happened, I had to keep my job until I started to show and Mr. Barker fired me. I had to endure it. John and I needed every penny. If I laced my corsets tight and wore loose clothes, I might be able to hide my condition until the sixth or even the seventh month. After that, I would only be able to do piecework at home, making match boxes or ladies' fans or men's shirts, taking in laundry and ironing. There was also my nest egg: the ninety dollars I had saved at Violet's, plus the ten dollars she had sent on to cover my last week's wages. One hundred dollars in the bank. That would pay for the lying-in and tide me over until I could hand the baby over to a hired girl and go out to work again.

Today was Wednesday. On Friday I would tell John. I twisted my mother's ring round and round my finger.

〜 Thursday I got sick at work again. Thursday evening, as we were getting ready to leave, Mr. Barker called me into his office. "I'd like to have a word with you, Miss Albrecht." That was the first time he had called me Miss Albrecht. *He knows,* I thought. *He heard me getting sick.* I assumed he was calling me into his office to tell me I was fired. Hopefully he would at least be decent enough to give me my full paycheck for that week. If he didn't give me a reference, I still had the old one from Violet, and John could help me forge a new one. Maybe it wouldn't be too late to get another job before I started to show.

"Please sit down, Miss Albrecht." He showed me to the straight-backed chair where I had sat during our first interview. He went to close his office door, then came back, folding his arms and standing over the chair, looking down on me. "You're awfully pale this week."

"A touch of the flu," I said, knotting my hands in my lap. "It has been going around, sir."

"In your particular case, Miss Albrecht, I think it's the sort of flu that lasts for nine months."

I got up from my chair.

"Sit down," he said. "Did I give you permission to stand?"

"I have an appointment, sir. I must go."

"You'll go when I tell you to go." He wasn't shouting. His voice was very quiet. "The other girls are decent girls. They come from good families. You set a bad example. I'm surprised they even let you stay at the Young Women's Christian Association. Do you think you're fooling anyone with that dime-store ring of yours?"

He laid one heavy hand on my shoulder. With his other hand he started stroking my hair. His fingers were like fat greasy sausages. I felt his breath on my forehead. Hot and heavy. Cigar smoke and expensive brandy. He took off his pince-nez. His pupils shrank to tiny black points. "This can be easy, or this can be very, very hard on you." I think that's what he said. That's where my memory closes like a curtain. That's where everything shuts down. Just fragments remain. Pieces of something that was broken.

≈ I remember walking down Nicollet Avenue back to the Y. Walking as fast as I could without breaking into a run. I didn't want to draw attention to myself. I remember it was dark and terribly cold. Snow was falling. When I was a little girl, my mother told me that Frau Holle lived in the sky. When she shook out her feather bed, it snowed on earth. Feathers falling from her downy quilt. The snow settled on my hat, on my coat, buttoned all the way up, not just for the cold, but to hide my torn blouse, the bruises on my arms and shoulders. I had put up a fight, the best fight I could. *Falling.* The falling snow covered my tracks.

≈ Back at the Y, I locked myself in the room with the bathtub and scrubbed until my skin itched and chafed, until the bathwater was gray and cold. I washed everything except my hair. It was far too cold to wash my hair. Then I toweled myself dry without looking at my body and got dressed again as quickly as possible. Only when I was clean and dressed did I reach into my coat pocket and take out the wallet of tooled Spanish leather. A man's wallet. A *rich* man's wallet. Once I was a girl like any other. Now I was a thief. I counted the crisp ten- and twenty-dollar bills.

There were even a few fifties. It was more money than I had ever seen. That bastard had thought he could boot me out the door when he was finished with me, but he had reckoned wrong. I had snatched the wallet from his pocket. I had snatched it, hit him, and run away as fast as I could. Once I was soft, but now I was hard. Now I had a baby to think of.

☙ Once you start falling, how do you stop? You don't. You fall until you hit bottom, and then you break. After my bath, I went directly to John's, but his door was locked. He was still at his night class. I felt around the stoop for the loose board and the key hidden underneath and let myself in.

So cold inside that room. So dark.

First I lit the kerosene lamp. Then I picked yesterday's newspaper off the floor, stuck it in the potbellied stove with a few lumps of coal, struck a match, and started a fire. When the room was warm enough, I took off my hat and coat, took off my shoes and lay on his unmade bed, pulling the covers over my face. I closed my eyes and tried to sleep. I wanted to block everything out, make myself numb, so I wouldn't feel anything anymore. Turn myself into a stone, a statue, a block of wood.

☙ Once there was a girl who lost her mother. She was taken in by a stingy woman who made her do all the work while her own daughter sat idle. The orphan girl had to spin and spin until late in the night. She spun until her hands were bleeding. "You awful girl!" her stepmother shrieked. "You have dirtied your spindle. Now you must wash it." So the girl took the bloody spindle to the well, but as she bent to dip it in the water, it slipped from her hand.

"Useless girl! You threw that spindle in the well. Now you must get it out again." So the girl threw herself down the well. She fell and she fell until she hit the bottom and shattered. Like a vase dropped on a flagstone floor. A thousand pieces of her strewn all around.

But she wasn't dead. She had just come apart. She was in another country. In the land she had left behind, it was winter. Here it was summer. Flowers and herbs grew everywhere. The very herbs she was seeking. Poleiminze and Gartenraute. But she walked past those plants to a tree covered in shining flowers like gold rain. In the world she had come from, this tree only bloomed for one week a year, but in this place it bloomed eternally. On and on and on. At the end of that flower-starred meadow was the most beautiful house she had ever seen. A sorceress lived there. She was so afraid of that place, that its beauty would blind her and burn her, yet she stepped forward. The only way to get her spindle back was by going through that door. A woman waited for her at the threshold. Frau Holle, the sorceress. She said, "Come and live in my house for a year and a day."

For a year and a day, the girl dwelled in the sorceress' house. Every morning she shook out Frau Holle's feather bed until the feathers flew and it snowed in the world she had left behind. When the year was over, Frau Holle held out her magic wand. The girl stepped over the wand, and her lost spindle flew from the sky. She caught it in her hand. Then the sky opened and something poured down on her, warm and soft like feathers, except it was gold. A shower of gold rain. The girl took another step forward and found herself back in her step-mother's house. She was golden. She shone like the sun, so radiant that she made her stepsister look ugly as dirt.

The stepmother sent her lazy daughter down that well so that she could be golden, too, but this was the bad girl, the terrible one who did everything wrong. Everything she touched, she ruined. When she came to Frau Holle's house, she tracked mud on the beautiful carpets. When she shook out her feather bed, she knocked crystal ornaments off the dressers and broke them. As hard as she worked, she only destroyed things. Finally Frau Holle sent her packing. "Now, girl, you will get what you have coming." She made her step over her wand. The bloody, broken spindle fell out of the sky and landed in the muck at her feet. Then the sky rained down pitch, pitch that coated her from her hair ribbons to her shoes. No matter how hard she scrubbed, the stain would never come off of her. Not for as long as she lived.

≈ *"Kathrin!"*

When I felt his hand on my shoulder, I screamed and slapped at it until I was fully awake and saw it was John's.

"Kathrin, what happened? What are you doing here?" He was sitting on the edge of the bed. I sat up. Too quickly. The blood rushed out of my head. Everything was shadowy, blurred. I could hardly focus on his face. My stomach rising to my throat, I thought I would be sick. "I got fired today." My voice was so high and thin, it sounded as if I were laughing.

"The second time in three months, Kathrin?" He was beginning to lose patience with me. "Are you at least going to tell me what happened this time?"

"My boss fired me because I was getting sick at work. I am pregnant, John."

It wasn't the whole truth, but it wasn't a lie. Part of me longed to tell him the whole truth, but I couldn't. To speak of what had happened in Mr. Barker's office would bring it back to me. I would have to remember, and I didn't want to remember. To tell him, I would have to relive it, ripping the bandage off the open wound. Things like this you keep hidden. Exposing your shame makes you even more shameful.

The fire had gone out. I was so chilled, I couldn't imagine being warm again. I wanted him to take me in his arms and tell me he loved me, that he would marry me. *We would be happy together for the rest of our lives.* But he just looked at me as if I had addressed him in a foreign tongue. His eyes were deep wells. I could not see to the bottom.

"Why didn't you tell me before? If you were getting sick, you must have known for a while."

"I was going to tell you this weekend." I wondered what to say next.

"Well, I guess this changes our plans, doesn't it?" His voice was hollow. "We'll have to get married a little earlier now." He sat down heavily on the edge of the bed and took my hand. His hand was cold from the walk home from the streetcar. *His gloves are too thin,* I thought. From now on, I would see to it that he always had thick gloves to wear in winter. His icy fingers found my ring. "Where did you get that?"

"It was my mother's. Her wedding ring." I tried to make a joke of it. *If I could just make him laugh, I could break the numb spell that had fallen on him.* "See, John, you do not even have to go out and buy me a ring.

I already have one."

He smiled faintly, then rubbed his face. His eyes were red. Downcast. *He will have to quit night school. With my news, I have taken away his dreams for the future.* I should tell him about the money, that I had enough for him to pay his debts, enough for us to keep a roof over our heads and support his uncle and the baby, too. But how would I explain where I got that money?

"Don't worry about the money," I told him. "I have been saving. I can still do piecework at home. Everything will be fine." I was the one who had to comfort him.

"Piecework!" He looked stricken. "Piecework is what you do when you're really poor. Oh Jesus, what's going to happen to us?"

"Listen, John. We will not be poor. I have money. I was able to save a lot at Violet's."

"Fifty dollars? Seventy-five?" He looked at me and shook his head. "That's not going to make much of a difference."

"I have more money than you think! You know, she wanted to send me to college."

"Kathrin, please. This is no time for make-believe." He got up from the bed and walked to the other end of the room and back. "Jan was right. We should have waited."

So cold in that room.

"Are you blaming me?" I felt like taking him by the shoulders and screaming, like wrenching Barker's wallet out of my coat pocket and waving the money in his face. But how would I explain another man's wallet? When I thought of Barker, the nausea returned. I covered my mouth with my hand and willed myself not to be sick.

"No," he said. "I'm blaming myself. I wasn't careful enough." He sat on the edge of the bed again. I felt too sick to speak. "I guess this was predictable," he said after a few minutes had passed. "It happens all the time, but I never thought it would happen to me."

Upstairs something hit the floor and shattered, knocking brittle flakes of plaster off the ceiling. As I watched the loose plaster falling like snow, I imagined a teapot falling from Mr. Jelinek's trembling hands. "Do you think he heard us?" I whispered.

John's eyes went dark. "You know how thin these walls are." He glanced desolately around the room. "My God, we're going to have a baby in this place."

I looked at the cracks running down the walls, at the broken-down bureau with the varnish rubbed off the knobs, at the fallen plaster on the floor. Mr. Jelinek called John's name.

"Oh God," John muttered, his fingers digging into the rumpled bedclothes. "I can't talk to him now." But Mr. Jelinek called his nephew's name more insistently, and finally John lurched to his feet. On his way out the door, he faltered for a second, letting the freezing air drift into the room. Then he quietly closed the door behind himself. Something inside me sank as I listened to his resigned footsteps climbing the stairs. *How can we begin our life together like this?* I felt so sore and used. Bruises covered my shoulders and arms. My breasts ached. This was so awful. At that moment, I hated my body for the humiliation it had brought on me.

Shivering, I put my shoes back on. Upstairs Mr. Jelinek's voice was rising. He wasn't speaking English. The only thing I could understand was my name. John was speaking English, but for once his voice was so subdued that I could not make out more than a few words. My imaginary family. Once I had dreamt we could make each other so happy. *Even Barker's money can't save us,* I thought. How could we build a future on stolen money? If John ever found out where it came from, I would fall apart.

I reminded myself that I was the one to start all this, coming to John's bed that night. I had set this whole chain of falling dominoes in motion. Barker's words came back to me. "The other girls are decent girls." Things like this don't happen to decent girls. The priest at St. Francis droned in my head: "What do you call a woman who cannot keep herself pure?" Even Lotte's voice tore at me: "How could you be so *stupid?*" I felt polluted. That place between my legs felt like a wound that would never heal. The nausea crept up my gullet; my mouth tasted of bile. It was all I could do not to run out into the alley and vomit until there was nothing left. My body had betrayed me. My body was to blame for everything.

Gradually John's voice rose to match his uncle's. "Of course, I'm going to marry her! I *said* I would marry her! Don't you dare start telling me about *responsibility.*" As I listened to their voices, I decided I could not stomach another degradation. I would not have him marrying me to placate his uncle. I wanted to make my body mine again, and the only way to do that was by taking drastic measures. I *could* rid myself of this. The nausea would stop and also the shame. I could step out of my bruised and hurting skin, start over. It would almost be like getting my innocence back. I was in motion before I realized. The men were too caught up in their argument to hear me slipping out the door. I left a note on a piece of torn paper on John's bureau.

> John, you are right. This is no time for make-believe. I will go away and take care of things. Maybe one day we will get married, when we are ready, but not like this. One day we will have another chance.

~ *Albrecht.* How well the name suits me. Al-brecht. Brechen is to break. Alles bricht zusammen. Everything falls apart. Except in German we say zusammen. Everything falls together. Back at the Y, lying awake in my dormitory bed, I tried to decide how I would do it. I would not go to some back-alley abortionist. For one thing, they robbed you, and they were nearly always men. It would be like Barker all over again. No, I would do it myself. Rent a room in a cheap boardinghouse and do it there. Not in my old neighborhood. I didn't want to bring shame on Lotte. What method? The gin and the hot bath. That was probably the least damaging. Once I had that gin down, I wouldn't feel much. Gin and scalding water would open the gates of blood, that warm red sea. What if I drowned there? What if I botched the whole thing? Anything strong enough to kill the baby could also kill me. What else could I do? Go away with Barker's money and have the baby on my own, hand it over to an orphanage? The more I mulled these things over, the more confused I became. But I knew that in the morning, I would leave. I absolutely had to get away from here. As long as I stayed at the Y, Barker would know where to find me.

As I packed my suitcase, the girls gathered around me in a tight, excited knot. "Kathrin, are you leaving?" I hadn't been very good at making friends while I was here. A thing I now regretted. A friend or two would be nice.

"Where are you going?" one of the Swedish girls asked. I smiled at them, from one face to the next. They had no idea how lovely they were. Innocent, like snow that had never been stepped on. "There is a friend I am going to visit," I said. Sirppa, the Finnish girl who had seen me getting sick in the bathroom, gave me a hug. "I hope this *friend* takes very good care of you." She was so big and brawny, she nearly cracked my spine. Everyone wished me luck, even the Croatian girls who could barely speak English.

Hidden between the pages of my English grammar book was Violet's letter with her new address. What I had commanded myself to forget, I now longed to remember. I let memory wash over me like rain. Not my memory of the night I had tried on her robe, but of the days and weeks before that, back when I was still as innocent as those girls at the Y. I would try to find her again. It was too late to go back to her house on Summit. I would go to her other house, her cabin. What we did hardly seemed to matter anymore. I would go to her and beg her forgiveness. Because of the secret we shared, I would be able to tell her everything. If she didn't hate me for leaving the way I did, if she didn't hate me for that cowardly letter, she would comfort me. She would take me in her arms like a mother. I was falling, sinking. She would raise me up again. I needed her like I needed to breathe. I needed a woman, older and wiser. A woman I could tell my story to. If I could tell her my story, I would be saved. If she forgave me for what I had done, I could forgive myself.

4 ≈ I have no recollection of boarding the train and getting off in Larkin, Minnesota. I only remember loose, wet snow. It was a mild day, the temperature straddling the freezing point. I tied a shawl over my hat to keep my hair dry and put on my old shoes to slog through the ankle-deep slush. I followed the dirt road past the handful of blank-faced clapboard houses out of town, the road that led to her cabin.

Half a mile out of town, the houses trickled off, slowly becoming forest, dense and wild-looking. The wet snow dusting the pine trees was so beautiful, I wanted to cry. After two-and-a-half years in a city, to suddenly see forest again, and *hills.* Minneapolis was so flat and exposed. This looked like the land I had left behind. I could almost believe I was home. It felt as if I would turn a corner and find a wayside chapel with flickering candles in red jars, a house of old black timber with green shutters on the windows. Up and down the hills I walked, dragging my suitcase. The air was sharp and clean, but my breath was labored. I was so tired, part of me wanted to build a bed of pine branches, lie down and sleep until winter was over, hibernate like a bear. My suitcase felt heavy enough to tear my arms out of their sockets, and every muscle in my body hurt. I wondered if this would be enough to make me miscarry.

My mother had miscarried twice. I must have been eight the first time it happened. Memory dawned on me slowly, like opening a door into a half-familiar room. I had awakened in the middle of the night to voices in the kitchen, Mama crying. I crawled out of bed and crept barefoot across the cold floorboards to the kitchen doorway. Then I saw the iron wash pan full of bloody towels. I didn't see my mother, because my father stepped in front of me, blocking my view, shooing me back to bed.

I could no longer remember her face, but I could remember her body. Spreading hips, flat feet, thick waist. Always a baby at her breast or a baby growing inside her. I could remember my five lost sisters, too weak to survive an influenza epidemic or a hard winter, and the silent resignation with which my mother bore and buried them. I couldn't remember her face, but I remembered her legs. The few times I got to see them, they were swollen and covered with a net of dark knotted veins, like rivers. I remembered the way she walked in the last month of pregnancy, half swaying, half waddling, rough hands supporting the small of her back. The noises she made when she went into labor, more animal than human, as in the stories of people being possessed by the devil. My mother never raised her voice at any other time. She harped and scolded, to be sure, but in a quiet way. My father was the one who shouted. Uncle Peter had sent me to America so my life would be better than hers. What would he think of the mess I had made of everything?

Big wet snowflakes kept hitting my face. I was so thirsty, I opened my mouth to swallow them. I let my family fade in the distance like a diminishing landscape seen from the window of a train. I kept seeing Violet's face, that look she had thrown up the stairs at me when I had told her to go with her sister and nieces and leave me behind. I thought of the last look we had given each other. What would I say to her now, how could I explain myself? I would just knock on her door and wait for her to open it. Knock on her door and pray.

   ➤ Her cabin was at the end of that road, six miles from town. I reached it as the light was fading. The temperature had dropped in the last hour. The cold wind cut through me as a knife cuts through bread, and my shoes and socks were soaked from the slush that was now hardening to ice. The cabin was girt by a weathered fence. I let myself through the gate. It had no lock. On the porch, the windows were dark, the curtains pulled shut. No smoke came out of the chimney. I put my suitcase down and knocked. The snow kept falling, soft snow turning hard, each flake a stinging needle. Yanking off my glove, I pounded on that oak door until my knuckles were raw.

My knocking was the only noise in that forest.

When I finally stopped knocking, I heard nothing. Not a bird. I closed my eyes. Everything was black. Everything shifted and lurched, shattered and converged. Everything gone, like the enchanted houses in Russian legend. The doors only open if you say the right charm, if you are worthy. The houses are set on hen's feet. They revolve. The doors are never in the same place.

I remembered Violet's talk of South America. I could see her vividly as if she were just a few feet away, except she was thousands of miles away, walking through the streets of some distant city. Where she had gone, the sun was shining. I knew from my uncle's atlas that if you went far enough south, the seasons were reversed. Where she had gone, it was summer; trees were flowering. Gardens of red roses and white jasmine unfolded with splashing fountains in shady courtyards. The air was loud with birds. I could see it before me, as if looking inside a magic lantern.

Some people say your soul can leave your body, and not just when you die, but during life. Some people have special powers. They lie in bed perfectly still, their eyes closed, and you think they are sleeping. But they are flying. They can fly like witches in fairy tales. They can fly like wild geese. It's their souls that are flying. At that moment, part of me flew away, leaving that miserable girl behind, that creature bent double over the porch rail, weeping as if she had just lost her mother, that girl throwing up, polluting the fresh snow. I cut myself off from her. I was flying free. A dove bursting through a glass pane. Bursting through pain. The shattering, the shards and splinters. I flew through it all. Flew up through the dark snowy air to a warmer place. Full of light.

But the rest of me was heaving and rocking back and forth, my hands clasped to my belly to protect the child that was growing there. First I had thought of aborting. Now I was rocking that thing inside me like a baby already born. In the end, it was my womb that anchored my soul in place. It was that poor child who saved me and brought me to my senses.

It was too late. I couldn't go back to Violet, couldn't even go back to the station and catch the train to the city. The next train didn't leave until the next morning. I was too tired to haul my suitcase back to town in the darkness. If I tried, I would collapse somewhere on the roadside. I would hurt the baby. I had to find shelter for the night.

If you're cold and desperate enough, it's not that difficult to force a window open. Using my shoehorn to pry the casement, I crawled in, then unbolted the door to get my suitcase.

The cabin was like a doll's house, one tiny room opening onto another. But as in a haunted house, the furniture was covered in ghost-white sheets. I rummaged around until I found a lantern to light. The matches from John's room were still in my pocket. I kept the curtains closed, so no one would see the light. I didn't think many people came down this road, but I was afraid of attracting attention. I had no right to be there.

I didn't make a fire in the stove or the fireplace. Even if I hadn't been afraid of being found out, there was nothing to burn. I just wandered with the lantern from room to room and drew back the sheets. If I couldn't see her, it was at least a comfort to see her things. She hadn't left very long ago. It wasn't that dusty yet. Nothing was mildewed. I lifted the sheet that covered her desk and opened the drawers, one by one. I didn't think she would mind. Here were the Russian dolls. I pulled them apart. Looking at that row of glittering wooden faces took my mind off the cold. I could hear Violet's voice. *You think she's crude and simple, but she's not.* I put them back together again, doll inside doll, like a magic charm, a prayer. I was trying to put myself back together, too, all the broken parts of me. And there was her journal, the one she had kept during my time in her house, those pages of her handwriting, black ink on onionskin paper. The flame inside the lamp was too dim and unsteady for me to read much. It kept flickering, guttering in the icy draft. Everything began to lurch like a ship at sea.

Weaving my way through the doll-sized rooms, I found the bed, but no linens on it, just heavy wool blankets to keep off the dust. I pulled off my wet shoes and socks, my slush-fringed skirt. Then I crawled under the blankets, pulling them over my head, warming myself with my breath, rocking myself until I stopped shivering. I was on her broad oak bed, her marriage bed, on which we had slept side by side, on the hills and valleys of the old mattress, that forgotten landscape. I didn't sleep so much as step backwards into a lost world.

↝ She was wearing her white dress, opening the door for me. I had come to her house to find my lost spindle, except my spindle had been desecrated. It was bloodied and broken. I had a vase of wilted red roses that had no fragrance, only thorns. I pricked myself and filled the well with my blood. I was about to hurl the vase of roses in the mirror, but I couldn't destroy anything that belonged to her. She stepped into the room, took the vase from my hands, and set it on the windowsill. She took me in her arms and held me like a mother. She took me to her bed. Pushing me down. Gently. Kissing my hair and then my mouth. At first I tried to resist her. She was parting my clothes, but I only wanted to cover myself, I was so ashamed. Didn't she see I was ruined, a stained sheet, a broken vase? My clothes were torn, I was bruised. But she took my torn clothes away and put camphor on the bruises, which vanished with her touch. She kissed my nakedness. She kissed me everywhere, even the parts of my body I had grown to despise, with each kiss erasing what Barker had done to me, as if it had never been. She kissed me until my soul rose out of my body to touch the stars on the ceiling. She kissed me until we were crying into each other's hair.

She was an enchantress. She could work magic. I thought she had the power to give me back my maidenhood, turn me back into the girl I had been before I left her. I thought she would be able to undo the pregnancy, but instead she wrapped me in red silk. Red, not white. *Red is your color, Kathrin.* And gave me her red silk shawl to wrap the baby in. *Love is a thing there is no cure for.* She gave me an oak cradle carved with briar roses. She gave me the Russian dolls. She said, "Kathrin, feed her. She's hungry." As soon as she had spoken, I was holding my baby in my arms, opening my blouse to give her my breast. She rooted for the nipple. I felt her hunger, her tug on me, smelling of milk and innocence.

◈ I awoke in the middle of the night curled tight like a fern frond, curled like the child in my womb. Crying because it had been so real. She had *held me.* She had come back from wherever she was to comfort me. It wasn't just a dream. I twisted in her bed, the woolen blankets rubbing my skin through my clothes. *That was the night I surrendered.* The night I knew I loved her. That I would love her until the end of my life, even if I never saw her again. *I am the girl in the sorceress' house. She gives me the flame from the living tree, the flame that consumes me, shooting through every part of me, the flame that fills me like the light inside a lantern. I give off sparks. I am radiant. I am a burning wheel, burning for you, all the way down the mountain. I cradle the flame inside me, the fire hidden away like treasure in the deepest part of me.*

I stroked my belly. That was the night I first sensed the life inside me, the night I knew she would be a girl. The night I fell in love with my daughter, madly, against all reason. I thought I was as desolate as a barren field in November, but something inside me was blossoming, a red flower unfolding, a fire kindling. My little girl. There would be no gin, no lye. I would birth this child, with or without a husband.

December 7, 1914

Dear Violet,
    If you find this, please know that I came back to your cabin to try to find you. My dear, I am so sorry. I will never stop being sorry. When you come back, please write to me in care of Mr. Jelinek. I will love you always. I will never forget you. Please forgive me for everything.

Very sincerely,
Kathrin

I attached that note to her Russian dolls. I had no idea how long she would be gone, but when she came back, she would find my message. I wrote Mr. Jelinek's name, not John's. I had no idea what would happen between me and John. When I left to catch the train, I took her journal with me. I think if she had been there, she would have given it to me herself. This was the flame I took with me when I stepped back out into the cold.

I read her journal on the train. Not in order. Opening it at random, I read what was there. When one part grew too beautiful or painful, I turned to another.

> Spent the evening on the porch talking to Kathrin. It's funny. I keep thinking of her as someone out of a fairy tale. Such an inexplicable girl. If Arthur were alive, he would agree. What would he make of an orphaned mill girl from a place called Höllental? Valley of hell! Like a daughter of the underworld. Arthur would call her the embodiment of Persephone.

> She *has* to go to college. She has to make something of her intelligence. I can't passively sit by and watch her marry the wrong man.

> She is so beautiful, she has no idea. Once she pointed to the laburnum tree in the back yard and told me that in Germany they call it Gold Rain. She is as lovely as that tree. She's going with the young man from the bookstore. It's none of my business, yet I fear for her. I saw the way he looked at her when he came to fetch her at the party. What he saw was a lovely girl in a blue dress, but that's all he saw. He didn't look inside her. Each time I look at her, I see that golden tree.

> Margaret came by this afternoon just to rail at me. Her head was full of the most ridiculous nonsense. Simply because I have this girl living with me under my roof, she thinks I shall disgrace myself again, disgrace the whole family. Why is she always digging up buried skeletons? And because of Kathrin? It's too absurd. That quiet girl who spends the whole day typing and translating. Kathrin is the most unlikely girl in the world to ignite a scandal.

> While sorting through old papers today, Kathrin managed to unearth Lynnette's picture. I thought I'd lost it, lost her image along with everything else. The photograph brought back such sadness, I thought I would break down, but I couldn't in front of Kathrin. I was amazed how calmly I could speak of her. Time heals all, as they say. Maybe it *is* healing, slowly. Maybe now I can finally let the dead rest in peace.

The night after the party, I heard these awful cries ringing through the house, the eeriest thing I have ever heard. Kathrin was having a nightmare. She said she dreamt of her dead mother. She was in such a state, clinging to me and crying, I was afraid to leave her alone. Eventually I took her up to bed with me, but she still kept having her nightmares until I held her and comforted her. Then she fell asleep as peacefully as a child. She slept the rest of the night in my arms. I swear my intentions were innocent, and she is so innocent, but when she wrapped her arms around my neck and hid her face in my hair, all I could think of was Lynnette. I couldn't fall back asleep, because my heart was beating too fast. I thought that if I did fall asleep, I would dream of her. Then I would be the one to wake up in a state, and Kathrin would have to calm me down.

The next morning I brushed my hair and let her sleep. When she's asleep, she looks even younger. She could pass for sixteen. She was so lovely, I couldn't bear to look at her. I just brushed my hair, but then she woke up and, without much preamble, took the brush from my hand and did it for me. It was too uncanny. Our eyes met in the mirror. Her eyes were so soft. Guileless. Completely open to me. I am falling in love with this girl. I swear, it can't be helped. Does she have any idea of what she awakens inside me?

I can't help being reminded of Lynnette, of how she used to be. I take that back. She doesn't remind me of L but of my own lost youth.

No, she is her own. Her life is her own. I have no right to efface her with such comparisons.

What am I doing with this young woman? I have no right. She needs to be with people her age. She needs to have friends and a life of her own. Her life is just beginning. I am middle-aged. My youth is over.

I told her about Lynnette today. I told her about the scandal. I thought she would shy away, but she *threw her arms around me.* Did she truly understand what I was telling her? Is it possible? But the way she embraced me—I was overwhelmed.

I can't believe her goodness, her absolute loyalty and trust. She eclipses Lynnette. I have never been this deeply in love, ever. *This girl has redeemed me.* She has healed my wounds, buried that old skeleton forever.

If I were a man, I would buy her a diamond ring and beg her to marry me, but I'm not a man, so I'll send her to college.

Live with the old, and you become old. My years with Arthur made me wise, but they aged me. He saved my life, but I lost myself somehow in the bargain. Yet she is giving me back my youth. She is making me young again. It's a second freedom that's coming back to me.

I'm certainly no maiden. Those days are gone forever, lost. The gift of motherhood eluded me. Shall I spend the rest of my days a batty, pedantic widow, writing treatises on Arthur's work? A dead man's life and a dead man's dreams. Is it too late to live the life I have always longed for? Don't women, older and wiser, freed of the constraints of family, have a certain enviable freedom, for all their loneliness? The things I could do if I had the courage. Travel again, leave this dead house. The cabin up north. Taking out the old skis. The snowshoes through the woods. Going even farther north where you can still hear the wolves howling at night. Dare I dream of pleasure, a life of adventure at my age?

This is Kathrin's gift. I shall finish Arthur's last project, let Lynnette rest in peace. Now I can begin again.

The strangest thing happened yesterday. I went to Jelinek's Bookstore, and, for the first time ever, there was a young woman in the shop. One of those factory girls you see on the streetcar sometimes. Bone thin and shabbily dressed, but hauntingly beautiful. She was staring at me. Why would a strange young woman do such a thing? What was I to her? She had the most arresting eyes I have ever seen. Huge eyes. Greenish-hazel with flecks of gold in them. As soon as I looked her in the eye and returned her stare, she blushed and hid her face from me. I still can't get her off my mind. The incongruousness of it. A factory girl in a university bookstore, bashful as a deer but staring at me with her lips parted, as if she recognized me from somewhere but couldn't quite place me.

That girl Violet had been writing about was a different person, a part of me that was no more, a part of me that had been lost. I could almost remember what it was like to be that girl. The girl Violet had loved and told her deepest secrets to. No matter what happened to me, I had this. A relic of her love and the life we had shared, my time in her house. I think the love she gave me in those five months went deeper than the love most people experience in an entire lifetime. My father had never loved my mother as Violet loved me. I was as beloved as Juliet, as Helen of Troy. Her love made me a heroine.

❧ I had lost her. Now I would find her again. Seek her out and call her back. She couldn't have gone to South America just like that. It was nearly Christmas. No one would leave on such an arduous journey before the holidays. She would have to say good-bye to her family first. There was still time, but I had to hurry. As soon as I got off the train in Minneapolis, I would find a public telephone and ask the operator to look up her brothers. I was afraid of her sister, but her brothers had seemed less intimidating. What a task it would be for the operator, looking through all those Andrews! I would tell her to look up Robert Andrews, who lived in Morningside. I remember Violet telling me he had a telephone. He would tell me where I could find her. The train was still twenty miles out of Minneapolis, but very soon, I would hear her voice. Opening her journal, I skimmed the pages. The river of her handwriting ended abruptly the day I left her. Then she had stopped writing, put the journal away. This final entry I had saved for last. I knew that it would be the most wrenching to read, but now I had enough hope in me to bear it. What I was not prepared for was the change in her handwriting, the jagged slant the letters had taken, the way the ink clotted and spotted the page. It was as if another person had wrested the pen from her hand and written this passage for her.

> I didn't think I was harming her. She was so shy and sweet, she made me cry. Now she's gone. I never learn, do I? It was differ-ent with Lynnette. She was my age, my peer. But K? I can hardly bring myself to spell out her name. What did I want from such a young girl? Did I want from her what Arthur wanted from me—a malleable child to shape in my hands like clay, someone who would adore me uncritically? An immigrant mill girl! My God. She is not my peer. The stakes were com-

pletely uneven. Those things I told her about L, how could I have ever expected her to comprehend? Margaret was right when she called me a hypocrite and deceiver. Taking advantage of a naive girl no older than Emily, a girl who trusted me. The only thing I can do now is go looking for her and make whatever amends I can, but I can't

Here the ink trailed off and spattered.

She must despise me.

The book fell shut in my hands. *Naive girl, malleable child.* I wasn't even sure what the word *malleable* meant, but I knew it was nothing good. *Immigrant mill girl. Not my peer.* The words flew through my head like poisoned arrows. She couldn't have meant them. It was Margaret's doing, Margaret's nagging. I held her journal in my lap and stared out the window at the bare white landscape flying past. My face was wet. Why was everyone on the train staring at me? Couldn't they mind their own business? *Taking advantage of a naive girl.*

Her voice came back to me as if she were sitting beside me. *There's real love, and then there's infatuation. It pays to know the difference. It's no good being too starry-eyed and naive. Once you step over a certain line, everything changes.* Perhaps it wasn't John she'd been warning me about but herself. I couldn't condemn her, not even now. I had to find her again, even if it was only to scream at her and force her to explain herself. *How dare you let me live in your house, share your table and bed, and tell me I'm a child and not your peer?* How could this have been written by the same person who wrote those beautiful things—by the same woman who had said I was like a golden tree?

In the train station, I clutched the telephone mouthpiece and waited. "Mr. Robert Andrews in Morningside," said the operator. "I'm putting you through." I bit the inside of my cheek. A young man answered the telephone. A boy a few years younger than me. "May I please speak to Mrs. Violet Waverly?"

"Aunt Violet?" He sounded puzzled. "She doesn't live here."

"Do you know where she is?"

"She's gone away." His voice seemed to shrink. "Who is this?"

I squeezed my eyes shut. "Where has she gone? Do you have her address?"

"She doesn't have one. She's traveling."

"How long?" My voice rose in panic like a child's.

"I don't know. Who is this, anyway?"

In the background I heard an older man's voice. "Who are you talking to?" He took the receiver from his son. "Hello. To whom am I speaking?"

"I am calling for Violet Waverly." I tried to sound calm and reasonable, tried to hide my accent, but whenever I attempted to suppress it, it came out even more conspicuously. "Do you have an address where I can write to her, sir?"

"Who *is* this? Are you that German girl?"

"Yes, sir. Sir, I just wanted—"

"Don't bother this family again." He hung up.

Hanging up the dead receiver, I picked up my suitcase and started walking under the strings of colored lights, red and green. The Salvation Army Band was playing "Joy to the World," and the crowd pushed around me, their faces closed and indifferent. *You stupid, stupid girl. Do you believe it now? She was rich, you were poor, and she used you.* I walked out of the station and into the cold and darkness. The half moon shone cruelly clear in the sky. Sharp and bony like a skull. The head of Death, the head of Judgment. The venom in her brother's voice. *Don't bother this family again.* What he meant was, "You are something awful." They knew all along! How I hated them, those falsely smiling brothers and their wives. The only honest person in that family was Margaret.

Had I really made that journey to her cabin, spent a goodly portion of the money I should have been saving for my baby to try to find her again? Would she have made such an effort for me? If she had really wanted to find me, she would have. Even after that letter saying that I never wanted to see her again. If she had really loved me. But she had cut her search short. Given up after two attempts.

All that running away from her, my hiding and guilt. I should have faced her squarely. I should have thrown that vase in her mirror. What's one broken mirror to a woman who owns a mansion? The college forms she had left with Jan—had she intended them as some kind of pay off? Even if I hadn't run away, but stayed and let her send me to college, it would have ended badly. She had her family's reputation to think of. She would have grown ashamed of me. We had no chance of a life together. *Hypocrite and deceiver.* To think it had taken me this long to see behind her elegant sleight of hand.

Where would I go now? To Lotte's? Brace myself for her litany of I-told-you-so's? I was so afraid of the way she would judge me. Instead I went to John's. I owed it to him to at least have another talk with him now that he'd had a chance to calm down. His door was unlocked, but he wasn't there. I lit the lamp and stove. Just a little fire. I had to warm up. Where could John be on a Saturday night without me? It struck me how little I knew about him and the whole other part of his life that went on when I was absent. Any port in a storm, Lotte had said, but what if there were no port, no refuge, at all?

Upstairs I heard Mr. Jelinek. He must have heard me come in. I shrank at the sound of his voice. What must he think of me now? The door of the upstairs apartment opened, then I heard footsteps coming down the stairs. *No,* I thought. I could not face that old man. Surely I'd broken his heart with this mess I had made. The door flew open without a knock. If I could, I would have turned to vapor. But then I froze. It was John. "Where *were* you? I went to the Y yesterday, and they told me you'd gone away." His voice was raw. He came to me and put his hands on my shoulders, tried to make me look into his eyes, but I couldn't. "I'm sorry about the other night," he said. "I was shocked. I had a right to be shocked, didn't I? That didn't mean you had to go running off. Where did you sleep last night?"

"That is none of your business." I was astounded that I had at least a shred of self-possession left.

"None of my business? We were worried sick about you." He let go of my shoulders and touched my hair as tenderly as Violet used to.

"Don't," I whispered, pulling away.

"From that note you left, I was so afraid you went off to hurt your-self." He touched my hair again so gently, it made me cry. But I didn't want to cry; I wanted to be hard as stone, so no one could ever hurt me again. "Just tell me where you went."

I fingered a crack running down the wall. "You are right. We made a mistake."

"Oh, God, Katie, you didn't!" He took my face into his hands, so I couldn't look away. "Katie, just tell me. I promise I won't judge you. Please." So humble and beseeching. Why hadn't he been like this last time? What if I had never made that journey to her cabin? What would I tell him? What truth? What lie?

"I did . . . I did not do it. I thought I could . . . take care of things by myself, but I could not go through with it." My face was hot. Feverish. He kissed me and held me against him. I let him rock me in his arms. Such comfort after so much ugliness and loss. *He cares for me. He really does. Did she care, at all?*

"Just imagine if you'd gone through with it and were all alone somewhere bleeding—"

"*Please,* let's never speak of it again."

"If you promise never to run away from us like that again. Every-thing's going to work out. Jan and I have already been making plans. He's going to hand the business over to me. We'll get married as soon as we can fix a date. We have to be happy from now on, Katie." He brushed away my tears. "Let's go upstairs and tell Jan you're all right. Don't cry in front of him," he whispered. "His health hasn't been so good. He was so worried about you, he was having palpitations. He loves you, Katie." John took my hand and led me up the stairs.

Jan was waiting at the door. Before I could say a word, he embraced me like a father and wept. This undid me completely. I thought I would fall on my knees. For a long time I held him and rocked him as John had held and rocked me. "I'm so sorry I made you worry," I whispered. John put his arms around me and his uncle. For one moment, the three of us were wrapped in a single embrace.

"Kathrin must be hungry," said John. "Do we have a can of soup some-where?"

To accompany our dinner of soup and toasted bread, Jan took a bottle of yellow wine from the cupboard. "I've been saving this up for years," he said. "I was waiting for the right occasion. To your wedding!" Sitting together at the round table, we drank the wine from tumblers. The sweetest wine I ever tasted, it made me laugh and forget the pain. Even the shabbiness of their kitchen was comforting and dear. Unlike her house, everything was exactly as it appeared. No secrets, ghosts, or intrigues waited to leap out at me.

Except you, a voice inside me said, *you are concealing something.* Her journal was still in my suitcase, hidden behind the torn taffeta lining. What would John do if I told him where I had slept last night? *Don't think about that now. Forget all that.* The sweet wine made me forget. John was holding my hand. I had my future to think of, my baby's future. The three of us clinked our glasses and laughed, our laughter chasing away sadness and misfortune. These two men were my peers, my people, my family. This was where I belonged.

Jan went to bed early, leaving me and John alone. John rifled through one of the drawers in the sideboard and took out a velvet-covered box, which he placed in my hands. I gazed into his eyes and laughed. So wonderful being able to laugh again, I simply couldn't stop. He laughed, too. "Aren't you going to open it?"

I lifted the lid. Inside was an old-fashioned ring of gold filigree with a tiny sapphire. "It was my mother's," he said. The silver band was still on my right hand, European style, but John put his mother's ring on my left hand, the American way. Now I had two rings. One from my mother, whose face I could no longer remember, and the other from Nadja, the woman in the old photograph who looked like me.

5 ☙ We were married on February 1, 1915. I still have a copy of our wedding portrait tucked away inside my journal. When my daughter's old enough to understand these things, I'll show it to her. One day she'll want to know what her father looked like. John and I are sitting on velvet-covered chairs in the photographer's studio on Fourth Street. John is wearing his dark gray suit, and I am wearing a pearl-gray dress, but in the photograph, it looks white. I could pass for a virginal bride. I am holding a bouquet of silk roses. In the middle of winter, artificial flowers are the easiest to be had.

This is what I remember of our wedding. Putting John's father's gold wedding band on his finger, the kiss he gave me in front of the altar. Stepping out the church door into the gray winter light. Our handful of guests circling around, pelting us with rice. Jan, Lotte, three friends of John's I had never met before, and their girlfriends, who cooed over my sapphire ring. Lotte inspected me at arm's length. "You look very pretty, considering," she murmured. "It hardly shows."

☙ We had the reception in the store, which stood empty. Jan and John had moved the books to the back room. The job had gone more slowly than John had anticipated, because he kept interrupting his work to pull books off the shelves and stacks, and show them to his uncle. "Remember this atlas? This was the one you let me bring to school. Remember how you made me read *Oliver Twist,* and I didn't like it?" When all the books and shelves had been removed, John seemed to genuinely regret their passing. He walked around the empty storefront in a daze. "This place looks so strange now. I don't recognize it." There

were black stripes on the floor from where the bookcases had stood
unmoved since the shop was founded, in 1891—the year of John's
birth. I used a broom and dustpan, and then scouring pads, scalding
water, and ammonia to clean up the grime that had accumulated over
twenty-four years. In the weeks before the wedding, John sanded and
polished the floorboards. He and Jan painted the walls dark green.
Green in the dead white of winter. The color of wealth and success. We
were all a little giddy from the paint fumes and ammonia. The window
glass and wainscoting shone from the scrubbing I had done. We had
made everything brand new.

John was using Barker's money to start up a stationery store, something with a quick turnover that would make a decent profit. He tried
to impress on Jan and me that a stationery store was the next best
thing to a bookstore. "Aren't these beautiful, too?" He showed us marbled ledger books, bottles of ink, India rubber, and gold-nibbed fountain pens. "They're also useful. People need them. They're going to
come in and buy them. This way our business has a future as well as a
past, Jan, and our children will remember you as the one who founded
the store."

≈ We sat down to our wedding dinner in a mood of hard-earned cel-
ebration. Lotte had gotten up early and skipped morning mass to help
me with the cooking. There was roast goose stuffed with apples and
chestnuts, bowls of mashed potatoes and creamed spinach, and white
cake with lemon frosting. We had a jug of sweet wine, some bottles of
beer, and John's friends had brought enough whisky and brandy to last
the whole night. I sat beside John, ate my goose, and listened to him
talking to his friends. He was telling jokes that made everyone laugh.
I was proud of him. But I had trouble eating the food Lotte and I had
worked so hard to prepare. Slicing my goose breast into smaller and
smaller pieces, I could barely get it past my lips. This late into my pregnancy, I was still feeling nauseous. Maybe I'd just had a little too much
of the wine.

John's gramophone sat on the counter next to the cash register.
One of his friends put a record on and wound it up—"The American

Beauty Rag." His friends banged their forks on their glasses until John and I got up from the table and danced. It had been so long since our last dance, I had nearly forgotten the steps, but John remembered. He was still agile and lean, swinging me around in circles. The music was so fast, by the time I had reacquainted myself with the steps, the song was over. Then John let go of my hand to dance with the other women, and I danced with the other men.

I did not know what to make of his friends. He had met them at night school. They sported slicked-back hair, mouths full of chewing gum, and slang I couldn't understand. There was something hard and brassy about their girlfriends. Not brassy like Lotte. They didn't wear rouge. They dressed like ladies in challis wool, lace at the collars and cuffs, charm bracelets at their wrists. Yet I sensed something mean, even vicious, hidden beneath the surface, like a flashy pink peony. You pick it and put it in your best vase, only to discover that it's full of ants. They threw back their carefully coiffed heads and shrieked with laughter as John twirled them around.

Finally my turn came to dance with Jan. "I've had enough of this modern music," he said, putting another record on the gramophone. An old-fashioned waltz. His hand in mine, his arm around my waist. A waltz is a moving embrace. Banishing everything else from my mind, I closed my eyes and let my head rest on his shoulder, felt his pulse through his worsted wool suit, his breath ruffling my hair. He held me as if he wanted to shelter me and my baby from everything ugly. I squeezed his hand, lifted my head from his shoulder to smile at him. It became suddenly silent in that room. John's friends had stopped their chatter. The only sound was the violin music on the scratchy old record, and the slow movements of our feet across the wooden floor. Then John burst out laughing. "Look at the two of you. This should be your wedding."

Jan and I stopped dancing. We stared at him, too dumbfounded to speak. His friends laughed nervously. Lotte fumbled with her cigarette. "It was only a joke," he said, moving the muscles of his face into a smile. "Come on, Katie. Can't you take a joke?" I made myself laugh. Everyone laughed, relieved. Jan retreated to an empty chair in the corner. Then one

of John's friends put the ragtime music back on, wound up the gramophone, and the dancing started up again. Commanding myself to remember all those lost steps, I danced with John, danced with his friends,
strove to laugh louder than any of the other girls. This was my wedding
dance! I laughed until I was hoarse, danced until my feet were too sore
to stand on. Then I threw myself in the chair next to Lotte, took one
her of her cigarettes, and struck a silly pose. "Look who's tipsy," she said,
rolling her eyes. "Remember the old days when you were too high and
mighty to drink a glass of beer?"

I handed her back her cigarette and shrugged. Something crossed
my cousin's face. "Your wedding present!" She started digging through
her shiny red purse, pulling out a tiny perfume flacon covered in pink
cellophane.

"That's sweet." I gave her a peck on the cheek. Peeling off the cellophane, I admired the design of the tiny bottle and was about to pull
off the stopper and smell what was inside, when a wave of dizziness
washed over me. I clutched the arm of my cousin's chair.

"What's the matter?"

"I'm not feeling so well, but it will pass. Keep talking to me. What
do you think of John?"

"Very handsome."

I squeezed her wrist. "I'm happy." Then I sobered. "I'm just worried about Jan. He has heart trouble."

"He's old," she said. "Did you think his health would be perfect?"

"I hope everything works out for us."

"Why wouldn't it?" Lotte eyed me quizzically. She took the cigarette I had been holding and lit it, staining the smooth white paper
with her painted lips. "At least you put that other thing behind you."

That other thing. My eyes stung from the smoke. I rubbed them,
shutting out the light.

"You haven't heard anything more from her?"

"No." I stared into my closed fingers. "I don't think I ever will.
She's gone away." I spoke derisively.

"Be thankful," said my cousin. I lowered my hands to see her taking a vigorous drag on her cigarette. "That's the best thing that could

have happened. Kathrin, you don't look well. You should go upstairs and lie down. John will understand."

~ I steered myself across the room to where John was sitting with his friends and discussing his business plans. This was his fairy tale, the one he told again and again. "There's no way I can lose. I'm still keeping my job downtown, just to play it safe. The old man can make himself useful in the shop. Meanwhile I hooked my boss into giving me a raise. I told him, 'I'm a married man, for God's sake, with a brat on the way. I need another five dollars a week or I'm out the door.' And you know what? He gave it to me." He paused for a minute to take in his friends' muffled cheers, then he glanced up and noticed me.

"John," I whispered. "I will go upstairs for a while and lie down."

Evidently I didn't whisper softly enough. One of his friends pounded on the table and roared. "Nine o'clock, and she's ready for bed. She can't get enough of you, John!"

Another friend grabbed the brandy bottle and filled every glass on the table except John's. "Wouldn't want to ruin your wedding night." They all guffawed. John tried to snatch the bottle for himself, but they held it out of his reach, passing it down the table.

"Give it back, you bastards!" he yelled. Then he looked up at me again, his laughter subsiding. "I'll be up in a bit, Katie." Taking me by the nape of my neck, he pulled my face to his, giving me a tongue kiss that made everyone howl.

~ Carrying the tiny perfume flacon and my bouquet, I went out the back, through the room that had once been John's. In honor of our wedding, Jan had moved into it, giving us his room upstairs. I hadn't wanted him to give up his room for our sake, but he had insisted. "Married people need their privacy." Now it was full of books. Somehow John and Jan had managed to cram the entire unsold inventory of the old store into this little room. "They're your books," John had told him. "You don't have to worry about selling them anymore. This is your private collection." Tottering bookcases lined every wall. Stacks of books on the dresser and wardrobe and crates of them under the bed. I gently fingered a row of dusty leather spines before going out the back door and up the outside stairway to the kitchen.

Away from the cigarette smoke, I was already feeling a bit better. If I rested up here for half an hour, maybe I could go back down and join the party again. Pulling out a kitchen chair, I sat in front of the sideboard and looked at Jan's old photographs. I'd forgotten to say good-night to him. No matter. I would go down later. Better not to let him see me when I wasn't feeling well—it would only make him fret. He'd fretted enough when I had given the apartment a top-to-bottom clean, washing the walls and windows, scouring the floor on my hands and knees. "You should not *worry*," I whispered, picking up the photograph of Jan as a young man. Even then his face had been melancholy. In the picture, his eyes were far away and yet sharply focused, as if he were looking at something visible only to him. He was a man from the last century who had never reconciled himself to this century. He had squandered his youth on unrequited love. Here was a picture of Střibro, his hometown in West Bohemia. "Střibro means silver," he had told me. Long ago there were mines around that town, veins of silver under the steep hills. Once the town had been rich, but now the silver was gone. Now there was only lead, which was being made into bullets for the Austrian army.

I found Nadja's picture, taken when she was young and unmarried. He had crossed the ocean the day after she married his brother. How could the love of one woman justify a life of exile and regret? She certainly had been lovely, though. What you couldn't see in the picture was that she had been a gifted pianist. If she had been a man or had come from a well-to-do family, how different her life would have been. In a later picture, she posed with her one-year-old son in her lap. I searched her hands until I found the sapphire ring I was now wearing. Holding the photograph close to my face, I looked into her eyes. They were hollow, opaque. That luminous tenderness had desert-ed them. Some inner light had gone out inside her. I could not find a single picture of her husband, not even their wedding portrait. Jan must have gotten rid of them. He must have decided he would have no picture of that man in his house.

A hysterical squeal from downstairs made me cry out in shock, nearly dropping Nadja's picture. One of those stupid girls had made that noise. What were they doing to her, anyway—poking her in the ribs? I put the photograph down as the dizziness gripped me again, then slowly dissipated. Lotte was right. I should lie down.

I opened the door to the bedroom. The kitchen had been warm from the stove, but here it was freezing. I should have left the door open during the day, so the kitchen's heat could warm it, but I hadn't thought of that. Setting the perfume and bouquet on the walnut dresser, I sat on the edge of the bed and hugged myself, trying to get warm. I let down my hair, let it fall over my face. It stank of smoke. I went to get Lotte's perfume to rub into it. Perfuming my hair on my wedding night, like a heroine in a dime novel. I had to laugh at myself. What scent had Lotte chosen for me? Apple Blossom? Lilac? Magnolia? The bottle was no bigger than my thumb, and the writing on the label was so small, I had to hold it under the lamp and squint to make the letters out. *Wood's Violet Leaf Perfume.*

How could she? I stared at the tiny black letters the size of crushed gnats and tried to reason with myself. It was a coincidence, no hidden meaning intended. She probably hadn't even read the label. Her eyes were worse than mine. She'd meant to get me Pink Carnation and picked the wrong bottle by mistake. Unscrewing the cap, I held it under my nose, expecting it to smell sickeningly sweet. It wasn't. Sweet, perhaps, but not sickening. Not sickening at all. I inhaled deeply before screwing the cap back on. What was I doing? I stuck the little bottle at the bottom of my sewing basket, then undressed for bed. Huddled under the covers with the lamp still burning, I said my prayers and waited for John.

6 ☞ "How much flour will it be today, Mrs. Jelinek?" Mr. Larsen, the grocer, directed his voice and eyes to my burgeoning belly. It was the end of May. I was four months married and eight months pregnant. People spent more time looking at my belly than my face.

"Five pounds," I said, more briskly than necessary. "Make it Pillsbury," I added, out of loyalty to Lotte. "And two cubes of yeast and a box of raisins, please."

"Baking again?" asked Mr. Larsen as he pulled the items off the shelves and put them into my shopping basket. "Your husband's a lucky man. You must bake three times a week."

"Raisin bread," I told him. It was Jan's favorite. My mother had only baked dense rye, never white bread. White bread was for rich people, but I had Jan's teeth to think of. Each time I went to the grocer's, flour was a little more expensive. The war kept driving up the price, but I had to bake at least twice a week. It was my condition. I craved the smell of baking bread the way some pregnant women crave sardines and sour oranges. I kept that little apartment as clean as a hospital, but it was by baking that I could make it feel like a home.

"How's the shop going?" Mr. Larsen asked as he rang up my order. There was a note of envy he tried to hide. Times were hard with the war and the inflation, hard for everyone but the steel and munitions industries. *They* were doing a very good business. But somehow our stationery shop was flourishing.

"We cannot complain," I said modestly. "My husband left his office job. Now he works in the store full time."

"That explains all the pretty young females going in there." Mr. Larsen thought he was being amusing. "A good-looking fellow, your husband. I'd keep an eye on him if I were you." His eyes still hovered on my belly. I managed to divert them by pulling the money out of my purse. "Raisin bread," he mused as he counted out my change. "My wife used to make lovely cream puffs, but she doesn't bake at all anymore. Arthritis, you know."

I never knew what to say when people talked about illness, especially illnesses that couldn't be cured, but it would have been rude to say nothing. "Tell her to try some wintergreen liniment. I heard that helps." Mrs. Larsen's ailments made me think of Jan's. "Oh, if you have some valerian tincture, I will take a bottle of that, too, please. The big bottle."

"The old man's heart," said Mr. Larsen, climbing on a stool to get the amber bottle down from the top shelf. "That'll be fifty cents, ma'am." I cringed at the price. John told me I should haggle, but it seemed in poor taste to be fussing about the cost of Jan's medicine. I laid two quarters on the marble counter and put the valerian in my shopping basket.

"Things are sure sparking up across the water," said Mr. Larsen, sweeping the coins into his palm. "Did you hear the Germans are using nerve gas now?"

"We sell newspapers in our shop, Mr. Larsen. I know very well what is going on over there." I must have spoken too sharply. He ducked his eyes and pushed one of the two quarters back across the counter to me.

"Tell you what, Mrs. Jelinek, I'll give you a discount on the valerian. Just bring me some of your raisin bread next time. And tell the old man to look after his heart. For a man his age, he works too hard."

"Thank you, Mr. Larsen. I will tell him that." As I put the quarter back into my purse, I managed to smile.

"Bye now, Mrs. Jelinek." He pronounced it the American way, with a hard "J," making it sound like a kind of marmalade. John kept threatening to change it to something like Smith or Henderson. "Something American that every fool knows how to say." At least it wasn't

German. I had succeeded in getting rid of my maiden name. If I could only get rid of my accent.

On my way home from the grocer's, I had to pass the motion picture house. It was that or take a significant detour. But my groceries were heavy, so I ended up walking past it. I didn't want to look at the marquee and the posters in the glass cases. The first war films were coming out. Black-and-red posters, stock caricatures of spike-helmeted Huns with dead nuns at their feet, blood dripping off their bayonets.

In all this time, I hadn't heard a thing from my uncle, even though I had mailed him a copy of my wedding portrait along with the news that I had a baby on the way. I hadn't heard from him since the war began. Sometimes I wondered if my letters even reached his hands. The newspapers said that every man under forty had to report for service. But he was a pacifist. He would go to prison first. Maybe he was in prison. Maybe that's why I hadn't heard from him. But maybe he wasn't. What if he had marched off to war like everyone else? What if he wasn't writing me, because he was too ashamed? It was either military service or prison, unless you were lucky and had connections and could prove you were doing something important that supported the war effort, like driving supply trucks or working in a munitions factory. Maybe they would spare him because he was a schoolteacher. But each time I passed those motion picture posters, something cold ran through me. When people talked about the mustard gas, something died inside me. Why hadn't I heard from him in so long? For all I knew, he was already dead, and no one from the village had bothered to write me about it.

Every night John brought the unsold newspapers up to the kitchen. We read them after dinner: the reports of the Germans launching poison gas at the Allied lines at Ypres, the sinking of the Lusitania, the suffering in Belgium. The pictures in the newspapers gave me nightmares. Last week there had been a photograph of French children from a village near the front. They were lined up in a row, wearing gas masks. Yesterday a picture of flag-waving German schoolchildren singing "Deutschland über alles." *These are not my people. I do not belong to them.* I didn't speak German in public anymore, not even with my cousin.

John would have liked to erase the fact that he had been born in Vienna. The United States wouldn't join the war for another two years, but we already had a big American flag hanging in the shop window to prove where our loyalties were. I was convinced that as soon as Jan was dead, John really would change our name to Henderson or Smith. Our daughter would be a real American. No taint of foreignness about her.

Now I was standing across the street from our shop. The façade was newly painted. Gold letters on dark green wood. Paramount College Stationer's. John had made a deal with his old boss at Paramount Office Supply. He would use the Paramount name and sell their merchandise. In return, they would give him the best wholesale prices. John's night classes had served him well. He was a genius when it came to business. He had taken the money I had given him and planted it like a seed, and it had grown and grown. Even with the wartime inflation, I could afford to bake several times a week. Every other day we had meat on the table. But the shabby old bookstore I loved was gone. A display of gleaming typewriters and boxes of paper clips had replaced the old Bohemian glass goblets in the front window.

After waiting for the milk wagon to trundle past, I crossed the street. Through the reflections in the glass, I could see people moving inside the shop. Strange to be on the outside looking in, when it was our business. I wanted to work behind the counter, but John told me it would look bad. "What would our customers think if I made a pregnant woman work?" When we were first married, I had been determined to prove I could be a help to him, a partner and not just a burden. "At least let me help with the bookkeeping." The night after our grand opening, I'd hauled one of the typewriters from stock up to the kitchen table and started typing up balance sheets. "This is exactly the same work I did at Barker Metals. My boss said I was good with figures." John had to admit I had a knack for it. From that day onward, I had done the bookkeeping out of the customers' sight.

Standing in front of the window, I observed my husband leaning over the counter and chatting with some college girls the way Mr. Larsen had chatted with me, except, unlike Mr. Larsen, John was young and handsome. In the store, he was his most attractive self. He made a point of learning first names. The walls in our building were so thin, I often listened in as I ironed his shirts or washed out his underwear. "Good morning, Leona." I imagined him smiling into her widening eyes. "Tell me what I can do for you today." *Leona, Margery, Norine, Gwendolen, Blanche.* Their names reminded me of shampoo. Not so long ago, it was me he used to tease. Once he had sent red roses to a girl with mermaid hair who lived in a Summit Avenue mansion, like a fairy tale princess of his own creation. I was no longer that girl, would never be a girl again, but the city streets were full of young girls brandishing their startled eyes and innocence in his face. "Don't waste your time worrying about it," Lotte had told me. As far as she was concerned, it was harmless banter. No real infidelity was taking place. "You're the one with the wedding ring," she said. "That's the only thing that counts." If I confronted John, he would tell me he was working hard to get the business going to support me and Jan, and that meant being friendly to the customers.

Peering through the plate glass, I appraised those girls. It doesn't take much to outshine an eight-month-pregnant woman with swollen ankles and dishpan hands, but to me, they looked faceless, bland and insipid, like the little ballerinas you find inside music boxes. By now I knew what *malleable* meant, and they were as malleable as putty. Girls like that were so easy. All you had to do was flatter them, dazzle them, show them passing kindness, and they melted. Then you could twist them into any form you wanted. Turning away in disgust, I unlocked the side door and dragged my basket of groceries up the stairs.

⁓ Eight steps from the door at the top of the stairs to the kitchen table. Three steps from the table to the stove, five steps from the stove to the sideboard, another five steps from the sideboard to the back door leading to the alley. This was my kitchen, the room where I spent most of my waking hours. Lotte kept telling me how lucky I was. "I'd give anything for a kitchen of my own." While I unpacked my groceries, she was sewing flour bags. "You're a lady of leisure now, Kathrin. Some of us don't have it that good." She kept telling me how lucky I was until I wanted to stop my ears.

Whenever I was alone the kitchen, my thoughts began to wander in dangerous directions. Listening to John downstairs, his laughter as he conversed with those girls, I began to wonder how it would have been if I had never married him, if I had taken Barker's money and gone off on my own, had my baby without a father. Unspeakable thoughts, but it was my condition. In the last months of pregnancy, women are particularly prey to mad imaginings. This would get me nowhere. I should listen to my cousin's advice. *Quit moaning and be grateful for what you have.* Whipping the oilcloth off the kitchen table, I cleared the space to mix my dough. I took off my rings. First my mother's ring, then my wedding ring. You couldn't wear rings when you were mixing bread dough. They got in the way.

I sifted flour, cinnamon, and salt together, then added it bit by bit to the bowl of yeast, sugar, and warm water. The flour was soft as baby powder on my wrists. The raisins went in last, but I took a few from the box and held their sweetness between my teeth and tongue. I loved the feel of dough. Something firm to hold on to, to shape in my hands. My bread took elaborate shapes. Sometimes the loaves were round; sometimes they were braided. For Easter I had baked a braided wreath. But I had already wasted too much time dithering in front of the shop window, so after letting the dough rise, I quickly patted it into standard loaf pans and stuck them into the hot oven. The most gratifying moment came when the yeasty cinnamon smell of baking filled the whole kitchen and floated out the open windows. No one in the shop below or the street outside could escape the smell of my bread and the hunger it awakened. Even those ridiculous girls would smell it.

≈ I liked to have the bread ready to take out of the oven at a quarter to eight. That gave it fifteen minutes to cool. The shop closed at eight, and we ate dinner when John and Jan came upstairs. To go with the bread, I had soup made from the previous day's chicken with some potatoes, celery, onions, and carrots thrown in, all very filling and economical. John would have to congratulate me on my thrift. "I baked you raisin bread!" I called as Jan came in the door. He was always ten minutes earlier than John, who was locking up now and emptying the till.

Jan looked haggard that night, more so than usual, the skin around his mouth tight and pale. Though he never spoke of his sadness, I knew that losing the old bookstore had hurt him as much as losing a child. But he never complained. He had promised to hand the shop over to John the day he married me, and he had kept his word. His loyalty never wavered, but I could read his grief in the lines of his face. Having to spend the last years of his life taking orders from his nephew, packing away the books he had loved in order to sell cheap yellow pencils, chewing gum, Hershey bars, and reams of flimsy typing paper—it ate him away.

"Sit down." I drew out his chair for him, got the bottle of valerian, and poured a teaspoon into a glass of warm water. As he drank it down, he made a face. He didn't like it when John and I mentioned his bad heart. He hid his symptoms from us and swallowed the medicine I gave him just to humor me. If I offered any advice about his health, I had to do it in a roundabout fashion. Touching the back of his neck and trying to ease the stiff muscles, I bent to whisper in his ear. "You look a little tired. How about taking a day off tomorrow?" Even that was too direct. It made him stiffen up even more.

"Day off! What would I do all day if I didn't work?"

"You could read your books," I murmured, turning away to take the soup off the stove. Jan got up and followed me. "I didn't mean to snap. Don't bother about an old man's temper. You're so good to me, dear, and you spoil me with this baking. *You* should ease up for the baby." Jan also looked at my belly when he talked to me, but in a different way from other people. He made me feel cherished. "Have you been thinking of names?" he asked.

"My cousin says I should name her after John if it's a boy and after my mother if it's a girl, but my mother's name was Waltraud. That is no name for a little girl. I think I will call her Jana." I said it to tease him. We both knew John would want an American name. But the lines in Jan's face eased for a moment. Without saying a word, he took me in his arms, held my head against his chest, his hand stroking my hair, his heart thudding against my ear. When he held me like that, it was hard not to cry. I felt as if I were going to crack open and let everything spill out, all my confusion and regrets, but then the baby shifted inside me, jarring me. I touched my belly and took a deep breath.

"Did it kick?" asked Jan. I nodded, took his hand, and guided it to my stomach so he could feel her, too. Our eyes met, and we broke into smiles. At that moment John came in the door. "What's for dinner?" he asked, looking at me sharply.

"Soup." I carried the pot to the table and filled the bowls. "And fresh bread. Mr. Larsen knocked twenty-five cents off my bill today. I haggled."

"So you just baked an extra loaf with the money."

"It is for the Larsens. Mrs. Larsen has arthritis and can't bake any-more."

"Striking a bargain isn't the same as paying for groceries with bread, Kathrin. If you're going to be buying all that flour from him, you should ask for a discount. The way you're going now, that man will be a millionaire by the end of the year. He can close up his shop and retire."

"You *like* my bread."

"That doesn't mean you have to bake for the Larsens. You should buy in bulk. Fifty pounds at a time. And make him give you ten per-cent off."

"How am I going to carry fifty pounds of flour home from Lar-sen's?"

"You buy so much from that man, he should deliver it to our door."

We would have gone on like this for half an hour if Jan hadn't broken in. "It's still cheaper than buying bread from the bakery, and Kathrin's tastes much better. Before you joined us, dear, we never had a decent meal. We were eating out of cans every night."

That shut John up. Lowering his head, he ate his soup like a scolded child. I didn't know what disturbed him more: that Jan had bested him or that Jan had taken my side against him. I cut a thick slice of bread and passed it to him. "Here, John."

"It's a nice mild evening," said Jan. "The two of you should go for a walk together. I'll do the dishes."

"Jan," I admonished. "You don't have to do the dishes."

"I don't mind. Some fresh air would do the both of you some good. You'll be tied to the cradle soon enough, Kathrin. You should get out of the house while you still can. When's the last time the two of you went walking?"

"I spent the whole day working," said John. "So if you don't mind, I'd like some peace."

"I think we'd all like some peace," said Jan, his anger breaking to the surface.

John laughed at him. "Who's paying the rent around here?"

"We're *all* paying the rent," said Jan. His fist struck the edge of the table with more power than one would expect from a seventy-year-old man. The whole table trembled from it. He and John stared at each other, mute and deadlocked. Then, exhausted from this effort, Jan crumpled, sinking back in his chair.

"Jan?" John leaned forward. "Jan, what is it? Aren't you feeling well?"

"It's just indigestion. My stomach isn't what it used to be."

"You hardly ate anything." I reached out to touch Jan's face, but he pulled away.

"Kathrin, let him be." John got up and stood over his uncle's chair. "Why don't you have a rest on the sofa?"

"I want to go downstairs."

"Then we'll go downstairs," John said pacifically. I watched him helping Jan to his feet and guiding him out the door. Their voices echoed in the stairwell.

"This time will you please see a doctor?"

"I told you it was indigestion."

I cleared the table, filled the sink, and began to wash the dishes. The dregs of the soup stained the water, turning it murky brown, like a stagnant ditch at the end of summer, a place where mosquitoes bred.

"We're going to switch rooms again." John's voice rose through the floor. "You're too old to be going up and down those stairs all the time." Jan's reply was in Czech. I didn't understand a word, but it was an angry mouthful. John returned to the kitchen shaken and drained. We glanced at each other, then he collapsed in the armchair and lit a cigarette.

"How is he?" I whispered.

"The same story. He won't see a doctor."

"I think . . . I think for a man his age, maybe he works too hard."

John stabbed out his cigarette and glared at me. "Is that my fault? Is that what you're trying to say?"

"No."

"I don't *make* him work."

"John." I turned and looked at his downcast head, his hand clutching at the stubbed-out cigarette. "I did not mean—"

"Leave it alone." He looked up at me and swallowed. "Just leave it alone for once."

I nodded, retreating to the opposite end of the kitchen.

"If you can't help," he said, "you can at least stay out of the way."

I wrapped the extra loaf of bread in a clean dish towel. "I am going to the Larsens," I told him before walking out the door.

The Larsens also lived in the apartment upstairs from their shop, except they had lace curtains in the windows and flower boxes with yellow and purple pansies. Not that I could see them in the dark, but I had often stopped to admire them in the daylight. I walked down the back alley and up the stairs to their back door, my footsteps lost in the phonograph music drifting out the open window. Some romantic ballad that people their age liked, probably a song from the days of their courtship. They had married too late in life to have children. Maybe that's why Mr. Larsen stared at my belly. By the time I got to the top of the stairs, I was out of breath, so I stood there a second, listening to the music and their voices. They were laughing about something. A lilac bush grew at the bottom of the stairs near the garbage cans, the odor of its flowers mingling with the smell of onion peels and coffee grounds.

When I knocked, Mrs. Larsen answered the door. I smiled steadily at her face, so I wouldn't have to look at her knotted hands. Her cheeks were permanently red, not from rouge, but from a fine net of broken capillaries below the skin. "Good evening. I hope I am not disturbing you. I baked bread, and there was one loaf extra. I thought you might like it."

"Why, thank you, Mrs. Jelinek. That's awfully nice. Won't you come in?"

I shook my head. "No, I am afraid I have to get back right away. I have a cake in the oven." It was the only excuse I could think of.

"That lucky husband of yours," Mr. Larsen called out from the kitchen table. He waved at me.

Mrs. Larsen looked at me closely. "You know," she said in a voice too low for her husband to hear over the phonograph music, "if you want to chat some time, woman to woman, you could come by in the morning. Any time you like." Her gnarled fingers touched my arm. I felt their warmth through the thin cotton of my sleeve. She saw right through my nervous smile, my eagerness to be gone. She could see right inside me. "I know how hard it can be for a young wife. They say the first year is the hardest. Sometimes it helps just to talk."

It was like having a pail of dishwater thrown over my head. The realization that this woman with the crippled hands felt sorry for *me*. She and her husband looked at me and saw a forlorn young woman, eight months pregnant after four months of wedlock, a young woman whose husband had an eye for every other female in the city. They saw a pathetic creature whose only pleasure was baking. She touched my arm with such solicitude, like a mother. I couldn't bear her sympathy. "Thank you, ma'am, but I still have that cake in the oven. Good-night now. Hope you like the bread." Before she could say anything more, I rushed down the stairs.

It takes so much work to build a façade, smoothing fresh plaster over eroding brick and rotting wood, covering the whole thing in shiny paint. It demands so much labor, but it always crumbles in the end. The plaster cracks: first a little hairline crack, then bigger cracks, then a web of fault lines, until whole chunks fall off, revealing the leprous brick underneath.

I walked as fast as I could without breaking into a run. I could do this only because it was dark. In the light of day it would have looked far too foolish. Pregnant women did not bolt like frightened horses.

What did I think marriage was going to be? Some unending state of rapture and bliss? *Things will be different when the baby comes.* That was what everyone said. Who couldn't fall in love with a new baby? I had crocheted a yellow blanket for her. I imagined wrapping her in that blanket and placing her in John's arms, waiting for his eyes to soften and change. Everything would be good between us again. Yellow was the color of hope.

 I stood in the alley outside Jan's door and waited in the darkness for my breathing to return to normal. Your pain you hide away. You don't burden other people with it, certainly not seventy-year-old men with weak hearts. Smoothing my hair and face until I could pass as calm, I finally opened his door after a brief tap to signal my presence, but his room was empty. He had left the lights on. Sometimes he was forgetful that way. He'd probably gone upstairs to use the bathroom. John was right. We would have to move down here again and give him back the upstairs room.

Standing in the middle of his room, I regarded the bookcases rising around me like a sheltering grove. I'd wait here until he came down again. In the meantime, I could read. Pulling an old atlas off one of the shelves, I leafed through the colored pages of continents and polar ice caps, of tropical islands in the vast blue ocean. Then I found myself staring at a map of South America.

I was about to return the atlas to its place on the shelf, but I didn't. Lowering myself onto Jan's bed, I leaned against the headboard to take the weight off my back. I held the atlas in my lap. When I closed my eyes, I saw blinding colors and stars. My fingers traced the long curving spine of the Andes. If you stare at a map long enough, it becomes a door. What landscape had she chosen for herself? The mountains, the pampas of the south, the tropical jungles cradling the Amazon, or the deserts of Northern Chile? The mountains, I decided. In the mountains the air is clearest. You have the best view of the stars. Nothing stands in your way or blocks your vision. In the mountains, you can look so far into space, you can see the Milky Way.

A gate was opening into that lost garden. I needed this vision to

sustain me, even if it was a cruel hoax. The woman I would never forgive. I must be mad, but I needed her. Her journal was still hidden
behind the torn lining of my suitcase. I could not bring myself to
either destroy it or throw it away. Her words had become a part of me.
Her words and her name branded invisibly on my flesh. The kiss of a
ghost. She was a sorceress. Marked and branded, I belonged to her.

John's flirtations with those silly girls were nothing compared to this.
Here I was, burning up over a woman I would never see again. Here I
was, a pregnant woman in thrall of a phantom, a grown woman weeping over an atlas. It was so absurd—*depraved*—the way I was falling apart
on account of some spoiled rich woman. She was at the other end of
the world, having adventures and a free life. Did she ever once think of
me, left behind, bruised? She was not worth this much pain. I made a
move to pull myself together, but it was too late. Jan was standing in the
doorway. "What is it, dear?" He sat beside me on the bed and put his
arms around me. The lines in his face were so deep, they looked as if
they had been etched in charcoal. I searched for words, but there were
none. I could not speak. This was the spell she had cast on me. Jan
stroked my hair. "I heard him shouting at you after dinner."

"Oh, Jan." My voice finally returned to me, hoarse as a crow's. I
shook my head. "That was nothing. He was worried about you." I
forced my mouth into a smile.

"Neither of you are happy."

The false smile died on my lips.

"It's been downhill," he said, "ever since the wedding. I'm going to
have a talk with him. It can't go on like this."

"Don't! That would only make things worse." I took his hand and
squeezed it. "Today was just a bad day."

"We can't even sit down to a civilized meal anymore." He stopped
short. I bowed my head and listened to the footsteps coming down the
stairs. John came in the door and stood a few inches inside the threshold. "What's going on?" His face froze and then contracted when he saw
me sitting with Jan on his bed, our arms around each other. Jan faced
his nephew squarely. "I found your wife crying down here all alone."

"Jan," I pleaded. "It is all right."

John pressed his lips together. "What were you crying about, Kathrin?" His nerves were already stretched so thin, he could simply not cope with another crisis or demand. He looked as if he wanted to throttle me. Under his gaze, my throat went dry. I clasped my hands and blinked. "Nothing."

"Nothing," he echoed flatly. "You came down here to cry about nothing. Why don't we go upstairs and let Jan get some sleep?"

"We have to talk," said Jan with weary authority. "Things in this house have to change."

"You're right about that," John said, throwing a tight-lipped smile at me. "Some things around here do need to *change*. Right, Kathrin? Come on," he told me. "It's late." To his uncle, he said, "In the morning, we'll talk all you like."

❧ "What did you think you were doing?" John demanded in a strangled whisper. "Carrying on like that in front of Jan. Don't you know how much you upset him?" We were upstairs in our bedroom with the door closed. "You really want to wreck this, don't you? The same way you messed up everything else. I can't believe the talent you have for wrecking things. You're so good at feeling sorry for yourself, but you never think about anyone else, do you?"

"John, please!" I wanted to shout, but like him, I only whispered.

"You're trying to ruin everything between me and my uncle. He's the only family I have, and you—"

"I would never hurt Jan."

"What do you think you did tonight? Before you came along, we did all right. We didn't always agree with each other, but mostly we got along. It was never this bad until you came."

"Now everything is *my* fault?" Cracking open, I covered my face. John could crack me like an egg. No matter how bitter and distorted his words came out, there was an element of truth to them I could not look away from.

"If you would just learn," he said, "not to do any more *damage.*"

"And you?" I asked. "What about the way you talk to him? What about the way you carry on with your . . . college girls?"

"Jesus, Kathrin." He was about to say something else when we heard a noise downstairs. A book falling off a shelf. A hollow thud as it hit the floor. A half-swallowed cry. "Oh, God," I whispered.

John blanched. "You stay here," he told me, before going down the stairs to his uncle.

7 ❧ Despite Jan's protests, John called the doctor in the morning. With the doctor's backing, he told Jan he didn't want him working anymore. Four days later, Jan collapsed in his room. John was in the shop. He didn't hear him fall. I was at Larsen's buying flour and eggs. We didn't know anything was amiss until John went to call him for dinner and found him dead on the floor. When I heard him cry out, I went running down the stairs, forgetting to take the bread out of the oven. It burned, filling the apartment with smoke that made us cough and gag. I opened the doors and windows. John locked himself in the bathroom. On the other side of that bolted door, I listened to him throwing up. He sounded as if he were choking to death. I cried his name and rattled the door knob, but he wouldn't let me in. I listened to him pounding his fists against the walls. When he finally came out, his knuckles were bleeding. He stood a few feet away from me. I was crying, numb and noiseless. He rubbed his bleeding hands and looked past me, looked through me as if I weren't even there.

He went to get the undertaker. He hung a cardboard sign in the shop window. *Closed due to family death.* He put an ad in the paper. *Rare collection of antiquarian books for sale. Inquire at Paramount College Stationer's.* Then he packed the books away in boxes. Neither of us could bear to look at them now. At the funeral, we stood three feet apart, like strangers. As I watched the men lower Jan's coffin into the earth, part of me was buried with him.

There were no more fights. We were worn out from fighting, swollen with grief. We hardly spoke, but his unspoken blame of me hung in the air like a poisonous cloud. This silence was more damning than

Mary Sharratt   212

the most brutal words. Silence smothered everything. May bled into June, humid and stifling. It became too hot for us to sleep in the same bed. When I grew so huge that I covered the entire mattress, John went downstairs to sleep in his old room.

Was it the thing inside me that made him turn away and reject me? I was the poisoned apple he had bitten into. I had poisoned everything. If I had been a decent woman, if I hadn't been crying for her on Jan's bed, if I had kept up my façade, could things have turned out differently? All Jan had wanted was for me and John to be happy together. He was the one to pay for our mistake. My mistake. If only I had never come to John's room that night in September. If only we had never conceived a child. The doctor's words kept echoing in my head. *Too late. It's too late to do anything about it now.* I was too broken to show my face to anyone. Those three weeks, I hardly left the apartment.

It was too late to salvage anything. No innocence was left inside me, no hope, either. I could not see beyond this baby's birth. I had lost everything. Violet, John, and Jan. Lost my beautiful illusions of the woman with the wand, my dream of a happy marriage and family. I was too battered to go on believing in fairy tales, and as for fairy tale characters, they did not exist. There was no sorceress, no prince, no wise old man to save me. There was no redemption. Only human failure and suffering.

The sun was setting slowly, staining the sky outside my bedroom window with blood. This room was as hot and airless as I'd always imagined hell would be. Everything shimmered and converged. I was being turned inside out. Even when I closed my eyes, I saw blood. I was drowning in it, sinking below the surface. I would never come up again. I was falling down a long dark well, the only way to get back to her house. I had to return to her house to get back everything I had lost. I was the bad stepsister, the dirty girl who did everything wrong. "Take your bloody spindle," she spat. She had Violet's face and Margaret's voice. She held out her wand for me to step over, but all I could do was stumble and fall. *I am covered from head to foot in filth.*

Someone stuck a wet washcloth in my face. I opened my eyes and saw Lotte. What was she doing here? "You keep shouting that woman's name." She didn't touch me with her hands, just went on prodding me with the wet cloth.

"Hold me," I begged her, not even knowing what language I was speaking. I tried to reach out to her. "Lotte, please. Just hold me." More than anything else, I wanted someone to hold me before I died, but she only yelled, "Kathrin, the doctor's telling you to push. For God's sake, would you stop moaning about that woman and push?"

In the land I had left behind, they used mustard gas that burned people alive. Men lived in holes and trenches like rats. On both fronts, women and children were starving, beaten, and raped. Little children wore gas masks. The world was a dirty, dirty place. How could I bring a new life into it? A kitchen table abortion would have been more merciful. It was time to leave, it was. The child's soul was innocent, even if mine wasn't. I didn't care what the priests said about limbo. This little girl would go straight to heaven. She would never suffer. Even if I burned in hell, she would be safe and unsullied.

I had always imagined Death as a man, but it was a woman's face I saw, decaying skin peeling back to expose the bone underneath. Was this my mother's face, the skull I had seen in my nightmare back at Violet's house? Had she come to take me home? It was time. Even Lotte saw that it was time for me to go. I heard her telling John to get a priest.

"Mrs. Jelinek, can you hear me? It's time to make your peace with God." He held the silver crucifix above my lips and made me kiss it. He sprinkled me with holy water and mumbled over me in Latin. "Is there anything you want to ask forgiveness for?" I tried to answer him, but I could only weep until the tears ran into my gasping mouth. He thrust that silver crucifix in my face. Stříbro means silver. If I called Jan's name, would he hear me? I was so close. I just had to step through that open door to the other side, but then I couldn't, because John was making so much noise. What was he doing, cursing over my bed? He was cursing at the priest. "Get out of my house with your mumbo jumbo! You're making her cry." *John* was crying. I must have been delirious. He was crying for me. "Katie, I'm so sorry. I've been so stupid, but I'm not going to be stupid anymore." He took my hand and said, "You're not going to lose your baby. It's stuck, but the doctor's going to pull it out with forceps. He'll give you chloroform for the pain. Tell me you're going to hold on. Just move your head if you can't talk. Give me a sign. Think of your baby. A child needs a mother, Kathrin."

The doctor came with the chloroform. John stroked my hair. "This is the last pain you'll feel." He said it like a promise.

8 ✎ When I opened my eyes, my daughter was lying beside me, wrapped in the yellow blanket I had crocheted for her. There were pink roses on the bedside table, nearly as pink as her sleeping face. John was holding my hand. "Here's your little girl, Katie." He placed her in my arms. When her eyes opened, I felt such a stab of love, I wept. To think she and I had both survived this. It was a miracle, like the stories you read of in the lives of the saints. Like Catherine of Alexandria. They tortured her on a wheel, but when the pain began to overwhelm her, an angel came to break the wheel. John kissed me more tenderly than he ever had. "Let's call her Jana," he said.

He brought me back. He brought back my soul. Just as Violet's husband had done for her, when she thought everything was over.

✎ In the jungles of the Amazon, there are orchids that can stay dormant for a whole year. You see the plant, and you think it's dead. Then one day it bursts into bloom, the most beautiful and fragrant flower you have ever seen. John had been so afraid I would die. The doctor said he could save the baby, but he couldn't save me. John bullied him into giving it one last try. I have John to thank for my life. Lotte was afraid, too. Risking the loss of her job, she missed three days of work to stay and take care of me. I don't know if I ever felt so cared for. Our bedroom was full of flowers. The pink roses on the bedside table and a vase of daisies on the dresser. John played his uncle's old waltz music on the gramophone because he knew I loved it. The smell of fennel tea drifted in from the kitchen—fennel tea to bring my first milk.

John rocked our daughter in his arms and sang to her. Neither of us wanted to remember, let alone discuss, what we had gone through in the weeks before her birth. We wanted to erase that sadness and pain. Jan was dead, and the past had died with him. From now on, there would be no more looking back, no vain regrets. We had suffered and made our mistakes, but we were young. We could change, both of us. We would look forward into the future, that world of possibility and hope, his hunger wedded to mine. This whole new life we would build together. We were a family, Jana joining us in a bond of blood and flesh. A new beginning. I was ready to do what Lotte had been telling me to do all along. Put Violet behind me. What point was there in mourning what had been lost forever? I wasn't a girl anymore. This harrowing passage into womanhood had freed me from her spell, her claim on me. I had escaped her tales. Nothing could hold me captive anymore. It was not she who had the power to punish or reward.

"Get your rest," said John, drawing the sheets to my chin. "You need to build back your strength." As I drifted in and out of sleep, John and Lotte sat in the kitchen and talked. He had to talk to someone about the whole ordeal, so he talked to her. Fragments of their conversation came to me like slivers of dreams. In the late afternoon, I awoke to hear him asking Lotte why I had been crying out for Violet. She told him. Told him everything. I listened to her and writhed under the sheets. My cousin did not set out to betray me. There was nothing malicious about her. John had asked the question, and she had given an honest answer.

John came in and sat on the edge of our bed. He held my hand as he had before, but his face was in a knot. He stroked my lank hair. One of us would have to speak first, but both of us were terrified. Our throats were silted up. The only sound was our breathing. I gazed at him and imagined tracing every contour of his face. His eyebrows. The vulnerable corners of his lips. I was the one who finally broke the silence. "What were you and Lotte talking about in the kitchen?"

He looked at me and shook his head. "I had no idea what she was going on about. Half the time I can't understand her. Her English is so bad."

What Lotte told him, we never spoke of again.

Book Three

CRONE: MIRRORS OF A SORCERESS

1 ❧ In the following weeks and months, we went walking every evening, John pushing Jana in her buggy. We wore our newfound happiness like shining garments. Mrs. Larsen was so impressed, she came by to visit. "You see, dear, I told you the first few months are the hardest. Once you make it past the rough part, you're home free." By the time our daughter was one year old, we moved to a bungalow in Prospect Park, a respectable neighborhood close enough to the shop so John could walk to work. I could take Jana out along the Mississippi, except we called her Janey to make her sound more American. We made the down payment on our house by selling Jan's books to rich collectors. The saddest thing was that Jan had been sitting on a fortune all those years without even realizing it. John had told him he couldn't make money off old books, but then he had made hundreds of dollars off them simply by knowing how to advertise and sell. Everything he put his hand to prospered, like the king in the story who can turn everything he touches into gold. The shop broke even and started bringing in profit. We fixed up the old apartment above the store and rented it out to a pair of young stenographers.

Around this time, John told me he didn't want to have any more children. "I wouldn't want to put you through that much pain again. If there's just one child, there'll be more for her. Janey will have the best of everything." I went to a special doctor who fitted me for a pessary. If the device itself seemed strange, I felt very modern and daring about it. I would certainly never wind up a brood mare like my mother, though sometimes I wondered if this precaution was necessary. John was coming home late these days. Since moving to the new house, he and I lived in separate worlds.

Though they were not nearly as beautiful as Jan's old books, I discovered that library books could transport me to a place vaster than this house, which I kept as immaculate as a shrine. John approved of the neat stack of borrowed books. "My wife reads poetry," he told our new neighbors and his new friends, for it seemed to impress people, to make them think that I was a cut above the ordinary housewives, that I was a woman of class and distinction. Who would guess, looking at those volumes of Sandburg, Dickinson, and Whitman, that I had once been a mill girl? The truth was that I read poems because I only had the leisure to read in brief snatches, stolen moments, or late in the evening, fighting drowsiness, after I had finally coaxed Janey to bed. "The Brain—Is Wider Than The Sky." Emily Dickinson's poems were like riddles; I read them again and again, imagining her dressed always in white like a bride, even as she shrank deep into her father's house, never leaving it. Then I read Whitman's poems that praised ferries and locomotives.

One day I felt so restless that I broached the subject of working in the store again. John was flabbergasted. "Katie, why would you want to do that? You'll never have to work again. Why aren't you happy? Don't we have everything now?" When he put it that way, I felt like an ungrateful wretch.

Lying awake in bed at night while he slept, I listened to the freight trains. We were a long way from the tracks, but on quiet summer nights with the windows open, I could hear them. That rushing noise they made, the muffled roar of longing. Finally I had a home that was mine, four solid walls around me, and I could only dream of trains.

But there remained the griefs one never spoke of. I finally deduced that one of the girls living in our old apartment was his mistress. He mumbled her name in his sleep. *Sarah.* Once I spied on her. She was waiting for him in the alley behind the shop. I could see her, but she didn't see me. Her eyes were too distracted, thinking of him. She wasn't what I expected. Not an insipid doll like the Leonas and Gwendolens. No painted-up tart, either. She had beautiful auburn hair and tawny eyes. Her face was incandescent with brand-new love, innocent and hopeful. Her innocence, I think, attracted him even more than her beauty. What hurt me most was how much she looked like me when I lived in Violet's house, before I fell from grace. She was the woman I had wanted to be for him.

I told no one, not even Lotte. I was too ashamed, and I wanted no one's pity. John thought I knew nothing, and I let him go on believing that. What good would a scene do? What if I delivered an ultimatum and he chose her over me? I had no desire to jeopardize my daughter's future. If I kept my end of the bargain, he would keep his. He would stick by me. He might not be faithful, but he wouldn't stray too far. He had his business and reputation to think of.

In 1917, when the United States joined the war, we changed our name to Henderson. John, Catherine, and Jane Henderson. We were as American as anyone else. John joined the Minneapolis Minute Men, a group of businessmen who worked together to sell Liberty Bonds. I joined the American Women's League and knit socks and scarves for the young men going to fight overseas. We flew a flag in our front yard and invited the neighbors to our Fourth of July picnic. I spoke only English to our daughter. It was hard to ignore the signs posted everywhere, from the public library to department store windows: *Don't be SUSPECTED. Use American language. America is our home.* Lotte stopped speaking German, and Schmidt's Tavern changed its name to The American Eagle. Even religious services held in Norwegian were considered seditious. Those who denounced the war or attempted to evade military service could be arrested by the Public Safety Commission. When Congressman Charles Lindbergh gave antiwar speeches during his gubernatorial campaign, people pelted him with rocks and rotten eggs.

John's friends who had come to our wedding enlisted right away. The neighbor's husband was conscripted. Each time I saw the postman coming, a prickle went up my neck, and I wondered if this would be the day John's conscription notice arrived. I pictured him in uniform, our last kiss on the railway platform before he went overseas. What if he returned only to be buried at Fort Snelling? I would wear black for a year and remember what was good in him. Death erases betrayal. But he was never called for service.

Sepp was drafted and went to France with the Thirty-sixth Infantry. Lotte said he lasted a month before dying in No Man's Land. Although she had parted ways with him shortly after my daughter was born, the news hit her hard. She left the mill and went to work for the Minneapolis Steel and Machinery Company. With so many men overseas, they had started hiring women. Working on the assembly line building tractors and railway cars, Lotte earned more than she had ever seen in her life. She moved out of the boardinghouse to a rambling apartment she shared with three other women from her new job. She cut her hair short in the new style and went to the picture show with her friends every Saturday night. She bought herself a bicycle. Of the two of us, it was Lotte who had become the modern, emancipated woman.

I still hadn't heard from my uncle. Sometimes I liked to think that he rode his bicycle off into the forest and never returned, like in the old legends. Sometimes the forest swallows a person. If you continue long enough down the path that leads to the thickest part of the woods, it leads you away from this world and into another world. Once you go that far, you can never come back. Violet had gone the same way as my uncle. She was a cavity inside me, an emptiness. From this distance, the whole episode with her seemed so improbable. Sometimes I questioned my own memory and wondered if it had ever happened at all.

🍂 June, 1918. I was making potato flour on the back porch. Since wheat flour was needed for the soldiers, I cooked as much as possible with potatoes, even baked potato bread. The sign in Larsen's Grocery said, *"Be a Potato Patriot. Every spud you eat is a bullet aimed point blank at Kaiser Bill."* Making potato flour was hellish work. It took five pounds of raw potatoes to get enough flour to bake one loaf of bread. You peeled the potatoes, grated them as finely as possible, and soaked the shredded mass in a basin of cold water. After a few hours, you scooped away the shreds that rose to the surface. Then you drained what was left to get the fine potato flour, which sank to the bottom. I still had another two pounds to grate, but Janey was clamoring for attention. She had just turned three. Everything good in me and everything good in John had blossomed in her. I thought she was smarter than both of us put together. Fiery and precocious, she had all of her father's boldness and some of his temper, too. Every sacrifice I made and every misgiving I swallowed had been for her. She would grow up to be everything I was not. In time, I thought, John and I would be able to afford to send her to college.

"That's where the *witch* lives," my daughter declared, pointing to the tower just visible from over the top of the hedge that enclosed our back yard. The ornamental water tower stood on the hill up the street. Because of its conical roof, people called it the Witch's Hat.

"Darling, there are no witches. You have witches in stories but not in the real world."

"I want a story," she said, pressing her head against my knee and grinning up at me. "I want the *witch* story." My daughter loved fairy tales, and her favorite was about the witch in the tower. Although I did not want to fill her head with too much nonsense, telling her fairy tales was the only way to get her to sit still long enough for me to finish my work. "A long time ago," I told her, "there was a poor miller's son who was in love with a girl who was beautiful and rich."

The only mills my daughter knew were the big flour mills. Lotte told her stories about them, and so did I. Sometimes, when the weather was nice, I took Janey over in the streetcar to show her St. Anthony Falls, the mills, and the Stone Arch Bridge. In my story, though, I tried to conjure up the image of an old-fashioned water mill. I described it for her, the water pushing the big wooden wheel.

"The miller's son asked the rich girl to marry him, but she was very proud."

"What's proud?"

"Stuck up," I said, throwing my nose into the air. My daughter giggled. "The rich girl laughed in the poor boy's face and said, 'Yes, I will marry you, but only if you bring me the sun, the moon, and a star.' The boy was very sad when he heard this. How could he bring her the sun, the moon, and a star? Any other boy would have told her, 'I'm very sorry,' and gone away, but this boy was in love. He had more love than sense. So he went on a long journey through faraway lands to bring the girl what she asked for. He met people who were rich and people who were poor. The rich people could not help him, because they were not very clever and not very nice. The poor people could not help him, either, because they had too much work to do. Then he made friends with the lowest people, the tramps and the gypsies, who were hated by the rich and poor alike and who wandered through the world without a home, just as he did. These were the smartest people he ever met, but they could not give him the sun, the moon, and a star. Finally he came to a very old tower on a hill.

"From that tower he heard someone crying in terrible pain. He went to the tower door to see if he could help whomever was inside, but a man from the nearby village stepped in his way and said, 'Do not go in that tower, young man. A sorceress lives there, an evil witch. She is dying, and the devil has come to take her soul!'"

Janey cackled. She liked the scary parts best.

"But the boy still wanted to help the witch, so he went inside the tower. He climbed the steps of the tower until he came to the top room, and there on the floor, on a bed made of straw, was a lady. Once she had been very beautiful, but she had been ill for a long time, and now she was dying. When she saw the boy, though, she stopped moaning and turned head to him. 'Finally you have come!' she cried. 'I have been waiting so long. I will give you the things you are looking for—a star, the moon, and the sun itself—if you promise to help me. The *second* I die, you must take my hand and bless me. Then you must take this bottle and throw it at the foot of my bed, because that is where the devil is waiting. The contents of this bottle will chase the devil away.'

"She gave him a bottle of holy water, and the boy promised to do exactly what she said. Then, in terrible pain, she got up from her bed and went to get her three magic mirrors. 'Open the window,' she said. 'I must be able to see the path of the sun, the moon, and the stars as they move across the sky. Now give me your hand.' She held the boy's hand, and with her other hand, she began drawing funny symbols in the first mirror. She mumbled words the boy could not understand. She cast a magic spell. After a while, there was a bright point of light in the mirror that got bigger and bigger until it turned into a star.

"'Here is your star,' said the witch. Then she took the second mirror and began drawing symbols and whispering secret words, but this time it took longer. She did not have much strength left, and this was a harder spell than the first one. But very slowly a silver point appeared in the mirror, and the silver point grew bigger and bigger until it grew into a moon.

"'Here is your moon,' said the witch. Her lips were white. The boy saw how close she was to death. Sweat ran down her forehead in big drops. She could hardly breathe. 'Why did you come so late?' she asked the boy. 'I don't know if I have enough strength left for this last spell.' She took the third mirror, drew the symbols, and whispered the words. This took much, much longer than last time. This was the hardest spell of all. The boy felt very sad as he watched her. This spell would kill her. He wanted to tell her to stop, but it was too late. He began to sweat, and his face went white as the witch's. Just as he gave up hope, there was a golden sparkle in the mirror, and that golden sparkle grew and grew until a golden sun filled the whole mirror.

"The witch gave him the mirror and said, 'My heart is breaking. Remember your promise.' The boy's heart was breaking, too. He helped her to her bed, held her hand, and blessed her. Then, the second she died, he took the bottle of holy water and threw it at the foot of the bed. And guess what happened?"

"The devil!" Janey shrieked in delight. "He hit the devil!"

"Yes! The bottle of holy water went smack into the devil's face, and he flew out the window. He screamed very bad things, and the whole tower was full of bad smells. But the devil did not get the witch. Her soul was safe. The boy knew it was time for him to go home and give the mirrors with the sun, the moon, and the star to the rich girl so that she would marry him. He would be a hero, and she would finally love him back. But suddenly he knew that he did not love her anymore. She was too selfish and spoiled. He sat for a very long time in the tower, holding the dead witch's hand and thinking about the strange things he had seen. He asked himself, 'What will I do with these mirrors, and where will I go now?'"

Janey wasn't listening anymore. She was halfway across the yard, running toward the woman coming through the back gate. When I saw the way the sunlight glanced off her white muslin dress, my throat went tight. I couldn't even look at her face, just that dress, and then the dress itself began to blind me. I blinked rapidly, but she jolted me from my reverie with a loud whoop. Grabbing Janey under her arms, she swung her around in circles, around and around, until they were both giggling and dizzy. "Don't get Lotte's dress dirty," I called out to my daughter, but neither of them seemed to hear. Janey was hanging on to Lotte's hand with both her own and chattering away about the devil and his bad smells.

"Has she been telling you those crazy old stories again? Kathrin, really! You poor kid." Her English was much more colloquial than mine. She had learned it not in a textbook, but from the women she had been working with for the past year. Since she worked double shifts most days of the week, they gave her Friday morning off, and that's when she usually came by. "I bought this for Alma's wedding," she said, coming up to the porch to show me her new dress. She turned around, so I could see the pearl buttons in the back. Then she spun to face me again. She wore a necklace of bright glass beads that caught and refracted the light. Her cropped hair fell in soft waves that came to her chin. It made her look years younger. She wore crocheted white gloves to hide the machine oil under her fingernails. "You look lovely," I said. I felt Lotte's eyes resting on my house dress and stained apron. And on my hands, red and raw from grating potatoes.

"Do you want some coffee? There is a pot on the stove. And yesterday I baked a cake."

"With potato flour?" She laughed and went into the kitchen to help herself. Janey followed her, clinging to her hand. Lotte had seen the inside of our new house plenty of times. The shining oak floors and kitchen cupboards, the big china canisters that held flour, sugar, coffee, and tea, but she no longer commented on these things. The only thing of mine she envied was Janey. Returning to the porch, she settled in the wicker chair opposite me and set her cup down to allow Janey to clamber into her lap. My daughter fingered the glass beads of her necklace. "Make rings for me," she begged.

I looked up from the potatoes I was grating. "Rings? Janey, she cannot make rings."

"She means smoke rings." Lotte lit a cigarette and began to blow a chain of evanescent white circles.

"Daddy can't do that."

"Can't he? Do you think your mother will come to the pictures today?" Now that she was earning good money, Lotte went to the pictures every chance she got. "There's a matinee today," she told me, "with Charlie Chaplin."

"I am too busy."

She gave me one of her looks.

"We have company tonight. I must cook for five."

"Another one of those dinner parties?" She pulled a face that made Janey laugh.

I nodded and went on grating potatoes.

"He never seems to be home at a decent hour unless you have company." Lotte tapped the ash off her cigarette. The gray clump fell to the porch floor, smoldered briefly, and died. She was worse than John, the way she let her ashes fall everywhere. This would leave a burn mark.

"He is very busy," I said. "He works very hard. After he closes up the shop, there is still the bookkeeping to do."

"You know something?" She looked at me through the haze of dissipating smoke rings. "You look exactly like your mother."

My hand slipped on the potato grater when she said that. I nicked my finger.

"In that apron," she said, "with your hair pulled back. You look just like her."

"Do I?" Raising my bleeding finger to my mouth, I sucked at it. I couldn't even remember my mother's face, yet Lotte said I was a replica of her.

 After Lotte left, I paged through the new cookbook John had bought me. Tonight he had invited his colleagues from the Liberty Bond campaign. I had to serve a four-course dinner, and I had to dress Janey up in her best frock and parade her in front of the guests before farming her out to the woman next door for the rest of the evening.

She was not permitted to eat with us when we had company. Although I resented the work and bother these dinners entailed, in a perverse way, I also liked them. It was one of the few opportunities I had to wear my silk evening dress and feel young and attractive again. Even if John's new acquaintances bored me, it was amusing to pretend, for at least one evening, to be an elegant lady.

Everything in the kitchen had to be finished by five-thirty. The roast in the oven, the vegetables already cooked, so I only had to warm them up when the guests arrived. The soup simmering on the stove. The table set with freshly ironed napkins and polished silver. John came home at six-thirty. That gave Janey and me an hour to bathe and change clothes. Janey loved watching me dress up. She perched with her rag doll on my bed as I put on my green silk dress. Tissue-thin, it rippled like water. It left my throat bare. I let her pluck my best necklace out of the jewelry box. A pearl choker that looked real. She watched my reflection in the vanity mirror as I fastened the necklace and put my hair up with the alabaster combs John had given me for my birthday. Then I gave my face a light dusting with powder and rouge—otherwise my skin was too sallow.

As we stood in front of the wardrobe mirror, her eyes were big and wondering at the way I could transform myself from a housewife in a spattered apron into a pretty lady. She thought I did this by magic. My hair was perfectly arranged, piled on my head like a crown. The alabaster combs would catch the candlelight at dinner. But something was incongruous. Something marred the perfect illusion. My hands. Not the hands of a lady but of a woman who did her own gardening and housework, someone who had spent the morning shredding potatoes. No amount of rose milk would soften them. Averting my eyes from the mirror, I turned to my daughter. "Let's put on your nice dress." She made a face, digging her heels into the rug. If she loved watching me dress up, getting her into fancy clothes was another story. But I made sure she was properly dressed by the time John came home.

The three of us stood on the front porch and welcomed our guests. We made a very pleasing picture, John and I, posing in front of our new house with our little girl. Two young people from the humblest of backgrounds who had worked their way up to *this*. This perfect image was what fueled John, what drove him to work so hard. When our guests came, he put his arm around my waist and said, "This is my wife, Catherine, and our daughter, Jane." I shook hands with Mr. Fogard and Mr. Timmins. They had come by streetcar, but the third guest, the one who arrived last, drove up in his own automobile. When Janey saw the black Ford coming to a halt in front of our house, she let out a yell and raced off toward it. I caught her under her arms to restrain her. Knowing her, she'd try to climb on the car. "Come on," I said. "Let's go to Anne's." Anne was the neighbor woman who took Janey for us when we had company.

➥ When I returned, John had shown our guests into the parlor, our best room, which we used only for company. He was pouring out glasses of California champagne. Taking my arm, he introduced me to the man who had arrived in the car. "Catherine, I'd like you to meet Mr. Robert Andrews. Mr. Andrews, this is my wife, Catherine. I'm afraid you just missed our daughter."

As I shook his hand, a shock went through me. His black hair, his gray eyes. It was almost like seeing Violet. It was her brother, the one who had told me never to bother their family again. How had he entered my house? Why had John invited him? Then it occurred to me—the men did not remember ever meeting before. Maybe Robert didn't even recognize me. It had been four years. But when I looked into his eyes, he went brick red and stiffly let go of my hand. "How do you do, Mrs. Henderson."

2 〰 When everyone was seated at the table, I brought out the soup and ladled it into each bowl. I tried to keep my hands from shaking. *My ugly peasant hands. They would give me away yet.* John and the other men were having an animated discussion. Only Robert and I were conspicuously silent. As wooden as he tried to act, his eyes kept slipping across the table to stare at me. I wanted to glare at him as coldly as Margaret used to glare at me. He looked at me and saw a mill girl masquerading in a silk dress. With each look, he tried to read in my face what I had done with his sister.

"Mr. Andrews." John had to shout down the table to get his attention. "Mr. Timmins told me there was a fund-raising venture you wanted to discuss."

"That's correct." He was too flustered to say anything more. I remembered those dinner parties in her mansion, when I was the one who sat tongue-tied and intimidated.

"You're not involved, from what I understand, with the Liberty Bond Campaign." John prodded him patiently, as if coaxing a timid child. "Why is that?"

Robert took a nervous sip from his water glass. He did not touch the wine John had poured him. "With all due respect, Mr. Henderson, I think more than enough war bonds have been sold. The government will always find the money to finance this war." An uneasy silence fell over the table. I could see that John regretted asking. "What do you and your friends on the Liberty Bond campaign intend to do about all those crippled and shell-shocked boys coming home?" The effort of getting out those sentences had covered his face in sweat. I watched him mopping his forehead with one of my linen napkins.

Timmins intercepted. "What Mr. Andrews is trying to say is that he wants to raise money for a new veteran's hospital."

"That's a very worthy cause," said John. "But why do you think that a veteran's hospital is at cross-purposes with our campaign?"

"It's a personal matter. There's been a tragedy in my family." Robert looked directly at me, as if to indict me. A hollow echoing filled my head. If I closed my eyes, I could see her carrying the chrysanthemums into her house, the graveyard flowers. She had picked them herself, beginning my nightmare of the river of blood, the drowned girl, and the woman whose face was a skull. The tragedy he spoke of—that night I had seen it and dreamt it.

"A tragedy," said John, regaining his poise. "I'm very sorry to hear that."

"My son came home three months ago," said Robert. "I suppose I should be lucky he's still alive. He has shrapnel in both legs. Can't get through a single night without screaming and trying to take cover. There's no cure for shell shock."

His son, not his sister. That boy who had answered the telephone when I had called, that must be the one. I could still hear his voice. *She's gone away.*

"Many of these boys," he said, "are sent . . . out of ignorance . . . to mental institutions, but they don't get better there, either." He was about to go on, but Timmins gave him a signal that this should be the end of his speech.

I was crying, my hand in my mouth. This man had just described the unspeakable damage the war had left on his son, and I was sobbing in guilty relief that no tragedy had struck *her.* John would be mortified, but when I glanced in his direction, he looked at me approvingly. I was showing exactly the right response. "Mr. Andrews, that is so sad." I looked into his eyes. Then I said, meaning every word, "I am very sorry about your son."

"Thank you for your sympathy, Mrs. Albrecht." *Mrs. Albrecht!* With those two words, he gave us both away. Raising his hand to his forehead, he corrected himself. "Mrs. Henderson." John threw me a baffled look. When I got up to clear away the empty soup bowls, he followed me into the kitchen. "How does he know your maiden name?" he whispered. "Does he know you from somewhere?"

"I met him at my old job," I whispered back, hoping he would think I meant my job at Barker Metals. Before he could ask me anything more, I carried out the tray of salads. Nobody dared to mention Robert's son again. No one wanted to reopen that well of grief. The conversation drifted off in all directions as I took away the empty salad plates and brought out the main course, but I could not speak. If I tried, I would choke on things that were caught in my throat. Robert had only spoken to me twice, but both times he had been hostile, blaming me not only for the episode with his sister, but also for what had happened to his son. My attempts to make myself American were useless. Fathers of war-damaged boys would only see me as German. I kept glancing up from my plate to catch him staring at me. When I met his eyes, he looked away. The other men were beginning to notice. With these covert looks passing back and forth, they would think we had been lovers. John caught my eye, his jaw tightening. What was he thinking? He knew there had to be more to this than two flustered people exchanging glances. "Mr. Andrews," he said. "Tell us some more about your fund-raising proposal."

"It's a two-fold project." Robert still had difficulty speaking. "I have just received and endowment from . . . a donor . . . who had stipulations." He glanced around the table, avoiding my eyes. "My donor is of the opinion that it's not enough to help the returning servicemen. There are also the civilian victims of war."

Timmins took over for him. "Mr. Andrews' donor has already contributed five thousand dollars. Half that money will go toward a new veteran's hospital and the other half toward the Red Cross humanitarian relief mission in the war-stricken countries. Mr. Andrews would like to raise at least enough to match his donor's contribution."

"Five thousand dollars," said Mr. Fogard. "That's quite a sum. May I ask who this donor is?"

Timmins was about to say something, but Robert gave him a

silencing look. "That," he said, "is neither here nor there. What I want
to know is if any of you are willing to help."

"Why won't you name your donor?" Fogard asked. "Did he request
anonymity?"

"I don't see what difference a name makes," said Robert, "as long
as the numbers add up."

"A name makes a big difference," said John, "when you're asking
for contributions."

"I assure you it's no one famous." Robert was sweating again. "It's
a relative who was deeply affected by what happened to my son."

"A relative you can't name?" asked Mr. Fogard. "That seems very—"

"Mr. Andrews," I blurted out. "One of the ladies I know in the
Women's League said you had a niece who wanted to train as a Red
Cross nurse. Is she overseas now?"

Robert looked at me, flushed and dazed. "Yes, she is. She's working behind the lines in Montdidier."

"Let's return to the subject of the donor," said Mr. Fogard, clearly
vexed at the way I had interrupted. "How can you expect us to take
your project seriously if you can't even name your donor?"

Robert hesitated. "If it's so important for you to know." Although
he was addressing Fogard, he pointedly locked eyes with me as he said
it. "It's my sister, Mrs. Arthur Waverly. The widow of the ethnologist."
My mouth began to tremble. That hateful man! He had stripped me
naked in front of my husband, had done it on purpose. John set his
glass down abruptly, spilling red wine on the white tablecloth. Both of
us stared at the stain. John's face was as heated as mine.

"Oh, yes," he said. "I think I've heard of her." He was too furious
to even look at me. I felt his rage emanating in waves of heat and
knew that I would have hell to pay. To get out of this mess, I would
have to go down on my knees and plead with him, pour out my confession, as I should have done years ago. Would he forgive? Maybe if I
told him it was entirely her doing, that she had used me. The only way
he would forgive me would be to make her out as a villain. But then
he would remember the way I had been crying her name in childbirth. The marks she had left on me were no longer invisible. My flesh

had been branded. John's eyes burned into me like a skull on fire. "Why don't you bring out the dessert, Catherine?"

I sprang from my chair and noisily cleared away the beef-stained plates, making further discussion impossible. In the kitchen I took the bowl of heavy cream from the icebox and started whipping it, but I could barely hold the wire whisk. I heard Robert saying, "My sister has been traveling abroad for the past three-and-a-half years, but when she heard what happened to my son, she wanted to do what she could."

Everything falls apart, or falls together. As I struggled to whip the cream, she came into focus. Not a ghost, not a sorceress, but a woman. She had not been home in all this time. I realized this sojourn was not a field trip or a wealthy lady's adventure. This was exile. She was an outcast in her own family. Despite the lavish donation she had given to her brother's cause, he could barely speak her name in polite company. Like me, she belonged nowhere. In these three-and-a-half years, she had become just as rootless and orphaned as I was. *See, Violet, we are equals now. You can no longer say that I'm not your peer.* With bitter triumph, those words rang through my head. I whipped the cream until my wrist ached, but it refused to thicken. I dawdled so long in the kitchen that the men abandoned the dining table. I heard their chairs scraping against the floor, their departing footsteps.

She was utterly alone in the world. She thought I despised her. I had judged her very harshly. She was never ashamed of me but of herself, ashamed of how passionately she had loved such a young girl. That starry-eyed girl was dead and buried. That girl I had been had died the day her brother hung up the telephone on me. Only a housewife with red peasant hands remained.

I stood in the empty dining room and listened to the voices in the parlor and the other voices coming from the front porch. Through the lace curtains I saw John and Fogard under the porch light. Each had a cigarette and a glass of brandy in hand. John had taken the decanter with him. Crossing the front entry hall to the parlor door, I stopped short. I wavered. I nearly turned away, but then I walked through that door. Timmins had cornered Robert into some intense discussion. Both men looked up, startled and a bit aggravated as I entered the room. I made myself smile into Timmins' eyes. "My husband is serving brandy on the front porch." Robert hadn't touched a drop of alcohol, but Timmins had. I knew he wouldn't refuse an offer of brandy. Robert made a move to follow him out of the room, but I blocked his path and seized his arm. I stared straight into his eyes. No longer a mill girl who could be dismissed. "Would you please give me her address?" I whispered.

He was so taken aback by my nerve, it took him a while to find his voice. "She's still traveling. She has no steady address, and even if she had, I wouldn't give it to you." He tried to pull away, but I held him fast. Finally I understood—her family was afraid of me. Afraid of what I knew about them and their sister, afraid of my power to bring down their good name. But I was also the one who had the power to call their sister back. The wand was in my hands. Call her back and forgive her. By forgiving her, I would redeem us both.

"Tell your sister I wish her well. If you write to her, can you at least tell her that?"

Robert looked at me and looked away, as he had done all evening. I was no longer intimidated by him or even angry. I could feel his pain, just like my pain. His heart was breaking over his son and now this. "You really cared for her, then?"

"*Yes*," I said. "Yes, I cared for her. What did you think?" That I had been after her for her money? Is that what her family had thought? "Why do you think I called you that night?" I was in tears again, but it didn't matter anymore.

"I didn't know that," he said. Even his voice sounded like hers.

"Will you tell me now?"

"Mrs. Henderson," he said in an urgent whisper. I turned and saw John standing in the doorway. My hand fell away from Robert's arm. "Excuse me," Robert murmured, and walked past him out of the room.

John stared at me, speechless. I had seen him mad on plenty of occasions, but I had never seen him like this, his face the color of ash. A

look passed between us. He was reliving each moment of our courtship, unraveling my secrets. He was remembering the way I had praised
her and the way I had run from her, run to him. Remembering the
way I had cried like a girl who had lost her mother when he first made
love to me. Remembering the way I had come apart whenever he
mentioned her name. The cards were on the table. Neither of us could
ever look away from this again. It was more telling than what had come
from Lotte's mouth, for he had heard it coming from me. Most unforgivably, I had made my confession not to him but to a strange man at
a dinner party. He looked lost, completely devastated; I wanted to go
to him and take back everything he had just heard. I took a step toward
him, but he turned abruptly and walked away from me. I retreated to
the kitchen.

Tying my apron over my good dress, I filled the sink with water and
started the dishes. My hands were shaking, as if they did not belong to
me. They disappeared beneath the scummy water, so numb I could not
feel whether the water was hot or cold. Over the noise of the clinking dishes, I heard the kitchen door opening, footsteps coming toward
me. "John?" I bit my lip. Then I turned and saw Robert.

"I came in to say good-night." He lowered his voice to a whisper.
"The last address we had for her was in Ecuador, but she's moved on
since then. She promised she would be home for Christmas, though.
There's a magazine called *The New Pandora*. She wrote an article for
them, the April issue, I believe. That will tell you everything else you
need to know."

"Thank you," I said, wiping my hands dry. "Thank you." I took off
my apron and followed him to the front door, where Fogard and
Timmins were saying good-night to John. Robert went to him and
shook his hand, acting more gracious than he had the whole evening,
congratulating him on the work he had done for the Liberty Bond
campaign. John couldn't even pretend to hold on to his dignity. He
couldn't look at Robert, could barely mouth the words *good-bye*.

As soon as the guests were gone, he stumbled out to the porch and
stood in the dark, staring into nothing. I knew that deep inside him

something was being decided. I had to get Janey back from the neighbor's, but I couldn't even bring myself to walk past him, so I went out
the back door, across the back yard. The moon, nearly full, rose over
the Witch's Hat. Its radiance flooded the sky. I held out my hands and
saw the silvery cast the moon gave my skin. I was suspended, hanging
by a thread. What would I do?

⌘ Janey was already asleep. I scooped her off Anne's bed and carried
her home, slowly walking toward our back door. All the lights in our
house were burning, illuminating the flowery yellow curtains in the
kitchen window. I looked at those curtains as though I were seeing
them for the last time. The house was so quiet. I was sure he had gone
out. For a moment, I could breathe again. Laying Janey in her bed, I
managed to slip off her frilly dress without waking her. I untied her
hair ribbon and unbuckled her shoes. For once she could sleep in her
chemise. When I pulled back the covers and tucked her in, she woke
up and whimpered. "Hush, darling. Hush." I stroked her hair and
kissed her. "Go back to sleep." In the cellar beneath us, something hit
the wall and broke. Unsteady footsteps climbing the stairs.
    "Mommy?"
    "Sleep." I kissed her forehead. *"Sleep."* I shut off her lamp, tiptoed
out of her room. He was waiting in the hallway. The drink on his
breath. I recoiled. His fingers sank into my arm. "Not outside her
door," I whispered.
    He pulled me into the kitchen, cornered me in the narrow space
between the pantry door and the cellar stairway. "Is it true?"
    I nodded. It took all my courage to hold his gaze. I waited for him
to explode, but he only stared at me in silence until I couldn't bear it.
"I'm sorry," I said.
    His eyes were dull flames. Down the street, a dog bayed at the moon.
    "I was just a girl when I came to her house. I tried to forget her. I
wanted to love *you.*"
    A flicker of his eyelid. His upper lip curled back. I realized what I
had said. Admitted to his face that I never really loved him, just tried
to, wanted to. He was going to say something. I saw his jaw working,

his cheeks drawing in, his lips moving. No words emerged. Only the hot spray of his spit hitting my face. Finally the words came pouring out of him. "You make me sick!" He took me by the shoulders and shook me until one of the alabaster combs fell out of my hair and clattered against the linoleum. "You ruined me tonight. Now the whole world will know I married a . . . a . . . What the hell are you, anyway?" He pushed me up against the wall. "Did she give you money for it?"

I was so appalled, all I could do was gape like a schoolgirl. Tears running down my face. In those tears he saw my love for her, and he wanted to twist that love into something horrible.

"So that's where you got all the money. That's what you brought into our marriage." He paused, looking in my eyes before continuing. "Your *whore* money."

Something in my throat was stretched as tight as it would go.

"Your whore money," he said again. "You were just some rich lady's—"

The flat of my hand struck his face, silencing him. His head twisted to one side. I saw the imprint my hand had made, the outline of my fingers burning in his cheek. He would go to work tomorrow with that red mark. It took him a second to get over the shock, but then his hands were at my throat. For a moment, I couldn't breathe. He tore at my necklace. I felt the snap of the string breaking, the imitation pearls rolling off me like rain. They rolled past our scuffling feet as I struggled out of the corner he had backed me into. I was about to break free, when he grabbed for my arm. Swerving out of his reach, I stepped backwards, losing my balance. And I fell down the stairwell. It happened so fast. A brutal somersault, my skull and spine striking the bare wooden stairs. My body slammed into the cellar floor. Damp stone against my face. Like the inside of a cave. For a moment, there was pain. I tasted my blood, sweet and salty at once. Then the darkness enclosed me like a fist.

I was rising, weightless and unencumbered, gazing with detached sorrow at that woman slumped on the stone floor. I saw him, too, looking down at her. Rubbing his face and trembling, he moved one inch forward, unsteady, uncertain. Would he go to her, go down those stairs, touch her, speak her name, try to revive her? The sight of her unmoving body was too much for him. The blackness swallowed her. She was no longer there. He closed the cellar door to make her disappear. His haunted footsteps beating a retreat.

≈ I was in a dark forest. A valley so deep, the sun could never reach the bottom. It was night. Moonless. But a woman stood over me with a torch. I looked up and saw my mother's face. The torch shone in her eyes, hazel and gold-flecked, like mine. The eyes I had passed on to my daughter. *You look just like your mother.* She said, "Come." And held out her hand. I looked at my mother and saw her face, saw my own face, more clearly than I ever had. A presence so palpable, I could reach out and embrace it.

≈ Screaming reached me from far away. Calling me back. My daughter. Tearing through the house in search of me. In the kitchen she could only find the scattered pieces, my fallen comb, the beads of my broken necklace. I had to go to her, had to answer her cries, but I was at the bottom of a well, trapped down so deep. How would I ever rise to the surface? An incredible splitting in my head—coming back meant returning to that pain. My palms clutched at the damp stone. Just a thin strip of light under the door broke the darkness. She was shrieking like a child possessed. A noise came out of my throat, more animal than human. Moving my lips, I managed to croak out her name. Trying to heave my body off the floor, I collapsed. Everything spun. Nauseated, I dragged myself up the stairs on my hands and knees. I thought this would take a century, but finally my hand turned the knob and pushed the door open.

She stood barefoot in her white shift among the scattered imitation pearls. Her eyes were huge. She did not recognize me. I had blood on my face. That made her back away from me and scream. Lurching across the kitchen, I groped for a dish towel to wipe the worst of it away. I could still walk, even if it hurt. No bones were broken. What dark angel had saved me? I sank to my knees and held out my arms. "Darling, come to me. This is your mother. Come." She threw herself against me and wailed something incoherent. I held her as tightly as I could and kissed the top of her head. "I know," I whispered. "I know." As I stroked her hair, a breeze touched my face. I glanced at the back door. He had not shut it when he left. That door was wide open.

⌇ I stepped off the train in Larkin, Minnesota, retracing the journey I had made in the winter of 1914. My bruises hidden under powder and a veiled hat, I walked up and down those back roads with my suitcase and daughter until I found a cheap cabin to rent only three miles away from Violet's old cabin. This was where I ran into the landlord who wanted to turn me away on account of my German accent, and this was where I stood my ground, fabricating the story of the American husband who had fallen in Montdidier. As for my real husband, I left him a note on the bureau, along with his mother's sapphire ring: *I am never coming back.*

⌇ Once I lived in a mansion with stars on the ceiling. Once I wove pale blue ribbons in my hair and wore a floating muslin dress. Now I found myself in a rented cabin with a Liberty Bond calendar on the wall. Alone in the woods with my little girl. I dyed my clothes black and let everyone think I was a war widow. People generally respect grief, as they do an eight-month pregnancy. Strangers gawk and wonder, but they leave you in peace. What if she didn't return for Christmas? What if this were just another scrap of false hope, something her brother had said to placate me? What if I were just a bruised and forsaken woman waiting in the woods in vain? Although it was summer on earth, it was winter in my soul, the harshest and most desolate of Februarys. "When will we go home?" my daughter kept asking, sometimes fearfully and sometimes petulantly.

"Jana, we *are* home." Since we lived alone in the forest, I called her Jana again. I tried to make a new home for us with the stories I told her, stories of girls who weren't afraid of fire, weren't afraid of the dark, weren't afraid of the devil. I told her about Baba Yaga, flaming wands, and burning skulls. After I tucked her into bed at night, I stepped outside and stared at the trees as they rustled in the moonlight.

One night in July, I went out, and there was no moon. I stared into that blackness until my eyes hurt. In that blackness, there were stars. I had never seen so many. This far away from the city, they shone more brilliantly than ever before. My face tilted toward them; I began to cry. Not in sadness but in awe. *I could see them.* For the first time in my life, I could see the patterns in the stars. It was there in the night sky, everything I had ever longed for. If you go far enough into the darkness, you touch heaven. Everything Violet had taught me, all that magic, flowed back, down from the stars and into my hands. Except now it was my magic. If I had become a crone before my time, at least I'd gained a few grains of wisdom in the bargain. Day by day, it returned to me, everything I thought I had lost forever. The broken scattered pieces—I wove and stitched them back together. This was my redemption. Night after night, I sat with Jana in the rocking chair and told her the stories Violet once told me.

If the Virgin is Violet's sign, the Scorpion is mine. It's not a beautiful or pleasant creature, but one that can survive in the desert. A woman strong enough to raise her daughter without a man. I am the serpent that devours her own tail—her own tale. If you tell a tale well enough, it becomes a path to follow. *I shed my skin and begin again.* I am walking through the thickest part of the forest. There is no moon, but I hold a flaming branch in my hand. I am walking. This time I won't get lost on the way. If you tell a tale true enough, it becomes a map. And now, for the first time since I stepped off the boat in 1912, I know exactly where I am going.

Epilogue

≈ THE GOLDEN TREE

The New Pandora called itself "The Journal of the New Woman." Finding a copy of the April issue wasn't easy, but toward the end of August, the librarian in town managed to obtain it for me. Violet's article was illustrated with a grainy photograph of women standing around a well in a dusty village square. The women were large, big-boned, strong-looking. They wore wide skirts and small fedora-like hats. Their hair hung down in braids. Standing in front of the well was a woman barely discernible from the others. She wore the same peasant clothes and her face was darkly tanned, but she was smaller than they were, and her hair was cut short. Nothing like my memory of her. No longer a lady in her mansion.

> The Incas called themselves the Children of the Sun. They honored the sun as their supreme deity and engineered sophisticated solar observatories and temples. The descendants of the Incan Empire still celebrate the solstices, and to this day mirrors are holy, because they reflect the sun. In the nearly four-hundred-year-old church of San Francisco in Old Quito, round mirrors are placed strategically to reflect the sunlight coming in the windows. This was one of the tricks the Jesuits used to win the indígenas to Christianity. Quito itself is built on the foundations of the great Incan city that Pizarro came to conquer, believing it to be the legendary El Dorado, the city of gold. Rather than surrender their city to the conquistadors, the people burned it to the ground. The Spanish built their new city on the ruins of a vanquished civilization.
>
> It was my curiosity about these lost and buried worlds that brought me to Ecuador. For me, it was not enough to see the

sights of Quito. I wanted to go off into high Sierra and learn all I could about the indígenas. For nearly three years, I traveled on horseback from mountain village to mountain village. After my first Andean winter, I learned to dress as the local people do, in a long poncho which doubles as a bedroll at night. I stayed in each village long enough to befriend the women and win their trust, so they would share their stories with me. This was no easy task. They did not know what to make of me.

What would drive a woman, a Yanqui, to travel on her own, without the protection of her family? How had my people allowed me to wander the world alone like a vagabond? When I told them I was a widow, I began to earn their sympathy. I went to mass at their churches and celebrated their fiestas, always remembering to pour the last drops from my glass on the earth as an offering to Pachamama, the earth mother they still worship alongside Christ. Yet I realized I would always be a gringa to them, a voyeur on the outside looking in. I might have come no further. My saving grace is that I am a storyteller. I thought that if I told my story to them, they might consent to tell their stories to me.

The story I chose was the Greek myth of Demeter and Persephone. I did not tell it as myth from an archaic culture, but as if it had happened to me—as though it were my story. I narrated the tale in first person, putting myself in the place of Demeter. I was the bereft mother cloaked in black and wandering the world in search of that lost maiden the underworld had swallowed. The gods above and below were in a conspiracy to keep me from ever finding her again, and the earth itself was barren and bleak, mirroring my desolation. Often I moved my audience and even myself to tears. I told that story in so many villages that it indeed became my story. Then, one by one, the women and girls began coming to me with their stories. They told me ancient folk tales: the stories of Pachamama and her two sisters; the unhappy story of the boy who captured a Star Maiden and made her his wife only to lose her. They also told me stories from their lives, pouring out confessions that will never reach the ear of a priest: stories of lost children, lost love, secret desires. I do not know what a proper scholar would make of this outpouring of women's stories I have gathered, but I wrote every one of them down.

Perhaps my biggest adventure during my Ecuadorian sojourn was my encounter with the curandera. Every village,
from the highlands to the coast and the Amazon basin, has its
traditional healer, which can be either a man or a woman. The
curanderos and curanderas work with a combination of folk
magic and herbal medicine, utilizing potent local plants such as
chinchona bark and coca leaves. The traditional Quechan heal-
ers believe that each individual has two bodies, not one. There
is the outer physical body, which other people see and touch,
but hidden inside the outer body is the soul body, visible only
to seers and spirits. If the equilibrium between these two bodies is disturbed, illness results. I did not glean this information
through scientific observation but direct experience. I contracted dysentery, and there wasn't a medical doctor to be had.

The curandera laid me on the floor in front of her altar with
the statues of Jesus and Mary and the terra-cotta figurine of
Pachamama. If one is seriously ill, it means that the soul has left
the body to wander in the spirit world. The curandera's task is
to call the soul back into the body; to be healed by a curandera,
one must believe in her magic. She called on the Holy Trinity,
then the Blessed Virgin and a long list of saints, but I am not
Catholic, and the good woman's prayers were wasted. She gave
me vile-tasting potions to ease the fever and diarrhea. The
potions made me see bright colors and rainbows which undu-
lated like snakes. She called on Pachamama and the old mountain gods, and then she began to call on the sacred animals: on
Condor, who carries back straying souls, and on Fox, the
Trickster, who outfoxes evil spirits. As much as I honored her
myths, however, I did not share her belief in them, and so they
could not bring me back, either. When she had reached the end
of her repertoire of prayers and invocations, she thought to call
on Persephone from my story. Using all her powers, she called
on the spirit of that maiden, and that was the shock which
jolted my wandering soul back inside my body.

Violet, I am calling you home. I send out my soul each night, flying
through the dark sky and following the path of stars until I find you
again. Your brother has mailed me the key to your cabin, and now I
shall see to it that you have a place to come home to. I have opened
the windows that have been shut for four years. I have cleaned out

every room. Everything is prepared for your return. In the wild grass surrounding your cabin, my little girl and I have planted over a hundred bulbs. Odd that autumn is the time for planting. You think of it as the time when everything withers away, but the bulbs are safe underground. Come spring, they will rise and push out of the thawing earth. Snowdrops, crocus, hyacinth, daffodils, and tulips. You called these spring flowers ephemeral, yet they rise each year like a promise that is kept.

The days and weeks pass so quickly now. I have left my sorrow behind and decided to do everything differently. Do you know the Torvola sisters? They run a dairy farm and seed catalogue business they inherited from their parents. That's why people call them the Torvola sisters, even though the older sister, Taina, is married to a man named Vernon Lauwers. He's overseas with the war, and the sisters run the farm and business by themselves. One day I went over to buy Mason jars.

Taina, the older sister, came to the door when I knocked. I'd interrupted her in the middle of baking, and her hands and apron were all floury. I was going to ask her about the Mason jars when something else slipped out of my mouth. "Ma'am, I am looking for work." Her face colored when she heard my accent and saw my black dress. No doubt she had heard the gossip about me. Her eyes darted from me to Jana and back again, finally resting on my face. "I heard," she said, "that you lost your husband in Montdidier." Her voice was hushed, and she shivered as she said it. "My husband's not too far from there. Come in." She led me into a big farm kitchen, which was clean but wildly disordered with seed packets, invoices, orders, and receipts all over the counters. After we had told each other our names, she poured me a cup of coffee and gave Jana a glass of fresh milk from her cows. "What kind of work can you do?"

"I can type," I said automatically. Then I glanced again at the jumble of invoices and orders. "I could help you with your bookkeeping. I could put your paperwork in order." Then I told her about the work I had done for Barker Metals. Taina began gathering the papers and stacking them on the kitchen table. "We really could use someone who knows about bookkeeping. Stay for supper. I want you to meet my sister."

Taina's sister Sirppa was much younger than I had expected—just seventeen. She reminded me of another Sirppa I knew when I lived at the YWCA in Minneapolis. In Finland, where their parents were born, it's a common name. When the war is over, Taina wants to send Sirppa to the university to study horticulture. Already she's experimenting with grafting plants. She wants to make new hybrids that can thrive in this climate. At supper that night, I also met Taina's four children. The youngest girl is Jana's age.

The next morning I started my new job, and have been working for the Torvola sisters ever since. I type up balance sheets at their kitchen table in the middle of the activity and noise: the children playing, the sisters tramping in and out, the soup simmering, and the bread baking. My daughter has stopped asking me when we'll go home.

When I was a mill girl and I came to live in your house, you gave me a whole new world of learning and beauty and fairy tales. This time I have a new world I can give to you, full of children and growing gardens and big farm suppers that Taina, Sirppa, and I cook together. Some evenings we read to each other or tell stories. Taina plays Sibelius on the phonograph: *The Swan of Tuonela* and *Lemminkäinen's Return*. She knows all the old Finnish legends. One day she will tell you about the forests in the far north where the sun never shines in winter and never sets in summer. I read Emily Dickinson aloud. Once I thought her poems were riddles, but now I am beginning to unravel them. I can understand Whitman, too. How he could find beauty in steam engines, in railway workers, in bridges, in dirt and grass. Don't think I've grown dull; my mind is sharper than it's ever been. All day long I do figures and calculations. I'm learning about botany, too: the propagation of plants, the different types of soil. One day when Jana is a little older, I would like to be a teacher. Like my uncle. I think I would make a good teacher.

By now, Taina knows my story. I didn't tell her everything at once, but over days and weeks, revealing one thing at a time. When I told her why I left John, she held me and cried. And I told her about you, that you are my beloved friend. Though I did not spell it out explicitly, I know that she *knows*. She's too wise not to know these things. Taina has taught me all about running a farm and business and standing strong. She is waiting for her husband to come home from the war, just as I wait for you. She is strong even as she waits.

⤳ At night, after I've put Jana to bed, I think about the letter I will write to Lotte. I'm not sure what she will think of the choices I've made, but one day soon I'll write her. I also say a silent prayer for your nephew, that the shells will stop exploding in his head. Then I light a candle and stare into the flame until the walls of this room fall away and, with them, the miles that separate us. I stare into that flame until I can see your face. Until I can speak to you and hear your voice. I am no longer that shining girl you remember. You will see from the breadth of my hips and the way I stand with my feet flat on the ground that I have borne a child. But you will take one look at the hunger in my eyes and know that I have loved you in secret, that I have planted the seedling you gave me, planted it inside me. You will take one look at me and know that I love you far more than that girl in the blue muslin dress could ever imagine. You will take me in your arms, and I will cry into your hair. My soul touches yours, and in the place where our souls touch, a golden tree will grow. You said I was like Persephone. But who is Persephone now, and who is Demeter? You wander the world like a maiden, and I am a mother. I have prepared a home for you and planted a meadow of spring flowers. And you, like Persephone, will return.

BIBLIOGRAPHY

≈ FAIRY TALES

Früh, Sigrid, ed. *Märchen von Hexen und weisen Frauen*. Fischer, Frankfurt am Main, 1996.

Hall, Nor. *The Moon and the Virgin: Reflections on the Archetypal Feminine*. Harper & Row, New York, 1980.

Hetmann, Frederik and Leonardo Wild, eds. *Indianermärchen aus Südamerika*. Fischer, Frankfurt am Main, 1997.

Olesch, Reinhold, ed. *Russische Volksmärchen*. Rowohlt, Hamburg, 1991.

Rüttner-Cova, Sonja. *Frau Holle, die gestürzte Göttin: Märchen, Mythen, Matriarchat*. Sphinx, Munich, 1998.

von Franz, Marie Louise. *The Feminine in Fairy Tales*. Shambala, Boston, 1993.

Woeller, Waltraud. *Deutsche Volksmärchen*. Insel, Frankfurt am Main, 1985.

HISTORY/BACKGROUND

Faderman, Lillian. *Surpassing the Love of Men*. William Morrow, New York, 1981.

Freier, Anna-Elisabeth. "Dimensionen weiblichen Erlebens und Handelns innerhalb der proletarischen Frauenbewegung." *Frauen in der Geschichte, Band III*. Annette Kuhn and Jörn Rüsen, eds. Schwann, Düsseldorf, 1983.

Gilman, Rhoda R. *The Story of Minnesota's Past*. Minnesota Historical Society Press, Saint Paul, 1989.

Hobsbawm, E.J. *The Age of Empire: 1875 – 1914*. Sphere Books, London, 1987.

———. *Age of Extremes: The Short Twentieth Century: 1914 – 1991*. Abacus, London, 1995.

Koppelman, Susan, ed. *Two Friends*. Meridian, New York, 1994.

Lass, William E. *Minnesota: A History*. W.W. Norton, New York, 1983.

McBride, Theresa M. "The Long Road Home: Women's Work and Industrialization." *Becoming Visible: Women in European History*. Renate Bridenthal and Claudia Koonz, eds. Houghton Mifflin, Boston, 1977.

McDougal, Mary Lynn. "Working-Class Women During the Industrial Revolution, 1780 – 1914." Ibid.

Meier, Peg. *Bring Warm Clothes: Letters and Photos from Minnesota's Past*. Neighbors Publishing, Minneapolis, 1981.

Morton, Frederic. *A Nervous Splendor: Vienna 1888 – 1889*. Penguin, New York, 1979.

Perrottet, Tony, ed. *Ecuador*. Apa Publications, Hong Kong, 1995.